domestic *affairs*

domestic
affairs

A Campaign Novel

BRIDGET SIEGEL

WEINSTEIN
BOOKS

7/12

Printed in the United States of America.
For information address Weinstein Books,
387 Park Avenue South, 12th Floor, New York, NY 10016.

ISBN-10: 160286-164-1
ISBN-13: 978-160286-164-0

First Edition

10 9 8 7 6 5 4 3 2 1

For my mom and my dad,
who gave me the world and then
taught me to reach for the stars

domestic
affairs

THE WAKE-UP CALL

Olivia opened her hazel eyes, her vision still blurred from the night before. She glanced at the clock lighting up the hotel room: 7:03. She'd been working campaigns long enough to understand that an extra chair beside the bed in a hotel room in Iowa made that room a presidential suite. She thought the bed felt a little softer than the one in her own room, which, as she connected the dots, she realized was downstairs. Her room barely allowed space for a bed, let alone a chair. And there was no way she could have overslept on that rock-hard mattress. This room was painted dull beige and above the bed was the obligatory landscape portrait that hung in every hotel on the road, the painting of the idyllic view that should have been outside the window but was not.

This hotel in particular was in the parking lot of a strip mall. Literally. Right smack in front of a Super Target. Which actually, Olivia had thought when they pulled in the night before, was pretty great. That was campaign frame of mind: you pulled up to a hotel that had a totally useful store nearby, and it far outweighed the fact that you would be sleeping in a parking lot.

I should probably stock up on some stuff I need, she thought. *I wonder how much I could fit in my suitcase. Probably not much.*

When traveling with a candidate on commercial flights Olivia did not check luggage. That lesson, Campaign Lesson #5 in politics, became crystal clear the first time she traveled with a gubernatorial candidate. Only a year out of college and thrilled to be filling in for her sick finance-director boss on a two-day trip to Texas, she had packed in preparation for any and every situation that could possibly arise. She would never forget the annoyed look on the candidate's face as they waited for her luggage on the carousel. She was new then so he didn't scream, despite the fact that her bag was the very last to come across the conveyor belt. Threw off the entire day's tightly–packed schedule. Now, four years later, equal to about sixteen campaign years, if she made a mistake like that, the politician paying her salary would blast her so severely that an on-looker might suspect imminent murder. Needless to say, Campaign Lesson #5 was to pack light. Wrinkle-free suits could look totally different with a new shirt, and a black shift dress worked for everything.

Maybe I could fit a small box of Q-tips and the Neutrogena face wash I like.

The buzz of a BlackBerry shifted Olivia out of her Target trance. The blinking red light beckoned. It couldn't be anything that bad. She had checked her messages before falling asleep two hours earlier. Post-sex BlackBerry check. It was the campaign equivalent of a postcoital cigarette, though admittedly far less sexy. Still, the thought of what awaited yielded a flurry of worries.

Where are we on the budget? Do I have enough calls scheduled today for the governor? Will Henley come through with the fifty he promised? What if Alek's check doesn't get here in time?

She reached for the BlackBerry and as she shifted, the arm around her pulled her back in. God, his timing was good. He tightened his hold on her slender waist and she decided to let him. Usually, on most mornings after, she'd feel as claustrophobic as Scarlett Johansson in *He's Just Not That Into You* when her boyfriend in the movie, E from *Entourage*, is sprawled on top of her and she can't escape. But with him it was different. There was a space right between his chin and broad shoulder where she fit perfectly. She thought his body was flawless, strong enough to hold her tight but not so muscular that he bulged out of an oxford shirt. Even the feel of his steady snore was sexy to her; it was more like calm, heavy breathing and it just took her over. He was it, everything she'd always wanted in a man. In these rare moments of closeness away from the craze of everyday campaign life her insecurities washed away, and she knew this was love for both of them.

Rrrrriinnnngggg.

"Go away," he mumbled as he pulled her closer. He ran his hand across her stomach and then her back as she turned toward him. "You're going to make me answer that, aren't you?" His eye was half-open. "Wouldn't it be better if we just found something else to do until it stops ringing?"

"Noooo. I'm afraid not," Olivia said. "No time."

"Think of it this way," he said, grabbing her by the hips. "I'd be in a much better mood. And that would be good for everyone."

She pushed him off. "Pick up the phone."

The truth was that she wanted him as badly as he wanted her. Or more. But the hotel phone was never a good thing. It was a given that everyone kept a constant eye on their BlackBerry, so if someone was using a landline, it was urgent. He took her advice, as he did most of the time. She could barely hear the voice on the other end and yet the caller might as well have had a megaphone to her ear.

"You've been caught with your pants down."

"I what?"

Suddenly they were both very awake and very aware of their surroundings. As the terror sank in, a flutter of emails, texts, calls, and moments whirled through Olivia's mind. *Which message did they find?* This feeling of terror was exactly as she had always imagined it would be: instant and crashing.

"What is he talking . . ." She didn't have to whisper. Words were barely coming out of her mouth and his face was flushed white.

"The trade deal. They know we spoke about it in Colombia."

And breathe. Well, for her. He switched into yell mode. It was amazing how quickly he did that. She wondered if it was a guy thing to be able to switch emotions as easily as shifting gears in a car.

Regardless, her breath resumed and it was back to reality and the start of a day. And the realization that it was 7:18—past the hour when it would be safe for one of them to slip out of the other's room, way past the hour when she could afford to be daydreaming. She jumped out of bed. She hated this part. It was the instant 180—one moment would be perfect and the next, reality would come crashing in, leaving her sneaking out of a room she shouldn't have been in to get away from a man she shouldn't have been with.

She glanced over at the man who had left her world. He was yelling so intently that he barely noticed her slinking around the bed looking for her bra. *Just as well,* she figured as she grabbed up the rest of her clothes and tied back her hair. A kiss good-bye or a "See you at work, honey" didn't seem appropriate anyway. It was time, yet again, for the ultimate walk of shame.

As Olivia slipped into the hallway the significance of the late time hit her. This hotel had two elevator banks and she wasn't supposed to be walking out of this one. Not such an issue at the usual four a.m., but it was now seven thirty a.m., and the news of her walk back to her room could spread around the world as fast as a sex tape featuring Kim Kardashian.

Please, let the world be still asleep. Please, please, please. She pleaded with the universe.

As the elevator doors opened she put her head down and pretended to read her emails. But she couldn't help taking a quick peek up. Reflex.

Shit. She put her head right back down.

Jacob had a seat at breakfast with a prime view of the elevator, waiting, no doubt, to catch her boss before someone else did. He was the worst-case scenario; he would know exactly where she was supposed to be and where she was coming from. Head down, she turned a quick corner, confident that he hadn't noticed. But her heart raced, shaken that she had come so close. As she power-walked to her room she kept her eyes to the floor. Now she was in an appropriate part of the hotel, but it didn't matter—she knew the path she had just taken was wrong.

What am I doing? By the time she reached her room, the shame and fear had boiled up from the knot in her stomach into warm tears. She leaned against the closed door and slid down to the floor as she cried.

Seriously, Olivia, seriously? She berated herself. *What am I doing? How did I get here?*

She knew how she got here. It was like it had happened yesterday. And a lifetime ago.

ONE

Could we maybe try a different route?" Olivia half-shouted through the Plexiglas to the cab driver as she hung up from what had seemed like an endless conference call. She looked down at her BlackBerry and watched the time turn to 4:04 p.m.

Traffic never failed to appear when she was running late. *More like Parked Avenue.* She looked down at her watch, annoyed that she had not left herself more time.

Well, at least Jacob is used to my being late. He'll know to make up an excuse for me.

Jacob Harriston and Olivia had worked together on a congressional campaign in Connecticut five years back. Right before he started working for Landon Taylor. Campaign colleagues were a lot like summer camp friends. Some you kept in touch with more than others, but either way, there was a bond that couldn't be entirely broken regardless of space and time. They had been through a war together. Slept on the floor of a dirty office while doing the seating for concert halls full of supporters, huddled together while getting yelled at by candidates and donors or both, did shots together as thunder rumbled minutes before huge outdoor fundraisers. They were in constant contact for months in a row.

Still, a year could pass after a campaign with both people being too busy to ever check back in. Jacob's call two weeks ago had caught

Olivia completely by surprise. They needed a national finance director for the Landon Taylor presidential campaign, he said. Olivia had first assumed he was calling her for a referral to someone she had worked for. It had not even crossed her mind that they would be offering the job to her. "I've told them I think you could do this better than anyone," Jacob said. She stammered through a response, assuring Jacob she could raise many millions of dollars in eighteen months, without actually thinking about whether or not this was true. In reality, she had worked on only three campaigns and had not even attended two national conventions, let alone been responsible for getting a candidate there—she had only just reached her twenty-seventh birthday. The job of national finance director of a presidential campaign was reserved for someone with greater seniority, management skills, and experience. She had heard buzz that Jacob was taking the reins of the campaign, stepping up as the unofficial campaign manager and bringing in a younger, fresher staff, but she couldn't believe he would go this far.

The two weeks since that call had catapulted Olivia into interviews, e-mails, and an emotional tizzy that left no time to reconsider anything. Not that there was anything to reconsider. This was her dream job. Being the national finance director of a presidential campaign was the apex of a fundraiser's career. She couldn't remember ever hearing of anyone near her age doing it. *Youngest national finance director in political history,* she proudly thought at least three times an hour, imagining the headline in the paper, the bio box that would hang next to her head when she was called in to comment on her favorite CNN show. This was it. The big leagues. The presidency. And not just any presidency, the imminent presidency of Governor Landon Taylor, her political hero. This would be the first time she actually met Taylor, so he could sign off on the hire that Jacob and the rest of the upper-level staff had approved—her. One of the most important days of her life, and she was running late. *Only five minutes.* She looked down at the clock on the dashboard. *Seven minutes.*

"I'll just get out here," she yelled to the driver, seeing the hotel a block away. She jumped out and checked the seat to make sure that she hadn't left her BlackBerry, the nightmare she had the habit of living through when she was in a rush. And she was always in a rush.

As she waited for the crosswalk light to change, she took a quick look down at herself and realized what a mess she was offering. The conference call had lasted the entire cab ride, so she hadn't had her usual five minutes to tuck in her shirt and slap on some makeup. Everything in Olivia's makeup bag was smudgeable, meaning it could be put on with fingertips rather than brushes in the dark or in the backseat of a moving cab, or, if need be, both. She was never much of a makeup girl. She left that type of thing to her older sister. So being able to apply it while in a cab, otherwise known as Campaign Lesson #8, made the whole process more bearable. Or at least less of a waste of time.

Thank goodness for Brooks Brothers wrinkle-free, she thought as she carried her bags, tucked in her shirt, and crossed the street all at once. The shirt was her saving grace. It stayed crisp no matter what hell she put it through. She didn't know who invented iron-free technology, but whoever did should win a Nobel Prize. And why hadn't every other designer followed suit? Why would anyone make non-wrinkle-free shirts anymore?

Why would I buy ones that weren't? Why do I only have one? I'll buy another one this weekend, she pledged to herself, knowing full well she wouldn't be making it out to the stores. *Focus, Olivia.*

She ran her hands down the sides of her brown pencil skirt, trying to force out some of the old-school wrinkles. It was one of her few classic go-to outfits and she was glad she had picked it. It made her feel better about the fact that her only makeup was a glop of Juicy Tubes lip gloss, smeared on as she walked in the door. She touched at the ribbon tied around her straight brown hair, literally *long* overdue for a haircut.

At least Jacob won't make fun of me for overdressing for Taylor.

Landon Taylor was not like other politicians. He was not one of those awkward-looking men who ran around DC in ill-fitting suits, concerned only with the sound of their own voice. Taylor stood six feet tall and had high cheekbones and youthful blue eyes that complemented his prep-school hair. He always looked like he should be standing alongside the Kennedy brothers in a black and white photograph, staring out at a horizon that only a few leaders would ever really see. When he spoke, his Southern accent blended with a sharp intellect to create the right mix of smarts and accessibility. And although a few years of campaigning had left her with a degree of jadedness, Olivia found her adoration for Landon Taylor was untouched.

Her senior year in college, only five years earlier, she had written a paper about the impact of his campaign speeches on the American dialogue about poverty, and later, while she was interning for the Democratic convention, she had the chance to see him in person. She remembered it like a girl looking back on her first kiss. It was one of the rare moments in politics when the world quiets down enough so you can truly listen to another person. The moment he began speaking, the massive, chaotic convention hall hushed, becoming more and more rapt with every word. To this day, Olivia couldn't imagine anyone hearing that speech and not being moved to do something more with their life. Of course, near the end of the speech she was jerked out of her trance by a donor asking for a ticket to the Maroon 5 party the next night.

"What a waste of time," the donor had said. "Does anyone really think this guy has a chance against the Republican machine in Georgia?"

She wanted to raise her hand to the sky and scream, "Me! I do!" but she knew Taylor didn't have a chance. She had been following his race as closely as if she were working on it. Every poll, even his internals, had him down double digits and he was being outspent three to one. Every hired political gun was urging him to center his message, but he stuck with his passion. For Olivia, as he spoke with fervor about everything she believed in, his impending loss was a substantiation of what she had just started to articulate to herself: that there used to be real leaders who could silence the world enough to argue for truth, but now they were all quieted by the circus that politics had become.

But something had happened with Landon Taylor. After an explosive surge in the last two weeks of his campaign for governor, he won, by more than a few votes, the race that everyone agreed he couldn't win. True, his victory was mostly due to the revelation of his opponent's insider-trading scandal, brought to light by that candidate's third wife. But still, *Landon Taylor won*. That was enough to keep alive Olivia's hope that a decent man, a real inspiring leader, could succeed. Since then he had gained accolades for the Georgia state government and consequently was selected as the vice presidential candidate in the last election. Though the ticket had lost (something she blamed entirely on Taylor's running mate), the publicity and exposure left him in an ideal position for a future run for president. He was an inspirational long shot who had beaten the odds to become someone with a real chance at the White House. Just thinking about it left Olivia with a renewed belief in the existence of the type of politics that had filled the posters on her old dorm room wall.

She studied him like an ongoing thesis project, picking up every fact, big or small. From his antipoverty speeches to the kind of shoes his gorgeous wife wore—Christian Louboutins, of course—Olivia knew the governor inside and out. He stood in stark contrast to the transactional candidates she had come to know in the last few years. They changed positions on major issues when public opinion shifted, made bland speeches so as not to ruffle any feathers even when the feathers clearly needed to be ruffled, and would say just about anything to get a donation. But with someone like this, like Taylor, her fundraising could serve a cause, not just her résumé.

So here she was. Running late, half-put-together, but as excited as she'd ever been for this life-changing meeting in the misleading calmness of the Brinmore.

The Brinmore was one of the most exclusive hotels on Park Avenue. It used to be the place ladies went to lunch, but fundraisers in New York had turned it into a political cafeteria. Its dining room, lined in dark wood and deep red fabric, had enough of a library feel to project gravitas, and it was just overpriced enough to make a politician feel fancy, yet affordable enough to not seem excessive to the donors, who always picked up the check.

Jo, the hostess, was a short, well-put-together woman who could best be described as a yenta, except she never gave away the gossip she collected. She ran the place with a gracious composure. Her control over where people sat at breakfast made her one of the most knowledgeable and powerful women in New York. Knowing who wanted to be near, or far, from whom gave her insight into every friendship, political alliance, affair, and divorce, often well before the heartache flamed up. Yet she held that power through a combination of intelligence and withholding. She never gossiped, never gave a single detail away. Not to anyone. When Jo knew something about you, her subtle glances and moves told you she did, but they never seemed to tell anyone else. She also had an uncanny knack for knowing exactly who someone was meeting as soon as they walked in.

As Olivia turned the corner into the restaurant area of the hotel, she gave a quick smile to Jo, who blew a kiss, called her "sweetie," and knowingly pointed to the back of the dining room. Olivia looked and saw the two men sitting in the large, couchlike chairs at a table in the back corner. The governor was laughing as she approached and Olivia caught herself smiling along. He had a nice way about him. His hair bounced lightly over his blue eyes, which could be seen from a mile away. There was something much more familiar about him than she had expected. She switched her coat and two bags to one hand and smoothed out her hair in an effort to condense the mess that she felt she couldn't completely contain.

"Hello." The governor stood and reached for her hand. "How are you today?" His Southern drawl was the perfect add to the smile. It was clear why everyone was drawn to him, she thought. He took her hand and clasped it with his other hand, holding on just a little too long.

"Sorry I'm late."

"We wouldn't expect anything else," Jacob said, chiming in with his normal dose of candid humor.

Olivia turned and hugged Jacob, struck by how much he and the governor looked alike. Jacob was a little taller, standing at about six foot one, but he had the same sandy brown hair and effortlessly charming smile. She wondered if he had let his bangs grow a little long so they would flop over his brown eyes just like the governor's did. As Olivia sat down on the couch next to the governor she wondered if campaign staffers spent so much time with their candidate they could actually start looking like them, the way people said dog owners did with their dogs.

"Nooow, sit down here," Taylor said with an extra-slow drawl, settling back into his chair and ushering Olivia with an outstretched hand. "Jacob here tells me that you are interested in education reform. Do you know that down in Georgia we've started to build communities that are working toward complete integration with every public school?"

Olivia knew but found herself hardly able to respond, she was so mesmerized by his desire to start off on policy. He fed right into the part of her that still believed in changing the world.

From as far back as Olivia could remember she'd gotten the same rush of excitement when a politician spoke with flair that most girls got from the high school quarterback's waving to them from the field or from buying a new bag. She wasn't immune to cute boys or new bags and was the first to admit she wanted a big white wedding dress and lots of kids. Five to be exact. But she had yet to meet anyone who could make her feel as alive as she did at a political rally. That was a foreign thought to the kids at her suburban high school, who'd rarely signed her petitions or even known when Election Day was. In her seventh-grade English class, Olivia was the first to volunteer to read her essay on love aloud. "Darkness cannot drive out darkness; only light can do that. Hate cannot drive out hate; only love can do that," she said, quoting Martin Luther King, Jr.

She continued on talking about love's role in civil unrest. It wasn't until she sat back down that she noticed the giggling around the room. The next forty minutes had seemed like forty hours. Olivia sank into her chair, feeling more alienated every time a new classmate got up to talk about Justin Timberlake, Britney Spears, or David, the star of the junior high basketball team.

Though her parents supported what she did, they never quite understood where it came from. Her father was a Republican, her mother a Democrat, but neither had a strong enough attachment to either party to keep them from voting for Perot in '92, despite Olivia's best arguments.

"Born that way," her mom would say when asked why her twelve-year-old daughter, Olivia, was protesting about environmental issues outside the middle school. Her sister's good looks and her brother's natural talent for sports were much easier to appreciate, even for Olivia, who herself had no explanation for why she loved politics. It was understandably simpler for her parents to come to school to see her sister in the school play or her brother in the state championship basketball game. A protest wasn't really the kind of thing they could pull up a chair to or invite the grandparents along to. Working on campaigns, though, had been the home she had always been looking for. She could eat, sleep, and breathe world events. The age-old question of why she had not yet found a long-term boyfriend was answered not by the incomprehensible idea that she would rather change the world than fall in love, but by the simple fact that she was just too busy.

The governor leaned over to her with that stare she had only heard about. With quiet earnestness he said, "This world needs people who believe in the promise of a better day—not just in words and in rhetoric, but in every step we take. We're going to build something that will reroot this country in the freedom and justice it started on." She was sold. He would do something about poverty, about justice, the issues that literally kept her awake at night, aching with a desire to stop the suffering. Amazingly, she thought, there wasn't anything corny about what he said. And his hand was enveloping her bicep to emphasize his sincerity. Hook. Line. Sinker.

"My man," a voice bellowed a few feet from the table.

Governor Taylor looked over her shoulder and got up with a huge smile. He moved to hug the enormous man looming over them.

Olivia shook off her rapt haze as she recognized the statuesque man.

"How are you, man?" Taylor was saying. "You remember Jacob, right?"

"Of course." Dikembe Mutombo casually threw a fist-bump toward Jacob. "Jacob introduced us!"

"And this," the governor said as he put his hand gently on her back, "is Miss Olivia Greenley, the most sought-after political fundraiser in New York."

Olivia shook her head in humble disagreement but she couldn't hide her smile. She knew it was a typical political embellishment, but she didn't care. Here she was being introduced to one of her favorite athletes by one of the nation's most famous politicians as "sought after." She hated to admit it even to herself—as a hardened staffer she was supposed to be above the celebrity factor of it all—but this was Dikembe Mutombo and she was excited. "Olivia, this is—"

"Dikembe Mutombo." She cut him off, trying her best not to sound like a schoolgirl.

"Ahhh, a basketball fan in our midst apparently."

"More specifically, a Hoyas fan. Class of '06." Olivia smiled.

"Gotta love a Hoya," Dikembe replied. "Sorry to interrupt, but I was just telling my office to reach out to yours. I have a charity event coming up next month and we'd love to get you out there. Three-on-three for kids. All the old Hoyas are in—Touomou, Owinje. David Henley is hosting."

"Done. I will be there. Jacob, let's make sure that's on my calendar. I'm shocked that Henley hasn't mentioned it already."

Dikembe looked a bit confused. He said, "Oh, I thought he was going to tell you about it, Governor."

"I bet he's already emailed me and I missed it," Jacob said, falling on his sword as all good staffers reflexively do. "Let me get the details from you." He smiled.

Olivia knew exactly what Jacob was thinking. She was thoroughly aware that he knew full well that the governor would not be going to that event. A good deal of staffers' time was spent "getting things on the calendar" and then breaking the news to people when they didn't stay on or, more likely, had never gotten on in the first place. Politicians had an uncanny ability to cancel and move things without reprimand. If Olivia or Jacob had gone into film or finance or anything else after college, either one of them would probably have given life and limb for a meeting with Jamie Dimon, Orin Kramer, Harvey Weinstein, or even Dikembe Mutombo. Olivia would have probably have shown up an hour early to any of those meetings.

Instead, Olivia knew that Jacob, at the age of twenty-nine, was as accustomed as she was to calling his financial idol to tell them that his candidate wasn't going to make it to the lunch that started in twenty minutes, but they could squeeze the financier in later in the day for a forty-five-minute coffee (to which Taylor would undoubtedly be fifteen minutes late). If that had been a business meeting of the highest importance, a call like that would have been answered with a dial tone and a cancellation of all future business. But this was politics, so the response usually sounded something more like, "Perfect, see you soon."

"I have all the paperwork with my staffers over there," Dikembe said, pointing toward the lobby. All of a sudden, he seemed more like a schoolgirl than the seven-foot-two basketball superstar that he was.

"I'll come grab it," Jacob said. "I'm pretty sure we have a Habitat event the same day as your event but let me get the info and double-check."

That was another trick that any good staffer used to smooth the we-can't-make-it message: tell people that there was something else scheduled on that date from the get-go. If the governor had seen the specific date before he said yes, that always made it a little more diffi-cult. But for a staffer, looking at an invite and saying, "I know we have yada yada on that date but let me see if I can try to move things around," crafted a win-win situation. If the boss didn't go to the event in the end, it was clearly because there was something important on the calendar. And if by some off chance the candidate could go, the staffer was the hero who moved things around to make it happen.

Being a hero to the donors definitely garnered privileges. Donors needed contact with the candidate to feed their egos. And wealthy donors' thank-yous for that access ranged from tickets to sold-out con-certs and sports games (like the ones to last year's Final Four that Olivia scored), to Hermès bags, to weekends at their Caribbean homes. While those staffers working in government offices were limited in what they could accept (Jacob's friends on the Hill couldn't even be bought more than $20 in drinks), campaign workers were completely unrestricted in what they could accept.

Jacob followed Dikembe to the lobby. As he disappeared out of sight, Olivia joked with the governor, "Jacob seems so smitten by Dikembe. Are you worried he's over there asking for a job?"

The governor laughed with ease. "Please, he could never leave—his grandmother loves me. Plus, there's more basketball on this cam-paign than in any of Dikembe's days. Seriously, did you see the last Dick Vitale March Madness scouting report?"

"No, but I'm interested in working on any campaign that prom-ises good basketball talk. Where does someone even get the scouting report? Is it part of your presidential-run briefing?"

"If I had my way it would be! Dick did some events for us down by Chapel Hill and I figured getting on his scouting email lists might be even more valuable than his fundraising."

"So you adhere to God, family, and then college basketball as the natural order of things? I love it."

"Something like that." He smiled like a five-year-old boy. "Here," he said, flicking through his BlackBerry, "I'll add you onto his list. What's your email? Consider it a welcome to the team."

She spelled out her email address, beaming.

Taylor barely looked up, seamlessly turning the conversation from basketball back to the campaign. "This is a big job we have here," he said, hitting the SEND button. "You really ready for this?"

"Definitely." She tried to disguise her total insecurity in the answer.

"This is going to be a good one. We're going to change the world."

Even now Olivia felt as if she were reading a really good book about the beginnings of a great social movement or a heart-shaking romantic tale, one she would get so lost in that she could believe the world really was the way she wanted it to be: the man really does come running back for his true love; and the woman overcomes her fears and admits she adores him too; and a kiss at sunset promises a long and happy life together. Olivia was a political romantic and those moments—which had become fewer and farther between—when she could really believe, as she could with Governor Taylor, made her feel completely high.

Jacob returned with a T-shirt draped over his shoulder. He dropped a handful of papers about Dikembe's charity on the table.

"Papers for you, shirt for me. See," he said, showing Olivia the extra-large neon tee complete with a caricature of Dikembe on it, "this campaign gets the good stuff!"

Another cup of coffee later, Olivia's job was solidified, the final approval in, and Jacob was eyeing their next meeting, who had just walked in the door. Knowing the look on Jacob's face from firsthand experience, Olivia understood that he was concerned with transitioning from one meeting to another. She said her thank-yous and excused herself from the table.

The governor stood and shook her hand. "Welcome to the team, kiddo. Get ready for the adventure of a lifetime. I can't promise we'll win, but I promise we'll change lives."

"Be careful of that one, sweetie," Jo said to Olivia as she said good-bye to her in passing.

"Okay, thanks!" Olivia might have said the words too cheerfully and too quickly. She turned back to ask what Jo had said, realizing she hadn't really heard the exact wording of the warning, but Jo was already showing someone else to his table.

As Olivia walked out of the hotel, the day seemed more vibrant than it had been when she walked in. She had gotten lost in the dark library-like dining room and even more so in the governor's gaze, which seemed to have a magnetic quality to it. She felt almost flustered by his genius.

She grabbed at her BlackBerry, which had been out of her hands for longer than she was accustomed to, and read down the thirty-two new messages. *Ugh,* she thought, *back to life.*

By the time she got to her apartment, a cozy junior one—or at least that was the way the ad had described the tiny one-bedroom apartment—it was six p.m. It was much earlier than she got home most nights. Her soon-to-be-ex-boss, the newly elected district attorney, was traveling this week, so she could savor a few early nights. He was off to California until Tuesday, partially on vacation, but with a few meetings squeezed in. It was a trip she would usually have gone on, but with no need to fundraise so soon after the election, she had talked him out of taking her. Though she liked having a little time to herself and the relative quiet of a post-election fundraising job, she had to admit she missed the craze of a real campaign and was excited to start a new one.

She reached for the box of pasta that sat on the counter because her cabinet could only accommodate two boxes of cereal and threw her culinary specialty on the stove. As she waited for the water to boil she began to Google Governor Taylor. The articles were endless, and that was just from today. She couldn't wait to be an official part of the team that would "re-dream America" and get to work.

TWO

W *hat a waste of time,* Jacob thought as the next meeting slid into the chair at their table. Lori Sanders adopted her signature perfect posture as she unbuttoned the jacket of her maroon tweed suit, which looked like the ones his grandmother wore whenever she saw the governor. "Proper church clothes," she called them. Lori's blond hair was tied up in such a high bun on top of her head it looked like it pulled her eyes skyward. *Hah! Probably her attempt at a cheap face-lift!*

Jacob sat back and began rewinding the meeting with Olivia as the governor and Sanders began their small talk. For a second, Jacob let himself admit that it wasn't the smartest plan to bring his buddy into the campaign.

When he'd first suggested Olivia he wasn't completely serious. He and the governor had been through three fundraisers in the last year, all of them unable to keep pace, and they weren't getting any traction from their other prospects for the job. Their main opponent, Senator Kramer, was the former head of the Democratic Senatorial Campaign Committee, and since almost all good fundraisers went through there at some point or another, he had close ties with just about everybody. Jacob had tried them all—Dara, Annie, Dennis, Jill, Allison, Meredith, Emily, Stephanie, Rachel, Leigh, Hildy, both Jennifers, Jordan, Lenny,

Jamie—the list went on and on. People didn't necessarily want to work for Kramer, but they didn't want to work against him either.

She can do it, he thought, trying to reassure himself, remembering that Olivia had pulled rabbits out of hats to get the new DA boatloads of money. Plus, she was one of the hardest-working people he knew and she seemed to still have that idealistic shtick going.

Then he let his mind slip to the thing that hovered in the back of his thoughts. Olivia was a friend and he knew the governor's effect on people, especially campaign people. He could draw them into his world with a grip tighter than any of Jacob's old wrestling chokeholds. And he knew how hard this campaign was going to be. *It won't get tough for a while,* he thought. She'd have time to learn to be the highest-powered campaign fundraiser in history before she really needed to set historic fundraising records. He reminded himself of one of his favorite sayings: *Campaigns and long-term thinking don't really go hand in hand. Relax,* he thought, *it will all work out. And having her around couldn't hurt the governor's mood.*

Jacob wondered if there was any project in life other than a campaign that relied so heavily on the mood of one person. Whatever the long-term strategy or policy ideas were, on a day-to-day basis, especially for—but not exclusively for—the "body guy," in this case him, the candidate's mood was the most essential part of everything they did. An annoyed candidate would cancel meetings, events, calls. An angry candidate could easily fly into a rage and upend the staffing or power structure of the entire campaign in an hour. At his worst, a mad or tired candidate could slip up in public and say something explosive in front of the press. And in the new age of the Internet, a small mistake could cause a big downfall.

All campaigners had their way of dealing with candidates. Jacob's friend, who was Governor Ashton's body guy, once told him Ashton wasn't a morning person, but a crowd could turn him around in a minute. So on particularly tough mornings, his staff would set up rope lines—rope-and-stanchion setups to keep crowds at bay, or in this case to build crowds behind—wherever he was. A minute into walking down the aisle of any rope line, the governor would shed his morning grumpiness, and the staff knew they could start the day.

For the senator whom Jacob used to work for, Senator Marks, all Jacob had to do was mention a car part or something similar that Marks could fix. Staffers could stop him in his tracks in the middle of berating someone with a quick, "Do you hear that clicking noise?"

On one road trip that was filled with painfully long and eminently annoying events, a Marks adviser brought along an old-school leaf blower that no longer worked. Sure enough, after the first day of events, Marks was near implosion, snapping at Jacob as soon as they ducked around any corner. To this day Jacob could picture the senator grabbing at his arm and asking if Jacob "planned on being useful at all." Then, before the last event, where press would be observing, the staff took the senator to a conference room for an hour's break. To Jacob's surprise, out came the leaf blower.

"I don't know what's wrong with it," the adviser said, as if it were the most normal thing ever to have a huge, rusty old piece of lawn equipment cradled in her overnight bag.

"Let me see that."

An hour later the leaf blower was in working order. Two hours later the senator gave one of his most acclaimed speeches and happily bought drinks for the staff afterward.

For Governor Taylor, the key was pretty girls. Like all mood-changing secrets, it was never anything spoken aloud. But it was what it was—whenever a beautiful woman interested in what Taylor was saying was around, fewer people got yelled at, more events stayed on schedule, and speeches were better. There wasn't a science to it, but as far as Jacob saw, it was a fact. Of all the vices Taylor could possess, Jacob thought, this wasn't so bad. The governor was never inappropriate, and his wife, Aubrey, had a real hold on him. That was another mystery Jacob didn't care to investigate too deeply, as it also worked for him as a campaign staffer: America loved the Aubrey-Landon romance. *Use it, don't excuse it* was the philosophy Jacob had come to adopt over the years. While it sometimes felt odd to Jacob that he questioned the basis of their marriage so much, he had real reason to marvel. Why would Landon decide to love her? Sure, she was pretty in a way where you could see she was once beautiful, and Jacob could rationalize them as college sweethearts—she, the beloved Miss Georgia, and he, the brilliant, passionate quarterback who had the world knocking at his door. It all made sense in theory, but in reality, well, Jacob thought, she was just a bitch.

Jacob knew Taylor saw her mean ways: He heard her scream at interns and staffers, saw her throw tantrums when a driver was one min :te late. But aside from the rare moments when Jacob could watch her obvious disapproval cause the governor to almost twitch his eyes downward with what seemed like a pang of sadness, the governor really didn't seem to mind at all.

He's too focused on the world to care, Jacob always thought. *The two of them together could make an impact on society, and that is more important to both of them than love.* It sounded weird even to say it in his head, but he knew it was true. He knew it because Taylor had practically said as much. It didn't really make sense, but Jacob had come to accept that's just how it was for Aubrey and Landon. And thankfully, the world bought in big-time. Aubrey and Landon were America's version of royalty.

So who cares if the attention of a pretty girl who thinks the world of the governor makes him feel better about things. Why not? Besides, in this case, the pretty girl was a friend and a fundraiser, two things Jacob sorely needed on the campaign.

Jacob glanced at Lori, for once grateful that the governor didn't know what an ass she truly was. Usually, Jacob would be annoyed at Taylor's insistence on talking to people whom Jacob thought of as, quite frankly, a waste of blood. But today, when he had three meetings cancel and he had to fill their time with whomever he could get at a moment's notice, the governor's naïveté became fortunate. To his credit, the morning had been filled with great fundraising meetings, so really it wasn't too bad that he had occupied the empty afternoon slot with Lori Sanders, who was now going on and on about how much money she was going to raise for the campaign.

Jacob considered Lori a Blowhard, his term for someone who always promised to raise $50,000 and then never had more than 5K when he showed up at one of their events with his candidate. Blowhards were never short on things to say, especially when it pertained to themselves or their fundraising skills. After wasted appearances happened twice, any self-respecting staffer would never rely on the Blowhard again for anything other than filling time. Jacob had actually thought about using the few hours that weren't chock-full to catch up on work he knew they both probably had, but idle time on a candidate's schedule was never left alone. Even if he knew Lori was a waste of time, at least the meeting kept them in the hotel and was completely containable. He rolled his eyes thinking about a campaign's knee-jerk need to schedule every moment, knowing he wanted this campaign to be different from the others. Long-term planning always took a backseat to putting out fires and rearranging minute-to-minute activities. Today was a perfect example of Jacob himself doing it. When the union meeting had been canceled the day before, he had immediately called Lori instead of sitting back and thinking about what else could have gotten done or referring to a list of the big-picture things that needed scheming. *Campaigns and long-term thinking don't go together well. But they should. This one will. I'll change that.*

Eight years earlier, before anyone in politics knew who she was, Lori had hosted a presidential fundraiser at her town house on the Upper West Side. It was one of the first events of that cycle and the campaign packed it with their celebrities. It had become the hot ticket. The event wound up raising 1.2 million, an outrageous sum when you consider it came in $2,000 increments. And although the fundraisers knew Lori was only actually responsible for about $10,000 of it, everyone else credited her with the whole 1.2. So the myth was born, and Lori made the most of it.

For a few years she could still get a few of the celebrities and contributors she befriended to come to her house. She could pull off a fairly decent event. But, as was true for most future Blowhards, it was a slippery slope. Within a few years, Lori could never be counted on to raise more than $10K or so, the only amount she'd ever actually raised. And $10K or so at Taylor's level was chump change. In his case $10,000 could be raised in a two-minute phone call made during one of their scheduled call-time sessions.

Jacob peeked at his BlackBerry and replied to a few emails. One of the nice things about being on the road with a candidate as his gatekeeper was that no one ever seemed to mind your constant

BlackBerrying, even if it flew in the face of manners. It was as if people just assumed urgent business called. In meetings like this, Jacob relished the slack. He couldn't stand to hear any more about how connected Lori thought she was.

"Oh, I can definitely put you together with Gerry," she was saying. "We're super close. He and Becky would probably love to do something at their Southampton estate. Have you seen it? I mean, it's absolutely gorgeous."

Jacob laughed inwardly, hyper-aware that extent to which someone quantified how well they knew someone else was usually in inverse proportion to how well they actually knew them. He thought for a moment about telling Lori that her "super-close friends" had sold their Southampton estate over a year ago but held his tongue.

That's why I could never be a candidate, he thought. He watched Taylor listening to her next story as if they were negotiating world peace. *He has to have heard this story at least as many times as I have and yet he appears to genuinely enjoy this shit. I wonder if he actually does.* Jacob's BlackBerry buzzed.

SophieMoore14@gmail.com: *I can do 10:30 but I warn you I may be sleepwalking.*

Keeper, he thought. He had only been on one date with Sophie but really liked her. She wasn't a "political groupie," as Jacob liked to call the girls who hung around political campaigns, willing to do just about anything to be close to someone close to the politician. He had heard DC called "Hollywood for ugly people" many times before, and politicians anywhere, particularly those with Governor Taylor's status, were its stars. Jacob's proximity to Taylor made him a prime target for the groupies, something he'd prized at first but had soon tired of.

The tricky part, when it came to dating, was finding not only someone he liked, but someone who was okay with ten thirty p.m. dates, constant BlackBerry checks, and absurdly timed calls from a candidate. Jacob was scheduled to leave New York that night after staffing Taylor at a dinner ("staff" being a campaign term for clinging to the principal and serving his every need), but he had convinced the governor to let him stay the night and go to a morning meeting with

Olivia. "She could really use my help," he had said. It wasn't a lie, *exactly*. His help wouldn't hurt.

As expected the governor had gladly agreed to the proposal provided Jacob could be back in Georgia in time for the County Democratic dinner the next night. *Brilliant plan,* Jacob thought, congratulating himself, since it had left him free to meet up with Sophie, just as he had devised.

Jacob@LTaylor.com: *Brinmore?*

Dates at the Brinmore were the other thing he would have to explain at some point. He could "buy" her fancy food and drinks as long as he wasn't actually paying for any of them. The campaign had its various perks but his salary was not one of them. The majority of his meager paycheck went to a large, rather ugly, and wholly unfurnished apartment in Atlanta in which he spent maybe twelve hours a month. *I should try to rent it out. Or just give it up. I could get a hotel room for the two days I'm in town each month. I guess I'd need to get a storage unit for my stuff. That might cost just as much. And when would I pack?*

"Everything okay over there?" Taylor asked, nudging him.

"Ah, yeah." Jacob knew how to bounce back quickly when caught like this. "Yes. Sir. Just making sure I have your messages correctly."

He smiled a bit, knowing he had just lost a round of the game he and Taylor played, catching each other daydreaming and then calling one another out on it. Time to pay up by getting him out of this meeting.

"Actually, Governor, I hate to cut things short but you have to get on the press call in ten minutes." Donors and press were an amazing pair in politics. The donors were in awe of the press and would let a politician out of anything to go talk to them. And the press were not deferential to anything except a politician's need to be with donors. It was another one of those things that made no sense, but worked so well in Jacob's favor that he didn't dare question it.

"Yes, yes, go," Lori said as she put her black American Express down to pay for the meal.

The governor thanked her, making it seem like he didn't want to leave. He followed Jacob out through the restaurant, stopping to shake hands. He thanked every waiter and server and, of course, Jo. As soon as they got into the elevator, Taylor relished his win.

"Nice of you to leave that little fantasy world of yours to get me out of the meeting."

"You seemed to be enjoying it so much I didn't want to get in the way of the fun."

The ribbing continued as they walked to the governor's "dayroom," a small suite that hotels customarily lent politicians who spent the day taking meetings in their restaurant. A politician could use the space to freshen up between coffees and meals and do calls as if there actually were a press call. The day room was a helpful, necessary, secure place to store the campaign staffers' collection of small black carry-on luggage and to have the many conversations that were not appropriate for public places. It somehow made Jacob also feel a little less like the nomad he had become.

He went into the bathroom to splash water on his face and liked the idea that he could reach for the towel with water in his eyes and know where it was. He wasn't sure if it was the comfort of recognition or just the momentary break from having to think of something new, but whatever it was, it made him smile.

The owner of the hotel was a big Democratic campaign supporter and over the years, Jacob had developed a relationship with him and his assistant, Deirdre. Now that Jacob was working on a presidential bid, all he had to do was make a quick call to Deirdre to reserve just about anything he wanted.

Taylor and Jacob settled into the room. Taylor began checking his messages, and Jacob turned the TV to CNN, loud enough for them to hear but quiet enough to deal with other business. A quick call to Deirdre had extended their use of the dayroom without question, or charge, to an overnight stay, completing Jacob's plan.

We're in the room till six thirty p.m., he rationalized to himself. *It's not like they could've rented the room out anyway.*

⊙ᙏᙏᎧ

"Why are we eating at the Brinmore?" Sophie asked. She had a stitch of reluctance in her voice.

It wasn't that the hotel wasn't good enough. Just the opposite, in fact. It was *too* good. Good as in expensive. Really expensive.

"Whoa. You weren't kidding when you said we were going a step up from two-for-one margarita night," she said. She surveyed the menu with a confused look and started listing items on the menu.

Should I ask her to marry me right now, or would that be too forward? This is only our second official date. She hasn't even experienced my man parts yet. I wonder if tonight that will change. Oh, shoot. She's talking. Pay attention.

"Or maybe the chicken with prosciutto and sage—which do you prefer?"

Say something safe.

"You really can't go wrong with either choice."

"Either choice? I gave you three choices. It's only our second date and you're already tuning me out?"

Shit. So much for that whole man-parts thing.

"I'm so sorry. It's just that I have a ton on my mind with work. The governor is supposed to give a lecture on the financial crisis at the University of Georgia in a few days, and I promised I'd shoot him some analogies he could use to simplify things."

That was technically true but also bordering on dishonest, intellectually at least. It was one of those "I'm trying to impress someone" résumé lies. The governor or some economic policy adviser would likely be the one to come up with the analogy, but the governor did tell Jacob to give it some thought. To be sure, Landon Taylor was not sitting at home waiting for Jacob to write his UGA financial-crisis speech, but Sophie didn't need to know that. Not yet at least. Especially given he was just caught paying no attention to what she was saying.

Jacob thought he had mastered the art of making yourself sound as important as possible without lying. He was convinced every political staffer did it. As time wore on, he "wrote" a speech he'd helped edit, embellished an encounter with a celebrity, and even, on occasion, inserted himself into a story he had heard about so many times that he might as well have been there. *Harmless,* he thought. *Saved time.* And he had a pretty darn good idea where all political staffers learned the technique—from their bosses.

"Well, I certainly don't understand the financial crisis at all, so I'd love for you to try some of those analogies out on me tonight."

I'd prefer trying out other things on you, but I guess I'll have to settle for financial-crisis analogies.

Sophie was adorable. Jacob had dated plenty of adorable girls, but there was something decidedly unique about this particular five-foot-four, black-haired beauty who taught public kindergarten in the Bronx. Dressed in what looked like inexpensive jeans, a simple black tank top, and a funky green knit hat, she was everything that everyone who sat at the surrounding tables was not—unpretentious, unimpressed by net worth, and dressed for two-for-one margarita night.

She was from Connecticut, although she had a kind of Southern charm about her that Jacob was looking for in a girl. Hell, it was one of the reasons he was excited to move to Atlanta after having lived in New York for a few years post-college. He'd never imagined he'd actually meet someone like Sophie in New York.

She didn't love her job as a kindergarten teacher. She originally wanted to be a nurse and even put in two years of nursing school that she personally paid for. Certified Nursing Assistant by day, bartender by night, with some nannying and housecleaning thrown in for good measure. Having too much on her plate led her to teach little guys. Sophie felt she had let herself down. Jacob thought she was doing something wonderful for society.

Jacob and Sophie had met running around the reservoir in Central Park a few months earlier. Jacob and the governor were on what was quickly becoming a semi-monthly fundraising pilgrimage to New York City. The governor liked to schedule at least two hours of downtime to run and regroup every afternoon. Schedule-wise, Jacob was more than happy to oblige. He could use that time to work-out, make a dent in his seemingly endless voicemails and emails or, more often than not, just catch his breath from the craziness of what he deemed the PCIT: Presidential Campaign in Training.

Looking back, he was exceptionally glad that that particular downtime du jour had him waiting in line post-run at the Central Park reservoir water fountain. Right in front of Ms. Sophie Moore. Known to his friends as a "starter," not a "closer," he was able to strike up a conversation as usual.

Only a couple months had passed since that sweaty initial encounter, so he remembered the exact line of engagement, not one that he was necessarily proud of, but it had had the intended consequence: "You lucky enough to run around this reservoir every day?"

Jacob was always looking for an opening to tell a stranger what he did, especially if it was a cute, fit, young lady. How many twenty-nine-year-olds got to travel with a presidential candidate? His parents definitely thought it was cool.

Shoot—call Mom. She's left like seven messages and wants to know I'm still alive, he remembered thinking.

"You don't live here?" Sophie had asked, almost with disappointment.

Then her coolness transformed itself into the excitement he had anticipated after he said, "No, I'm on the Taylor campaign. But we get to town every couple of weeks."

He let her cut him in line for the fountain, and after they exchanged pleasantries, they agreed to meet for a drink that night at Becky's, a bar on the Upper West Side, near Sophie's apartment. Fortunately for Jacob, the place was not too far from the Brinmore, where he and the governor were staying. The drink went well enough and each was sufficiently intrigued and attracted to the other that they exchanged an awkward kiss—he was ten inches taller than she—and agreed to meet again the next time Jacob was in New York.

"I know I'm going out on a limb here, but a bottle of Frog's Leap for you and your lovely guest?" Marco said with a smile. Marco had been waiting on Jacob and the governor for years. In the lounge after a long day of politicking and fundraising, Marco would bring them a bottle of Frog's Leap Sauvignon Blanc to take the edge off in front of whatever game was on the flat-screen TV. Jacob always thought they should be drinking something more manly than white wine, but it was the governor's favorite, and Jacob obliged.

"Absolutely," Jacob replied, then quickly backpedaled, remembering he wasn't sitting with Taylor. "Well, assuming you like sauvignon blanc, Sophie?"

Frog's Leap wasn't the cheapest bottle on the menu, but it was close. It was expensive enough that you wouldn't embarrass yourself for ordering it but cheap enough, by New York standards, not to warrant an internal audit by the chief of staff, Billy Wortherlin. Jacob found himself cross-examined by Billy after nearly every trip to New York. Although Billy was on the government staff, he watched the campaign finances like a hawk and always gave the governor and Jacob agita for what they spent on the road. Billy liked to sit down for hours, meticulously going through details, which drove the governor and Jacob, who liked to move at the quickest pace possible, mad. Given that Jacob wasn't even with the governor on this particular night, he knew he'd get interrogated by Billy when he returned to Georgia. Small price to pay for not having to admit to Sophie he couldn't even afford to take her to the two-for-one-margarita-night restaurant down the street.

"Is it red or white?" Sophie asked sheepishly.

Jacob was surprised by how off guard the comment caught him and found himself feeling a bit embarrassed in front of Marco. This was strange, given how her question was exactly the type of thing he had thought drew him to Sophie in the first place.

And his bank account was bordering on the red, so who was he to judge? Not caring what other people thought was a trait he tried to embrace but never could quite live up to. And, unfortunately, the characteristic seemed to be getting worse. The more traveling he did with the governor, the more he wanted to look, speak, and act right. Even though his dad was a well-off doctor, at home growing up, they knew the difference between Sprite and 7Up, not sauvignon blanc and Riesling. A spicy Italian foot-long from Subway was a great night out.

As if he were psychic, Marco replied, "Until I started working here, I had no idea either. I once served someone who said they wanted 'a nice pinot' a bottle of pinot grigio instead of pinot noir and almost got fired. Who knew that was grounds for firing? Sorry. That was a long-winded way of saying, it's white, miss."

Sophie smiled at Marco, clearly appreciating his friendliness. "Yes, white sounds great."

"Wonderful. I'll bring it right out. Are you ready to order before I go for the wine? The usual, Jacob?"

I always order a cheeseburger and fries and I just got embarrassed that Sophie didn't know if sauvignon blanc was white or red. What's wrong with me?

"You know what? I think tonight I'll change it up. I'll take the chicken with prosciutto and sage. Sophie, you can pick from one of your other two dishes and we'll share." Jacob winked and smiled. "Just as long as it's not shrimp. I'm actually allergic to shrimp and my EpiPen is in Georgia. And, although they keep it immaculate, I'd rather not spend my night on the bathroom floor."

Shoot. Too much?

"I'm allergic to shrimp too!" Sophie yelped, as if they had just found a winning lottery ticket.

"Okay, so no shrimp. Miss, what can I get for you?" Marco attempted to finagle his way out of playing the role of Chuck Woolery on *Love Connection.*

"I'll have the cheeseburger, medium rare, with fries, please."

"Very well, miss." Marco turned to walk away so only Jacob could see his face when he silently mouthed, "She's a keeper."

"So to what do I owe this pleasant surprise?" Sophie said, raising her shoulders. "I thought you were supposed to go back to Georgia this afternoon with your boss."

"Hmmmm . . . you want the truth or a lie?"

"Oh, definitely a lie. I love it when guys lie to me." She rolled her eyes.

"Actually, I can give you both, all wrapped up into one."

"That's what makes me nervous about you."

"So tomorrow morning I'm supposed to meet with David Dowling. He's a BSD. Olivia, my friend who I mentioned to you, the one I just hired onto the campaign, she had a meeting with him scheduled tomorrow and invited me to come along." *Don't lie. You like this girl,* he reminded himself. "Okay, so I kind of invited myself so I could stay the night and see you," he admitted.

"BSD?"

"Oh, sorry, campaign speak. Big Swinging Dick. The type of guy who does what he wants, when he wants. And can raise *a lot* of money for a politician, if so motivated. We're hoping to get him going. I think he could be one of Taylor's biggest fundraisers for the upcoming presidential, if he so chooses."

"Are you a BSD?"

"I'd call myself more of an MSD . . . you know, Medium Swinging Dick." If that man-parts thing came to fruition—and Jacob was thinking the potential had reemerged—he didn't want there to be a letdown.

"You guys sleep together?"

"Me and the BSD? Look, I get impressed by that stuff, but not that impressed."

"Nope. You and Olivia."

"Ha! No."

"I saw *The West Wing* once and couldn't understand a lick of any of the political crap they were talking about. All I took away was that everyone was either sleeping with each other, used to sleep with each other, or wanted to."

"No, Olivia is just a good friend. We haven't laid a finger on each other, scout's honor. We met back in the '06 campaign."

"It's so funny how you do that."

"Do what?"

"You never speak in years, just campaigns. Like there you said you met her in the '06 campaign and when I asked when you moved to Georgia you said during the '08 campaign, and that cut on your arm you got at the start of the '04 campaign."

Jacob laughed, impressed she had remembered all that, but also that she had caught something he never noticed about himself. It was true. His life, at least for the last decade, was divided into campaigns. "I do do that," he said.

"It's kind of like parents who relate everything to their kids' ages. You know, my mom always says things like, 'Oh, the spaceship went up when Sophie was five.'"

"Campaigns are kind of like kids."

"Okay, so which years does this one cover?"

"This one really got started about three months ago, in February, although we did spend a year as a PCIT, 'Presidential Campaign in Training.' Technically—well, hopefully—it runs through next November, but actually the big test is coming up this February, just nine months away."

"February?"

"Yeah. We've put all our eggs in one basket, so to speak, and the basket is the Iowa Caucus. It's the first contest of the primary season and if we win that, we sail through to November."

"With just one primary?"

"Yep. Iowa for us is like the first domino. If we win, we've been promised certain endorsements, a few political and, more importantly, some of the major unions. So all roads lead to the Iowa Caucus."

"Wow. So he could really be president, huh?"

"He really could." As many times as Jacob said it, he always found himself a bit surprised and excited by the statement. It was truly colossal.

"So then you would go work in the White House?"

"That's the plan."

"Has that always been your plan?"

Jacob sat back. He thought about it for a second.

"Actually not at all. The plan was business school, corporate America, and early retirement. Pretty basic stuff, you know? Figured I'd have my corner office at Goldman by thirty-four and my plane by thirty-six. Working in politics was just a way to bide my time until I could cram enough GMAT information into my brain. But then I met the governor after he gave this amazing speech at the Democratic convention and, well, everything changed."

"Yeah, now you're flying in private planes and sitting in corner offices at twenty-eight."

"I guess so." Jacob smiled. He shook his head, thinking about how much his plans had been altered in the past few years. He had always thought of himself as much more of a realist than an idealist. No one who knew him would have ruled out politics as a career choice—he was, after all, always voted best personality or most sociable, and though not the class clown, he had an innate talent for lightening an awkward room with a joke. But if you asked his family, still holed up in the sub-urbs of Chicago, or his fraternity brothers at Michigan, any of them would have pegged him for running within the Republican Party, not the Democratic one. His turn from the captain of the wrestling team and all-around complacent but fun-loving kid to the maestro of liberal politics often surprised even him. "I know it sounds corny but those things just seem like such small potatoes now."

"From corporate America to world domination."

Jacob laughed. Logically he knew it sounded crazy, but actually it was what they were fighting for. Landon Taylor was going to change the world, and Jacob was going to be by his side the whole time. He ridiculed himself in his head and shook himself back to reality. "Don't get me wrong, I still plan on getting my corner office and plane. Just may take a few extra years."

"Do you think he'll win?"

"Yeah. This guy, Sophie," he said sincerely, "he's not like the others."

By the time the food came, Jacob had given her a crash course in campaigning and had sounded, he thought, at least smart enough to get his man parts back in the running for the evening. Dinner after that was as smooth as one of his best-planned events. After a long meal with plenty of wine, Jacob walked Sophie home. He had tried to get her to stay at the Brinmore with him, but she said she wasn't comfortable sleeping in a hotel in her own town, reminding him how weird it ac-tually was that he lived most of his life in a hotel. "Sketchy" was the word she had used. As he kissed her good night and walked away he found himself not even bothered that she hadn't seen his man parts. She was pretty and fun and reminded him what it felt like to be normal.

THREE

The email showed up like a mass email, but then Olivia noticed there wasn't any subject.

LET@LTaylor.com: *Hey, Hoya, what's your pin?*

Pin? What did that mean? Was it for her? Was it him? He couldn't actually have that email address, could he? She felt a flurry of nervousness in her stomach.

LivGreenley@gmail.com: *My pin?*

That seemed like the only thing to write back. That way, if he didn't mean to send it to her or if it wasn't him she could figure it out. She stared around her office, a small room left over from the district attorney's large campaign space, which, aside from her, had since been emptied. It was packed with boxes on their way to storage and remnant posters, as well as clothes she needed to take home. She waited impatiently for the blinking red light.

LET@LTaylor.com: *Press reply then type in "mypin" and then hit the space bar.*

She followed the instructions and when she pressed the space bar the "mypin" turned into the red letters and numbers that she assumed were "her pin."

Cool, she typed, still not understanding what the heck a pin was. As the little arrow in the corner started to send the message she flinched.

I probably should've said, "Nice to meet you. So excited to work for you."

Or something. Jeez. Near leader of the free world and that's the message I send? "Cool"? But before she could think another thought, her Black-Berry lit up. A red message stood waiting.

PIN 317323: So you ready to raise me millions or what?

Olivia smiled. She could almost feel his smile through the text.

PIN 678018: Hmmm. Depends really. You ready to pay me millions?

Her "pin" was sent back in red. She wasn't supposed to be this casual. She knew that. *But he did start with "Hey, Hoya," right?* She hated these mini nervous breakdowns between messages. You were supposed to be able to discuss and analyze these with at least three friends before replying.

PIN 317323: If hope and inspiration are currency in your world then yes.

Ahhh, I get it. A "pin" is how people who totally have you pinned send you a message. Before she could come up with something to write back, another reply came in.

PIN 317323: I hear you officially start here in a month. How about we pull a test run a little early next week? You, me, and the NY donors.

It was all starting.

Olivia walked down the hall to the office of her current boss, newly elected district attorney Tom Adams. The whole floor looked, as most state government offices do, like a midlevel law firm designed and decorated in the eighties, with brownish carpeting and cream-colored wallpaper that was probably a little brighter, maybe even white, when it was put up. Each new occupant changed a picture here and there, the Democrats adding Clinton's portrait, the Republicans Reagan's. But all in all, it stayed exactly the same. Olivia peered into some of the offices, saying her hellos to those she knew from the campaign, all of whom seemed eager to get right back to work. Fundraisers were the most popular kids at the table up until the election, but the minute it was over—win or lose—they lost all worth.

Olivia told her boss she was going to take the day to help Governor Taylor with meetings. When she originally let him know she would be leaving his office entirely to work for Taylor, Adams had flinched, but there wasn't really any question of whether or not she should stay nor negotiations he could offer her. As expected, Adams was actually glad to let her go. Even he was surprised that she had been offered the high-ranking job, and with Taylor on the brink of possibly being president, having a former staffer on the inside was a total coup. Also, it would connect the two of them in the donor base, and Adams, like any politician considering a future run, saw the upside to that. More specifically, Adams relished the possible access to Taylor's lists.

Lists. Campaign Lesson #12: Political fundraising lists are hot commodities. Olivia understood the idea of it: political donors who gave to one person were most likely to give to another of the same ilk. The weight that candidates put on those lists, though, seemed completely irrational to her. They would spend hours going through them, picking out names they knew or making connections to how they could get to them. The candidates' view was, almost across the board, that the money raised directly corresponded to the number of people on a list. Statistically that made sense, but the truth was that cold-calling a list, no matter how good it was, would warrant only two or maybe three contributions you wouldn't have gotten anyway.

Adams was an extreme version of the politician who dreamed that every new list held a fortune just waiting for his campaign coffers. He was obsessed with other peoples' lists. Olivia was constantly having to download other politicians' filings and translate them into usable formats—a horribly laborious task. For their last event they'd mailed to twenty-two thousand people and got two hundred and fifty donors, none of whom came from anything other than Olivia's core list anyway. Even the thought of it made her cringe.

Plus, the truth was that Olivia had just about overstayed her welcome at Adams's PAC, and given the continued failure of her resolutions for the past four New Year's—to go teach skiing in Colorado—they both knew she would need a new job soon. *PAC, political action committee— what a stupid name. It isn't political, it rarely takes action, and there's never any actual committee.* In practice, a PAC was more of a holding company that allowed politicians to either keep paying the staffers they didn't want to lose between campaigns or to offer those staffers a needed cushion between Election Day and a new administration job. Adams knew, with four years before his next serious election, that her time with him was about up and that Taylor would be a great new place for her to land.

Walking out of Adams's office, she didn't even wait until she reached the water cooler before enthusiastically grabbing at her pocket for her BlackBerry.

Looking forward to it, she pinned the governor, doing her best to play it cool, and then immediately started plotting out what she would wear.

⟋⟋⟋

Getting back to Georgia after a New York trip usually left Jacob with almost a hangover feeling, but the past two days had been different. Getting Olivia on board meant the campaign could really start moving, and his date with Sophie had left him unable to stop smiling. He loved the adrenaline of both. The pieces were falling into place.

He paced with antsy steps outside of the governor's office, waiting for him to get off whatever call was taking him so long. He flopped down on the visitors' maroon leather tufted couch that had become more comfortable as it got a little more worn in and stared up at the framed map of Georgia that hung across from him. Offices in the South seemed so much more regal than those up north. Almost an extension of Southern manners, they were decorated with a certain grace and tradition that just wasn't found in New York. The ceilings were high and each corner had a beam that seemed like it had been taken off a plantation. Of course, Taylor had added a wall of Georgia sports heroes and the ten-foot mural of himself, Aubrey, and the kids, both of which detracted a bit from the elegance of the place. *Classic Taylor,* he thought, *Southern tradition with a twist of superstardom.*

"What is taking him so long?" he mumbled under his breath.

The governor's assistant, a thin woman, probably in her sixties, named Arlene, who talked with a particularly slow drawl, glanced up almost as if he had yelled the question. She was a career assistant who had been passed down from one governor to the next, with seemingly little concern paid to who they were or what they stood for. "Hard work is the yeast that raises the dough," she would say, addressing everyone as if she were talking to one of her sixteen grandkids. It probably was the multitude of offspring that armed her with a knack for hearing what people said under their breath. "The governor sure does have molasses in his britches today," she said, concurring.

"Yeah," Jacob replied, enjoying another one of her classic sayings, and then quickly corrected himself. "I mean, yes, ma'am." Something about older Southern people made him acutely aware of his habitually poor English. He picked himself up from the couch, deciding to take action.

He peered into the office, trying not to lose his cool. "Governor, we really have to leave." They were late again for the morning briefing, which would undoubtedly make them late for the rest of the day. Aubrey had already texted Jacob twice, not-so-subtly explaining how "unhappy" she would be if they were late to the Habitat for Humanity event. It was his least-favorite phrase of hers. "Jacob," she'd say with a big break after "Ja-" and a loud emphasis on the "-cob," like she was auditioning for Meryl Streep's role in *The Devil Wears Prada,* "I will be ra-ther unnn-happy if he is a minute late to myyyy event today." He had heard it so many times he could detect the passive-aggressive emphasis on each syllable even in an email or text. Her insistence on getting the schedule every morning was one of Jacob's big lost battles. She would comb through it, picking apart every detail, and would often call for an explanation of why something had been put on or why something else had been left off.

On some level Jacob appreciated her intensity, and lord knew they needed her on the trail. He just wished she didn't always have to be so mean about it. Inexplicably, to anyone who knew her well, she was beloved everywhere in the country, aside from the campaign, of course. Her smiles and hair flips were enough to win them at least five to ten points in the polls, and having her stump could always pull them out of whatever hole they were in at the moment. She was happy to do it too. Sometimes it seemed she liked campaigning more than Landon did.

And she was definitely more ambitious about winning. Aubrey had been measuring the White House for curtains for years now. The inside joke on the last campaign was that the presidential candidate threw the election because he knew Aubrey carried a pocket knife that she wasn't afraid to use to make Landon president especially if he were next in line. Her ambition, though, in Jacob's view, was flawed in its stubbornness. She didn't only want them to win, she wanted them to win her way, and when they weren't doing it her way, heads would roll. Jacob had mastered the art of keeping her happy and the perhaps more difficult art of making her seem happy to the rest of the world.

"I'm on it," he had responded via email. "Like white on rice today!" He said it as he typed, trying to push a strained smile through the airwaves.

White on rice that insists on being purple, he thought as he leaned on Taylor's door and waved his hands in a speed-it-up motion. They actually needed about an hour more in their morning to make it to the event on time and there really wasn't anything he could cut from the schedule. His plan was to pull his boss from every room ten minutes early and to do that, he needed to start pulling him twenty minutes early now. The governor looked over, annoyed at being hustled along. But he obligingly hung up.

"Sorry, sir. We just have to go."

"Yeah, yeah." Taylor lightened up. "I've heard I'm on a tight schedule today."

Jacob smiled, realizing the governor had probably heard about the event twice as many times as he had. Some days Aubrey's nagging would put Taylor in an awful mood, a fact that would never be alluded to in front of him by anyone except Jacob. At first Jacob never said a word, keeping his subtle eye-rolls, as all staffers did, strictly behind Taylor's back. Half of his career had been spent putting out fires she started, and he had gotten used to it. A few years back, though, he'd had a particularly rough go of it. It was in the middle of the last campaign, and Aubrey was aggravated that Jacob had taken over her daily schedule, which until that point had been the job of Mary Elizabeth, Aubrey's just-out-of-college, naïve assistant. With great regularity, Aubrey hired, and fired, assistants young enough to tolerate being ordered around, but who would not make a single decision—including when to take a bathroom break—without express approval and direction from their boss. Rather than talk to Jacob, she jumped unannounced onto the weekly staff call, which included about thirty-five campaign workers in six different offices.

When the call turned to Aubrey's schedule, Jacob began to walk everyone through the stops she would be making. They included "retail meet-and-greets," where she would shake hands with people coming and going from stores. In grand Aubrey fashion, she piped up, without warning, when they got to the main stop of the day.

"Now, why the fuck would I stand outside a Target all day? Do any of you know how fucking cold it is in Iowa in October?!" she screamed into her speakerphone. Jacob, shocked to hear her on the call at all and trying to control the outburst, immediately fell on his sword.

"Mrs. Taylor, that is my fault. Let me call you offline right now and we can get this fixed." He made the statement in his most controlled voice.

"You can't fix this, Jacob. It's shit. The whole schedule is shit. I'll just have to go and clean up your mess like usual."

"Clean up your mess" in Aubrey-speak meant nothing more than her canceling every well-planned stop of the day and, most likely, heading off to the salon instead.

Jacob had literally held the phone away from his face, looking in disbelief, then started to apologize.

"You know what, Jacob?" she shouted loudly, her voice then rising into a shrill scream. "The next time you get the urge to schedule something, *go chew on a pencil*." And then the beep of a caller getting off the call hit the line like a slammed door.

Jacob felt the need to put his fist through the nearest wall but resisted. "Okay," he said, ending any gossip before it started, "I screwed something up this morning here, that's all that was. Sorry about that."

He took a short unnoticed breath and went on with the business of the call. When they had finished the teleconference, Jacob asked everyone to pick up their phone off speaker. "Listen, people," he had said. "We are a family and some days we all lose it. I have seen all of you lose it at least once and you have all seen me lose it more than once. We can laugh and joke about it and move on. It happens. But Mrs. Taylor's image," he argued to everyone, while also reassuring himself, "is as important to the campaign as the governor's. Our bad day might piss off our family or our loved ones. Her bad day could piss off a country. So, as a family, we are going to respect the fact that she has a bad day every once in a while and we are going to have her back. It's not going to become gossip. It's not going to become a joke. Even between us. You have to remember the scrutiny we are under. One person overhears something like this, and we all go down. We're in this together."

Silence followed.

"Not to mention," Jacob said, "I assure you that if something on this campaign is leaked, I will find out where it came from. I promise." Jacob was only twenty-four then, and he had surprised even himself by taking such complete control. Of course it helped that campaign workers revered the team mentality. Campaign lessons varied from person to person and campaign to campaign, but lesson number one was always loyalty.

To this day he felt proud of that moment and took credit, internally at least, for the fact that there had been no subsequent leaks. He had also come up with his words of steel, as he termed them: *calm, contain, control*. According to him they were the keys to making it in campaigns, especially when it came to handling people like Aubrey. And so far, they'd worked. The country never suspected that even a single curse could pass Aubrey's lips, much less the daily serving she actually provided.

As he and the governor walked to the car, Jacob laughed thinking of that episode. And he remembered how the events of that day had changed a great deal for him, and for Taylor as well. Jacob had been working late and around ten forty-five that evening when the governor came into his office and sat down. He threw his feet up on Jacob's desk, an occurrence that had not yet become familiar, and said, "So how was the day?"

"Good," Jacob replied as he listed several of the accomplishments and updated him on endorsements, half wondering if he would be fired as a result of Aubrey's anger.

"Good, good," the governor replied. "Oh, hey," he added, "I got you something." He placed a box on Jacob's desk. Jacob looked down at the box of pencils and laughed.

Ever since then the two had running private jokes about everything. Including Aubrey.

CRUD

Amazingly, Taylor made it to the Habitat for Humanity event only fifteen minutes late, and Jacob let out his first sigh of relief of the day. Habitat fundraisers were their signature event and accordingly second nature. Aubrey and Landon actually had been two of the organization's first supporters when it was just a small, faith-based community group in Georgia. It was also at a Habitat event where the Taylors met Billy, the governor's trusted adviser, longtime friend, and now chief of staff. He was a young staffer to a congressman then.

On this May morning, Aubrey and Billy were waiting at the entrance to the site when the governor's car pulled up. The governor and Jacob opened their doors and stepped out in tandem. Jacob forced a smile, pushing back his annoyance at Aubrey, who stood with her hand solidly at her hip, where it often seemed Krazy Glued. Obviously out of public eyesight, she turned her cheek to Taylor's kiss.

"You're late," she said, shooting a stare Jacob's way.

And you're a joy, Jacob said sarcastically in his head as he turned on as much charm as he could muster. "So sorry, Mrs. Taylor, we did everything we—"

She began talking in the middle of his sentence, and Jacob stopped, knowing he wasn't supposed to give an answer and kicking himself for trying. Aubrey looked at Landon with a smile that Jacob thought was more of teeth grinding than happiness.

"Darling," she said, transforming that faux smile into pursed lips, "the Angevines are here. Please remember her name is Danielle."

The governor gave a "Yes, dear" head nod, and Jacob could see one of those momentary pangs of timidity in his eyes and wondered how long it would be before Aubrey let the governor live down not remembering Danielle's name one time last year.

Billy stood back, hands folded in front of him, as always, with the unfazed look of someone who had been watching this same movie for twenty years. Jacob surveyed the chief of staff's face, unsuccessfully trying to picture him twenty years younger. Billy was one of those men who seemed stuck in time, a statuesque African-American man with grayed hair that one couldn't imagine him without. He was always dressed meticulously in a three-piece suit without deference to occasion or weather. Jacob imagined he had little choice in the matter, having met Billy's wife, Martha Ann. Martha Ann had edicts that would not be broken, and among them was, breakfast should consist of porridge, and a man should be properly dressed at all times. Jacob felt forever awkward in her presence, but especially at their first meeting, when he thought she was kidding about the porridge thing and had made a joke that was, retrospectively, not very funny. *Okay, not at all funny.* In his defense he wasn't aware porridge was something people other than Goldilocks and the three bears ate.

Martha Ann had since come to like Jacob—well, at least he thought she did. *Maybe "tolerates me" is a better term,* he thought, remembering the searing look of disapproval she'd given his khaki pants the last time they were in church together. *Must work on that,* he thought, piling it onto his ever-increasing list of resolutions. *Impress Martha Ann and Billy.* He smiled, knowing it was a near-impossible task. They were as elegant and meticulous as Billy's old three-piece suits.

The governor approached Billy and the chief of staff leaned in a bit, speaking with his usual calm. "Senator Del Giudice is here. He's warm on section 2A of the spending bill."

And that goes on the list too, Jacob thought, watching Billy ask the governor to do something without ever actually asking a question and vowing to adopt the technique. Jacob constantly felt as if he were begging for something to be said or done. Billy had a way of just mentioning a fact that would immediately spur Taylor to do just what he wanted him to do. *Of course,* Jacob thought to himself, *he also always has every domino piece in place before he asks for the push.* Like his perfectly put-together outfits, Billy laid things out well before they ever needed to be done. Everything he did was slow and methodical—one might say painstakingly slow—but he was always prepared.

Jacob often wondered how Billy managed to stay with Taylor, who was basically his polar opposite in terms of planning things out. *Opposites attract,* he thought gratefully, as he also couldn't imagine Taylor, or any of them, without Billy. Everyone loved Billy, even Aubrey, who now interrupted their conversation to say, "Thank goodness for my dear man Billy. Otherwise I would have been here by myself."

Billy smiled, ever the peacekeeper, and stayed a careful three steps behind the governor and Aubrey. He turned to Jacob and began speaking again, not exactly in a whisper but in a tone that only the person he wanted to hear his words could make out. "Good job, kiddo. I thought we were in for at least twenty more minutes."

"We almost got here early!"

Billy grinned again and continued walking quietly behind the governor.

Jacob sprinted ahead to Taylor and began grabbing the business cards that the governor was receiving from all sides and slyly passing off. When Jacob saw Aubrey grab the governor to pull him over to the Angevines, he knew he'd have at least five minutes to himself and he took the opening to run up to the stage, which was built out on the side of one of the houses under construction.

Double-check there is water on the podium. Yes. The mic level has been adjusted. Check. The right amount of chairs set. Check. The Taylor sign perfectly straight on the front of the podium. Check.

He rushed back to the Taylors' side just in time to hear them moving on from Aubrey's friends. *Calm, contain, control,* he reminded himself as he watched Billy, still steps back, clearly and serenely catching each person he needed to talk to. Jacob watched him move closer to the governor as Senator Del Giudice approached him. He barely looked as if he was moving but when the senator said, "Hiya, Billy!" sure enough they were so near to the governor that Taylor simply turned his head and was in the conversation.

When the speaking program finally began, Jacob walked back behind the hundred or so people crowded in the middle of the four houses that were being built and slid back, leaning onto one of the erected support beams. He looked around at the scene in front of him, thinking it was an exact replication of every Habitat event they had ever done, including the very first. Not that Jacob was there, but he had heard about that first event so many times, it was clearer in his mind than some of his own memories. He wondered if maybe the stories had evolved, as all political stories do, with the passing of time; it seemed less likely that they would be able to re-create the same event so many years in a row. Although they did have it down to a science. Even their stage positions stayed the same: Taylor at the podium, Aubrey stage left looking adoringly at him, Billy in back of the crowd listening intently. It was like an old rock band playing a thirty-year-old hit song live. They could do it in their sleep, but the crowd still loved it, and so did they.

Billy, who met Taylor at that first event, explained the scene to every interviewee that stepped into Taylor's offices, including Jacob, as if describing a Norman Rockwell painting come to life. "It was a cool Georgia day unsuspecting of its imminent importance," he would say. The high school quarterback, now the matured law professor, was at the podium with his beautiful wife by his side. Her blond hair blew in the subtle wind as she looked intently at him, nodding as if he were preaching her life's religion. The half-built house in the background and the hammer that Taylor had accidentally taken up with him and clumsily placed on the podium as he was speaking seemed unprofessional to Aubrey, who apparently later scolded, "Can't you juuuust fuckin' keep it together at least for the pictures?" Billy never told that part. To him the scene was "directly analogous to the country's house—desperately needed, but only half-built—and Taylor held the hammer to get it done."

Billy, then in his late twenties, was the legislative assistant to an elderly congressman whom Aubrey, a young, self-proclaimed trophy wife, just a year out of UGA, had convinced to be the featured guest speaker of her event. Aubrey could convince anyone of anything without their even realizing they had been convinced. As far as Jacob could tell, even before she won the Miss Georgia crown, the spotlight seemed to follow her around. *The universe is probably under direct orders never to let the light dim*, Jacob thought, recognizing he had spent more time than he cared to admit trying to figure out what it was that made her unacceptable behavior so acceptable to everyone else.

He was sure that it was more than just her pretty face framed by locks of always-perfectly-sculpted blond hair, though neither of those things hurt. It was something inherent in her personality. When she demanded things, people treated her as if she were doing them a favor. And as far as Jacob could tell, it was a talent she was born with.

"She kept me working!" Aubrey's mother was known to say. Which was actually fact, he had found out, not just a cute phrase. Aubrey's mom had once told Jacob that she planned on being a stay-at-home mom but went back to work because when Aubrey was in the second grade, she had marched downstairs, one hand on the hip of her frilly beauty-queen dress, and announced that she would "no longer put up with a public school education."

"Charming!" people would say when the story was recounted by Aubrey or her mom. Spoiled and obnoxious seemed more like it to Jacob. But like all things Aubrey-related, that was not something one said aloud. He sometimes wondered if it was an emperor's-new-clothes kind of thing.

Habitat for Humanity, Aubrey admitted to Jacob on the way to an event years ago, was her least favorite of the social organizations.

"I prefer anything with less dirt. But Landon really enjoys it."

And with that Aubrey had lasered in on the potential. The cause would have great mass appeal and the group was new enough that the Taylors could be a significant part in its growth, giving them the public platform they needed to get press coverage. Jacob wasn't sure how certain Aubrey had been that she had found the perfect building block for a gubernatorial or even a presidential campaign, but Jacob was sure that selfish motivation was the driving force. Any alpha girl knew that you couldn't reach the socialite apex without demonstrating real leadership, if not ownership, of a philanthropic organization. So Habitat it would be, and Aubrey walked into the organization just as she had entered the world of private schools: with the understanding that there was no other place she wanted to be.

Together Aubrey and Landon were an unstoppable force, just as she planned. Landon organized the volunteers, adding legions of his students to the workforce, then managed the crews with a roll-up-your-sleeves-together motivation. Aubrey had tapped into her social address book, inviting everyone with a name or a checkbook to the "Raise the Roof Party" she had put together on the open field next to one of the houses Landon was building.

By the time the first event kicked off, Aubrey had over five hundred people at the tented affair, all of them happily snacking on canapés arranged on pieces of lumber and Georgia peach pies on decorative step stools. She had raised more than five times the organization's entire budget. She had astounded even herself with the speed and ease with which she and Landon took it over. In the third month of planning, with half the money already raised and the Taylors footing all the bills, the founder, a minister they knew well, insisted they list themselves prestigiously on the invitation as the group's chairs.

"Only if it's helpful to the organization," Aubrey had said, probably with her usual absurdly fake sweetness. She added in the next breath how "wonderfully perfect" Landon would be as the emcee.

Taylor, then an unassuming adjunct law professor, was indeed the perfect emcee. He gave a rousing speech, saying, as Billy would recite verbatim, "We live in a world where we have taught our children to pick up litter off the street, but we have left them unconcerned with the man, the woman, the child on the street. It's time to re-instill in the new generation the idea that the purpose of life is not just to enjoy the world they were left, but to leave that world in a better place for those around them and those to come."

Now, nearly two decades later, Jacob looked back over at Billy, who seemed to emphasize his own earnestness by nodding along with the parts of Landon's speech he had written or just really enjoyed. Jacob wondered how Billy could still find fresh emotion in any of the speech. It was unquestionably one of the good ones in Taylor's repertoire but Jacob could recite it himself, and Billy had to have heard it at least fifty more times.

Billy turned his head and gave Jacob one of his typical knowing, fatherly looks. Jacob smiled and mouthed the words as the governor said them.

"I may have stumbled across Habitat for Humanity, but Aubrey put it on the map."

Billy conceded a smile when Jacob mimed a hand wave and tilted his head, exactly mimicking Taylor.

FOUR

T he day of tryout meetings with Governor Taylor came more quickly than Olivia wanted. She felt like she needed a month to plan for it. And at least another week after that to plan out her look. She slipped on her black Theory dress, which fit perfectly around her waist and hips and had a high scoop neck and knee-length hem that made it suitable for business. Her black Christian Louboutin stilettos, with their signature red soles that made Jimmy Choos seem cheap, finished out her look. She had gotten them in exchange for a scarf that Aaron and Angela, two of her favorite donors, had given her one holiday. She still couldn't believe a pair of plain black shoes could cost $590. She could barely pay her rent.

It was exchange only. And the shoes do make every outfit so much better.

Of course, she probably shouldn't have worn them as much as she did. Okay, she probably shouldn't have *run* in them as much as she did. Her first boss in politics, Gabrielle, had taught her, among other things, Campaign Lesson #6: Always have walking shoes and standing shoes. Flats to walk in and Louboutins to stand in. It was actually brilliant in theory and Olivia really tried to do it, but the number of times she was running late, literally *running* late in the heels, far outweighed the times she was prepared enough to have the walking shoes with her.

She looked at the clock. Seven fifteen. *Shit.* The first breakfast wasn't until eight thirty but she really wanted to get there early and be über-prepared. She gathered up her binder and folder. Her type-A personality had gone over and above on this one. She had the governor's schedule printed out along with extensive briefings for each of the six meetings. Each briefing had background info on the person's business, family, and anything else she could find, as well as all the money they'd given to anyone ever. She actually liked doing the research; she'd been with the district attorney so long that his briefings lately consisted of her whispering a few key points to him as they walked into a meeting. She tried to skim through the pile of papers just to triple-check for mistakes as she left her building for a much-needed coffee.

"Woo-hoo. Looking pretty there." Harun, who held down the coffee cart outside her small walk-up brick building, was the cornerstone of her every morning. Not only did he provide the essential caffeination, but he always found something to compliment her on. Even when it was tough. "Looks like you're working hard; good job, kiddo," he'd say on particularly rough days.

Her BlackBerry buzzed with a message from her sister: *Good luck today.*

She knew that Marcy didn't really want her getting into another campaign, but she was sweet enough to remember that this was a big moment for Olivia. Olivia also took the text as a warning: "I remember. Thus be prepared for a lecture or two to come on why political campaigns are bad for your health, ability to relate to the human race, and love prospects."

Thanks, Olivia wrote back, literally skipping down the subway steps. Nothing could deflate her glee on this day. She jumped through the open doors of the subway and chose to stand even though there were empty seats. She was too excited to sit. Olivia was the type of kid who always loved the first day of school, and this was that times ten.

When she bounced out of the doors ten minutes later she wasn't even fazed by the fact that she had gotten six new messages in ten minutes. She scrolled ahead to the two from Jacob.

Jacob@LTaylor.com: *How'd the 7 am go?*

Olivia felt a stroke of panic as she grabbed for her schedule and switched to the second message from him. Could she have read it wrong? Did she miss a meeting? The first meeting?

Jacob@LTaylor.com: *Just kidding. Have fun today.*

Olivia let go of the death grip she had on her papers as the blood flowed back to her fingers.

LivGreenley@gmail.com: *Soooo not funny. Almost had heart attack in subway.*

Jacob@LTaylor.com: *Sorry, but it was a little funny.*

⌒↬↬↬↫↫⌒

Jacob cackled as he threw away the empty Domino's boxes and made his bed down in Atlanta. He pictured Olivia having a nervous break-down outside of the Brinmore. She became such a spastic freak when she was nervous. He probably shouldn't have joked with her like that. But he was in such an outrageously good mood. Having her staff the day was a total coup.

After two weeks of talking every night on the phone, Jacob had convinced Sophie to come down to Georgia and visit. With a friend, of course, since Sophie told him two weeks was not sufficient time to warrant a weekend alone despite his argument that in campaign time, that was equivalent to at least three months. She and her best friend, Jane, would come down on Jacob's air miles, of which he had hun-dreds of thousands thanks to campaign travel and no time to use them himself thanks to campaign work. He needed at least a day to clean be-fore she got here. Which he would, of course, cram into an hour. He looked at his TV, embarrassed that his cable had been turned off. Even if he were trying to be organized, he probably wouldn't have caught the bill or the second and third notices with all the traveling. And he wasn't trying. Every once in a while he got the urge to get on top of his finances. Okay, well, that was really only when he started dating someone new or when he had been dating them long enough for them to get on him about it. It was too much to be organized for the gov-ernor and the campaign and then care about his own life on top of that. In fact some days he felt like a part of him was purposely rebelling by leaving his house a mess. It was the only part of his life that could be like that.

Even a week earlier, Jacob would have never even thought about missing a trip with the governor—not even for his grandmother's eightieth birthday party, which he'd skipped for work the year before. His grandma Lee didn't mind, since Jacob was helping the governor, or "my Landon," as she referred to him.

But his anxiety about how the governor would accept his minutely concocted justifications for staying in Georgia had been unnecessary. The governor hadn't even waited for the full explanation, complete with manufactured to-do lists. When Jacob had said Olivia would staff the day the governor answered with a simple, rarely heard, "Okay."

⌇

"Okay," Olivia said to herself, straightening her posture to walk into the Brinmore. Jo was, as always, greeting and maneuvering people at the door. She smiled at Olivia; threw her a kiss; mouthed, "Hi, sweetie"; and motioned her toward the corner table in the lobby.

"Crap," Olivia muttered when she saw Governor Taylor sitting comfortably, already on the last sips of his orange juice and, from the looks of it, into at least his sixth newspaper.

Why do all the candidates I work for have to be morning people?

"Good morning, Governor," she said as she reached the table.

"Hello there, Miss Olivia." He stood as he moved some papers off the chair so she could sit.

"Early start to the day?"

"I try to get up and run at six," he said with that drawl. "Leaves me enough time to get to the papers before the meetings start. Though admittedly," he added contemplatively, "it doesn't always work."

Olivia resisted the urge to make a joke about running and tell him that she hadn't run since high school soccer, as he suddenly appeared more formal and intimidating without Jacob by his side. She took a breath and composed herself.

"So what do we have on tap today?" he asked, as if he hadn't had a schedule faxed, emailed and handed to him at least four times already that morning. "Do you want a coffee?"

"I'm fine, thank you." Olivia hated eating or drinking at meetings, although she would have benefitted from the savings in food costs. She never knew what was too much or too little, and the men always deferred to her to order first. Usually she just got a Diet Coke, in meetings when it would be too awkward not to have anything.

"We've got a full schedule," she said, pulling out the folder and trying to sound her most businesslike. "I think some really good potential supporters."

"You feel good about it?"

"Sure, of course." She was unaccustomed to the question. Most candidates didn't have time for or interest in how she felt about a schedule, or anything else for that matter. At the same time Olivia realized how proud she was of the day she had put together.

"Great, great," he said, looking at her as he flipped through the pages. "Thanks again for staffing this day. I'm so glad you're coming aboard." Then he paused and looked down at his BlackBerry. "I've just gotta make one call before eight–thirty. Billy—he's my chief of staff. You've met him?"

"No, not yet. Spoke to him on the phone though."

"He's the greatest. Really good." The governor began to dial.

Olivia handed him the briefing and began to look around for Yanni, the first meeting. As she scanned the room, Jo caught her eye and came over.

"Hi, Jo."

The governor, remembering his Southern manners even during the phone call, stood and kissed her hand.

"Hello, hello," Jo said in a motherly whisper, so as not to actually disturb the call. "We have you guys set up at a corner table in the main dining room whenever you're ready."

"Thanks so much, Jo." Olivia smiled.

The governor had already gone back to his call.

Olivia sat trying to look busy without making herself so busy that she would lose her focus on him. She used the time to study him, his voice, his movements, see if she couldn't get into a rhythm that would assure donors it wasn't her first day by his side.

"Okay, okay, I understand what you're saying and I have to go to these money meetings, but do me a favor, Billy, just check the wording in that bill. It's the paragraph on top of page twelve I'm concerned with. I think we can do this better. Let's get Senator Saujani on it too. She'll help here."

A candidate who reads bills. Olivia hadn't been sure there were any of those left and adored him for actually being interested in governing, not just the politics of it.

"Okay, let's do this," he said as he hung up the phone and started to the table in the dining room.

"Just one thing I wanted to be sure you saw on this first meeting." She had watched the governor glance at his briefing but knew he couldn't have read it through. "Most likely Yanni will talk your ear off on banking issues, but just in case"—she paused, trying to consider a euphemistic way to say it—"he's had a bit of a family shake-up recently, so I'd stay away from the personal side of things."

"That's a nice way of saying what?"

"The short story is his wife just left him. For his brother's wife."

"What?!" His eyes popped so far out of his head she had to giggle.

"Governor." A brusque voice called him over to a table off to the left as they walked, cutting her explanation short. It was Stephen Bronler, the king of BSDs. Though in his case, he was at least justified in claiming that title. He had built up a small film company from scratch and had become the ultimate titan of the movie industry.

"Stephen!" The governor moved in for a big hug. "How are you, man?"

Stephen stood and threw his muscular arms around the governor. Though only an inch or two taller, he appeared to tower over Taylor because of his robust build. Olivia knew from having written countless briefings on him in the past that the cool mix of colors in his skin was a product of his Indian mother and Moroccan-Russian father. He confirmed her long-held belief that children of mixed ethnicities were, without fail, gorgeous. "Good, good. That production tax-credit law you signed for us in Georgia was huge."

"Win-win, man. We've had more state revenue off that bill than we ever imagined. If you hadn't brought that to my attention we would have missed out on a lot of good money. You know they did *The Blind Side* in Georgia?"

Olivia tried to slip into the background. She had worked with Stephen on the last presidential campaign but there was no way he could have remembered her.

"You know Olivia Greenley?" Taylor asked.

Olivia wondered if she had not kept her inner monologue to herself.

"Of course," Stephen said, moving forward and grabbing her arm. "This girl is a winner. You working for him now?" he asked, and without waiting for an answer to the somewhat awkward question, continued. "Why don't you guys come in and see me tomorrow morning? Let's talk about doing an event for you."

Olivia barely heard the rest of the conversation due to the mix of pride and relief clouding her brain and hearing.

Again characteristically not waiting for an answer, Stephen said insistently, "Ten a.m. She knows where the office is. This is going to be great."

As they walked away, Taylor turned to her and said, "Tell Jacob to make that happen. My schedule tomorrow doesn't work anyway." He hesitated, then said, "And find out how long we have to wait after the bill signing to take a contribution."

"Thanks," he added. He smiled, seemingly remembering that she wasn't yet a peon on his team. Not officially anyway.

As they proceeded to their table across the room, the governor stopped to say hello to nearly every person along the way. *Some days the Brinmore could use a rope line,* Olivia thought. The tables were filled and bustling with not quite the elite of New York City, but definitely an array of movers and shakers, just as they were every morning. In the corner booth sat the African-American politician always running for something, although no one ever seemed quite sure for what. Olivia actually loved to hear him speak at events—he was inspirational and always talked with gusto about being a Freedom Rider and marching at Selma, two things Olivia often wished she had been alive for. His oratorical skill made it all the more disappointing that he consistently made himself an easy target for character assassination. He traveled everywhere with a woman he freely introduced as his girlfriend even though he was married, noticeably paid for everything in cash, and spent his campaign war chests on things like weeklong stays in a Four Seasons hotel out of the state he was supposed to be campaigning in. *And apparently a lot of it at daily breakfasts at the Brinmore,* Olivia thought.

She followed closely behind the governor as he moved toward the front two tables. These were reserved for the real social climbers and the new people, both of whom were determined to have their costly breakfast be high-impact. Today, one was occupied by a designer who talked loudly enough for Olivia, and probably everyone else, to hear about plans for an upcoming charity ball.

"Well, what would elevate the event to *that* level?" the designer asked carefully, stirring her coffee with her well-manicured, diamond-covered hand.

Olivia laughed as the designer all but blatantly asked how big a check she would have to write to get the legendary *New York Times* social photographer Bill Cunningham to notice. Though Olivia admittedly loved looking at the pretty dresses in the Style section as much as the next girl, she couldn't help but question the absurdity of the photographer being the kingmaker for charities in the city. Any fundraiser knew the phrase "Bill Cunningham will be there" sold more tickets to a charity event than anything like "One out of three children in America will go hungry tonight."

Another politician appropriately sat at the other "climber" table. Olivia stifled an eye-roll as the short, overweight man stood in his already crinkled suit to shake the governor's hand. He had literally made a career of running losing campaigns, including the congressional one he was in the middle of.

"This one really has that winning feel to it," she heard him say, and she wondered how someone 0 for 6 would know what that felt like. Rumor had it, understandably, that his wealthy sister continually encouraged and funded his campaigns in order to keep him out of the family business. He shook Olivia's hand as the governor started to walk away, handing her the same business card she had received at least a dozen times over the years. His committee was listed as "friends of" rather than specifying any year or office so he never needed to change it.

"So nice to meet you," he said so superficially that it would have been better if he had ignored her altogether.

You have met me a million times, Olivia thought. She faked a polite smile.

"So nice to *see* you as well," she said, changing out the words. She wondered why all politicians couldn't learn Campaign Lesson #9—always use the word "see" instead of "meet," just in case. She had to smile when Taylor leaned into her as she caught up to his side and whispered, "We should get his lists."

Their hellos had given Yanni Filipaki plenty of time to get settled at the table. He didn't mind that the walk around the room had made Taylor technically fifteen minutes late to the actual table, since that walk confirmed that the most popular kid in the cafeteria was ending up with him. Yanni was a Greek shipping heir turned trader, turned playboy, turned just about anything he wanted since he was worth billions. With an "-s." She had met him on the district attorney's race, where he had given over $150,000. He had also hosted events, and as someone always willing to lend a helicopter or one of his three jets, he had soared, quite literally, to the top of Olivia's PPL.

The PPL, or "private plane list," was an ever-important Excel sheet that listed all the important details about private planes that candidates might need to borrow. It had each plane's size, number of seats, whether or not it needed to refuel on a cross-country trip, and what the actual costs of its usage were on the off chance one needed to report it as a contribution. Olivia had gotten creative with her list while procrastinating one night, so it now also contained notes detailing things like "Yanni's biggest plane serves hot food" and that the hedge-fund manager and designer wife's plane had "the most comfortable couches and most spacious bathroom." Jacob was always prodding her to add a ranking column for the attractiveness of female flight attendants and X's for flights with the dreaded male attendants, but Olivia had yet to oblige.

From the instant they sat down, Yanni and the governor clicked. Olivia sat quietly through breakfast, marveling at the governor's ease in gliding between subjects—export, import, banking, jazz, and American history. They even seemed to have read and memorized all the same articles in Golf Digest. Yanni, medium height and medium build, sat back comfortably in his chair. He had a mop of curly black hair and matching bushy eyebrows that would probably have seemed more intense if not for his always perfectly tanned skin. Olivia wondered if that was his natural Greek coloring or if it was due to his weekend jaunts to the Caribbean. *Probably both,* she thought.

In meetings like this she often felt like a fly on the wall of a man date and tried to stay on that wall so as not to disrupt the flow of the breakfast. Only toward the end of the meeting, when the conversation turned to the Hamptons, did she chime in.

"Yanni has a palace out there and throws the best parties ever," she said, knowing it would please both men by boosting Yanni's ego and providing an easy segue for the governor to ask for an event.

"It's not as nice as my place in St. John but it'll do." Yanni played right into the ask. "We should do an event for you out there."

"That would be great."

"How much does one of those events have to raise?" Yanni asked, chomping on a piece of bacon.

Olivia jumped in, saving the candidate from having to say a number, something candidates across the board hated.

"We'd need it to raise at least a hundred thousand dollars to justify taking him out of Iowa."

Taylor glanced over at Olivia, clearly impressed with her gumption.

"But how much does it have to raise to be a good one?" Yanni asked.

"Depends how good you want it to be!" Olivia knew this game well and thought she could get him to at least $500,000 before the breakfast was over, but Governor Taylor was relatively new to Yanni.

Breaking the game of chicken, he piped up. "Our top raiser raised us about two hundred and fifty thousand dollars at one event in California."

Olivia was thrown by the low number, but she figured it would be an easy one for Yanni to top and she wasn't wrong.

"Well, then," Yanni said with a smile, "put me down for two fifty-one and let's get this thing scheduled. Can't have New York trailing Los Angeles. Who else are you meeting while you're in town? How long are you here?"

"We've got a full day of meetings," Olivia boasted.

The governor finished her sentence, proud of his newly scheduled morning meeting with Bronler: "And we just added on a meeting with Stephen." He glanced over at the film producer, knowing everyone recognized him simply by his first name. "So now we'll be here till tomorrow."

"Perfect. Well, now I've got your dinner plans," Yanni said without waiting to hear if the governor could even make a dinner engagement with Yanni. "We can wrangle some cohosts for my event."

As Yanni scribbled down a location for seven o'clock that night and said his good-byes, Olivia heard Jo receiving a boisterous greeting at the door.

Ugh. I know that voice.

Olivia looked to the door and confirmed the thought as Yanni left and Taylor sat back down to wait for their next meeting.

Chris, the former White House deputy chief of staff, whom she used to date, had walked into the room. *He moved to Manhattan just to torture me. I know it.*

She straightened, tense, trying to track his moves as he swept from table to table. He was, of course, caught up in a round of hellos. His hellos were always lively, something that had first attracted her to him. People seemed to love when he arrived, regardless of the people, regardless of the room. He had an infectious charm. And that was not just the biased opinion of someone who used to love him. Orin, one of her favorite donors, once commented to her that Chris's walking and preaching at events was such a natural fluid movement that he seemed more like an athlete than a politician. *Taylor has that too,* Olivia thought. It was a rare gift to be able to make a speech or a round of hellos look like a beautiful dance.

Of course in Chris's case, as Olivia found out over the course of two years, that art was used without restraint and was practiced on women even more habitually than it was directed at politicos. He had broken her heart in a cruel, unexpected way. Who was she kidding? It was a totally expected way. Intellectually expected at least. *Damn expectations,* Olivia thought. She hated the phrase "Keep your expectations low." *I wonder if that has ever made disappointment less hurtful or easier to handle for anyone.* Never that she could remember.

The low expectation she was supposed to have—the one she swore to everyone, including herself, that she had—that Chris was capable of being in a monogamous relationship (any Google search would have invariably demonstrated the low odds) did not make finding out that she was not his only girlfriend any less painful. *Lucky. You're lucky,* she silently repeated, like a yoga chant reminding herself that the now-married Chris had lied to her with great regularity. *I'm lucky he didn't pick me, I would not want to be married to him. I would not want to be married to someone who cheats.* Olivia held tight to the words in the hopes they would function like a shield and fend off his admittedly handsome eyes and smile. Sure enough, his deep blue eyes were upon them when Olivia looked up from her thoughts. Taylor stood to give him a hug.

"My man, the gov," Chris said, grasping Taylor's shoulders.

Damn it, even the cheesiest of lines sound perfectly acceptable when he says them. Their two minutes of niceties and conversation were lost on Olivia while she tried to focus on staying cool, calm, and collected. *Breezy. Stay breezy, Olivia.*

"Do you two know each—"

Chris interjected before the "yes" came out of Olivia's mouth. "No one steps into New York without knowing the beautiful Olivia Greenley."

He leaned over to give her a kiss on the cheek and she politely smiled with a tense edge.

"Always the charmer," she shot right back with a huge smile, knowing the only way to fight fire was with fire. "Chris is running this state these days. Today the mayor of the Brinmore, tomorrow maybe mayor of the city."

She tried not to let her smile turn to a smirk even though she couldn't help feeling proud of doing what she always noticed him doing. That thing she could never get quite right. It would probably be Campaign Lesson #10 or 11 if she could ever learn it. It was a political bomb—couching private information in a compliment so skillfully that everyone around would be impressed at the kindness; meanwhile the person receiving the "compliment" would sting from it and have to humbly thank the complimenter for being stung. In public.

In this case, she knew he wanted to run for mayor eventually, and no one wants political ambitions known before they are announced. It was a rumor that he was constantly working to avoid.

"That's what I'm hearing. Seems the whole city is singing your praises." Taylor played right into the compliment, going on about Chris's latest appearance on CNN. Chris's eyes widened a bit—he was seemingly caught off guard—but he continued to smile.

"Well, I'll let you get back to it. Time is money when Olivia is around." Chris nodded to her and ambled away to his own table, continuing to greet people along the way.

Time is money. Hmpf. She'd really have to practice her poker face.

"Nice poker face," Taylor said, again as if he had heard her inner monologue.

"Huh?"

He cut off her embarrassing loss of words as they sat back down. "Did you work for him?"

"Ummm . . . No. I mean I helped him but no, never worked for him. We're friends . . . I mean we . . ."

"And the full-sentence translation of that is . . . ?"

"We used to date." She lowered her head in defeat.

"Oh, really?" The governor sounded surprised.

"Yeah. During the '08 campaign. Well, if you can call it that. He, well, he pretty much lived life like he was on *The Bachelor,* you know; he dated a number of girls, narrowed it down to two, and then chose one at the last minute."

"What an ass. And I take it you were in the last rose ceremony?"

"Unbeknownst to me, yeah, I guess I was. Though instead of ABC, his surprise-to-me engagement was announced on Page Six. Good times." She laughed self-consciously. It was a story she rarely talked about, and saying it aloud still made her cringe with embarrassment. *Really, Olivia? Really? Why are you saying this to the governor? Why would you tell him who you dated? Why would you tell him you dated Chris? You never tell anyone this. Idiot. Subject change stat.* "Wait, are you telling me you watch *The Bachelor*?" Luckily, her surprise that he had recognized the TV reference supplied the perfect transition.

The governor smiled. "No, I get periodic briefings on trends and fads. Apparently it makes me more mainstream. You know, people like to feel they could have a beer with me."

"Wow. How sad is that?"

"That I have to be briefed to seem human? Very."

"No, no!" Olivia laughed. "That our country wants a leader who watches reality TV shows. I mean, I feel I lose brain cells every time I watch one. I want the person running our country to be way too smart for shows like *The Bachelor*. It makes no sense. Don't you want someone so much smarter than you deciding when we go to war?" She caught herself. "I mean not you as in you, as in people other than you." *Oy.* "Case in point."

The governor sipped his coffee, seemingly pleasantly amused as she flailed about in front of him.

"Anyway, you seem plenty mainstream to me even without the reality TV show knowledge," she added.

"We'd be in good shape if there were more voters like you out there," he said as he ran his hands back through his hair. "I'm getting the hang of it though. It's funny, I remember when I was a professor, thinking that same thing. Yelling at politicians on TV who were so blatantly dumbing down the issues. It seemed so fake. Remember when Jon Stewart did that bit about how screwed up it was that people wanted to vote for someone they could get a beer with when that person was a recovering alcoholic?"

"Yes, I totally remember that. You had to laugh. It was too scary to do anything else."

"Exactly. But I'd throw a fit about it to anyone who was listening. Or not listening. About how wrong it was that those were the standards we held politicians to. And that the politicians were complacent because they played along. Then I started campaigning."

"Do you feel like you became complacent?"

"No. Well, maybe, but I understand it's not what I thought it was."

"What is it?"

"People don't want to elect someone they can have a beer with—that's just press spin on people wanting to know you can relate to them. They want to see in your eyes that you understand where they are coming from. You don't have to have a beer with them, but you have to understand and recognize their need to have a beer at the end of the day. Take *The Bachelor*. I think most people actually do agree with you. They don't want a president who watches that show. However, they do want a president who accepts the fact that they watch the show as part of their life, not just a joke. Now, you can separate the two because you have thought through the idea on a thorough and intellectual level. But most Americans don't make a distinction between what they actually want and what they say. If I know what the rose ceremony is, then in a way I know the world they live in. It's really just a connection to their needs and their lives."

"You never seem to dumb down what you say though. It's a rare ability. That thing Clinton could do too—translate an idea into someone else's language without losing the intelligence of the original thought." Olivia had marveled a lot at this talent when she watched Governor Taylor in the past.

"Thanks, Olivia." He held her eyes in an earnest gaze that made her feel close to him in a new way. "I think it's probably more of a learned skill than a talent. But thanks."

He seemed to think for a minute before saying, "I'll tell you what, it was clearly a lucky miss for you, but I think Chris made a big mistake not giving you that rose." Then he whispered in a way that seemed far less inappropriate than the words were, "I mean, if I were twenty years younger . . ." He smiled, standing up to greet their next meeting.

She tried to stop the blood from rushing to her cheeks as he moved into the next conversation. What she wouldn't have given to have met him twenty years ago. Well, no, she'd have been seven then. But if they were both twenty at the same time. She would have definitely loved him. He was the explanation she had been looking for when her friends questioned why she, someone who bought wedding magazines just to look through and who had already picked out her wedding dress, cake, and flowers ten times over, could never manage to stay in a relationship for more than two months. "I'm too busy," she would always argue.

But the truth was right there in front of her. She was in search of her Landon Taylor, and she wasn't prepared to settle for less. She smiled, happy in the knowledge that the theoretical man on the pedestal in her head actually existed. Sure, he was older than she and already married, but his existence had to mean there were others out there like him.

As Jo ushered their next meeting to them, Olivia refocused on business and as she would continue to do all day, tried to push down the inappropriate thoughts of Landon Taylor as her perfect man. *You will not be the cliché girl with a crush,* she vowed, but Olivia caught herself more than once noticing how easy it was to be around him. She had even ordered a hamburger and fries when he jokingly pushed her to order food at lunch. "Just beyond your comfort zone," he had said, "is where all the good stuff is."

Even the donors seemed of a higher caliber around Landon. The last coffee was with Melissa Lowe, a businesswoman known for her temper, who spoke passionately about the work Share Our Strength was doing to bring school breakfasts to all communities. It was actually one of Olivia's favorite parts about political fundraising, being able to see hot-tempered CEOs and hard-nosed businesspeople in situations that they loved and enjoyed, where you were, therefore, more likely to catch them exposing a kinder side of their personality. Most people, she thought, really did get involved in politics for the right reasons—to do good, to help others, to make change. Especially when they were around the right candidates.

At the end of the day, the governor's driver dropped her off at home, concluding, for her, a perfect workday.

As she slumped down into her sea-green couch, a hand-me-down from her cousins that probably could be more accurately described as a very big chair, her head flopped back and her eyes landed on the poster hanging on the brick wall. She threw her feet up on the wood Ikea coffee table in front of her and considered the black and white photo of Martin Luther King, Jr. leading a huge march. Behind him stood a front line of people holding hands, each with a more determined look on their face than the next. She had gotten the poster in high school and it had been one of the few things to survive both the move to college and the bumpy U-Haul trip back from DC. She wondered if perhaps she had finally found her own movement, her own march, her own leader.

FIVE

Later that night her BlackBerry lit up with a red message. Being superstitious, she hadn't saved Governor Taylor's name into her contacts, but no one else in her life sent pins, so she knew it was him. *Note to self, find out what pins are!*

PIN 317323: Hey. Usually donors ask me to drop my staffers, not demand they come back. With some fans of yours. You busy?

Olivia's heart skipped a beat as she looked around at her half-baked French-bread pizza in the toaster oven; the computer, open to Adams's latest list, the one she promised him she would finish before officially leaving his employ in three weeks; and the DVR'ed *Colbert Report* playing on her TV. *Be professional. Sound busy. But not too busy. Write back quickly,* she ordered herself.

PIN 678018: For my fans? Never too busy. How can I help?
PIN 317323: Secondo, 51 and Madison. 20 min?

Yes. Of course she wanted to go. Obviously anything would have been better than going through another list, but this—this was her invitation to sit at the grown-ups' table. She picked up her phone to tell someone. Then she quickly put it down. Campaigns left little time for friends so she hadn't talked to anyone non-campaign-related in weeks. Okay, months. Any conversation now would have to be longer than a quick squeal about her night-to-be.

She could call her sister, who knew about the Taylor job, but then she'd have to turn down an invitation to go away this weekend, again. She could call her mom in Westchester, but then she'd have to answer for the fact that no, she had not yet called Dr. Henner to make her annual appointment, for the third year in a row. She shook her head in frustration. *Campaigns really turn relationships into a lot of work. Who has time anyway?*

She didn't even have time for a shower. Twenty minutes were barely enough to get to Fifty-first Street even if she took a cab, which she really didn't want to do. She'd already spent her self-imposed cab quota for the week. The quota she never kept to.

She glanced at her closet and groaned. It was full of useless items. Worn-out and mostly wrinkled—New York City dry cleaning was not a viable option on her salary—Banana Republic and J.Crew suits. All of which were about two sizes too big since she'd lived solely on Doritos and mochas on the last campaign. Surprisingly enough, stress and junk food made a better diet plan than Jenny Craig.

She looked at the Brooks Brothers shirt. *Wore that last time.* Then her eyes turned down to the black dress from earlier in the day that was strewn on the floor, amazingly not wrinkled. *Well, not too wrinkled. Just stick with what you had on,* she decided as she traded out the comfy sweats she had adopted the minute she walked in the door. *Definitely could've hung that up.* It would do though and kept her looking professional. Plus if she kept her outfit the same, her what-to-wear-freak-out might be slightly less obvious. *Probably not.*

She reapplied her makeup, which looked much better than it did when she put it on in the cab in the morning, and managed to get her too-long hair—*Must get haircut*—to look decent hanging down around her face. Her Chanel bag would be the perfect finishing touch. It was a ridiculous pink Chanel clutch. It cost three times a month's rent and it was, for the most part, totally useless. Aleksander Yerkhov, a fabulous Russian donor, had gotten it for her on her last birthday, and like all things Alek had presented to her, she had thought about returning it or putting it up on eBay. But in this case, her momentary hesitation gave way to frank understanding that she loved the purse; it was just too pretty and too completely fabulous to let go of. And in Olivia's convoluted justification on the day she received it, it did come in handy on nights like these, when she was off to meet people who owned one in every color.

She was not surprised that Alek had chosen something that delighted her. He understood women. He was a fruit importer, around sixty-five, but he always seemed to have a young woman on his arm. To Olivia, he never seemed anything other than fatherly. He loved buying treats for campaign staffers—bags, jewelry—because he said he remembered when he was a young man and all these wonders were out of reach. Plus, he said, he felt as if he were contributing to peace on earth since staffers "spent their lives trying to make se world better."

"I don't have se guts to give up my salary to do it, so least I can do isss support you kids who do," he would say in his thick Russian accent. "Bezides, I've got no kids and ser's already a school and a hospital, they name it after me. No reason not spend se rest behfore I die."

Who could argue with that? She ran her hands over the perfectly quilted pink leather and remembered that it was Jacob who first introduced her to Alek. He knew him through Governor Taylor, who had first brought Alek into politics. Apparently, they had met when Taylor helped him with some huge Georgia peach deal and they had remained close friends. Alek was always talking about his weekly trips to Atlanta. Add that to the list of positive things about the Taylor campaign.

She took a quick look in the not-quite-clear mirror that hung sloppily over her closet door, remembered to turn off the toaster oven on her half-baked French-bread pizza, and headed off to Secondo.

Secondo was one of the best Italian restaurants in the city. And for the BSDs it was a favorite for two particular reasons—first, the black truffles, some of the finest in the world, were offered on pasta in the way most restaurants offer Parmesan cheese. The amount of truffles ordered was in direct proportion to the amount paid. So it was one of the best ways in the city to sit at a table and show everyone how rich you were. The second reason, Olivia had learned was that to get in, you had to walk down a long flight of stairs. The restaurant below was windowless, so the BSDs stood a better chance of not being spotted dining there with women who were decidedly not their wives.

Now Olivia walked down the famed steps with confident enthusiasm and practiced in her head the words, "I am here to meet Governor Taylor and Yanni Filipaki."

The fantasized vision of belonging in this setting came to a crashing halt though as she turned the corner. Back in the L-shaped part of the restaurant was a long table. It was a table she knew well. She also knew the uncomfortable rush of insecurity flushing through her.

She could see the backs of real estate titan Matt and his best friend, the boisterous financier Chris, with their flavors of the month, this time former models turned B-list celebrities. Both women had that long blond wavy hair that made them seem as if they had just gotten off the beach—that is, if the beach had been staffed by stylists and makeup artists. Their couture dresses made the black dress Olivia thought was so hot before she walked in the door now seem like a nun's frock.

Yanni sat with the governor on his right, and on his left was Erin, a familiar-looking girl who had often been with him at events. She was not quite as beautiful as the models, but her last divorce had left her with enough money to stay well dressed and well made up at all times. Around the rest of the table were more of Yanni's friends, most of whom Olivia knew from previous campaigns. There was Stu, the short, stocky hedge fund manager, whom Olivia actually liked and thought was entirely sincere in his political involvement. Of course that sincerity could only be seen on nights like tonight, when his horrid wife wasn't yelling at him and everyone around him. Next to him sat Todd, the heir to a publishing company who, despite his title of president, never seemed to do any actual work. He had his arm around his Dallas Cowboy–cheerleader girlfriend, the one who had reportedly chased away his second wife. All of them seemed to be talking and laughing over one another, as always, with no regard to the experience of the rest of the patrons, who were clearly frustrated with the noise level.

The governor, with his back to the wall, was the first to notice Olivia. "Hello there."

She smiled, reminded of the first time she had met him in the Brinmore.

The seriousness of the workday had worn off for him, probably with the help of a few glasses of wine, and he had reverted to the man who had flustered her originally. His sandy brown hair dipped over his blue eyes as he rose from his chair.

"We were wondering if you'd show up."

Yanni got to his feet and grabbed a chair from the next table. With no regard for anything around him, he lifted it over his date's head. "Sit here." Yanni motioned as he threw the chair between him and the governor.

Olivia walked around the table saying her hellos and offering casual nice-to-see-yous to the women, who weren't at all embarrassed to be there as the dates of married men. As Olivia thought they should have been.

"Heya, beautiful," Todd said as he stood and greeted her with a hug that went inappropriately around her waist. She tried to chalk it up to his just being overfriendly or drunk. Nonetheless, his calling her beautiful gave her a little ego boost and she stood a bit taller as she shimmied behind Yanni to the empty chair. He lifted his head as she walked by and gave her a peck on the cheek.

"I like starting and ending the day with you," he joked.

"As do I." The governor stood to pull her chair out.

Olivia smiled, impressed that wine didn't seem to diminish the governor's Southern manners. She felt happy to settle in.

"You gotta catch up," Yanni said, pouring her a glass of red wine.

Curses. Red wine puts me to sleep. She immediately scolded herself: *Deal with it.*

"The wine is the best I've ever had. Yanni should be a sommelier." Taylor clapped his hand on Yanni's shoulder.

Olivia marveled at how fast these two grown men had seemingly become best friends.

"Let's get you some food," the governor added.

Olivia looked around at the plates of half-eaten salad as Yanni yelled out for help.

"I'm good, fine, thank you," Olivia said, trying to hush him, but the waiter was already there, ever attentive to the raucous table and probably pleased to be adding more to the bill.

"What can I bring you?"

Olivia looked around and quickly realized a menu wasn't in

sight. Wanting to take the focus off of herself as quickly as possible, she ordered the only thing she remembered they had.

"Fettuccine *ai porcini*, please." It wasn't really what she wanted, but it was definitely better than the Stouffer's French-bread pizza she had left behind. Just the sound of the caloric intake involved in the fettuccine caused the women at the table to squeal. Olivia smiled to cover her insecurity, wishing she could just once fit in at a table like this. Her mind instantly flashed back to being ostracized for ordering pizza at the cafeteria in the seventh grade. She had spent homeroom talking to her favorite social studies teacher about the Bosnian War and had missed the pact all the other girls had made to eat only carb-free items that week. She wondered if she would ever find that place between her need to save the world and her desire to just fit in, or if they were inherently, and forever irreconcilable.

Thankfully, the conversation turned to the campaign, and Olivia sat up a bit taller and took a sip of her wine. *Oh, so that's what people mean by good wine,* she thought, having never before tasted such a difference.

Yanni was asking about the primary opponents and Taylor summarized the bios of everyone even considering a run. He explained that Senator Kramer was their only real challenge, and that if they could beat him early in Iowa, they would clear the field. Olivia listened as the governor spoke about Iowa politics in such detail that it was as if he were talking quantum physics.

"Seriously," Olivia said, leaning over, when there was a break in what seemed like a university-length lecture, "if this guy raises five million and puts together union support, which, by the way, will come with the money, and we top it off with an Iowa win, you guys are sitting with the next president of the United States."

That kind of talk completely invigorated these BSDs. "Five million dollars? I'll have to throw two parties," Yanni crowed with a laugh.

"And don't think he's not already scheduled as a keynote speaker at next month's Harkin Steak Fry in Iowa." Olivia put down her wineglass with a confident, heavy hand. It made a clinking noise against the side of her plate. She was so sure of herself, she barely noticed Taylor's look of astonishment.

"So you know the steak fry." He gazed at her approvingly.

Neither her district attorney's race nor the rest of the jobs on her résumé required her to have an education in national retail politics, so he must have been startled by her knowledge of this minutia—and his speaking schedule. She could feel how much he liked this expertise.

"The Harkin what?" Matt asked.

"Harkin Steak Fry," the governor explained, still looking at her. "Senator Harkin's been doing this annual fundraiser in Indianola since before time. Everyone turns out for Harkin." His eyes went to the group. "It might as well be the opening ceremonies for the Iowa Caucuses."

"Indianola. I think that's where we refuel the Hawker on the way to L.A. when the Gulfstream is out of commission. Who knew I could have been stopping in for some fried steak?!" Yanni joked, waving his hand to get the waiter's attention. "One more of these," he yelled across two tables as he swung the empty bottle of wine in the air.

Olivia seized the opportunity, "How about you take the Hawker even when the Gulfstream is *in* commission and we can get off at your pit stop? We'll bring you back the fried steak. The Hawker beats Midwest Airlines any day."

Yanni laughed, continuing on to a different story, while Olivia sipped her wine knowing full well she would soon set that exact routine in motion.

"Well, when Erin and I started dating four years ago . . ." Yanni said as he grabbed Erin's shoulder. He started telling a story about how he had brought the head chef of Cipriani, Erin's favorite restaurant, on board to cook the first time she flew in his plane.

When Yanni turned to get Matt's attention for the end of the anecdote, the governor turned toward Olivia and pulled her in a bit, ribbing her under his breath. "Thought you said he got divorced this year. So much for you being the staffer who knows everything."

Olivia sat up a little, jolted by the touch of his hand on her shoulder but still holding on to the confidence of the last conversation. "He did," she whispered back with a grin that acknowledged the incongruous math.

Taylor gave a look that mugged extreme bewilderment.

Olivia couldn't help but laugh a little as the governor's hand fell down off her shoulder but didn't disappear.

Holy cow, it's on my back. She suddenly felt like there was a spotlight on her and that it was obvious to everyone that his hand had found a place on the small of her back. *The governor's hand is on my back. It's not moving. It has found a comfortable place on my back. Comfortable? No, not comfortable. What the hell? "Comfortable"? Why would I even call it that?* Olivia felt the sweat build up on her neck—which she knew meant she was blushing. *We're in public. Someone's going to notice. Will he say something? Is this inappropriate? When is someone going to notice? Has someone already noticed?* She looked around at everyone resuming their own conversations, totally oblivious to her panic. They seemed to move in slow motion, their dialogue making just blurred sounds. Olivia tried to focus on the words. *Concentrate,* she begged her ears as the table's volume slowly came back to a normal level. Governor Taylor had steered into a conversation on health care reform, seemingly without missing a beat.

Is this not weird? Should I be more pulled together? Yes. Pull yourself together. He's Southern. He's a politician, connecting with people, this is his job, it means nothing. It's a handshake.

She tried to stop the swirling in her mind when another thought hit. *It's nice.* She hadn't noticed how strong his hands were. She felt almost as if her back were resting on his hand rather than the other way around. As much as she tried to talk herself out of it, she couldn't escape the bubble she felt she was in. The bubble where the only thing that mattered was his hand on her back. The hand that moved gently when he laughed and tensed up when he spoke seriously. The hand that grabbed at the ends of her hair as he reached for another glass of wine. Every move registered with Olivia like she had her own personal Richter scale. How was it possible that she was in an earthquake zone and no one else seemed to notice the shocks? The only thing that helped was the wine, so Olivia downed it.

Three glasses and a healthy serving of truffles later ("More," Matt had said to the waiter, pressing him, "I just sold the Park Tower so we can at least afford a few extra truffles"), Olivia was bleary-eyed and exhausted. She had been working overtime to stay in the conversation with that hand on her back, the hand that had actually become quite comfortable there—yes, she would finally admit, comfortable.

By the time Yanni paid the $4,600 check with a scoffing, "Did we not drink tonight?" the hand on Olivia's back and no one's questioning of it emboldened her to almost feel like Taylor's plus-one. The night had been entirely entertaining, the conversation always finding its way back to the campaign, which Olivia was growing to love and feel a part of. For the rest of the table, all seemed as it always was: Matt and Chris's girlfriends had disappeared to the bathroom together, something they seemed too old to do. Stu had stepped outside after his wife had called screaming obscenities that the whole table could hear, all but confirming the rumors that she was probably abusing him on a regular basis. Todd and the cheerleader were engaged in a session of heavy petting that made the hand on Olivia's back seem familial. Yanni and the governor, fast friends, were far into an export-import conversation that shouldn't have been possible with the wine intake.

"C'mon," Erin said, gently tugging at Yanni's arm. "I think we've all had enough banking talk for one evening, right, Olivia?"

"Sure," Olivia said, acquiescing, as Erin stood up. Actually, she could have stayed there all night, but agreeing seemed like the right thing to do.

"We may take longer to get ready, but they take longer to get going!" Erin looked at Olivia and motioned for her to follow her lead out the door.

Again transported back to the seventh-grade cafeteria, Olivia eagerly shadowed the "cool girl at the table" toward the steps. The governor and Yanni followed suit and the others lagged behind. Up the stairs and back into the bright lights of the city, the world suddenly came into sharper focus.

Right, because I just spent four and a half hours in a windowless den of an alternate reality. Apparently the rest of the dinner guests felt the same way, each one standing up a tad straighter and soberly making their way into their chauffeur-driven Mercedeses and SUVs. Governor Taylor, looking ten times more sober than he had at the bottom of the steps, said his good-byes. He gave Olivia a peck on the cheek.

"Great day, Olivia, great day."

And with that he turned to walk the few blocks back to his hotel, leaving her in a weird state of proud confusion. She figured she shouldn't even try to process the evening. At least not until she got home. *Home. Gotta get a cab.* She looked down into her bag at the ten-dollar bill she had stuffed there before she left. The ten dollars that she had found in her jeans that was supposed to last her until her next paycheck hit in two days. *Coffee tomorrow or cab tonight?* She knew it should have been more of a decision, but the subway wasn't safe at this time, and there was no way she could bear the walk home, so she headed to the curb to wait.

"Olivia," Yanni called. She turned back to him. "What are you doing? Are you crazy? George will take you home. Erin and I can take her car."

Olivia looked over to the two black cars against the curb and Yanni's driver, George, standing by an open door.

"Really? Are you sure? That would be great. Thank you." *Coffee tomorrow,* she cheered silently.

"Please," he joked with a hint of sarcasm and a hint of truth, "thank-yous are for having the jet take you home. The car is easy."

⚬〰〰⚬

When the sun drifted in through the blue sheet tacked up as a temporary curtain beside her bed, Olivia still hadn't made sense of the night in her mind. She couldn't reconcile the feeling that she had been on the best date of her life with the fact that she had been at a business dinner. It was work and nothing more. *Politicians are warm, touchy-feely people. Right?* She scolded herself for even thinking otherwise. *Get it together,* she said, looking in the mirror. *These thoughts cannot even be going through your head. It was not a date. It is your job. The job. The job of a lifetime, which you will not ruin by having ridiculous thoughts.*

She considered calling her friend Katherine to dish about it, but every time she dialed and thought about what she would say, it sounded so stupid she hung up before the ringing started. Her non-boss put his hand on her back? That was a nonevent. She scolded herself, deleting the email she had written to her sister, the one that she almost sent a few times, asking if it was normal to keep a hand on a colleague's back for extended periods of time. Or if it was something that a married guy might do habitually since he was used to having his wife beside him? *His wife. Aubrey. She's perfect. They're perfect. It was nothing.*

✺

"Got a little bounce in that step, eh?" Her coffee-cart friend winked as he handed her a coffee.

She gladly took the compliment and the coffee, which was at its best. Some days Harun put in too much sugar or too little milk. But other days, like this one, he got it just right. She bounced down into the subway and reached the platform as the train pulled up. She loved days when the city worked with her. If you were a real New Yorker, she had decided, or maybe she had heard it on *Sex and the City,* the city melded with your mood. If you started in a bad mood, the coffee would be cold and the train would be late and crowded. But on a day like today, a good-mood day, everyone and everything was in sync with her. Her flawless morning left her outside Bronler's office with twenty minutes to spare. She was sitting on a bench across the street answering emails when one from her sister came in, reminding her she had never finished the email she had started more than a few times.

Marcygreenley@gmail.com: *You okay?? How was yesterday? It's been 36 hours! Email me back.*

Trying to recompose the email turned her giddiness into a flurry of nervousness.

LivGreenley@gmail.com: *Hey! Sorry, been crazed, wound up going to a dinner with the gov.*

She started to type *It was crazy and I think I love him,* but seeing it in her BlackBerry made it sound even stupider than it sounded in her head. She pushed herself again to stop the thoughts. She quickly deleted it and settled on *All good. All good.* Well, that was sort of right. Things were good, really good, even if she wasn't quite sure which side was up.

When the black SUV pulled up, she was already waiting in the lobby of Stephen's building trying to imagine how the morning would go. Would the governor say anything about last night? About his hand? *That hand,* she thought, remembering its steady strength. As he stepped out of the car she could see the businesslike look in his eyes—the same one he'd had that morning at the Brinmore. The one that grounded her then and made her stomach plummet now as if she were a kid realizing she was alone at recess. *Business,* she reminded herself. *This is business.* Her thoughts straightened up her shoulders as she approached the door and opened it for him.

"Good morning, Governor," she said, attempting to hide her nervous smile.

"Hey, kiddo." Alone at recess with her hair pulled.

Thankfully, the doorman stood up from his chair, excited to meet Taylor, sparing her from having to come up with chitchat in the midst of her disappointment. She had become "kiddo" again.

"I voted for you. And my mom, well, she just loves you," the slight, redheaded doorman was saying. "She's still in Georgia." He was so excited, he spoke without taking breaths.

"I 'preciate that," Taylor said in his sweetest Southern accent. "You tell your mama we'll be back even stronger this time and we're going to need her."

The young man straightened like he'd just been called to attention. "Yes, sir." He all but saluted as the elevator doors opened.

When they got in, so close in the small space, Olivia could feel her knees weaken a little, wondering if she should say something. *Anything.*

He broke her inner monologue.

"You know what I was thinking?"

That we should forget the world, get married, and have lots of beautiful political kids? Maybe I can get myself one of those shock bracelets to stop thinking like this.

"Yes, sir?"

"You should call Henley—he's our finance chair, do you know him?"

"Not well."

"Jacob can connect you guys. We should plug him into Filipaki's event. Tell him Jon, his business partner, should talk to him about his rail-freight deal. Jacob will know . . ." He trailed off, his words going back down into his BlackBerry as they walked off the elevator.

"Hi, we're here for Mr. Bronler," Olivia said to the receptionist.

"Your names?"

Ah, our names. Say our names.

"Sorry, ah, Governor Taylor and Olivia Greenley." She could barely compose her thoughts. Where was the person she was on a date with last night? And who was this person standing so formally beside her? What happened to their newly found coziness? Then her thoughts crashed in on insecurities. Could she have said something wrong? Was she acting too boldly? She didn't think she had had too much to drink last night, but what if she had said something inappropriate? She tried to replay every last word of every conversation, but there were parts she couldn't remember exactly. Or could she?

The frenetic thoughts continued well into the meeting in Bronler's huge office. Perched on one of the coolest streets in the Meatpacking District, the place overlooked the Hudson River and New Jersey. "Let's head into the conference room," Stephen said.

They followed closely behind him as he walked them the long way through the office so as to give them the full tour.

It'd be nice to have a long way through an office, Olivia thought.

As they passed walls covered with pictures of celebrities, one more famous than the next, Stephen explained the occasion for each photograph. Laughing with Barbra Streisand at his Empire State Building birthday party. Chatting with Leonardo DiCaprio on the set of *Titanic*. Andy Warhol, Basquiat, and Stephen at an art opening. They seemed never-ending.

"Here's my political wall," he said with a gruff arm-wave toward the back side of the office. It was covered with memorabilia, most of it signed, as well as pictures of him with the last four presidents. "I used to do movie nights with this one," he said. "He loved movies. We'd screen all the good ones at the White House. It was great; we'd invite ten or so people and sometimes even do a double feature. There's a great screening room in there."

"That's for damn sure. And it has the best popcorn this side of the Mississippi River." Taylor nearly slapped Stephen's back in kid-like enthusiasm. "I don't want to count my chickens before they hatch, but hopefully we'll be making good use of it soon!"

"With Stephen's backing you will," Olivia interjected, needing to say something to break her thoughts of watching movies with Landon in the White House screening room. *You will not be sharing popcorn with this man's hand on your back ever*, she thought, scolding herself. *Get a grip!*

It was at that moment that Stephen started talking about the black and white picture that hung prominently in the middle of the wall of Marilyn Monroe and President Kennedy sharing a whisper.

"That was backstage before she sang 'Happy Birthday' to him," Stephen explained.

"Wow. Do you know that was almost fifty years ago? May 1962. Man, what that must have been like."

The grip she had just forced upon herself slipped as quickly as it had come. *I wonder if Marilyn was happy. Maybe it's all backward. Maybe Marilyn was the real love of his life. Maybe Kennedy needed someone else. Maybe the governor needs someone else. Too bad I'm not a gorgeous, famous singer. Holy shit*, she snapped at herself, *I cannot be having these thoughts.*

"Recarpeting?" she asked, trying to change the subject to the dozen or so carpet samples that lay on the side table.

"Yup, the plane," Stephen said, as if it were obvious. "That reminds me, Lisette," he yelled to his assistant standing two feet away, "see if we can't get bigger samples of these. I've never understood how they expect you to pick a fuckin' carpet based on a square you can't even walk on."

"That's true," Olivia said, grateful to have a new ridiculous thought to focus on. Why were carpet samples always so small?

With that, Stephen led them into the adjoining conference room. Olivia tried not to drop her jaw to the ground in amazement, but the governor didn't hide his awe.

"Holy Moses! I have certainly picked the wrong field!" he yelled with a loud Southern twang.

"This is really amazing," Olivia said in agreement, trying to have her reaction appear polite without seeming naïve.

"You've never seen this, Olivia?"

"No, sir," she said, realizing the meetings she usually had with Stephen were quick and rarely passed the front office, much less the back two. The room was incredible. She guessed it was at least four thousand square feet. She had no clue what that really was, but she knew her apartment was six hundred and fifty and this was definitely five times the size, if not more. There were floor-to-ceiling windows on three walls, giving a view of the entire city, all the way up to the Chrysler Building. The only wall that wasn't windows was literally a snack counter from a movie theater. The governor leaned his head against the far window.

"Sakes alive, I'm not sure I'll ever get over how big all the buildings are here."

Olivia smiled, loving how free he was with all of his thoughts. She was so careful with her words, always conscious of how they seemed, how they made her seem. He, on the other hand, had such an expressive naïveté. She thought it must have been the fact that he was so clearly intelligent that made the naïve things he said, like how big the buildings were, sound honest rather than stupid.

They always said JFK was like that, with a natural curiosity. He was never afraid to ask questions. Her mind flashed momentarily back to Marilyn before she could bat the mistress idea out.

Stephen sat down at the head of the long glass table and the governor pulled himself away from the window and took the modern-looking black leather and silver seat next to him. Olivia and Lisette, Stephen's assistant, who seemed too pretty and too well dressed to be the person Stephen barked orders at, sat in the seats next to their bosses.

"Let's get some coffee." Stephen pressed down on a big button on a small, beige-colored square that looked weirdly similar to the garage-door opener Olivia's parents had before garage doors had codes. Within seconds, a man in his forties dressed in all black came into the room equipped with a small pad and pen.

"Yes, sir?"

"Uhhh, I'll have a skim cappuccino with extra foam. Gov?" Stephen looked to the governor, who hadn't yet lost his look of childish bewilderment.

"Hiya. How are ya doing today? I would just love a coffee with some sugar. Thank y'all so much." He bowed his head toward the waiter.

"You sure?" Stephen asked. "We can do mochas, lattes, anything. I swear they're better than Starbucks here."

Olivia wondered who "they" were and where "they" worked.

"Ma'am?"

Olivia looked up. "Oh, nothing for me. I'm good."

"Have something!" Stephen shouted. "Have a mocha. It's fuckin' great. Bring her a mocha. Everyone loves a mocha. And bring us some muffins. Thanks."

Olivia smiled. "Okay, sure, that sounds great, thank you," she said.

Lisette leaned back in her chair toward the waiter. "I would love a skim latte. Thanks so much, Jeffrey."

They had barely started talking when Jeffrey reappeared with the tray of drinks and muffins. Olivia lasered into her mocha, which did indeed look delicious, but was topped with tons of whipped cream. *Curses!* she said in her head, knowing there wasn't a chance anyone, much less her, the clumsiest and messiest person in the world, could drink that drink without becoming a disaster of whipped cream. The cream sat upright in the large round blue porcelain mug, complete with the Bronler logo. Jeffrey placed one small cloth napkin, also with the logo on it, next to the mug. *Super,* Olivia thought to herself, *that is going to be a gigantic help.*

"Now is that a fuckin' mocha or what?" Stephen said, banging his hand down on the table.

"It's incredible!" Olivia tried to figure out how to attack the milky enemy that seemed to stare mockingly at her from the table as Stephen rattled on and on about the summer event they would do in Martha's Vineyard—complete with rock star performances, movie stars emceeing. Suddenly the glitz of it all seemed to take a backseat to the work she was going to have to do to make it happen.

"Get a date," Stephen said to Lisette.

"Is there a specific month we want it in?" Lisette asked.

"I don't fuckin' care. Olivia will just fuckin' get it done."

Olivia nodded her head in agreement, giving Lisette a look of understanding shared worldwide by assistants. She wondered how Lisette stayed so polite with a boss who used the word "fuck" much more frequently than he did "please."

"Okay, honey?" Stephen asked Olivia, a seemingly funny follow-up to his more boisterous outbursts.

She smiled, knowing there was something nice about him. Actually, a lot. Even when he called you a fuckin' idiot, which he was bound to do at least a few times a meeting, he did it with a weirdly endearing sincerity. It was like he was in on the jokes about himself and by playing along, he allowed you to be in on them too. There was something "inside/outside the family" about it that actually made you feel more included with every "fuck."

By the end of the meeting, an event had been planned and the governor had given a ten-minute policy pitch on film incentives, but Olivia felt as if she had not taken a single real breath. She had not even officially started her new job and here she was sipping—well, clumsily inhaling was probably a better description, but nonetheless drinking her mocha in Stephen Bronler's back conference room and scrutinizing Taylor's every move. After saying their good-byes, Olivia silently escorted the governor out of the building, watching him type away on his BlackBerry. As the SUV drove away, taking Taylor back to Georgia, she wondered what world she had just entered and whether or not she should be dropping bread crumbs.

෬෩෨

Over the next few days, Olivia woke up feeling like she had given a cute guy her number and was waiting for him to call. She was back to working campaign hours, better known as "all of them," wrapping up things with Adams (which, she reminded herself, included getting the boxes that filled her small office into a storage space for keeping until the next campaign) and starting unofficially with Taylor.

She wished switching campaigns could be more like sports-team trades. The minute a professional basketball player got the call that he would be playing for the Knicks rather than the Bulls, his hat switched from red to blue; the former hat simply disappeared under a table at the press conference. With campaigns, there was always a window of a few weeks when two organizations considered her an employee—one excited to have her start and the other anxious about her impending departure, so both grabbed all the attention they could get. At nine-thirty p.m., when her BlackBerry buzzed with a private number, she reached down for the phone, assuming it was Adams, who had been calling regularly that evening.

"Hey, Hoya." The Southern accent on the other end of the line startled her and she fumbled with her BlackBerry.

"Hi. Hello. How are you?"

"Not as good as when I'm in New York."

"We feel the same way here." *What? "We feel the same way here"? What does that even mean? Who does?* She was so busy ridiculing herself that she completely missed whatever he was saying.

"Hello?" he asked as if the line had dropped.

"Hi. Sorry. You cut out there for a minute." It wasn't a lie. He had cut out from her train of thought.

"How's it going?"

"It's good, thank you." She could feel herself flustered and wondered if through the phone he could tell her cheeks were getting red. "How are you?"

"You know," he said with a campaign-like energy, "things are good. Really good. You see the *Washington Post* today?"

Washington Post? She could barely find the time to get through all the New York papers these days.

"I haven't. Not yet. Which article?" She held the phone to her ear with her shoulder and ferociously typed his name and "Washington Post" into Google News.

"Oh, you gotta read it. It's a great one. All about how our campaign is bringing back the younger generation. I have to tell you," he said with a pensive pause, "for me that's everything. For the first time in the history of this country, we may be at risk of leaving our children in a worse place than our parents left us. To me, that's incredible. And just plain unacceptable. I won't stand for it. We have to be able to ask ourselves if we're willing to pay the price tomorrow for the poverty and indifference we allow today. If I can get this generation to ask those questions, to believe in the power of politics to do good, to renew just a bit of their hope in government . . . well, that would really be success."

"I think you're doing that already." Olivia felt her own sincerity.

Forty-nine minutes and thirty-three seconds later, as so recorded by her BlackBerry, Olivia hung up the phone, once again unsure of what had just happened. She had listened intently to him speak about poverty in a fashion fit for one of her books on historical speeches, feeling as though she should be taking notes. She looked down at the pad in front of her where she had scribbled "We have to first believe that within all of us is the power to change the world and then we have to have the courage to use that power."

As she stared down, she wondered how they had moved so seamlessly from a book-worthy speech to stories of the biscuits his grandma used to make, to her need to play peacemaker in her family, a characteristic she rarely admitted, much less shared with others. He had told her he saw "a great spirit" in her. She had even convinced him that Yanni's party in the Hamptons the next weekend, though totally apolitical, would be worthwhile. There was an ease in talking to him—one that seemed more befitting of a friend, not her longtime political hero. It left her smiling as she closed the Adams list and opened a new Excel file of prospects for Taylor.

SIX

Jacob@LTaylor.com: *Hey. You're coming with us. We'll pick you up at 2.*

Olivia's heart fluttered as she read the message that popped up on her BlackBerry. The campaign had become like a new crush—every time it was mentioned, she felt giddy. She had been awaiting Jacob's text, knowing from her conversation with the governor that they would go to Yanni's party after the scheduled fundraiser in New Haven, but she wasn't sure Jacob knew that she and the governor had spoken. The campaign was doing a lunch at the Swannee. (Olivia Googled and figured out the Swannee was the Swann Club in New Haven, Connecticut. Campaign Lesson #7—no campaign staffer worth his or her salt ever says, "What's that? I've never heard of it.") She wasn't required to go, as she didn't officially start until the next week. But she had been hoping they would invite her. She tried to play it cool.

LivGreenley@gmail.com: *Huh?*

Jacob@LTaylor.com: *Gov wants you to come to lunch fundy w/ Stanton, then to Filipaki's in EH. Will RON and get back sometime tomorrow.*

She effortlessly decoded the campaign-speak: Manny Stanton—a big Connecticut-based trial lawyer who had the kind of goofy commercials where the badly made-up litigator looks into the camera and says, "If you've ever been injured in an accident and need help *now* call 1-800-GET-RICH"—was hosting a fundraising lunch in New Haven. Then they would head to Yanni's in East Hampton and spend the night (RON = "remain overnight"). It was going to be fun.

Before she could reply, another message from Jacob blinked on her BlackBerry.

Jacob@LTaylor.com: *And try 2 look good tonight. If I have to see that Banana Republic suit one more time, I'll blow my f*cking brains out.*

"Jerk," she said aloud, smiling ear to ear at the Banana Republic suit she had laid out to wear.

LivGreenley@gmail.com: *Jerk. I'm not one of ur lackeys that says how high when you say jump. Will try to move mtgs around and let u know if I can make it.*

She pressed SEND knowing damn well she was going. She figured she'd give it a few minutes. Besides, she needed to focus on picking out a new outfit. She grabbed the skirt from one of her Express suits and paired it with a white sequined tank top she had gotten at Forever 21 for $8.99, much to the chagrin of her friends. Olivia held tight to her addiction to the store despite the mocking it brought on. Aside from the store's being a big, chaotic, loud mess that she could get lost in, the clothes spiced up her boring suits, especially when she was reminded how boring they were. And yes, she understood that instead of buying ten of the $9 shirts she could buy one $90 shirt that would last longer than all of them combined, but the truth was she never really had $90 to spend on a shirt at once and the $9 at a time she did have could change her wardrobe rotation for three weeks. She remembered a line Jacob had once told her: *Campaigns and long-term thinking don't really go together.* Her shirts and her savings, or lack thereof, were good examples of that.

Focus, Olivia.

The sequined tank looked good, but she wanted to be sure she was professionally covered. She grabbed a black blazer and threw in her jean jacket for the Hamptons. It was dark denim, so it didn't seem too casual. The perfect work-at-nonwork-events look, something she had decided she had mastered.

Five minutes later she emailed Jacob. *Okay, mtg moved. Can come. Try not to look like u r going to ur bar mitzvah. I don't want you to embarrass me.*

⚭

As Jacob closed out Olivia's text in the backseat of the SUV, he looked down at his normal campaign garb. Semiwrinkled khakis, light blue shirt, blue blazer, and Cole Haan shoes. It was actually exactly what he had worn to his friend's kid's bar mitzvah last month. He tugged on the sleeve of the blazer, which was still a bit stained from when he'd put his arm into some mustard, reminding himself that it needed to be dry-cleaned stat. He wondered if Sophie had already seen this outfit more than twice. *She didn't seem bothered by it,* he thought, smugly reminiscing about her lingering kiss as he had run out the door.

He looked out the window to see the governor walking toward the car, stopping as always to say hi to every person he passed.

"Afternoon, Gov." Jacob started his usual rundown as the governor shook hands with Sal, the security detail deployed to drive them, and settled into the front seat. "Manny is hosting this at the Swann Club," he said.

Governor Taylor looked around the car. "Isn't Olivia coming with us?"

"We're picking her up—her apartment is right on the way to the FDR."

Sal nodded his head, confirming that this was the most efficient way to go, and then gave a little side glance and smile to Jacob. Though there was no guarantee you would get the same detail every time you went to a given state, Sal had driven them around New York during the presidential race and had become a confidante. A trustworthy driver, who was inevitably privy to all kinds of conversations and phone calls, was a rare and treasured thing. So Jacob had made a point of requesting him whenever they were in town. Sal appreciated the special request and had a good time with them, so he was quick to help out when Jacob needed backup on a plan change. In this case, Jacob knew Sal believed what he was agreeing to, which made it that much more convincing. The actual plan had been to pick Olivia up before they arrived at the governor's hotel, but Jacob wound up staying at Sophie's on the West Side, making it impossible to get to both of them and still be on time for the governor. *The kiss was totally worth it.*

"We'd be making a huge circle to get her first," Sal had originally argued. "Her apartment is literally on the street we have to go on. If she's waiting outside and we get a red light, we may not even lose a single minute."

Jacob rolled his eyes, hoping that explanation would hold his boss over and wondering why, after all this time, Sal still didn't understand that in the battle of logic versus what makes a politician's trip faster, the latter always won out.

Now, as long as the always-late Olivia is for once on time . . . Waiting never went over well with Taylor, or any politician for that matter.

"Okay," Taylor said, more accommodating than usual.

Jacob continued on with the briefing. "All the info is here." He handed him the page of notes. "And here are your remarks and some updates on the latest tort-reform bill in the Senate. Manny's wife Carol will be there, along with his kids: Manny, Jr. and Robbie. Cheryl and Blair are cochairs. They're the ones who actually raised most of the money, as usual. Also, wanted to make sure you saw that Ron and Doris Keller will be there; you helped get their daughter into Emory."

"Right, right, what's her name again?"

"Sally. She's a freshman, studying political science. She's an obligatory internship waiting to happen."

"Okay, who else?"

"Governor Marino and his wife, Donna, may stop by."

Sal interrupted. "Here, Jacob, right?"

Jacob looked up and let out a sigh of relief. Olivia waited on the corner, huge bag in hand. "Yup, that's her housing project."

He never understood why girls felt the need to pack for a week when they were going overnight. He had brought an extra shirt and an extra pair of underwear, and they fit in his computer bag. Why did girls require drag-along luggage at all times?

৩৩৩৩৩

Olivia saw the SUV pulling up and applauded herself for having made it down before they got there. It had taken all of her talent and time to get every plausibly necessary outfit into the smallest black bag she could find.

"Hello, hello, Miss Olivia," said the governor through the window.

She smiled. *See now, why can't anyone I know ever be walking by me at a time like this? Picked up by an SUV with Landon Taylor welcoming me out the window. I mean, it shouldn't be that much to ask. There's always an ex-boyfriend or high school friend available when I'm disheveled in Juicy sweatpants taking in food on a Friday night! I mean, I'm just saying.*

"Sparkly," Jacob said chidingly through the open door with a smile, "meet Sal."

Sal had stepped out to the back to help load in Olivia's bag.

"Hello. Thanks so much." Olivia handed over her bag and jumped in the car. "Good afternoon, Governor." A rush of nervousness swooped over her but she quickly lost it to the buzzing of her BlackBerry.

Jacob@LTaylor.com: *Sequins, really?*

"How?" she mouthed while typing back to Jacob, wondering how he even had the time to type so quickly.

LivGreenley@gmail.com: *Thought we were going to forgo the bar mitzvah garb.*

Jacob@LTaylor.com: *If only I had known we were going sweet sixteen instead.*

Olivia let a laugh out, conceding, as always, to Jacob's humor.

"You ready for a big day back there?"

"Ready, sir!" Olivia smiled. "I hear Manny has put together a great event."

"Who told you that—Manny?" The governor laughed. Even his laugh seemed to have a nice Southern twang.

"He's not so bad!" She pleaded his case. "He means well."

"Oh, please, Olivia, he's a DFTL." Jacob hit her on the shoulder. "Even *you* can't find the good in that."

"A what?" She loved Jacob's way of always coming up with nicknames and acronyms, but this one was new for her.

"You know, a DFTL, 'dirty fuckin' trial lawyer.' I mean, seriously, the only classes he could have ever actually passed in law school were Being a Spokesman on a Commercial 101 and Picking up Women in Hotel Bars 102. Glorified telemarketer. Haven't you seen his ads? 'He is ready and waiting to defend your honor!' Of course, the only thing he is actually ready and waiting for is your money, and possibly your wife. DFTLs."

Olivia laughed out loud, and the governor smiled.

Manny Stanton was indeed a dirty fuckin' trial lawyer. He was waiting at attention with his eldest son, looking as if they were expecting the Pope, as the SUV pulled up to the Swann Club. His combed-over hair was greased down across his round head and Olivia could see the Gucci logo all over his tie from twenty feet away. *He'll never come through with all the money he says he'll raise,* Olivia thought, happy that it wasn't her problem just yet. She lightly pinched her arm to make sure it wasn't all just a really good dream.

∾∽

Jacob had most of the responsibility on his shoulders. It was hard enough maintaining finance events when you were there to set them up, but on the road, it was nearly impossible. *It will be so much easier when Olivia starts officially,* he thought as he watched her nervously pick at her arm. He hated doing things half-assed. To prepare a good event required being on site for four weeks, or at least two, beforehand. But with all of his other responsibilities and constant travel, he had to leave a good portion of the work in the hands of donors and volunteers. And most of the time the only question in such cases was who would be less reliable. He had hired a new finance assistant, Addie, who had started the day before. But with only one previous campaign under her belt, she couldn't handle everything.

He and Olivia plotted their game plan for the event as they rode up I-95. She would "staff" the governor. Jacob would rush into the space, check Addie's progress, and do on-site advance. "On-site advance" was an oxymoron—it was called advance because you were supposed to do it in advance of the candidate's arrival. He and the governor joked that lately what he did would be better termed "on-site during."

He walked into the club, an old mansion decorated much like the people in it—expensive but without any real style. Both the club and the members seemed to be stuck between wanting to be part of an old, traditional country club and showing off their very new money. A huge maroon speckled rug covered a dark wood floor in the large lobby, and strangely modern wood chandeliers hung from the ceiling. Jacob said hello to the volunteers, who were seated at long folding tables that had been set up leading into the room and covered with white tablecloths. They seemed, as volunteers always do, more interested in where the candidate was than in their task of collecting the checks.

Jacob tried to get them to focus by promising that Taylor would take a photo with all of them at the end of the event. This would keep them in their seats working until the end. He double-checked the microphone level and made sure there was a bottle of water on the shelf under the podium and that it was moved in the perfect position, to the right where it would be easiest for the governor to grab it. He scanned the room and breathed a sigh of relief. Addie ran to his side looking for approval of her setup, proud to be handling her first event for the campaign.

"Looks good," Jacob said. "I want to make sure you meet the governor. I've told him so much about you. He's really looking forward to meeting you in person."

With the ease of a candidate himself, Jacob led Addie straight to Taylor. He needed to get him toward the podium and start the speaking program anyway.

"Let's get this show on the road!" Jacob said to Manny as he pulled the governor toward the microphone.

Manny proceeded up to the podium, with the governor following closely behind. He began speaking, telling an inane story Jacob had heard at least a dozen times before. It was an explanation of how Manny and the governor met. After hearing it for the fifth or sixth time, Jacob had determined that the story had no point other than to describe in detail the size of Manny's house.

"Ladies and gentlemen," Manny said boisterously, wiping the sweat from his brow, "I'm so happy to introduce my very good friend, the next president of the United States, Landon Taylor!"

The governor shook Manny's hand and walked to the microphone, where, Jacob thought, he really did look like the next president of the United States. As Jacob moved to the back of the room, confident in the job he had done, the governor reached down without a glance and easily grabbed his water.

⚬᷍

Jumping in a car to leave an event had the opposite effect of jumping out to start one. For Olivia, it was always accompanied by a feeling that she had left something behind. Getting a candidate out of a room was tough, especially a politician like Taylor, who always made it seem like he didn't want to leave. She sometimes literally had to tug at a candidate to make him or her drop the handshakes and stop the chat. Olivia was glad Jacob had taken over staffing Taylor after his speech as she never particularly liked the feeling of making someone leave a room.

By the time Jacob, the governor, and Olivia got settled in the car, it was as if they had been a team for months. They had already fallen into a rhythm, stepping around each other with the comfort of people who had been well choreographed together for years. Olivia looked at Jacob as she started organizing and counting the checks she had collected from the volunteers. *Different candidate, different circumstances, same us.* It was like picking up where they had left off in the last campaign.

"Sakes alive." Taylor exhaled as he pushed back on his chair. "That was a doozy. How'd we do?"

"Counting now, boss." Jacob glanced over as Olivia scribbled down the amount she had counted out, $36,250. "Forty at the door. Plus I have ten on my desk, so we're good."

Olivia knew Jacob probably had forty total. They worked the same way—there was always money to move around in their goals so the candidate would feel good about each event and, more importantly, continue to allow more fundraisers to be added to his schedule. They would tell each other the exact numbers, but no one else. They had learned it together from their old boss, Gabrielle, who had taught Olivia almost all of her Campaign Lessons. She would tell them over and over, "Say what you need to say to the donors and candidates to keep them happy, and tell the truth to your teammates to keep your donors and candidates." That was a Campaign Lesson that Olivia hadn't numbered yet. *Somewhere in the teens,* she thought.

"He said seventy-five to me at the door."

Jacob rolled his eyes at the governor's reminder. "He always does, boss. I'm leaving it at fifty and if he gets that extra twenty-five in it'll be icing."

"How ridiculous is that?" Taylor still seemed to be genuinely baffled by the language of the donors. "Olivia, you think that's normal? For him to fall short and no one calls him on it?"

"Normal, no, sir. But I don't think political fundraising has ever held any claim to normalcy."

"Yeah. I suppose." He shook his head. "Could you imagine a businessman saying, 'I'll buy the stocks for seventy-five thousand dollars,' and then only paying fifty? It's ludicrous. We should try to change it."

Jacob spouted out the laugh Olivia was holding in. The governor spoke with such levity, she couldn't tell whether or not he was joking.

"Laugh, Jacob. You're running this sham of a business!" he said with the sarcastic nudging tone of an older brother. "You're letting these guys pay you fifty thousand for the seventy-five-thousand-dollar stock. Maybe you should have taken the GMATs after all. I'm going to have a talk with your dad about that next time I see him."

Now it was Olivia's turn to snicker.

Taylor wasn't ready to give this one up. "Why don't you call Manny and tell him we have him in our budget for seventy-five? You told him that was his goal, right?"

"I did," Jacob replied dutifully.

"So," he repeated, "tell him it's in our budget and we need it."

"I'll get right on that."

"Don't placate me."

"No placation, boss. Just don't know how threatened Manny will be by our budget. It's not exactly a certified contract, and even if it was . . ."

"DFTL. I get it, I get it," Taylor responded, almost but not quite conceding. "Let's see if we can make the process more accountable. More truthful. If we're going to inspire change, we have to be willing to jump a little ourselves."

Olivia and Jacob smiled at each other in the backseat. Olivia recognized the happiness on Jacob's face as the same as hers—they were glad to be there, in the backseat of the SUV that contained their chance to inspire, to be inspired, and to jump.

As they pulled into the airport, they all three went back to their BlackBerrys, foreseeing the coming thirty-five minutes or so of inability to use them. The car pulled onto the street and over to the private terminal. Olivia had been on private planes before. Well, actually, she had been on two private planes. One was a small plane that she and Adams had taken with Bronler to his event on Martha's Vineyard when their flight was canceled. The other was a small prop plane that still made her nauseous thinking about it. Both times she had been so nervous about where they were going, who was picking them up when they landed, and the timing of it all that she hadn't really appreciated the experience of being on a noncommercial flight. This time though she was a passenger. Not just any passenger, but a part of Landon Taylor's team, his crew. She was at the cool table in the cafeteria, and someone else was taking care of the details.

As the car rolled toward the small freestanding terminal, Olivia began to gather herself up, ready to go in. She tried to put on her best "I've been to this terminal before" look so as not to seem the newbie that she was. Jacob, as he so often did, saw the effort rather than the effect. He gave her a subtle "chill out" look just in time to stop her from opening her door.

"We good, Sal?" He checked in with the driver, more for Olivia than anything else.

Hand on the handle, Olivia reconfigured herself as the car started moving toward the metal gates to the airfield.

"Ready for takeoff," Sal replied.

In front of them the metal gates began to open as a guard waved them through. Sal rolled down his window. "Thanks." He used the tone of formality that security types reserve for each other.

Of course. We're not going into the terminal. Landon Taylor gets driven straight to the plane, Olivia realized.

"That one's ours?" The governor pointed to a jet not much smaller than the commercial plane she had taken to Florida over the holidays.

"Yes, sir." Sal began to rattle off facts. "Gulfstream, wingspan is . . ."

"Cool." Taylor, for a moment, sounded like a young kid with a new toy.

Sal drove them as close to the plane's opened steps as they could get. Two men were standing waiting to open their doors.

"Thanks so much," Olivia said as one needlessly helped her out of the car.

Jacob sprinted up the steps like an Olympic runner.

"My pleasure," said the uniformed man to Olivia. "I'm Dan. I'm your pilot today."

"How are y'all?" Taylor took the man's hand.

"Very well, thank you. Honored to have you aboard today, sir."

Olivia smiled, wondering if there was anyone who didn't act deferential to Governor Taylor. She had spent time working for so many candidates and politicians, even former presidents, and all had an effect on people but none, that she had seen, had inspired respect so across the board.

The pilot described for Taylor in detail the engine, the wings, thrilled to be so thoroughly captivating the governor. Olivia walked toward the back of the SUV, where Sal was handing the bags to the copilot.

"Here, I can grab mine." She reached for her own bag.

Sal swatted her hand away. "No, no, darlin'. We got it here." With a chuckle, almost just to himself, he said, "You really are new to this team." And then with the tone of a sort of reminiscence he added, "Sweet."

Olivia stepped back, feeling a little out of place, as Jacob jumped out of the door of the plane.

"We're set up here. It's been advanced!"

"Best one-man advance-and-during team in the game." Taylor patted Jacob's shoulder as he walked up the stairs past him.

Olivia followed the governor. As she walked in, she tried not to gasp. The plane wasn't just huge, it was beautiful. It had two sets of enormous seats on each side with tables in between. Taylor strolled to the left, dropping comfortably into the window seat facing the front. Jacob had sat himself in the second set of seats behind the governor and had already sprawled out all his paperwork and books as if he had been there a week. Olivia smiled at the mess, walked quietly by the governor, and sat herself in the aisle seat across from Jacob.

Aisle seat? Why would I sit in the aisle seat?

As she mulled over moving to the window, a young woman dressed in a tight navy blue sheath walked by.

"Can I get y'all anything before we take off? We have a full bar and hot options as well as cold today."

"Diet Coke would be great if you have one, baby," Taylor said. It was strange to Olivia to hear the governor call someone "baby" and even stranger that she, Olivia, wasn't offended. Usually the feminist in her, who was rather large and loud on most occasions, would have righteously scolded anyone who used such a term. But with Taylor it was different. There was something about his sincerity and casualness that made the way he called people "baby" actually sound nice. Maybe it was just the accent.

⌒〰〜⌒

"I'll have one as well, please!" Jacob said, waving his hand. "And what kind of hot options are we talking about today?" He knew by now to take advantage of the food on Henley's planes. Henley always had his galley stocked with the best. It was the reason, other than the fact that Henley always said yes, that Jacob liked to ask him for the plane. Not to mention the flight attendants were beautiful.

I wonder if Olivia ever added that column for flight attendants to that private plane list she keeps. Probably not.

As the plane took off, Jacob bit into the Philly cheesesteak he had ordered and opened up his computer. He figured he could at least get a little work done before Taylor started in on his stories. It was like clockwork. The minute there was no signal left on the governor's Black-Berry, the boss would turn and start with the "Let me tell you a story" stories, which were all well and good but, at this point in their relationship, redundant and distracting. Jacob glanced at his BlackBerry and saw the bars of signal disappearing. Even when it got down to no bars, he saw the small arrow still working in the corner and knew he had a few extra minutes, as Taylor would try to get the last bits in as well.

When Taylor finally tucked his BlackBerry into the front pocket of his briefcase, Jacob started to close programs and move toward him. But instead of his usual "Let me tell you" statement, Taylor leaned across the aisle.

"Okay, new girl. Come on over here—let's get to know you if you're going to join this campaign."

Olivia looked surprised. She scuffled out of her aisle seat and moved next to the governor. Jacob leaned back and turned his computer back on, mentally high-fiving himself for having scored someone new to listen to Taylor's stories. He shook his head, listening to her giggle as she spoke. *Going to need to squash the schoolgirl crush she clearly has on him. Harmless,* he thought, and went back to work.

For the next forty minutes, with the governor and Olivia chatting away in the background, Jacob went through a week's worth of scheduling requests. He couldn't remember the last time he got that much work done uninterrupted.

He congratulated himself. *Brilliant! Now this is a campaign I can manage.*

⁂

Yanni's sprawling mansion was exactly what you would expect from a billionaire in the Hamptons. The latest TV series about the chic community had actually filmed most of its episodes in his backyard. A long gravel driveway led back through perfectly manicured lawns to a fifteen-bedroom estate. The outside was covered in gray shingles accented by bright white window frames. The ceilings inside were twenty feet high, at least, and windows covered the entire back of the house, giving every room a view of the two pools and the ocean beyond them. As they walked into the expansive white marble foyer, Olivia let her eyes dart off to the right, where the hall opened into a massive kitchen. A familiar-looking man stood spraying Windex on the counter. *Is it?*

As the man turned, she confirmed that yes, it was rock star Jon Bon Jovi, nonchalantly cleaning off Yanni's countertop. *Wow.* Jon Bon Jovi with a paper towel and a Windex bottle? Then the inevitable greeting panic attack whirled through her head. *I wonder what he goes by. "Jon"? "Mr. Bon Jovi"? "Mr. Jovi"? Is "Bon Jovi" one word or two? Is that his real name? Is it really "Jonathan"?*

"Jon!" Jacob strolled over. "Album sales this bad, man?"

"Album sales are this good!" Mr. Jon Bon Jovi stuck out his wrist to reveal an A. Lange & Söhne Tourbograph. As Jacob leaned in to get a closer look at the watch, which cost two times as much as the house he grew up in, his face was met with a playful spray of Windex.

"Even a manservant lives large in Yanni-land," Jacob said, wiping his cheek. "This flustered new member of our team is Olivia."

Olivia shot Jacob a squint-eye glance of fake annoyance and held out her hand.

"Hi," she said, opting for no name at all.

She heard Jacob behind her as she took in Bon Jovi's sultry eyes and his famed hair. "Jon, you remember Governor Taylor; Governor Taylor, you know Jon."

That kind of ease was what made Jacob the perfect staffer, she noted. It was a basic rule and first duty to enunciate the names of your candidate and whomever he or she was meeting immediately. In all cases. Great politicians had nearly flawless recall and some, like Governor Taylor, were known for it. So missing a name or a face because it was an off day or because they had just humanly forgotten was even worse than a regular person's lapse.

Olivia had learned this, Campaign Lesson #14, the hard way. In the last campaign, the presidential candidate hadn't recognized Ted Foyer, one of the bigger campaign supporters, and Ted subsequently withdrew all his support. "I raised you people four hundred thousand dollars, and the man doesn't even know my name! Why the hell would I raise you another dime?" he had screamed.

Olivia still thought of a new response every time she retold the story, but really it was ultimately symbolic of a simple truth: People in politics wanted to be recognized. They paid to be. The name rule was one that was particularly important when it came to celebrities, because if someone had 99 percent name recognition, like Jon Bon Jovi, political candidates usually made up the 1 percent that didn't recognize them. As Taylor reminded his top staffers on a regular basis, he had to know these celebrities' names. He couldn't be seen as someone who thought himself too high-minded for pop culture.

"High-minded pop culture" seemed to describe the rest of the evening perfectly. The party had been planned when Yanni had won, or actually, bid seventy-five thousand dollars for, the services of a catering company in a silent auction. Seventy-five thousand dollars to serve fifty or so people appetizers and drinks, Olivia figured. Add on the table of Nobu sushi and miso cod and it worked out to at least two thousand dollars per person.

In a rather unconstructive manner, Olivia sometimes liked to calculate the cost of a party or dinner she was at and think of what could be done with the money spent per person. At first it horrified her; thousands of dollars for a plate of sushi that she didn't even like definitely could have bought lunches for way too many homeless kids. After a few years in fundraising she had come to accept the cost for the most part, rationalizing the trickle-down effect of campaign spending. But she still found herself often weighing the alternatives. In this case it was bought at an auction for the local hospital, so it was a somewhat easier pill to swallow.

Low-income rent for half a year, she thought as she grabbed a mini egg roll and leaned against the wall.

She looked around the room and saw the man from *Hamptons* magazine taking pictures. She wished she had worn a more fun dress. Everyone seemed to be in cool, flowy satin numbers—most of which she recognized from the most recent issue of *Vogue*. She had stuck with the skirt and sequined top. It was fine, but clearly not as cool as she had imagined it being. Untucked, the white sequined shirt flowed over the black pencil skirt just enough to make the low scoop neck acceptable. Over it, she had thrown her favorite silver-locket necklace, which hung down perfectly on baggy shirts, giving them a little shape.

Okay, it's more Teen People *than* Vogue *but Rachel Zoe would definitely approve,* she thought, trying to reassure herself.

"Olivia!" Yanni yelled out as he entered the room, the governor trailing behind him. "Landon got the tour. Come drink with us."

Olivia walked over obligingly and smiled knowingly at the governor. She had been on Yanni's "tour of the house" a few times before and knew it included every nook and cranny. As Yanni ordered drinks, Olivia leaned in to the governor. "I forgot to mention Campaign Lesson # 23—always set a time limit before going on Yanni's house tour."

"That would have been really helpful *an hour and a half ago!*"

Olivia chuckled and pulled her head back, surprised by the impact of the scent of his soap. Freshly showered, he had a clean smell that reminded her of a fall day in Georgetown.

Yanni turned back to them and asked, "Patrón silver with three limes, right, Liv?" He smiled broadly, remembering her drink.

"Oh no, just a Diet Coke is fine for me." Not drinking around the boss was definitely Campaign Lesson #3. Or 2. Yes, Campaign Lesson #2.

"Oh, please!" Yanni flipped his hand at her and continued ordering.

"We're all off-duty here," the governor said, leaning his shoulder against hers. "Have a drink."

That's true. It isn't actually a fundraiser. But he is actually your boss. Well, not yet. Officially. Yanni passed her a drink as she debated the idea in her head. Needless to say, she drank obligingly, glad halfway through the first glass for its help in abating her nervousness.

Before she knew it, she was deep in a conversation on the sofa with Alberto, a brain surgeon turned best-selling novelist who liked to shock politicians by showing up to events in T-shirts like the one he had on tonight—a worn-out gray scoop-neck with a big marijuana leaf across the front. He had a subtle dark humor mixed with quiet sincerity. His beautiful wife, Sarah, a brilliant art historian, smiled adoringly in her husband's direction every time he spoke.

Far into a conversation about the media's take on Islamic extremism, Olivia leaned back, drinking her tequila and thoroughly enjoying the idea of an intellectual conversation at a party. It had become commonplace in bars for guys trying to pick her up to rattle on about a political event or issue they undoubtedly knew nothing about. Or for them to feel the need to explain why they hated her candidate or the Democratic party. Regardless of the multitude of clichés (no politics, no religion in polite conversation) people seemed to have no problem going off on baseless tangents about what she did for a living and what she believed in. It drove her crazy.

"What if I told you I wanted the stock market to fail?" she would retort to a stockbroker in an always unsuccessful attempt to explain the offensiveness of his latest antipolitical commentary. More often, lately, she would just tell people she was a kindergarten teacher, ensuring a subject change.

But here, sitting with Alberto, his wife inches away, which eliminated any pressure of trying to be picked up, Olivia relished having a real conversation just for conversation's sake. Midsentence, Olivia heard her name called and turned. Todd was standing around a table of sushi in the kitchen with Yanni, Matt, and the governor.

"Hey, Olivia," Todd called out, "come settle something for us."

"Sure." She started to politely excuse herself from the conversation with Alberto and Sarah.

"Go, go." Alberto pointed to the governor. "The boss beckons!"

Olivia nodded and walked over obligingly.

Todd continued talking. "First, what's your favorite charity?"

"Ummm"—Olivia turned and looked around, confused—"that would have to be Taylor 2012!"

"Love that!" Taylor said with a wink. "But we need something I don't profit from on this one."

"Okay, I'd have to say the Innocence Project."

"Okay." Todd clearly didn't care about the specifics of her answer. He gestured toward her. "Can PACs give to the Democratic National Committee? And if so, how much? LT here says you are the final word on this."

LT? she thought, giggling. They were like a bunch of college kids. "Is this a competition to see if I'm up on my campaign finance rules?"

"No, no, no," Matt interjected. "We just need the answer here, and your candidate is no help!"

Olivia smiled with confidence, glad that she had spent so much time looking up the limits before the last day of meetings. "They can give five thousand dollars annually."

"Yes!" Matt shot up his fist. "Todd here owes you ten thousand dollars for that Innocence Project thing."

"Huh?"

Todd shook his head and started scribbling on a pad of paper.

"This is how we bet. Loser gives to a charity." He ripped at the piece of paper with his credit card information on it and handed it to her. He had written "10k to Innocence Project" on the top and signed his name across the bottom. "Just call Miranda on Monday if you need other info. And see if I can get invited to some dinner or something for it!"

"And if he can just send the tickets to me!" Matt yelled about three times louder than need be.

Olivia looked down at the paper in amazement. "Really? Are you sure?"

"A bet's a bet. Besides, the Innocence Project is a good pick—I like that place. Last time Tina picked some weird animal shit organization, and now I get calls from them all the time."

Olivia laughed. She folded the paper and tucked it into the pocket of her skirt. She liked that despite their brazenness, they were all constantly giving generously to important causes. They cared. As she shook her head in astonishment at the latest part of a night that had already seemed like a movie, Yanni grabbed her arm and led the group of them outside.

"Jonny's going to play us a little something."

Sure enough, Jon Bon Jovi sat outside by the first pool with a guitar, taking requests. Olivia sank back on one of the white cushioned chairs waiting for someone to pinch her. The fact that she was completely out of place in this alternate universe seemed to be lost on everyone else. But she also had never felt like she fit in more. She looked over to Yanni and the governor standing by the pool. The governor's light brown hair flopped forward as he leaned in to talk to Yanni, who stood five or so inches shorter. The governor's hair looked so soft. She wondered if it was one of the things Aubrey fell in love with first. *I'm sure it was. It must have been so fantastic to fall in love with him. He probably courted her at perfect parties like this.*

She remembered reading an article in *Vogue* about their being homecoming king and queen of their college. It said they went to IHOP once a week. *I bet he was the coolest guy in the room, even before he was governor.* Suddenly all the facts she had learned about him—and she had learned them all—seemed insignificant. His grades in school, his organizing skills, the bills he passed—they all paled in comparison to his charisma. *His magic.* He reached up and put his hand through his hair, pushing it back and to the side. She felt like she was in a 3-D movie, desperate to reach out and touch the image.

"Awesome, huh?"

"Totally." She spoke, her eyes glued to his hair, before looking up to see Alberto and Sarah standing next to her chair. "Oh, yes, amazing." She quickly followed up, agreeing with what Alberto was talking about—Bon Jovi, of course. *Not the governor's hair.*

"Okay, well, we're going to take off."

She stood to bid them farewell and noticed the thinning crowd. She looked back over to the governor and Yanni, who had moved over to Bon Jovi. She could tell Yanni was telling jokes by the way his arms flapped around, while the governor laughed.

I wonder if I could marry Yanni. We could have one of those marriages they all have. He could go out, I could go out. I could stay in. Here. I wouldn't have to work. I could be Taylor's helpful donor. Who needs love anyway? Hmmm. She picked up one of the truffle fries on the table beside her. *I could be that shallow. I really think I could.* She gobbled down a few more fries, knowing she couldn't.

"Okay, it's Palm time." Yanni stood over her, waving her up with his hands.

Olivia knew the Palm well. It was a local, expensive restaurant where anyone from Billy Joel to Diddy and a half a dozen of their peers could be found on any given summer Saturday night. She looked at the heels lying by her feet. The thought of getting back up onto them seemed offensive at best.

"I think I'm going to let this be a boys' night out," she said, demurring.

"Oh, it will not be a boys' night." Yanni smiled mischievously.

"Right." Olivia laughed. She was clearly too tired to participate in any of this. "I'm out. The thought of putting heels back on is too much. Thank you so much for everything, Yanni." She added in the last part feeling grateful, more than anything, for being included. Yanni, of course, was out the door before the "you" escaped her mouth.

As soon as she stood up, she realized how right her decision to stay in was. She was either too drunk or too tired to get to her room, much less adventure to the Palm. Head spinning, she grabbed the staircase railing for a bit of balance. As the music began to fade into the background she became aware of her drunkenness. Campaign Lesson #2—no drinking at work. *Maybe that should be lesson number one. Focus, Olivia.*

True, Yanni's house was huge and her bedroom was on the far end of the second floor, but the walk couldn't have actually been as long as it now seemed. She grasped onto the shoes in her hand and straightened up her back, as if that would make her less drunk.

Finally she arrived at her assigned bedroom. She looked to the left for her black bag and her purse strewn against a corner (her trick for disguising her messy chaos in hotels and houses was to stuff anything she owned in a corner), which enabled her to make sure she had in fact made it back to the correct room. She could still hear the techno-hip-hop remixes playing downstairs.

Or is that just in my head? I should brush my teeth and wash my face, she thought as she flopped down on the bed. *Ohhh, but the bed is so soft. I'll go in a minute.* Closing her eyes, she sank into the sheets and wondered how many thousand the thread count was as the gravel spewed outside her window from the caravan of cars heading off to the Palm.

Olivia turned over in exhaustion, grateful she had decided not to go. She dozed off, awakened a few minutes later by rustling at her door. She tried to pick up her head but, as if in a dream, couldn't really get her head from the pillow. Her eyes opened with the sound of the door and suddenly she was awake.

"Governor." She felt her neck shoot up. "I . . . um . . . I'm sorry . . . oh my gosh, did I take the wrong room?" Her eyes darted to find the bag she swore she had already confirmed to be on the floor.

"No, no." He paused and looked around the room. "No, it's, uhhh . . . all me. Sorry. So sorry!"

"Oh." Olivia exhaled slowly. She stood and twisted back around the skirt that had turned during her flop on the bed. *Ohmigod. What am I even wearing? I'm a mess. And he's* . . . She looked at him standing so casually in her doorway. *He's perfect.* His shoulders pressed out against his blue jacket and the top two buttons of his shirt were open, exposing a bit of his skin. It looked so smooth; she hadn't noticed how smooth his skin was. *Stop noticing his skin!*

"Sir . . . Sorry . . . I thought . . . didn't you go to the Palm?"

"Nah. Figured I'd make Page Six work for their news this year."

Olivia tilted her head, trying to make the world stop spinning. *And totally virtuous. And that skin.* She glanced down. *Ohmigod I just looked at his crotch. Look up. Look up. He's your boss. Was it big? Could I glance back without his noticing? Did he notice already? Stop it!* She tried to stop thinking and focus on what to do with her hands, which hung down awkwardly by her sides.

Thankfully, he interrupted her spiral.

"What a day, huh?"

"Incredible. Bon Jovi did just play an acoustic set downstairs, didn't he? I mean I hear tequila is a hallucinogen but that seemed pretty real."

He laughed.

Holy shit. Who am I? What am I doing? Drinking? Talking about tequila? Looking at his crotch? Ohmigod, I just saw it again. It is big. Holy shit. I said that already. He is your boss. You are a professional. This is the job of your dreams. Stop looking at him, she begged her subconscious.

"Some days I'm sure someone will wake me up and I'll still be a law professor just daydreaming at my desk."

"You ever wish you still were?" Olivia stepped to the side a bit and lost her balance.

The governor noticed and stepped toward her, as if he were ready to catch her. He put his hand on her shoulder.

Embarrassed, Olivia tried to cover up the tipsy move. "Whoa, you know when you get up too quickly? What do they call that— 'head rush'?"

"I believe the proper term is 'tipsy'!" He laughed. He seemed to be making a point of not letting go of her elbow. "God, you have a great smile." He was actually saying those words.

She froze, looking up at him, aware of how close that smooth skin under his neck was. And his hand on her elbow. She awkwardly pulled it just a bit, needing to break away and regain her composure.

"Thank you, sir." She looked around, desperate to escape the inappropriate closeness between them, but as she did, he stepped away too.

"I'm apparently losing my mind today." He lingered on the "-ay."

She looked at him, trying to decipher his smile. *Could he have meant to come here? This couldn't have been a mistake. It didn't seem like a mistake. Maybe he loves me.* She quickly pushed the thoughts from her head. *What am I saying? I am insane.*

He apologized again, shaking his head, as if he were trying to get something out. Then he straightened up his body and switched his voice to a parental tone, a bit louder and less breathy than before. "Okay, then. So you get some rest."

"Okay, yup." As the door closed behind him, Olivia felt the room double in size and her own self halved. Unsure of what had just happened, she knew she should feel uncomfortable and possibly upset, but instead her stomach churned with excitement.

She flopped on the bed, her skirt spinning back around again, feeling that tingling that she felt when she first glanced at the sleekness of his chest. She closed her eyes, imagining what the rest of him looked like. Felt like. She grabbed a pillow and squeezed tight. *It's a crush. I have a crush,* she told herself. *It will go away. It has to.*

✺

Jacob shot up at seven forty-five a.m., long after he was used to waking up, but without the groggy exhaustion he should have had. He couldn't help smiling at the fun of last night. The Palm was obscene. That was the appropriately descriptive word. Models had flocked to the table Yanni had anchored with bottles of every type of liquor possible. Jon Bon Jovi had left because it was "getting out of hand." *I stayed at a party too out-of-hand for a rock star,* Jacob thought to himself with an urgent need to contact at least four or five people from high school to tell them.

And Jenny. Or Jackie. Shit, what was her name anyway? He had never done anything like that. Not that he did anything. *Okay, so we went swimming and she definitely was in her bra. But it was a just-look-don't-touch kind of thing,* he said to himself, feeling like he needed to defend the decision. *What should I have done? Looked away? Yeah, I should have looked away. Definitely. But that would have been weird.* And he couldn't deny enjoying the feeling of fitting in. Fitting in with the business guys, with the guys he wanted to be. The night confirmed all his suspicions that his proximity to the governor, the future president, would lead to his corner office. To his own table at the Palm. In past campaigns he was the peon but now he was at the adult table. Literally. As Landon Taylor's campaign manager.

Okay, so he was the body guy, not exactly the campaign manager, but for all intents and purposes he was managing the campaign. At least the road part. Billy would probably eventually hold the official title, but Jacob would do the work. Now that Olivia was on board to take over the fundraising, he could step into the role he really wanted. He knew they wouldn't give him campaign manager but he was sure he would get deputy campaign manager or road manager. He laughed thinking of how much like a rock band that sounded.

As he threw his rumpled and wet (*Who thought that two a.m. swim was a good idea? Oh right, Jackie. Jen, I mean Jen.*) clothes into his bag, he thought about the conversation he would have with Taylor. He heard

Yanni's voice in his head. "Step up, man," Yanni had said. "Wishing and hoping is for lazy people. Good things come to those who get up and grab them." That's what Jacob would do. He would step up and grab the reins. The reins of the campaign to the White House. *Damn, it's good to be me.*

⌒⚭⌒

Damn, damn, damn. Olivia woke up in even less of a real world than the one she fell asleep in. Her mind ran from yesterday straight into today as she focused on packing and practiced her "Hello, Governor" with Shakespearean intensity. She precisely folded every piece of clothing. She needed to get control over something. She longed to be zapped to the diner with her friends or to her apartment. Her couch. She'd rarely been so desperate to get back to the emptiness of her small home. *Why am I so freaked by this?*

It was nothing. Nothing. The more she protested to herself, the more she seemed to believe it was more than nothing. What was that thing about her smile? Why was everything so blurry? Why did she have that tequila? She had never been drunk at a work event before; she had barely ever drunk alcohol at one. And granted, this wasn't exactly a work event, but it was workish.

She looked at the day on her BlackBerry. Sunday. One day before she officially started on the campaign. Maybe she should get out of it. *Dream job. Not getting out of it. It will be fine.* Questions kept resurfacing. Was it really an accident that he stumbled into her room? Could it have been more than that? *Nothing,* she reminded herself. *It will be fine.*

She headed down to the kitchen, bag in tow, determined to seem more professional than ever. She just needed to survive an hour. Not even. The governor and Jacob would be on a plane back to Georgia in fifty-two minutes and she could go back to the city and regroup. Fortunately, as she stepped into the kitchen, Jacob and the governor were, as they always seemed to be, mid-conversation. They barely looked up at her, waving a bit only, and her practiced hellos became totally pointless as a chef-looking person put himself in her path before she got the first "H" out.

"What can I get you for breakfast?" He went on to offer her more choices than she would find at an IHOP.

Note to self: rethink marrying Yanni.

Actually she could have gone for an omelet and well-done bacon but there was no chance she would sit down for an awkward breakfast. Plus, she had already noticed that Jacob and the governor had half-finished coffees in hand and figured she should match their gambit. "Just coffee would be great, thank you."

Jacob smiled at her with a clearly hungover glaze in his eyes.

"You ready to blow this taco stand, Liv?"

"Uh, yes, sure. Bags packed."

"I'm sure Sal can drop you in the city."

"Oh no, it's okay. I can just grab the Jitney back."

"The what?" the governor asked, confused.

"The Jitney—it's a bus. It goes right into Manhattan." She answered this with more assuredness than she deserved to have, because she really had no clue if the Jitney even ran in May. If she hadn't been so obsessed with planning her hello, she might have had the notion of checking the schedule.

Sal came in before she could figure out how she would actually get back if the Jitney weren't running.

"Sal, aren't you heading back to the city after you drop us off at the airport?" Jacob asked.

"Yessir, I am," Sal answered. His crisp appearance—he wore his standard suit—contrasted starkly with the mess of the rest of them. They all seemed like frat kids after a kegger.

Olivia took a breath to explain she really didn't need the ride. She couldn't imagine having to make conversation with Sal the entire trip back to the city. *Being alone would be great right about now.* She tried to formulate a plan, but Jacob spoke before she could even put down her coffee. *Damn liquor really does slow your reflexes,* she thought.

"Can you take Liv back with you?"

"Would be my pleasure."

"Thanks, Sal," she muttered, accepting defeat.

⁐

The car ride to the Hamptons airport was painful. Jacob's head pounded and he thought for sure there was more in him to throw up every time the car took a curve. Taylor had chosen that moment to answer

Aubrey's call, something he rarely did before eleven a.m., and Aubrey had put him on speakerphone with the kids—Margaret Jo, who was eight, and Dixon, who was six. Taylor, like Jacob's parents, seemed to not really grasp speakerphones or cell phones, so when the two came together, it was a disaster. He yelled to them as if he were using a megaphone rather than a cell phone. It didn't help that Aubrey and the kids would unfailingly run around, going about their normal business. He wondered why she couldn't just sit them down for five minutes. Or pass the phone from one kid to another, or ask them to stand still for a minute or two. *Ha! Fat chance of that happening.*

That was one of those things Jacob decided he should make sure of before he settled down with someone. It could be his litmus on child-rearing. *How do you feel about children who can't sit still for longer than a dog?* He'd have to check with Sophie on that. *Sophie. Shit.*

The memories of the night before came crashing back. He rationalized, arguing to himself that the newness of their relationship didn't require monogamy. Still the guilt washed over him. Those girls had come back to the house to swim. *Yanni didn't give them money,* he thought, trying to erase the clear memory of its happening. And anyway, all he did was swim with them. They didn't even exchange a kiss.

He wondered if Olivia had heard them. There was no way she slept through their rowdy homecoming. *She must have. What must she think of me? Of us?* He raced through his mind trying to remember the details of the night. He glanced over at her. She stared straight ahead with an uneasy look that seemed cemented on. She didn't even wince while Aubrey yelled over the speakerphone. At this point the yelling wasn't even directed at Taylor. She was screaming at Eric, the lackey driver whom Aubrey had also turned into their all-around houseboy. He even changed lightbulbs.

"Kids! Don't run into the ladder like that!" he heard Eric sheepishly saying.

The governor barely seemed to notice. He spoke in a controlled manner and ordered the kids to sit down.

"I'll be home in two hours," Taylor told them. "When I get there, I want to know three things that you're each going to do this week to make a difference."

The kids yelled an "Okay, Daddy" in chorus.

Jacob rolled his eyes with a laugh, but Olivia didn't bite. She gave a half smile, in no mood for jokes.

Ugh, we better not have scared her off, Jacob thought. It had taken him too long to hire a fundraiser for this campaign. She had enough experience to be good enough to handle it. *Well, almost enough.* And she was young enough to want to take it on. That was the thing about campaigns. It was near impossible to get people with experience because no one lasted long enough to have it. The hours, the pay, the travel, the demands. It wasn't something anyone did for a long time.

Olivia was barely blinking.

We must've really traumatized her. Will have to fix that. Then he breathed a sigh of relief. *Landon will fix it. He can always come in and clean up any mess.*

⌘

Olivia stared in amazement at the private jet lifting off into the Hamptons sky. She felt as if she were in a coma. What did she say? What did she do? Was it as awkward for him as it was for her? Did he notice her looking at his crotch? Where did she stand now? Her head hurt and while she could have done without Sal's hour-long conversation about the Yankees, in the end, she was relieved to be in a car being driven back to the city as opposed to figuring out how to get on a Jitney. It was nearly noon. She emailed her sister, Marcy, remembering it was Sunday, when she, her sister, and a friend had a regularly scheduled meal.

LivGreenley@gmail.com: *Late lunch at the diner?*

Marcygreenley@gmail.com: *Obviously. We've been waiting. When do you get back?*

LivGreenley@gmail.com: *On my way. Meet at 1:15?*

The black SUV pulled up in front of the diner and Olivia got out fast. Sal started to open his door to help her with her bag, but she had put it on the seat right behind her.

"I got it. Thanks so much, Sal. See you soon." Her words hurried out of her mouth.

"No problem," he answered back. "See you next time, kid."

Her sister and friend were sitting at the table by the window.

"Fancy!" they squealed as she sat down. "Tell us everything."

"You guys first." She tried to adjust back to her normal surroundings. Listening to their stories—the date Marcy had been on with the Australian finance guy that had gone surprisingly well, how Katherine's on-again, off-again relationship was hitting another speed bump—brought her back to herself. Unconsciously, she breathed audibly into her ginger ale.

"You okay there?" Marcy asked.

"Yes." She laughed. "Just glad to be back to reality."

"Okay, so come on, tell us, what was the nonreality?!"

Olivia started explaining the trip from the start. "He gave this speech about poverty in America where he said—"

"Come on, get to the plane part!" Katherine said, interrupting.

Olivia smiled, realizing she had intended to repeat his whole speech verbatim and that it did not qualify as girl talk to any girl but her.

"It was awesome! We drove right up to the plane and it was beautiful. Really big. I was a total spaz picking a seat and then the governor had me come sit with him and we just talked the whole way there."

"As in all twenty-five minutes?" Marcy said with her normal sarcasm.

"Yes." It had felt like hours. "But it was amazing. I mean he's this guy I've studied. Literally studied. And it turns out he's the easiest guy in the world to talk to. Anyway, we got to Yanni's, which is insane, and Jon Bon Jovi was literally cleaning up the kitchen."

"Ohmigod, really? Did you meet him?"

"Yeah. I mean we all hung out. Yanni had this great dinner and drinks. Lots of drinks." Olivia still wasn't sure how she was going to frame the rest of the story. She wasn't even sure how she felt about it.

"Anyway, they all went out to the Palm, but I was dying and figured I shouldn't be completely drunk for my first weekend of work, so I went to go to sleep. And . . ." She tried to rush through the one part she needed to talk through at length. She figured the best way to say it was to blurt it. Rip off the Band-Aid.

"And the governor accidentally came to my room." She pulled her neck back, ready to be slapped.

Everyone stopped cold—Marcy put her drink down and Katherine's fork dropped from her hands. Both nearly did spit-takes, and Olivia had to admit it sounded ridiculous.

"*What?*" They almost looked angry.

"Nothing happened! Literally at all. It was just a weird moment."

"Seriously?"

"Yeah." Olivia already regretted the words coming out of her mouth. She should have just kept it to herself. It really wasn't actually anything at all.

"Isn't he married?"

"Yes." Olivia felt the weight of guilt double, then triple for even thinking anything about it. "And they have the perfect marriage. Everyone knows that." She backtracked. "I'm totally making something out of nothing. It literally was an honest mistake. He left right away." *He did.* She felt dishonest leaving out the part about her smile. The part she desperately wanted to tell someone. But it really wasn't anything at all.

"Nothing?" Marcy looked at her, one eyebrow raised.

"Nothing." Olivia became resolute in her answer.

"What a jerk!"

"Are you going to keep working for him?"

"He's totally a Spitzer or Edwards."

"Ew, politicians really are all like that." The comments came at Olivia like a spray of bullets, each one making her feel more guilty and more defensive. All of the years she had spent defending politicians crashed in on her. *I will not be the cause of this.*

"He's not. He's not like that. He's incredible. It will be fine. And yes, of course, I'm keeping my job. It really was just an accident. That's all." She sank down into the booth. "Let's talk about something else," she finally said, totally deflated.

"No, how do you feel about it?"

Olivia felt near tears. "I don't feel anything about it. I really like him. He's an amazing candidate. He's going to be president, and I'm going to be a part of that. This is the job I've been dreaming of since I was in kindergarten. This is the candidate I've been dreaming of since the first time I heard a political speech. It was literally nothing. He walked into the wrong room."

"Okay," they both said, knowing it wasn't an argument they would win.

Olivia wasn't lying about the job and the candidate. She would force herself not to ruin this. She would force herself to believe that the moment of intimacy between herself and the governor was all in her head.

As Olivia walked home that night she regretted saying any of it aloud and pledged to think before she spoke on a more regular basis. *Maybe that should be Campaign Lesson #1 rather than loyalty.* Tomorrow she would officially begin her job as the national finance director of Landon Taylor's presidential campaign. She would start new.

SEVEN

At eight forty-five the next morning, Olivia officially walked off the elevator and into the dream-job reception area. For the next year she would be working out of the offices of Jeremy Goldberg, a rich Texan who had moved to New York with his wife, Jenna, to run his family's hedge fund. The Goldbergs were friends of Taylor's finance chair, David Henley, who had arranged the workspace. Since federal law required a campaign to pay a "fair market price" for its offices, campaigners had two viable options—convince a donor with enough office space to let them "rent some rooms" or find real estate developers who had a great space that was under construction. The former was the chic option but not likely unless the campaign was high-profile enough. Like Taylor for President. For the latter, the mess didn't matter to the campaign—it fit the theme actually, and the developers could justify renting it to them at absurdly low prices. In both cases, the space was impracticable for anything but a campaign-type operation and as a perk, the companies had a possible governor, senator, or president as a tenant.

Big-time, she said in her head as she looked around silently thanking Henley for putting this deal with the Goldbergs together. The offices were beautiful—extravagantly stark, with white marble floors and crazy black leather chairs, low to the ground and almost hammock-like. Every office she went into these days had them, which seemed strange since they were so awkward to sit in. Maybe that was the point. Maybe it was some business mind game executives played to psych people out before meetings. *I could have people wait awkwardly here.*

She indulged in the thought for a moment, appreciating her new office but sure she would never actually think to do that. It was perfect. As an added bonus, she didn't even need to deal with setting up any of the basics, like phones and Internet.

This New York time, though, she knew, could only last so long. Campaigns grew at an insanely quick pace. If they won Iowa she would probably be hiring twenty or so people. They would have to get a huge space, and realistically, it would probably be at the campaign head-quarters in Georgia. The campaign life of pizza boxes, beers, and naps on gross carpets would be waiting in February. But for now, she was a *presidential fundraising executive on the twenty-third floor of the Lever Building in New York City.* She flipped her hair a bit, feeling empowered.

"Hi." She smiled to the tall Nordic receptionist, hoping the woman recognized her clout.

The receptionist smiled with pursed lips.

"You must be the political girl." The woman spoke barely above a whisper and emphasized the word "political" as if it were a disease, immediately bringing Olivia back to life. Her life. More standard executive psychological warfare, she figured. It was working.

Olivia pulled down on the edge of her suit jacket as if it might help tug some wrinkles out of the material. She realized that even though she had put on her newest Banana Republic ensemble she, as always, was clearly identifiable as the young, broke activist. She kept hoping she would walk into an office where they'd give her a makeover like the girl got in *The Devil Wears Prada.* Maybe they had a secret closet full of designer clothes. She'd be on the lookout for her Stanley Tucci for sure.

The receptionist whispered again. "Someone will be right with you. Please have a seat." It seemed more like an order than a suggestion.

As Olivia assessed the chairs, wondering how she could sit with-out flashing the receptionist or falling completely, a short, stocky man in his late forties appeared.

"Hi, I'm James, the office manager." He reached out his hand to her. "Come on back." From the looks of his pleated khaki pants and polka-dot button-down shirt, Olivia knew he would definitely not be giving her a makeover. Still, she was relieved to see a friendly face and hear a voice rise above a whisper. As she followed closely behind him down the hallway she realized that this would probably be the friendliest face she would encounter here. Office after office was as stark as the reception room. Indistinguishable young men sat at each desk, most of them on headset phones, surrounded by papers, and all looking haggard and well worn despite their brand-new suits. One or two looked up as she passed, but most didn't dare break their concentration. Olivia found herself almost tiptoeing for fear of disturbing them.

At the end of the hallway was an exact replica of the other offices except for the fact that it was void of anything but a desk, some file cabinets, and a big old computer. It wasn't quite the executive suite she had imagined, but it was definitely a large step above most campaign spaces. James flung his arm toward the desk.

"Your palace, madame!"

"Tha—"

"The one right next to you is for the other girl. She's coming, right?"

"Yes, Addie, she's starting Wednesday." Olivia was relieved she had decided to take the two days to herself to get acquainted with the new offices before Addie began. She had seemed nice enough at the Connecticut event, but Olivia had decided she needed to collect her thoughts before she had a deputy. And that was before she knew there would be so many thoughts to collect.

"Copy room down at the end of that hall, along with a kitchen. It's fully stocked, so help yourself! We put breakfast out around six. By 'we,' I mean me of course. Lunch goes out around noon. For dinner you're on your own unless the bosses are here late. Then we order up. Usually from '21' Club or Marea. Either costs more than my rent, so definitely take them up on it when they ask you to join. If you're here. I heard you work a lot. The boss said you work a lot. That you'd probably need your own key and stuff. You work for Taylor, huh?"

"I do." Olivia grinned proudly. She was still so excited to be able to say that. *And I love him.* She was determined to stop adding that in her head like it was a good thing.

"I really wanted them to win last time. And he's got that pretty wife. I knocked on doors for them in my neighborhood. Woulda been better if they had won."

"God, it's so true." She thought about that all the time. "The world would really be a different place. Hopefully, this time we'll do it right."

"I like it already. He'd be better as president anyway!"

"Thanks, James."

"Anyway," he said, going on with his tour, "this computer should work."

"Oh, that's okay, I have my laptop. Just as long as I can print from one of them."

"That should work. I'll have Luke, the IT guy, stop by to check on it. He doesn't get in till about noon most days. Not exactly an early riser. Tech kids."

"Thank you so much, James. This is great."

"No problemo. Let me know if you need anything else. I'm right past the kitchen." He gave her a kind smile and walked away, his arms moving at his sides like a speed-walker's.

Olivia sat down at her new desk and looked around at the empty office. There was a small window that looked directly into another building. It was so quiet, so different from her last campaign office, which was one of the real estate deals—an under-construction, mostly dilapidated floor of a building.

Sitting at the desk felt great. She had never been on a campaign that felt so invincible so early on. Sure, Taylor had a few good challengers in the Democratic field, but none of them really stood a chance. The only close contender was Senator Kramer, from Colorado, but the Democrats didn't need Colorado like they needed the South. A year from now, the Taylor bid would undoubtedly be the forerunning campaign for the president of the United States, and she was in charge of the national fundraising.

She looked down at the Google Alert on her BlackBerry, savoring the moment. "Taylor taps Greenley for Fundraising Role." Sure, her mom didn't know what Politico was, but her colleagues did. She did. And even her mother would understand the significance of a news organization writing about her getting a job. Ben Smith was reporting on her.

Sam Stein and Chris Cillizza, too. She warranted her own Google Alert. At twenty-seven she had made it to the top of her profession. She had flown through the lower ranks of fundraising teams in just three campaigns. Being put in charge of Adams's campaign was a fluke, but she had done well. Now she was changing the world at one of the highest levels. She should write an email to her political science professor and tell him. He'd be so happy for her. She scribbled down the idea in the new notebook she had spent three days picking out. The perfect notebook for the perfect job. Then a wave of panic hit as she remembered she had to actually do the job.

She opened her laptop to a blank Excel file and stared down at the paper next to her computer with the big number written on top of her to-do list. The one right above "write Professor Eigen a note."

Five million dollars.

Five million dollars and write a note. Spectacular to-do list, Olivia. Perhaps we should start with the money. She underlined "five million dollars." That's what they needed to collect before the Iowa Caucus in nine months.

She wasn't sure who had decided on that number. Whatever the reason, it wasn't really her concern. She just had to hit that mark, and in the course of three quarterly filings. She made a chart on her scrap paper. Half a million already in the bank. She would need to bring in another half a million before July 30. Another two million in September and then the final two million in January.

Olivia stared at the Excel sheet and thought about the numbers. This was her favorite part of the process—imagining the budget. Really it was just a theoretical list of numbers, but to her it was where she could do anything, raise any amount. Breaking it out gave her the road map to get to impossible numbers in impossible time. Down the first column she began typing in "New York," "Texas," "Florida . . ." and the cities she thought they could work in. She added in prospective hosts and within an hour she had the start to a road map.

As she began turning to her calls, her BlackBerry buzzed.

"Hey, Jacob."

"Livster! How's the first day?"

"It would probably be better if I had slept at all this weekend!"

"Oh, please. Your ability to operate well without sleep was one of the key reasons I hired you."

Olivia laughed, knowing that was actually probably true and wondering how she might phrase her unique abilities in the "Special Skills" section of her résumé.

"So what's up?"

"We need to talk about the budget."

"Okay." Olivia looked at the sheet, not quite prepared to go through the numbers, but at least having an idea of how she would get to five. Jacob paused a bit.

"So remember when we talked about raising five million before Iowa?"

"Ummm, yeah, my goal hadn't escaped my mind just yet. I'm not that sleep deprived."

"Yeah, actually we need it to be seven."

"What?!" Olivia shook her head and realized it was one of Jacob's jokes. "Very funny, Jacob." She imitated him making fun of her: "And I should wear my sequins when I raise it, right?"

Jacob's voice didn't waver. "You shouldn't really wear sequins when you do anything, Liv."

She stopped laughing as he continued on.

"This one's for real. We just met with the pollsters. If we can't run an extended media buy in Iowa, we can't move Kramer's negatives, and ours, the way we need to." Olivia looked into the phone as if she might be able to find a dose of reality there.

"Jacob, that's insane."

"I know, but we can do it. We have to."

"Jacob." She didn't even know what to say. How could they change her budget by so much in one day? Her first day no less. "Two million dollars is a lot of money."

"Yeah, the pollster thinks so too."

"Stop it. Stop joking around." Olivia stammered, more scared than angry, "Okay, I . . . I mean . . . I don't know if I would've even taken this job with that goal." She knew it wasn't true but changing the goal line by this much, this early, all just seemed so unfair. She had to protest.

"Really?" He sounded sincerely skeptical.

"No," she replied, "of course not. But it sucks! How often is this going to happen?"

"It won't anymore. I promise."

"Yeah, yeah." She rolled her eyes, knowing every minute she spent talking about the goal was one more minute she was psyching herself out and one more minute that she needed to spend working. "Okay, better get started." She hung her head backward over her chair and closed her eyes.

"That's the spirit!" Jacob yelled with sarcastic motivation.

"You're a pain in my ass, Jacob."

"You love me for it."

"Like a mailman loves a pit bull."

She hung up the phone and threw her head down on her folded arms. *Fifteen minutes ago I wasn't sure five was possible. How the heck am I going to get to seven?* A hopeless ache started to grow in her stomach.

"Hard first day?"

She opened her eyes and picked up her head to see James peering in the door. She rubbed at one of her eyes, remembering she was neither alone nor in the world she had just created for herself.

"Oh, hi. Sorry. No, not so bad at all! All good." She added in a thumbs-up. "All good" was such a useful phrase. People rarely pressed for further information after it was said. She wondered when she had started saying it. Probably in high school, she thought. It was so much easier to use those two words than explain all her protests and rallies to friends, who really didn't want to hear about global warming or Iraq anyway.

"Glad to hear it! Have some coffee! We have great coffee here."

"Will do. Thanks so much." She turned back to the Excel file and added ten more blank lines. That was her sole accomplishment for a solid hour. She simply couldn't get her head around the challenge.

By six that evening she still wasn't sure seven million was humanly possible, much less probable. The buzz of a private number calling on her phone was a welcome distraction. *Adams,* she thought with a smile. He had been calling all day with things he had "forgotten" to ask her before she left. The familiarity of his voice was a comfort. Plus the questions were easy.

But when she picked up the private number this time there was a silent pause on the other end of the line.

"Hello?"

"Hey, babe."

Olivia smiled, recognizing the governor's voice but not the familiarity, as embarrassment caused her face to flush.

"Hi." Silence filled the line as she sat nervously awaiting her boss's words. Just the sound of his accent excited her in a way she couldn't help but admit was more than professional.

"So." He paused. "Jacob thought I should call and make sure we hadn't scared you off this weekend."

Olivia made a sound that wasn't quite a laugh or a snort.

"I know."

He seemed to have a bizarre understanding of the sound she didn't comprehend herself. Did that mean there really was something odd to what had happened?

"Wait. Did you—?" She wasn't even sure what she was asking him. "Did he—?" *Stop it. Nothing happened,* she repeated to herself again, annoyed that she needed so much reminding of such a simple fact.

"He was worried Yanni and the party did it."

"Oh, no. I wasn't. It was fine." She laughed awkwardly, wishing she had a clue what he was thinking. And wishing, a little bit, that she hadn't been totally off base. That there was something more meaningful to his coming into her room than a casual accident.

"It probably should have," he said with a touch of introspective humor. "So we're still okay? You're not scared off?"

"I'm not scared off. I mean the numbers are a little scary, but when it comes to you guys, I'm good." She tried to lighten her tone.

"Are they realistic?" Word of the budget had swerved him immediately into business mode.

"Well, yes," she said, a bit unsure and unprepared to talk about it. "I mean, they're high. Really high. But campaigns know no other way I guess. I think if they were too realistic I'd be more worried. We need to make a splash, right?"

"We need to show massive numbers for this to work, but more

than that we need to not be surprised. If you can't get them, I need you to speak up."

Olivia thought about speaking up right then and there and then quickly thought better of it. The force of his voice jarred her into a memory of being in school and needing to have the right answer. "Okay. I know."

"Look, this campaign is about to expand by the minute," he said. "We're making decisions now based on the budget. Huge decisions— media-buy projections, consultants. Once we go down this road, there's no turning back. We can't change the budget halfway through."

Suddenly the numbers in front of Olivia that she had stared at all day became objects of even more intense trepidation. She was responsible for people's salaries and, more importantly, for whether or not those people would be able to do what they needed to win Iowa. Iowa. A huge national event that could determine the presidency was suddenly a tangible item on her scribbled to-do list.

"I put together the start of a plan today." She didn't tell him it was for two million off his goal. It was a big exaggeration. A lie maybe. But how could she not? "We can get there. I know we can. I can do this." The last sentence fell out of her mouth, but she said it more to herself than to him.

"You *can* do this, Olivia. It's going to be harder and bigger than anything you've done before and I'm going to push you more than you think I should sometimes. But it's because I know you can do this. You know, when I played football in college, there were a bunch of different trainers and everyone avoided this one guy, Barry. Barry always put twenty more pounds of weight on you than you could handle. He was tough and he made you feel like you were at the bottom of a ditch. But he was always my favorite. It's the guy who adds twenty pounds to your bar who really believes in you, who pushes you to be not the best you think you can be, but to be even better. That's who you want setting your goals."

Olivia exhaled, a bit speechless, as he continued on. Her inappropriate thoughts seemed to slip away. This was Landon Taylor—the governor she'd studied, the politician she idolized. And he believed in her.

Not because he thought she was pretty or because he liked her smile. Because he knew she could do the job.

"That's who I'm going to be for you. I'm going to add the weight, but only because I know you can handle it. I see something special in you. I'll be there spotting you. But you're not going to need me."

"I won't let you down," she pledged, as if she were joining the army.

"I know you won't." His words carried a sweet confidence. "What I do need though is for you to tell me if we're not on track. I need to know you are on the numbers, that you're keeping us on track to get to where we need to be. I need to trust you to be the person who will give it to me straight. It's an unfortunate truth, but money is the gas of this campaign. We need good parts and a good body, sure, but without gas we won't go."

"Okay." Olivia spoke with apprehension. For the first time since the Hamptons she was concerned only with the job at hand.

"And hear me when I say this, please." His "please" sounded like more of an order than a nicety. "I can change the budget early in the game, but I can't change it last-minute, so if we're not hitting our numbers, you have to tell me as early as possible."

"Okay." She was responsible for the numbers. She would have other superiors, but at the end of the day, she was reporting to Governor Taylor.

"We're going to do a finance committee meeting soon, right?"

"Yes, sir. Two weeks from tomorrow."

"Two weeks? That's soon."

Way too soon, Olivia wanted to scream. She had begged Jacob for more time to get herself organized, but he had put it in motion before she filled out her W-9 and refused to change it. *It. A national finance committee meeting.* Most campaigns did two, maybe three, of these in an entire election cycle. They were gatherings set up to woo and motivate the most important donors. For the Taylor campaign, it would be a day in Georgia, complete with a full briefing on the campaign budget, run by Olivia. There would be presentations by Billy and Jacob, as well as their pollster, Richard. Aubrey would be organizing a lunch at one of the Habitat sites.

Terrible reasoning, Olivia had told Jacob when he explained that they had to have a finance committee meeting early because the ball was already rolling. Still, she couldn't argue too hard about the schedule before she even had a desk. She had planned to bring it up with him again this very day but then had gotten sidetracked with the goal change.

"Yes, it is." She spoke without a hint of the concern she felt. "But Jacob and I talked in depth about it. We already have good people confirmed to attend, and I'll be on the phones to get everyone else we need there. We need to hit the ground running anyway, and it gives me a good excuse to introduce myself to people and get to know the group. I always like an extra reason to call and harass people."

She regurgitated all the reasons Jacob had given her when she had argued against the time crunch. As she spoke, she found herself becoming more and more committed to making it work.

"Yeah," the governor said in agreement. "That sounds smart." He left an awkward silence on the phone. She tried to think of something intelligent to say, but he continued on. "You'll be ready?"

"I'll be ready." By the time they hung up the phone, Olivia had taken full responsibility for the meeting in her own mind. She could do this. It didn't matter that she had never done anything so big before. Nor did it matter that she wasn't sure how to do it. She was never the smartest kid in the class, never the most talented on the soccer field, but she could always come out on top. Sure, she wasn't the very best at anything, but she could work hard enough at anything to be damn good at it. Her talents, as she saw them, weren't innate. They were earned.

"You just set your mind to it." She heard her mom's voice in her head. The same voice that encouraged her to try out for soccer in high school even though she had never played in any organized fashion. *"Keep your eye on the ball. With your determination, the sky's the limit."* The coaches had called Olivia the "Rudy" of the team, letting her join not because she could play (they told her in no uncertain terms that she wasn't very good), but because she had more heart than they'd seen in years. Sure enough, two years later Olivia had made varsity and all-county. *The sky's the limit,* she repeated in her head. *I can do this.*

EIGHT

The morning of the finance committee meeting, Jacob sprang out of bed at five fifteen a.m. He had never been an early riser, but the hours of sleep he needed seemed to lessen with the campaign's every passing day. He opened his laptop and began reading over the briefing Olivia had sent two days before. He scrolled down the list of expected attendees. All of their major players were coming as well as a handful of people Olivia was bringing into the campaign. He had worked the phones hard getting people committed to attend, all with a lingering feeling that he shouldn't have pushed this meeting on Olivia so soon. The meeting needed to run smoothly. They would all be there—the BSDs, the DFTLs, even a few of the SWs, or Starving Wives, all of whom were starving for something, mostly money and food.

In all aspects of campaigns, but especially with fundraising, Jacob had learned, spin and momentum were the name of the game. Their poll numbers were starting to gel in Iowa and New Hampshire. He knew if he could get the influx of money he needed into Iowa early, they would win the caucus. It had become, to him, as simple as a mathematical equation. The best county captains and enough field organizers, fed sufficiently well and hanging up the right number of signs, would equal a win. He knew the data and the people. His candidate was hitting his stride. Now all he needed was the money to make it happen. If only the rest of his life could be this straightforward.

He scrolled down the pages to Olivia's plan. She was about to tell all their biggest donors that her goal was for them to raise one million dollars by June 30. He shook his head with fear. *She's not going to be able to do that. She's too young. The number is too high. They're not going to take her seriously.* The number was higher than he had even set out in his original budget. One million dollars in five-thousand-dollar checks in two months. *She's insane. Which is a problem since she was my idea. I should've never agreed to the seven.*

His head immediately rushed to the worst-case scenario of their coming in under a goal they set out loud to a room full of people. And not just any people, their top donors. Even if they had raised a significant amount, a dollar less than the goal would signal something was wrong and could offset the race's momentum. He was so lost in thought he didn't even notice it was only five forty-five when he dialed Olivia's number. Fortunately she didn't notice either.

She answered with a chipper, "Morning, Jacob."

He looked at his clock. "Ah! I didn't realize it was so early. Sorry."

"Totally fine, I haven't been able to sleep a wink. They were kind enough to let me into the hotel restaurant even though it doesn't open until six. They said I had to wait till six for coffee, but maybe they just thought they should slow me down because they saw my knee jittering already!"

"Want company?"

"Yes! I would love to talk this stuff over so I don't make a complete fool of myself today."

"Be there in twenty." Jacob hung up the phone and got dressed, feeling better just knowing she was on the same wavelength. And happy to have someone in Georgia who also couldn't sleep. He had been in Georgia for a while but he still hadn't gotten completely used to the relative quiet.

Twenty minutes later Jacob slipped into the chair across from Olivia, who was downing her first coffee of what he predicted would be many. While it wasn't reassuring to see her so nervous, he was glad that at least she was visibly aware of how important today was.

"Thank you so much for coming over," she said. "I'm so happy to have someone to talk this through with before the meeting."

"We have to talk? I thought I was just getting a free hotel breakfast."

Olivia laughed, putting down her coffee for the first time since he walked in. "Right. Breakfast. I'm so hungry."

"I don't think I've ever heard those words coming out of your mouth."

"I got in late last night! I didn't have dinner. Plus I think if this campaign doesn't work out, I'm going to try to be a competitive eater."

Jacob laughed out loud at her serious expression. "Yeah, if there's a category for who could eat the least amount of food over the longest period of time, you would totally crush it." Jacob looked down at the menu, happy to have other options than the box of probably stale cereal in his apartment.

Olivia started her pitch after they ordered. "Okay, so this is the plan." As she laid out her ideas, even walking him through the Power-Point on her computer, Jacob started to relax enough to enjoy his waffles, bacon, and grits, a delicacy he was enjoying more with every passing week. Olivia looked up from her notes and watched him shovel in some grits. "Big change from our Sausage McMuffin mornings, huh?"

"Yeah, thank God. Another year with you and your McDonald's habit and I would have been at least double my size."

"Oh please, we all know you couldn't gain weight if you tried. Isn't that what your wrestling coach used to say?"

"Yeah, yeah. Liv, this is really good." He pointed to her presentation and tried to sound less surprised than he actually was. She spoke with such authority on the numbers, Jacob bought into it all himself, and he knew he was as cynical—if not more so—than anyone coming into that room.

"The grits? Ew. I am not trying those things."

"Yes, the grits are good. But, please, I know you better than to try to convince you to eat them. I'm talking about your presentation. It's really good.

"Really?" Her eyes widened with surprise.

"Really. I mean I had no clue how you were going to make one million plausible, and instead, you made it completely doable. Gabrielle would be totally proud." Gabrielle, their mutual former boss was their common standard bearer for all things fundraising.

"Well, I'm going to tell them the public goal will be seven hundred and fifty thousand, and one million is their inside goal. That way if anyone leaks, which obviously they will, they'll leak under one, giving me some room to fail."

"You won't fail," Jacob said, trying to reassure her.

"But my real goal is one point five." She smiled.

Jacob laughed at her audacity.

"That's awesome, Liv. You know how many bumper stickers in Iowa I could buy with that?"

"No, but I want to know!"

"Huh?" Jacob smiled, assuming this was sarcasm.

"Wait, no, seriously." She stopped his laugh. "Can you tell me the numbers on some of those things? Donors will love that."

"Seriously?"

"Yes!" She squealed with a delight that seemed incongruous with bumper stickers. "Seriously, Jacob, that's brilliant. Give them tangible things to fund. I'm not going to use it for this, but let's do that for online giving."

"I like it. Liv, really, this is great."

"Oh, thank goodness." She stopped and breathed a huge sigh of relief. "I'm so scared someone other than you will realize I have no clue what I'm doing." She looked down at her untouched breakfast and took the last sip of her second coffee.

"Olivia Greenley." Jacob looked at her sternly. "You do know what you're doing. You're even better at it than I thought you were. And I thought you were pretty damn good. Now you need a dose of self-confidence to go with it. You know BSDs; these guys see fear a mile away and love to seize on it for sport. Do not let them see even a glimpse of it. You know what I say—calm, contain, control. That should be one of those campaign lessons you're always counting."

"Yeah, yeah, I know." Olivia shook her head, looking like a scared kid. Jacob wondered if he had gone too far.

"Come on, it'll be totally fine." He took great comfort in actually believing what he was saying. "Eye of the Gabrielle!" He lowered his eyebrows the way their old boss used to do when she got serious and hummed "Eye of the Tiger." Olivia laughed and made the face with him. "Now, let's get some of that competitive eating going."

Olivia laughed as she took two small bites of her burned bacon, passing her grits over to Jacob.

༺◦◦◦༻

Fifteen hours later Olivia stood at the hotel bar worried that if she sat down she might fall asleep. The day, filled with everything from a tour of the Georgia capitol to the Georgia Peach Pie Shop, had gone incredibly well by all accounts. She glanced down at her watch as inconspicuously as she could, hoping no one saw her lack of enthusiasm for staying out.

After the last official event, a dinner at the hotel restaurant, most of the attendees, including Governor Taylor, had filtered into the old-fashioned bar. It was musty and had a lingering smell of cigar smoke, but there was something about it she loved. The dark wood tables were surrounded by chairs covered in all shades of velvet, and colored glass chandeliers hung down so low that some of the taller people had to duck to miss them. Olivia could imagine singers from the forties, dressed in feathers and sequins, standing by the piano that sat in the corner of the room. *It would be a great place to sit and read a book,* she thought. *Hah! Like I would have time to read a book.*

Yanni came up next to her to order a drink. He patted her back.

"This was great, Olivia. Really great. Thanks for including me."

"No, Yanni, thank you!" She smiled, full of pride. Her part, the one she had been practicing for days, the one that kept her up for three nights in a row, had been a huge success. When she stepped up to the podium, her hand had been shaking a bit, but Jacob had shot her an eye-of-the-Gabrielle look. *No fear,* she had reminded herself, and, head held high, she led the room of twenty-six men and three women through her plan to raise one million dollars. The flaws (she forgot the part about the pre–planning for next quarter's direct-mail program and she should have had them all introduce themselves before she started) stuck in her head. But really she was proud of the job she did. Her voice, in contrast to how she felt, had sounded completely confident and in control, a theory confirmed by her audience's reactions. The three women all complimented her directly and the men, without saying a word about her presentation, began speaking to her with a new frankness that was as obvious as a direct compliment. And no one had called her "kid" or "kiddo" all day.

She moved around the room, fending off her exhaustion and embracing her budding confidence. As usual, at one point in the evening she got cornered by Alek, who was plenty nice, but could talk forever. He stood facing her at the bar, his hand tightly gripping his tumbler of vodka. His hands were pudgy, like his face, but his fingers were perfectly manicured. His button nose was always red, as if he had just come in from the cold Russian weather he often spoke of. His eyes were small, black, and sunken in, and his wrinkly forehead seemed bigger because of the blunt black bangs that were usually stuck to the top of his head.

Twenty minutes that seemed like an hour into his story about the NASCAR race he and the governor had gone to together five years earlier, Olivia blinked and stuck her nails into her palm, a trick that was supposed to wake her up, but never really worked. She had heard this one at least three times before and hoped he would get to the part where they met Stephen Colbert soon so the story would end. Her head started to bob down, tired of balancing on her neck. As she picked it back up, her eyes met the governor's on the other side of the room.

Sitting diagonally across from her, in a booth with Henley, Yanni, and some others, he let his gaze momentarily meet hers and smiled empathetically. He lifted his eyebrows and winked. Olivia looked around the room, which was crowded with people talking and laughing, all of them completely unaware of his wink. It wasn't anything, she told herself, but her stomach stirred with their private moment. Henley, trading off between his cigar and his bourbon, pulled at the governor's arm to engage him in the conversation. The governor turned, not missing a beat, and she swerved back into her own conversation. She was wide awake now. A mere minute later she heard her name.

"Miss Ohhh-livia Greenley," Henley shouted from their booth. "Get your pretty little self over here." His Texas accent was much thicker than the governor's drawl and when he spoke, he always did so with a bit of a laugh that made his large belly jiggle. He reminded Olivia of what Santa Claus would be like if he were Texan. And a lawyer.

Olivia gladly excused herself from the conversation with Alek and walked toward them. Henley and the governor stood, as they always did when a lady was joining or leaving the table. As Henley made way for her to slide in, the governor pulled his large leather chair closer.

"Thought you could use a reprieve over there." Taylor spoke without any acknowledgment of the moment of silent gazing they had shared. She smiled and nodded, hyper-aware of how close he was to her. She felt strangely lost between career and the contrasting fluttering emotions.

"Now, let's get us some more bourbon and talk about these Texas events." Henley waved over the waitress.

"Could I have a Diet Coke, please, as well?" Olivia half-pleaded, not wanting to drink just bourbon on an empty, tired stomach. She would not make that mistake again.

The governor leaned over and said, "If we're going to talk numbers while drinking bourbon, I'm going to need some food." He smiled out of the corner of his eye at Olivia. "Sliders?"

"That sounds great." Henley piled on every other appetizer and the waitress headed to the kitchen.

The crowd began to dwindle as Henley boasted loudly about the events he would put together in Texas.

"You'll stay at my guesthouse. I think you should come out three weeks before. At least."

Olivia got her second wind with the help of the sliders and a spinach-artichoke dip that she finished almost completely by herself. She was scribbling names as he rattled them off. She had heard of most of his friends and colleagues. They were well-known trial lawyers and Democratic donors, but before she joined the Taylor campaign, they had always been just names on call lists that never called her candidates back. At this level, it was a whole other league of prospects.

"Do you think we can really pull off two-fifty? I think I can do fifty at a lower-dollar event but I'm nervous about putting his trip to Texas on the budget with a goal of three hundred thousand." She barely noticed the ease with which she talked about hundreds of thousands of dollars despite not having a single thousand of her own.

"We'll definitely do two fifty."

Olivia breathed out. Whether or not she believed him, it was good to hear it aloud and even better to hear someone say "we." It made her feel the tiniest bit less alone on the road to seven million.

"LT, focus, grasshopper! I need your pretty-boy ass hitting the phones." Henley reached over to grab the governor's arm to pull him away from Alek, who had made his way over. Henley regarded Alek, whom he often referred to as a "chicken with his head cut off," with an annoyed glare. Olivia caught the look and felt bad. Alek was a little peculiar but he really was a good guy. Henley continued. "Anyone staying for this conversation commits to raising another two fifty." Henley loved to assert his chairmanship by throwing out such numbers.

"Sat is too rich for my blood! I go." Alek laughed.

"Thank you so much for everything, Alek." Olivia stood up and hugged him good-bye, reminding Taylor that Alek had brought in two new people for this meeting, both of whom had committed to raising fifty thousand dollars. The governor followed suit as Henley waved his cigar in the air.

Olivia looked back at Henley and began gathering the papers she had spread in front of her. "I'll leave you guys to discuss."

Henley shot an incredulous look her way. "Sit your hot little ass in that chair. You're not going anywhere."

Olivia smiled at how his thick Texan accent made those words sound so much less offensive than they were.

"Damn," she said with one eyebrow raised and a grin. "I thought you guys could handle this part on your own."

"I have been around this shit enough to know a politician's word is only as good as what his staff writes down. Plus," he added, "you're not half-bad at this."

"Thanks, Henley." She was beginning to like him more every moment.

"That Yanni guy you brought, he's not so bad."

"Yeah, he's great. He's going to do two hundred in the Hamptons."

The UT fight song erupted from Henley's phone. "Shit, it's my assistant," he said. "Gotta take this. Y'all hold that thought."

Henley excused himself from the table and began to talk rapidly, waving his cigar around as he spoke.

"He's amazing," Olivia said.

"He's a good friend. He really is." The governor shook his head, closing his eyes in thought. "He's not going to do two fifty though. I love him but he can't do that."

"I only have him in the budget for one fifty."

The governor widened his eyes, seemingly charmed. "Good."

Suddenly she felt she needed to defend Henley. She wanted the governor to like him, and vice versa. Fundraising was the apex of people-pleasing for Olivia. She didn't just need the players involved to go through the transactional motions, she wanted them to actually like each other. She wanted to build relationships. "I think he might be able to get there though."

"That'd be great. That'd be just great."

Before she could respond, Henley came walking back in, cell phone pressed between his ear and his shoulder. He kept flinging around his cigar with every hand gesture. He leaned over the table, put down his cigar, and grabbed his tumbler of bourbon. He pulled his iPhone from his ear and rolled his eyes.

"I gotta deal with this shit. See y'all tomorrow?" His gruff voice barely lowered as he walked off, without waiting for an answer, carrying the bourbon.

Olivia sat back. "He's such a character." She smiled. "I feel like I've been transported to a smoky room in a black and white movie when he's around." She watched him motion to the waitress for the check and sign his name, all while yelling into the phone.

"Who else did he say will host his event?"

Olivia reached for the paper she had scribbled on, embarrassed at the mess. "Sorry, he started on names so quickly I didn't have time to pull out my notebook." She looked across the room at her large bag with the laptop sticking out among folders and papers, wishing it was closer and neater. "I'm going to transfer it all to Excel when I get to my room."

The governor studied the list and didn't seem to notice the disorder.

"Ugh. Harry. This guy is scum—you watch out for him. In fact, watch out for all the trial lawyers. Jacob has some name for them."

"DFTLs," Olivia said with a smile, remembering the acronym.

"Yeah, yeah, that's it. Okay, so this is about one hundred here. You have to get Henley to get you more than this. Ask Alek too. That man can come up with money anywhere."

"Right. Yes." *Shit,* she muttered internally. She had thought it was easily two hundred on that page. She took a deep breath.

"Do you have the budget with you?"

"Sure. Yes. Let me just get my bag." She walked over to the wall where she had stashed it and nervously pulled her laptop out. As she returned to her place in the booth she thanked him for standing when she sat.

"Sorry, it'll just take a few minutes to load up."

"No problem." He checked his BlackBerry reflexively.

As the computer loaded, she watched him typing away. Now that she felt more relaxed, she asked the question she had been too embarrassed to ask before.

"Hey, by the way, what's with the pins?"

He looked up, confused, and she instantly wanted to retract the question, but it was too late.

"I mean the pins rather than emails. What's the deal with that?"

He replied matter-of-factly, "Pins are device-to-device, no servers, so things aren't saved remotely anywhere. It's just a more secure way of communicating."

"Oh." Olivia thought for a second. That could be Campaign Lesson #20: No servers. As she noted the new rule in her head, her list popped up on the screen.

He leaned in, and they went down the budget as Olivia included names and numbers from the day. The math was starting to add up. She spoke, again, with authority on her plan. She couldn't remember a time she felt more comfortable in her own skin.

When the governor excused himself to go to the men's room, Olivia sat back and watched him walk. She caught herself smiling with more than a tingle of excitement. *He's perfect. This is perfect. I'm doing it,* she said to herself. *This is what dreams are like when they come true.*

Upon his return, the governor slid into the booth next to her. She caught her breath with the nearness of him. As he moved in, his hand gripped her knee. "We're really going to do this, kid."

Annoyingly, her leg flinched at his touch.

"Sorry." He looked up at her eyes.

"No, it's okay. It was nothing." She hoped he would believe her lie. The lie she had been trying to get herself to believe for weeks.

"It's not. I'm sorry." He looked down with a disappointed shame and said in a breath, "I forget myself around you."

It may not have been the nicest thing anyone had ever said to her, but in that moment, coming from Taylor, it was everything she had always wanted to hear someone say. She tried to reply but couldn't find the words. Her stomach did belly flops any time he was close, but that's how it was supposed to be. She was the kid with the crush. He wasn't supposed to feel anything. He went on with a sense of contemplation.

"That . . . losing myself around people . . . that doesn't happen to me." He looked at her like he was trying to find an answer. She was desperate to be able to give him one but couldn't find breath, much less words. She tried to remember the logistics of breathing. *In and out,* she instructed herself. But in between the "in" and "out" she was overwhelmed with excitement and nervousness.

"I mean, it's no secret that Aubrey and I . . ." He lowered his voice to a near whisper. "We haven't been in love for a long time, but it hasn't been something I've even thought of. The path we've been on together has taken the place of a relationship." He seemed to be working his thoughts through out loud more than telling her about his feelings. "The truth is, we were on a demolition path before the governor's race. We had even separated for a few months."

"Really?" Olivia didn't mean to say it so loudly, but she was caught so off guard. First of all, why was he talking to her about love at all? It was as if the whole time she had been wondering if his accidental stumble into her room had significance, he was already assuming something more. And this idea of Aubrey's relationship to him being strained . . . *No secret?* There was never even a hint of discord in the press or even in the campaign rumor mill about their marriage. *And what did he mean by saying "it" hasn't been something he's thought of? What hasn't? What's "it"?*

"Yeah. And we didn't get back together for the race. It wasn't a political decision. I think it reminded us of how we fell in love with each other originally. We had a shared ambition to take on life. When the race came up, we fell back into the comfort of having a goal we could get to together. We were great together at the job at hand."

"You are great together," Olivia said, correcting him.

"Yes. Yes, I know. And we got back the teamwork aspect. But the relationship, the love, didn't really come with it. I mean, the woman is perpetually disappointed in me." He thought for a minute and added, "Well, in everyone."

Olivia shifted, trying not to seem as uncomfortable as she was. This was out of her league on so many levels. She didn't even know what kind of ear she was supposed to be lending here. A friend, a coworker, a kid with a crush? Not that it mattered. She wouldn't know what advice to give on any of it. He continued, apparently not really looking for advice anyway.

"In fact, I sometimes wonder if the love was ever there. One time, at the start of the campaign, when we were getting back together, Barry, my trainer, who sometimes doubles as my life guru, asked what it was like when it was just the two of us alone at night. I said it was good now that we weren't arguing. We have the campaign to talk about at night now, I said. And it's true. We do. But if we didn't have that . . ." He was suddenly pensive and almost said the rest to himself. "If we didn't have the politics, I don't think we would have anything."

"Does it maybe just seem like that because the campaign is all-encompassing? I mean, I'm sure there's something. Do you remember the things you fell in love with at first?"

This conversation couldn't be happening. For all the times she had thought about Governor Taylor's loving her, she had never considered actually hearing that he wasn't in love with his wife. Did that mean he did love her? *Shit.* Her fantasized thoughts of his loving her were smacked with a dose of reality. If he did have feelings for her, the ones she had for him, the ones she secretly hoped he had for her, what would actually happen? She hadn't actually thought through her fantasy. *You're not supposed to think through the consequences of a fantasy! That's why it's a fantasy!* Her thoughts swirled. *What does that mean for Aubrey? They looked so happy today. The way she looked at him. Could I have gotten him so wrong? Does Jacob know?*

"I do, but I can't remember any of the reasons being her as a person. God, that sounds awful aloud. It was all about who we were together."

"Maybe that's enough. I mean, spark is overrated. Maybe the road to a common goal is a stronger force, stronger thread." Olivia felt she had to turn this around. He had to be in love with Aubrey. That was the way things were supposed to be. The alternative left too much open. Too much to think about. Too much to handle. She felt a bead of sweat on the back of her neck. His legs, weren't moving, but they seemed to have inched closer to her.

"You believe that?"

"I don't know. Well, I guess, yeah, if I think logically about it. I think so."

"There's a 'but' there."

She smiled a busted smile and let her head drop. "I'm a bad one to ask."

"Why?"

"I am a child of the Disney princesses, you know? I'm a romantic, but that's stupid. That doesn't last. You know, there's a reason the phrase is 'hopeless romantic.'" She crossed her legs away from him, wishing she didn't blurt out emotional things about herself like that around him. Wishing she could feel less attraction.

"Ahhh." He grinned, interested. "Is that why you're not married?"

"It probably is. I'm still looking for my Prince Charming. But Prince Charmings are about as realistic as glass slippers. You know what would happen if I really had a pair of glass slippers? When I stood on them, they'd shatter, and I'd cut my feet."

He smiled. "Then why are you still looking for the prince?"

"Good question!" she said. "I think my heart and my head don't often see eye to eye. My dad used to always say, 'The heart knows reason that the mind knows nothing of.'"

He grabbed her leg and shook his head with a muttered laugh. "That is exactly what my aunt Lil used to say to me. Where did you come from? God. If this was another lifetime, not even the physics of it would stop me from finding you glass slippers that wouldn't shatter . . ."

His words trailed off at the end, almost as if he didn't mean to say it. But Olivia heard every word. Her heart rose into her throat. The intimacy was palpable and felt, to Olivia, like a tiny current of electricity running through her veins. She shook her arm in an attempt to stop it from tingling. She looked around, realizing for the first time in what seemed like hours that there were other people at the bar, other people in the world.

He followed her gaze. "Okay. It's about time I get to sleep. Jacob gets mad if I'm tired in the mornings."

Jacob. Shit. He would kill me for this conversation. He would kill the governor. Jacob. She felt a rush of guilt. *Does he know this side of the governor? He would have told me if he did. How am I going to keep this from him? Lock it up, Olivia.* "Yes, yes, definitely."

They got up awkwardly. "I'm going to just check my messages." He didn't move away from the table.

"Okay, right, yeah." Olivia felt like she was on a balance beam. *Right, duh. We can't walk to the elevator bank together! He doesn't love his wife. He wants to find me glass slippers. Walk away.* She begged her subconscious to gain control. "Okay. Good night, Governor."

"Night, babe." He grabbed her hand and gave it a squeeze. "You did a great job today. Really. Just great."

"Thank you. Good night." *Said that already. Okay, bye.* She walked away unsteadily. The conversation swirled through her head. Nothing about it made sense. She didn't want it to. For the first time in her life she didn't want to have the answer.

☙

Upstairs, the alarm clock lit up her room with its red 1:21. *Four hours at the most,* she thought. It had been days since she got the coveted five hours of sleep. As she washed her face, she heard a knock. She grabbed a towel, wiping the suds from her eyes with a weird feeling that her conversation with the governor wasn't complete.

As strangely expected, Taylor stood in the doorway. Holding his jacket in his hand, his tie now open and hanging down on either side of his shirt, he smiled and his eyes locked into hers for what seemed like the millionth time of the day.

"Wrong room again?" She laughed. "You really are losing your mind!"

"Not the wrong room." He slid past her with a smoothness contradictory to the situation. "I just forgot to ask you something."

"What's that?" Olivia closed the door and followed him in.

The governor stood in front of her, closer than they had been even that night in the Hamptons. "Your shoe size." He didn't drop his gaze.

"My shoe size?"

"You know . . . in case I find those glass slippers."

Olivia struggled to find a response before the governor leaned down to kiss her. As his lips touched against hers, his arms wrapped around to her back. Without her heels, she was a good nine or ten inches shorter than him. And his grip around her sides was strong and steady. *Wait.*

"Wait!" She pushed him back.

He kept his arms around her waist.

"Wait. What are we doing? We can't . . ."

"Are you saying you don't want to kiss me?"

"I mean, no. Well, no, it's not that I don't want to kiss you." The words rumbled around in her head. What was she saying? Of course she wanted to kiss him. This was Landon Taylor. This was the fantasy.

"So kiss me." He drew her back in. "I've been wanting to since the day I met you."

Olivia's heart was pounding as the blood rushed throughout her body.

"Literally. Since that day at the Brinmore. I've been in a good mood since you came aboard. You can even ask Jacob."

"I think I'll probably leave Jacob out of this one." She laughed nervously, but it wasn't funny. She had just kissed the governor. She had crossed a line. A line she couldn't go back over. She would have to lie to Jacob. She looked down.

"Right. Yeah. Right. Okay." He reached for her chin and lifted it up until her eyes met his. "But, Olivia, I don't remember the last time I felt like this. It's not something you let go of."

"It is. It is something you definitely let go of." *I have to let go. But it's Landon. Landon Taylor. And those eyes. Do I have to?*

He looked at her without missing a beat. "Not possible. You know it as well as I do."

Olivia breathed. She couldn't even process the thoughts in her head. She wished she weren't so tired. *There's something sane to say here. I know it's there.* She scanned her list of Campaign Lessons in her head but couldn't think of anything other than flats and heels and servers. *And his blue eyes. There's definitely a lesson in them.* The governor stopped the rattling of her thoughts.

"Tell me something—if I weren't married, what would you be doing right now?"

"I think there's a chance I'd be kissing you back." The minute the words came out of her mouth she wanted to reach into the air and grab them back. *He's married. I just kissed a married man.*

"You already kissed me. And my situation—it's complicated but it's not a problem."

"Not a problem"? "Situation"? What is his situation? God, his hair looks even softer this close. "For who?"

"For us."

Oh my God. There's an "us." Stop it. I mean there couldn't be a way kissing him could be okay. Could there?

"How do you figure?"

"It is what it is."

"I ca—" Olivia turned away from him in an effort to break his searing stare. It almost seemed like that black and yellow swirl that cartoon characters see when they're under an evil spell. *That's what this must be—a spell. I'm not this girl. I'm not. I don't kiss married men. Hell, I barely kiss any men.*

He kissed her again, and she let him. It had been a while since she had been really kissed. His lips were as soft as she'd imagined they would be. But not too soft. Strong and powerful at the same time. She pulled away and again tried to escape his eyes. *My job. The job. He's my boss.* "I work for you."

His hand gently gripped her wrist, turning her back to him. "I know. And I need you. Not just for fundraising. I need you." Olivia felt the gulp. Why was this totally nonsensical conversation making perfect sense?

He is a good kisser.

As if he had heard her inner monologue, the governor moved in and kissed her again. Suddenly nothing mattered. Her insides went to mush, like a teddy bear whose only job was to be held.

"Liv," he said, as if they had known each other for years, "stop thinking on this one. Just for a minute." She wondered if he didn't know she had already just decided that thoughts were unnecessary.

༺✦༻

The next thing she knew, the buzzing of her BlackBerry on the night table woke Olivia. Her eyes opened, seemingly one at a time.

Dreaming. Still dreaming? The back of his head lay in front of her, still as could be. She closed and reopened her eyes, making sure it wasn't an illusion. She flashed back to his kiss. And to falling onto the bed, locked in his embrace. She remembered his arms wrapped around her, his breath on her neck. *Hours ago. Maybe minutes ago.* She couldn't be sure. She checked her shirt and confirmed the memory that all her clothes had been left on. She breathed a sigh of relief. His shirt was crumpled up, so that a bit of his back could be seen.

God, the skin on his back looks soft. She couldn't actually remember touching it. *I wonder if he has some Brooks Brothers wrinkle-free shirts. I wonder if they'd withstand this type of thing.* Shit. *Omigod, Olivia.* She gave herself an inner-monologue bitch slap. *This man. Can't be here. He's married. He's my boss. This cannot have happened. Campaign Lesson #1. This is Campaign Lesson #1.*

Her bitch slap must have reverberated, because he flinched and turned to her. His eyes seemed even bluer than before. *Do not look.*

"You have to leave." She whispered fiercely, still unaware of even what time it was.

"What?" He showed her the naïve smile of someone not awake enough to recognize the situation for what it was.

"You. Me. You have to—Someone will—" She couldn't get the

words to form a sentence. *Why does he have to be so good looking? He has to go.*

"And the translation of that is, beautiful?" He kept his incongruously calm smile and brushed back her hair.

He called me beautiful. He thinks I'm beautiful. She began to tilt her head toward her shoulder and then quickly picked it back up. *He can't call me beautiful.* "Ohmygod, crazy man. This is insane, and you can't be here!" She pushed him nearly off the bed.

"Do you always look this pretty when you wake up?"

"Leave. Leave. Leave. Go to your room or your house. Are you even staying here? Ohmygod."

He smiled. "Okay, okay, I'm going. I'm staying a few doors down. Knew it would be a late night." He went to kiss her, but she swiftly interrupted his move with a shove. He stumbled off the bed, pulling his shirt down, with a smug grin that seemed a response to her assertiveness.

As he left the room, he turned and looked back at her.

"You're amazing, Olivia. Amazing."

As the door shut, she fell backward onto the bed, turned her head into the pillow, and silently screamed.

She flipped back over, smiling. She held on to a pillow, unsure of what to do with herself. She rested her hand on her neck, remembering how he had held it so tenderly while they kissed. *Amazing. He thinks I am amazing.*

"We kissed. Oh my God, we kissed. Landon Taylor. I kissed Landon Taylor," she whispered to the ceiling. She had to say it out loud, as if to confirm that it had actually happened. It took a good seven or eight repetitions of that phrase before the excitement turned back to fear and guilt.

"Ohmigod, I kissed Landon Taylor. He's married. He has kids. He's my new boss. He's Landon Taylor." The trauma began to hit her like a brick wall. *Jacob is going to kill me.* What had she just done? What had *he* just done? Her breathing got tighter. She could feel every exhale press against her chest. She sat up on the corner of the bed and put her head on her knees. Her thoughts spun like one of those paint-splatter machines that people used to use to make sweatshirts in SoHo. The spinning core spattered totally incongruous and inappropriate thoughts. She flopped back down and tumultuously twisted and turned, trying to escape the shame. The worst part of it all was, despite the guilt, which she knew she should—and did—feel, more overwhelming was a feeling of happiness. She lay in bed, drowning in complete, reprehensible bliss.

⌒൜

Olivia hated early flights but relished the chance to leave for the airport at six a.m. and avoid seeing anyone, especially the governor, in the hotel. She spent every second of the cab ride, the waiting at the gate, and the entire flight going over in detail what had happened, in an effort to make some sense of it. For the last two weeks she had been envisioning that kiss. And it was even better than her fantasized version. It was real. Every time she thought of that kiss, those arms around her waist, she had to close her eyes and remind herself to breathe. But more alarmingly, the black and white picture of a perfect candidate had turned gray. She was disappointed, which was less comprehensible than anything. This was her dream. She should have been thrilled, but the truth was a part of her wanted him to be better than the man who kisses someone who is not his wife.

Back in her office she tried to distract herself with work. When, at eight the next morning, her phone finally rang with a private number, Olivia lost her breath a bit. She had had twenty-four hours to figure out what to say and she had not even settled on a greeting.

"Hello?"

"Hello there."

"Hi, Governor." She mumbled the word "governor," worried it was not the right way to go.

"Hiya. How y'all doing today?"

That voice. That same voice that called me "amazing."

"Ummm . .˙. I'm okay. I'm good. I mean I'm just getting back to stuff here. You know. I mean, following up on things . . ." Thankfully he cut off the painfully awkward conversation before she had time to stutter through another sentence.

"Olivia, I'm so sorry."

She felt a stream of relief wash over her as she let out a breath. "Oh my God." She said. "Me too." *Sorry?* She wasn't even sure what she was saying. What was he sorry for? Did he tell someone? Did she ruin every-thing? Would she be fired? It was a mistake.

"I mean, I don't know what came over me. I have never done that before." He emphasized every word.

"Obviously!" She felt like she had jumped outside of her body and was left without control of the words emerging. *Obviously? What am I, a Valley Girl? What's obvious? Nothing's obvious!*

He breathed a laugh, almost a sigh of relief, and Olivia followed suit. "That bad?"

"No! Bad, no! I just . . ." *More like the best kiss of my entire life.*

"I'm kidding." This time he was giving the breath back to her.

"Right." She felt the pressure to figure out the situation before ut-tering any other words. How was she supposed to play this? Magazine covers and quizzes whirled through her head, but nothing helped. *Why hasn't anyone written the article on what to say to your new boss whom you are madly in love with after he apologizes for hooking up with you? Okay, "madly in love" is an overstatement. An exaggeration. I'm not madly in love. Olivia Greenley, lock it up!*

The governor continued his stream of consciousness. "The thing is, I have spent the last six years in a frenzy of different worlds. Worlds that don't make sense even in context. And then you come along, and you just get it. With a charm that's just so mesmerizing. I was really taken aback."

"I—Thank you." *Fine, madly in love.*

"It's not a compliment. It's just the truth."

She wanted to tell him something, but there wasn't a word in her mind that didn't seem dumb and incongruous at the moment.

He stepped in. "But it was wrong of me."

"It was wrong of me too." She hurried to take some blame.

"No, I'm responsible. I'm sorry. Do you think we can move for-ward? I have to make this right." He suddenly seemed to have an un-natural desperation in his voice.

"No. I mean yes. I mean it's already right. It's okay. Really. I just—I've never done anything like that either." She stumbled on. "I'm sorry. I don't know what to say, you know?"

"I know," he said, the reassuring tone returning. "But look, you need to think about this—if you don't want to work for me, if you feel like you need to tell someone, I respect your need to do that."

Tell someone?! She remembered clearly how her sister and Katherine reacted just to his showing up in her room. She very decisively would not be telling a soul. This was ridiculous. It was a mistake and he was clearing it up and this was how it should be. *This is the job of a lifetime. My lifetime. My job. My candidate.*

"Governor Taylor"—she straightened up in her chair with a new directive—"this is the campaign of a lifetime. You are the candidate of a lifetime. Not only would I not do that to you and me, I wouldn't do it to the world. We made a mistake. It happens. You're going to change this world. Literally. And I get to be part of that and for that I am so grateful." As she spoke, her insecurity crashed over her like a wave. "I mean, that is, if you're still okay with me being here."

He jumped in. "Yes. Yes. Olivia, you are not like anyone I've ever met. I'm more than okay with you being here. You fill a hole on this campaign that I'm not sure I even knew we had."

"Wow—I—Thank you. I'm . . ." Now she really couldn't form words. "I want to fill it."

"Uh . . ." For a man known for not employing "uh" or "um" in his vocabulary it was a rare moment.

"That made more sense in my head. It really did."

And just like that he moved on.

"Okay. So it's settled. We move forward, win this thing, and change the world."

"Easy enough," she said. She found herself smiling but her head was spinning.

"All right, I'm going to run into this staff meeting. We'll talk later?"

"Yep. Yes." She corrected herself. "Yes, talk to you later." And then, "Governor?" she said reflexively before he ended the call.

"Hmmm?"

"Thank you." She wasn't even sure why she said it.

"Yes, you too."

She listened to the silence of the ended call for a good thirty seconds before putting down her BlackBerry, her body feeling drained and frozen in the moment. When her arm finally moved, slapping the BlackBerry onto the desk, she shook her head, attempting to shake some reality into it. The combination of emotions was impossible to decipher. *It was right. This is good. Pretend it didn't happen.* What was she even thinking? That he would leave his wife for her? That they'd fall in love and live happily ever after? That the press would be okay with it because they'd be able to see how in love they were? Yes. That's what she had thought. For at least a few fleeting moments. *Okay, more than a few.* She laughed at herself.

"Thank God," she said aloud. *Phew.*

NINE

Olivia squished into her window seat in the last row of the Jet-Blue plane. She grumbled at getting another seat that didn't tilt back at all. *What does the campaign get, five dollars off for putting me in the last row of every flight?* The campaign treasurer, on whose card all these economy flights were billed, probably had enough miles to go around the world first-class. She leaned her head on the window and thought of how Jacob used to say campaign years were like dog years. It must have been true since she felt sure months had passed, though the calendar said it had only been three weeks since the finance committee meeting.

She had already been in Texas and California setting up temporary offices and now she was going to Florida to do the same. Franchising, Jacob had told her. It seemed an appropriate term. She would have three days at most for each state. Best-case scenario was to get a cubby or two in the offices of one of the fundraising event hosts. If someone had the means to host an event, they usually had a pretty nice office too.

Although the "incident of the kiss," as she liked to refer to it internally, played in her mind every night as her eyes closed, it was a distant memory during the day. Stress and money-raising dominated her waking thoughts. Texas, she was sure, could do two hundred if Henley were pressured enough. California would do three hundred. She would set up two to three events a night in other cities. Add on Yanni's, Florida, and then the big shebang—Bronler's event in Martha's Vineyard that she would somehow get to six hundred.

With mail, online, and small events in Georgia she knew she could cover any drop-off and maybe even get the campaign between one and one point five million. The numbers, which she knew like the back of her hand, stood in stark contrast to her emotions about the campaign and Taylor, so she tried to focus only on them.

She leaned back on her immovable seat, pressing her head against the top of the headrest, in an attempt to stretch her neck. She looked down at her BlackBerry, which was still on. That was the one upside of the last row—the attendants barely came to offer water, much less check if devices were turned off. It used to make her nervous, the idea of going against the rule, and she would hide her BlackBerry in her pocket, sneaking looks at it whenever she was sure no one could see her. But now, the BlackBerry sat out on her tray in clear sight. She thought about her friend who always said, "If it really had any effect on the plane every terrorist in the world would buy an iPhone and a ticket."

She looked down at an unfinished email to her sister. The half-written e-mails seemed to pile up these days. She wanted to talk to her family and friends, but there was just never the time. And when there was the time, she didn't know what to say. Her sister's emails had gone from annoyed to passive-aggressive, to worried, and right back to annoyed. *I don't understand,* read the last email, *how it is possible you don't have five minutes in your day to call me. And if I hear one more "all good" from you I'll come to your campaign office and scream!* She read it again, to formulate a reply, but decided she was too tired to deal with her sister.

As she took the shuttle from the plane to her hotel, she called Jacob so he could fill her in on the intricacies of Taylor's relationships in Florida, as she did at the start of all her stops.

"Hello, Charlie," she said in her best Cameron Diaz voice, which, Jacob had pointed out many times, was not good.

"Hello, angel," he said, playing along. Then he added, "We gotta stop doing this. One day I'm going to answer the phone like that around Sophie, and she's going to freak."

"Oh, please. She knows us well enough by now to not care!"

"True."

"How are things going with her anyway?"

"All good."

"Right." She recognized the response and continued on. "Okay, so, Florida. I have Paul and Milo hosting the two big events but I was thinking of just putting them together."

"Yeah, that's a good idea if you're looking to shorten your life. A bullet to the brain would be less messy."

"Um, not such good friends?"

"Paul was married to Milo's sister and now he dates some twenty-two-year-old. Plus, now they are finance chairs of opposing sides in the gubernatorial primary down there, so it's basically devolved into color wars, with each of them at the helm."

"Got it." She thought for a minute. "Where do we fall politically on the race?"

"We're Switzerland."

"Perfect. So I can offer our support based on which team raises more?"

"Yeah, brilliant, Liv," he shot back sarcastically. "Screw up the second-most important state for us for a few extra dollars."

"Kidding, Jacob. Chill."

"Florida is a delicate freakin' balance. I'm petrified we'll have to actually pick a side in the primary. That would majorly cut into our base there. Senator Kramer would be all over it. One false move and the dominos fall."

"Got it, got it. So we do one from five to seven and one from seven to nine. What else?"

"That's it on Florida. Unless you want to put in a YP event late-night."

"Also messier than a bullet to the head. Not doing those until we need them politically." A YP, or young professional, event was a euphemism for an event with a low ticket price. "You raise five hundred dollars for every ten hours of work you put in."

"Good. Okay, so I'm emailing you the list of past Florida donors. Also check in with Theresa Chambers; she used to be our consultant down there."

"Wow. I haven't heard that name in a while."

"Yeah, she's laying low since that whole thing with Senator Traxton."

"Right." Olivia had heard rumblings of the story but had never heard someone say anything about it plainly. She tried not to sound as surprised as she was that it was clearly true. She always thought the rumor that had Senator Traxton's chief of staff driving Theresa across the state border for an abortion had to have been a campaign myth, but Jacob had known Theresa forever. He was stating it as fact.

"You know that asshole voted on the floor against a choice bill two weeks after she aborted his baby?"

"Yuck, that's outrageous. It's amazing that story never got out."

"Yeah. You know I worked on that campaign for a month, right?"

"You did? How did I not know?"

"I don't tell anyone about it. I try to forget it myself. What a freakin' mess that was. Everyone knew what was going on. I mean, he slept with every female staffer. I got right out. I'm not working for someone like that. That could ruin your career forever."

"Yeah." Olivia rolled her neck down, cracking it as it moved. *He is not like that. It was a kiss. Taylor is not Senator Traxton. He is not someone like that.*

"I mean look at the Edwards staffers—all of them have more subpoenas than the Madoff family. Doesn't even matter if they knew anything. Just being around for it won them each a lifetime of debt in legal bills."

Olivia squirmed, hoping he would stop talking. Lawyers' bills. She didn't even have money to pay her cable bill. What if someone found out? What if Landon told Aubrey? She'd be the downfall of everyone. Of Jacob. She would lie. No one could prove anything. They wouldn't ask if she had kissed him, only if she was sleeping with him. And she was not sleeping with him. Thank God.

"Ah. I gotta go, Liv. Can you start with that and then we'll go through Texas later?"

"Yeah, yeah, of course. Later."

"Later."

When she got into her room, Olivia bounced down on the bed, thrilled to be there. The hotel was a sister hotel to the Brinmore and since the Brinmore was her other family—her actual family would probably rightly say she spent more time there than with them these days—they comped her a room for two days while she set up the events. She looked around. The room was decidedly bigger than her apartment. And nicer. And considerably cleaner.

Before she could get comfortable, not that she would have even considered it, her phone began to ring—Jacob calling back with more background information on more donors. She talked while throwing her bag into a corner of the room, gathering up her materials, and heading back out.

Fortunately the Brinmore Miami was just as popular and convenient as the one in New York, so almost all of her meetings were right there in the lounge. Even her meals would be comped. Most likely the people she was meeting would pay the bills, all of them people who had more in their change pockets than she had in her bank account. Still, there was Campaign Lesson #4: Always have a backup plan—particularly on weeks like this when she couldn't be entirely sure her credit cards wouldn't be rejected.

She moved her meeting with the brother-in-law donor, Paul, back so as to make sure he wouldn't run into Milo and added on a meeting with the two college students, Peter and Mira, who wanted to talk about the young professional event she would not be doing. *That coffee I'll definitely have to pay for,* she thought, making sure to schedule it at a time that was decidedly not during a meal. She sat waiting for her first meeting—Wendy and Jason Silverman, also known as the apex of Florida society—drinking a coffee and wondering if she could go the full two days without ever leaving the hotel.

After her first two meetings, Olivia went back to her room, relishing the idea of having twenty minutes to herself and scheming to escape in a nice bath, something she hadn't had since she moved into her studio with just a shower only a few years ago. Once in the room, she started running the warm water, throwing in some of the hotel's soap to make it sudsy. It hadn't gotten more than a few inches high when her cell phone rang.

"Curses," she muttered, seeing Alek's name come up and knowing that she not only needed to take the call, but that, despite its larger-than-her-apartment status, this room was not big enough to conceal the sound of running water in the background. She begrudgingly turned off the water and answered the phone.

"Hi, Alek!"

"Se princess."

She smiled, enjoying his nickname for her. "How are you?"

"Good. Good. I have question for you."

"Yup?"

"Did se governor, he change his number?"

"His number? Umm . . . You know, Alek, I don't actually know. I never call him on his cell and when he calls me, it comes up as private." She could tell Alek was in the mood to talk for at least ten minutes, if not twenty. He was always in the mood to talk. She balanced the phone on her shoulder, pulled up the drain in the bathtub, and watched the bubbles dissipate. *Just as well. Who takes a bath in the middle of the day anyway?*

"Oh." Alek thought for a minute, sounding dejected. "I just call him and haven't heard back. I thought maybe . . ."

"Really?" She tried to sound totally surprised, even though she knew how bad Taylor was at calling people back. *And they've been so busy lately. I mean I don't even get to my calls these days.* She thought about her sister's message waiting for her on voicemail. *Landon must have a million times more.* "I'm sure he didn't get the message! You know how awful he is at checking his phone!"

Alek quickly agreed to the not-complete lie, as donors always did for fear of seeming like they didn't know him well.

"You know," she said, "the best thing is to call Jacob, and he'll get him for you. You have his number, right?"

"Um, yes. Actually, you give it to me one more time."

"Sure, of course." She scrolled through her phone looking for Jacob's number, which the ease of technology had spared her from having to memorize.

"You know Landon is my oldest political friend," Alek said as she searched.

"I know, Alek. He always talks about how long you guys have known each other. It's so great." The governor did talk about him frequently and

Olivia knew, despite the fact that Alek could be annoying to talk to, that Taylor genuinely liked him. She had heard him say so plenty of times. They were friends.

"I haven't seen him in ages. I know he's very busy, but, you know, I see him only now when he ask for money."

That stung. Not just for Alek, but for her own confidence. It was her job to make sure donors didn't feel like Taylor's personal ATM machine. To do her job well—the way she wanted to do it, where donors raised because they were part of something—Olivia had to make them feel a connection to the governor. It was one of the reasons she loved working for Taylor. He really had those friendships; she just needed to maintain them a bit while he was busy campaigning. She thought back to Adams, for whom she needed to actually forge the friendships. This was easier. Well, it was supposed to be.

"I'm so sorry, Alek."

She thought of Martin Luther King, Jr.'s quote about knowing a man's true character when he was at the bottom, but actually she thought it was a better sign of character to see how they acted when they were on top. That wasn't the case here, though. This wasn't about Taylor's character, which, she assured herself, was good, and more importantly, loyal.

"Every Sursday we would go to the peach pie place and the voman who knew us, she vould know exactly vhat we vanted."

He's just busy. Plus, Alek is annoying. It takes him a lifetime to get to his point.

Alek went on about the pies. "Now, no more!"

Olivia felt bad for Alek. Then she had a flash, wondering if this was how Marcy and Katherine talked about her, since she had not made it to Sunday brunch in at least a month. Campaigns were hard. It wasn't as if she didn't want to go to Sunday brunch. And it certainly didn't mean she loved her friends any less. She would much rather be at a meal with friends than glued to her computer in her office.

"I know he misses the time when he could do that. Really, Alek. We're all just doing the best we can." She couldn't figure out the war within her. She felt slightly annoyed at Alek and terribly sympathetic at the same time. She needed to help him but she wasn't sure if she was doing it to placate a major donor or to redeem Taylor. Or if she was trying to remind herself that long friendships mattered most in life. She hung up, pledging to get some time on the schedule for Alek. And also to get to Sunday brunch.

⚬⚬⚬

As the governor started speaking to the Pottawattamie County Democratic Club, Jacob moved toward the back of the lobby. He ducked quietly off to the side and into the kitchen, a small, musty-smelling room where a few people were puttering around, putting chips into plastic bowls. He sat on a stool by the counter and began to answer emails and make calls.

You could always tell how long a staffer had been around his or her candidate by where they stood during a speech. People on the trail for one year would be as close to the podium as possible, hanging on every word that dropped from the candidate's lips. Two to three years later they'd be in the room but paying little to no attention to anything around them. Three years or more and you could always find them sitting in an adjacent room, hiding out to do work, making calls, or just getting some food.

Jacob, now nearing his fifth year with the governor, knew every speech by heart. If he could have left the building completely, he might have. He answered emails, snacking on potato chips and ignoring calls until he saw Olivia's number come up. He had been missing her since they spoke about Miami in the morning and he needed to make sure everything was okay.

"Hey, angel," he whispered, and crunched down on a potato chip.

"Hey, Jacob."

She only called him Jacob when she was stressed. "What's going on? You okay?"

"Yeah, yeah. Just tired. Hey, I need to get Alek and the gov together for a meal."

"Ugh, why? I need him to meet around eighteen million people. We don't have time for the people he already knows." *She's out of her mind,* he thought, chomping down on two more chips. *I'm not having him sit through a four-hour dinner with Alek.*

"Please. I'll make it easy. I can get Alek down to Miami and we can do dinner with him after the event. Please make this work, Jacob. I promise it will be worth it."

He hated when she said "please" like that. He took a deep breath in, scrolling through the schedule. He had Taylor getting into Florida from Iowa at three forty-five, leaving barely enough time for him to get to the hotel, change, and race to the fundraiser. The Iowa day that preceded Florida was stacked, and the second day in Florida started at eight a.m. Adding in a late dinner made him tired on Taylor's behalf just thinking about it.

"Shit, Liv. He's going to be so tired."

"There's literally no other time I can do this. Alek says Taylor was his first friend in politics and now he can't even get a meal with him. He's feeling totally unloved, and unloved people don't raise money."

"They're donors, Liv, not girlfriends. They don't need to be loved." Jacob looked up from his emails and peeked into the room to see the governor tightening the top on his water bottle, a telltale sign he was about ten minutes from being done. "All right, all right, I gotta go. Catch ya on the rebound."

"Please try, Jacob," he heard Olivia say as he hung up.

"Just a few more," he whispered to no one in particular as he grabbed up another handful of chips. *I don't even like these,* he thought, wiping off the grease on the inside sleeve of his blue blazer. Clearly everyone in politics wore blazers like this because nothing stuck to them. *Well, at least in Iowa politics, where butter is more common than water.* He pulled the lapels together and started to button it before remembering that on the last trip here he had realized this particular blazer had gotten too tight. *Okay, so the tightness isn't particular to this blazer,* he thought, remembering that there was another Butter Burger stop on the schedule later that day. *Great. I'm getting a beer belly without even getting to have the beer.* He forced himself to walk around the room to where the governor was taking questions.

"What is your position on charter schools?"

Jacob recognized the tall, curly-haired lady from one of the school board events they had been to a month or so ago. Or maybe two months ago. Time really was flying, not to mention running together.

"Mrs. Stabile, it is so nice to see you again, ma'am." The governor stepped toward her. "Mrs. Stabile and I met at the Jefferson Middle School just a few weeks back, where we talked with parents about the importance of after-school programs."

Jacob shook his head, thinking he would never stop being impressed by the governor's ability to remember names.

"If you really look them in the eyes, right at the bridge of their nose, you can sear the face into your memory," Taylor had once told him.

Jacob had tried very hard that day to practice the new technique and had almost gotten slapped by a woman who thought he was checking out her plastic surgery. On top of which, he was so focused on staring at her eyes, he forgot to listen to her name or remember what color hair she had. There was no way he'd even recognize her, much less remember her.

"Harriston!"

The only thing he would have liked better than being able to remember people's names was being able to convince a few specific people to forget his.

"Hey, Joe." He grabbed the hand of the robust man standing before him in a plaid shirt tucked into dark jeans. Joe Ottingly was one of his Iowa county captains. He was fiftysomething, with spiky, short hair, a remnant of his military days, that was now almost completely gray. Joe stood too close and was always sweating more than seemed appropriate, but he was a hard worker, and Jacob needed him happy.

"Great event!"

"So good to see you, Joe. The numbers from your county are looking good!"

"Thanks, thanks." Joe wiped his brow, moving the sweat around rather than getting rid of any of it. "Listen, we need money for the vans."

"I know," Jacob said, pacifying him. "Let me get back to my desk and work out where we can get it from."

He knew where he would get it from, but this was a standard reply, promising, but without negotiating in person. He had been schooled in this process. "Y'all never commit money on the spot!" Henley had yelled at Jacob once, smacking the back of his head like a fraternity brother. Though the sting of the hit seemed harsh, the lesson was ingrained and he didn't commit funds ever, even though he knew Olivia could get money in for something as utilitarian as a van. *On my way to being a BSD,* he reminded himself. Then he thought about upping Olivia's goal yet again and emailed himself a reminder: *Schedule that dinner with Alek.*

৩৩৩৩

Jacob and Olivia jumped into the backseat from either side of the black SUV and closed the doors at the same time, like they had been doing since that first event in Connecticut, which now officially seemed like four years ago. As the car sped up Park Avenue in New York City, Olivia started counting the money, and Jacob placated the governor post-event.

Having settled into his seat and taken a swig of water, the governor turned back to Jacob, who placed the governor's BlackBerry in his outstretched hand, as per their routine. After the "Berry," as the governor liked to call it, had rung in the middle of one of his speeches, Jacob had been tasked with minding it during events. He would switch it to vibrate and look out for "must-answer calls," a.k.a. Billy and Aubrey. In recent months he had even gotten comfortable enough to answer some donor and political calls. *Only the ones the gov is never going to call back anyway. At least this way they get to talk to a human,* he thought, justifying it to himself, and, if they were calling for something, which they always were, there was a good chance he'd be the one asked to take care of the problem anyway.

The governor, now decently relaxed, took his BlackBerry and asked, "We good?"

Jacob looked slyly over at Olivia as she flipped through the last of the checks and shot him a thumbs-up. He smiled. Three events down and it wasn't midnight. And every event had hit goal.

"We're very good," Jacob said. "All three events went over goal today."

"Good, good," the governor said, barely raising his voice.

Jacob turned and smiled at Olivia. The lack of enthusiasm was actually better than enthusiasm, and they both knew it. The governor knew they would hit goal, expected them to because they had been doing it all month. His relaxed mood, after three events, was the best approval of their work they could ask for.

"Let's go over lists. Olivia, do you have time? Let's get some food too. I'm starved."

"That would be great!" Olivia blurted out.

"Sal, is there a place we could get a good steak around here? I'm fixin' for one."

Jacob couldn't believe his bad luck. He had promised Sophie he would be out to meet her by ten. It was another promise he would have to break, he realized as he watched the clock turn to eight–forty. *Hmpf,* he grumbled inwardly. *"Olivia, do you have time?" but, of course, there's no asking Jacob. No "Hey, Jacob, do you have a special date planned? A medical emergency? Is your house on fire?" Not only does it not matter, it's not even asked.* To make things worse, Jacob had made Sophie begrudgingly change her plans to be near the Brinmore and now he wouldn't even be there.

Olivia glanced his way and—as always—seemed to understand his expression.

"Actually, sir, I don't have all the lists with me. Could we possibly land at the Brinmore so I can print stuff out? Sorry."

"No, no, that will work actually."

Jacob shot Olivia a smile. Stopping at the Brinmore wasn't perfect, but it was definitely better than a restaurant somewhere farther away from his date.

Olivia was already clicking through her emails, no doubt trying to pull lists. Fundraisers seemed to have a greater supply of names and numbers than the white pages and an endless desire to go through them. She actually looked sincerely enthused. *Guess she's not getting laid.* Jacob laughed to himself, thinking about how easily campaigns substituted for sex for campaigners. He hadn't heard her mention any dates at all since she started. Maybe there was no one, or maybe she was seeing someone secretly. Those were usually the two choices on a campaign. *She did date Chris for a while. What an asshole that guy was.* He sat back, glad to be dating Sophie as it seemed like such a dose of normalcy. *I'm finally getting it right,* he thought, congratulating himself. *Perfect campaign. Perfect girl. Perfect balance.*

Olivia scanned through her emails looking for new lists sent from Addie, whom Olivia had assigned to constantly search for new sources of names. Olivia had tons they could go through but she wanted the perfect ones. Going over lists was a lot like playing Six Degrees of Kevin Bacon. With a really good list you could make connections from the donors on it to the governor in fewer than six moves. When the governor turned around to her, she tried not to let her panic at failing to be perfectly prepared show. He leaned back with a calm smile. "So how was Texas?"

"It was hilarious." Olivia had been wanting to tell someone how funny Texas was all week, but no one who didn't know Henley or the intricacies of campaign fundraising would understand. No one except Jacob and the governor. "First of all, I walk off the plane and outside the gate is none other than David Henley, cowboy hat and all, in his little red Tesla."

Jacob knowingly chimed in: "He looks like a kid in one of those motorized cars when he drives that thing."

"Exactly!" Olivia grabbed his arm, so glad to be able to say something and not need to offer further explanation. The more time she spent on the campaign, the more she realized how inexplicable her experiences were to anyone not on it. Her sister had stopped pushing her on the "all good" responses at least a month ago, and she hadn't even told Olivia where she and Katherine were going to meet the past two Sundays. Olivia was officially off the Sunday brunch list. She thought about her exclusion with a healthy dose of guilt, but also with a bit of relief. It was so hard to have to talk through her stress about a filing, a campaign issue—things they knew and cared nothing about. "I know it doesn't seem like a big deal, but to me it is," she would say to blank stares. It seemed the more she tried to explain, the less they understood. What did they want her to say? That she was in love with her boss? So they could talk her through it? There was no time for that. And more importantly, there wasn't time for the emotions she might find.

As Olivia continued on with her Texas stories, Taylor and Jacob laughed and listened like girls at a slumber party.

She told them all about how David had handed her ten one-thou-sand-dollar checks before he even said hello. She had sat in his little red sports car, knees squished together, while simultaneously trying to con-trol her hair flying in the wind and tightly gripping her large black bag ("the briefcase," as Jacob termed it) as they sped from Henley's law firm to every other law firm Henley knew. Olivia and Henley would walk into each, Henley strutting, his cowboy boots, complete with spurs, tap-ping on the marble floors, tipping his hat to the secretaries, whom he'd soon come back to take contributions from.

"Put a little hop in that step, darling," he'd yell to Olivia as she power-walked behind him in the heels she now regretted changing into back at the airport.

Without fail, they would go into the partner's office, talk about the latest trial, and switch over to the campaign, at which point he would lean over to Olivia and say, "This little darlin' is Landon's right arm." Then he would let out a roaring laugh. "And his left too!"

Olivia, of course, would play along, as she'd learned to, mention-ing tidbits about the campaign trail that made her sound even more of an insider than she was. When she had first started, she hesitated to name-drop until she figured out that it wasn't bragging at all. Letting donors think she was in close contact with Landon let them feel that they were too. Not to mention they would repeat whatever tidbit she had disclosed (Governor Taylor had to actually taste the fried butter at the Iowa State Fair!) to anyone and everyone they saw, transferring the experience so that the donor would seem closer. *And he's a fabulous kisser,* she longed to add.

With the partner suitably seduced by Olivia's fried-butter anec-dote, the three would then walk the halls of the law firm asking for con-tributions at each office door. Olivia had never seen anything like it in her life. She would quietly walk behind Henley and the partner, unsure if it was even legal to ask partners, associates, and even secretaries to write out checks.

"I think some of them actually think my name is Darlin'," she told Jacob and the governor.

Jacob chuckled. "So how much is in hand from your trick-or-treating-style fundraising?"

"Three twenty!" she gleefully exclaimed.

The governor put his BlackBerry down on the dashboard and turned around to Olivia, both eyebrows raised. "Seriously?"

"Yup! The trip is going to do four hundred."

"Holy crap!" Jacob smacked her on the arm.

"What he said!" The governor shook his head in amazement.

Olivia smiled. She was proud. It wasn't just the money. It was knowing she had found her niche. She was with people who understood her. She went back to pulling up lists and found herself subconsciously humming the song "Walking on Sunshine." She giggled with happiness, remembering her sister's theory that people always wound up humming songs that fit how they felt in that moment.

꩜

Walking into the Brinmore was always accompanied by a bit of relief for Jacob. He likened the hotel to an enclosed dog park where you could let the dog off the leash. The governor knew the place well enough that he could find his way from the lobby to the room to the restaurant on his own, a skill set that in other places proved more elusive than it should have for a presidential candidate.

"Y'all meet back here in fifteen? That good?" said the governor.

"That's great," Olivia said obligingly. Jacob smiled again at her, knowing she probably could have used at least twenty-five minutes to pull lists, but was clearly conscious of Jacob's need to get out as soon as possible. As the elevators closed on Taylor, Jacob and Olivia headed toward the business center.

"Loving you right now," he said, following her as she walked briskly.

"Oh, did you have something tonight?" Olivia turned back to look at him sarcastically, one eyebrow lifted.

He grinned, admitting he had told her maybe four too many times about the date tonight, along with each change in time and place.

"Yeah, I figured we weren't getting out of it." She turned into the business office at the hotel like it was her own. "So I decided we should get it as close as possible to where you needed to be for Sophie."

"I totally owe you one." He plopped down on a chair next to her as she went to work, once again pulling up lists.

"I'll just have Addie strike one of those lines on the drinks-I-owe-you poster I have on my wall."

"Deal. Do you need help here? Anything I can do?" He was already consumed with his own emails. If they could keep this relatively short, it might actually be perfect for him to get an hour of work done and then get out to Sophie.

"I'm good. Thanks."

"Okay. I'll jump out and get us a table."

"Cool. Be there in five." She spoke without lifting her head from the screen.

Jacob strolled into the restaurant, happy to see it almost empty. A family with a three-year-old sat eating dinner at a table in the center of the room. *Foreign. Alternate time-zone meal.* Behind them, two people were huddled over almost-empty drinks in the corner couches. *Definitely an affair.* When the man stealthily put his hand on the woman's knee after looking around, Jacob congratulated himself on his hypothesis, thinking he should be eligible for some sort of psychological degree in hotel personality assessment. He had spent enough time in them to be able to pick out every particular situation.

He walked straight over to his favorite corner table. It had four big leather chairs clustered together and a surface large enough to accommodate a good deal of spread-out papers. Plus the high and rounded backs of the chairs left them, as he liked to say, AHAP—as hidden as possible. He sat in one of the enormously comfortable, but not too mushy, just-right chairs. Marco, who really seemed to work the restaurant at all times, day and night, walked by.

"Hey, man. Just you tonight?"

"No, no, there's going to be three. The boss is on his way."

"Okay, okay, big-time." Marco straightened up a little even at the mention of the governor. "You want to start on something?"

"I would like to start on a vodka immediately, but I think I better stick with a Coke for now." Jacob smiled. "And actually lemme grab a menu from you, man. I'll get us going on some snacks. My plan is to get this thing over and done with in under an hour." One of the greatest parts of a place like the Brinmore and people like Marco was their ability to help Jacob stay within a time frame when he needed it.

"Hot date with the teacher?"

Jacob nodded. Marco knew more about his life than most of Jacob's friends.

"Ten-four. We'll have you out of here by nine fifty-eight. On it, man!" He handed Jacob a menu. Jacob knew the offerings by heart. He didn't think twice about ordering for Taylor or Olivia. Chicken tenders; a thin-crust pizza; an order of sliders; Kobe beef, of course; and truffle fries. He threw on a tuna tartare for good measure, knowing the chances of its getting eaten were minimal. Thankfully, Billy didn't get itemized bills from the Brinmore kitchen. He couldn't imagine the response he would get for thirty-six-dollar sliders and tuna tartare. *That would go over real well with voters,* he thought with a grimace as he got back to his Iowa emails.

Joe Ottingly needed $225 for the rental van to transport fifteen volunteers every day for a month. Jacob started to think about the fact that the bill tonight would undoubtedly be more than that and then tried to remember Landon's advice on compartmentalizing. "The worlds have to be kept separate in your mind," Landon had explained once on a plane ride. They were on their way from a rural farming town that was slowly dying to Alek's birthday party on a private Caribbean island that he had rented for a week.

"He rented the entire island?!" Jacob had asked incredulously.

The governor, newly elected, had taken the question and broadened it into an entire political theory, as he often liked to do. "You can't possibly rationalize one world in the context of the other," he told him. "It would drive you mad if you tried."

Jacob looked up from his email just as Olivia hustled into the dining room, almost panting, and sat down as if she had just finished a marathon.

"Okay." She exhaled the word as she dropped papers all over the table and started sorting them. "I brought a Florida list, a Democratic National Committee trustee list, and *Institutional Investor*'s top-paid hedge fund managers."

"And I got you chicken fingers."

"You're a god."

He laughed as she started to pull herself together, clearly nervous. "It's easy, because you and the gov have the exact same palate—a three-year-old's."

"Touché. Actually you will be happy to hear I have acquired a taste for sushi." She puffed out her chest.

"Holy crap, I never thought I'd see the day. How did that happen?"

"That art event at the Mastrimonicos'. Literally, Jacob," she explained, still dazzled by it herself, "they had all of Nobu in the kitchen. At least twenty workers, all in their Nobu uniforms."

"Oh! That's right! Where Ashley Mastrimonico actually ate." He laughed heartily. The Mastrimonicos were major Democratic donors. "Man, that stuff must have been really good."

"It was insane."

"Let me guess, to *diiiiie* for?" He said it with Ashley's exact accent and a toss of his imaginary hair.

"Exactly. She was completely binge-eating in the kitchen during the speech. And get this—I compliment her on her dress and she says, 'Oh, it's just a little nothing! Bergdorf is right downstairs, so when I don't have anything to wear—which is always—I just hop down in my robe, and they can always find the perfect thing. It's like an extended closet!' How crazy is that?"

"She goes to a store in her robe?"

"She goes to one of the most expensive stores in the world in her robe! And picks out clothes like it was her closet!" Olivia's eyes opened wider. "Sometimes she gets two of the same dress because she forgets she already has it. How much fun would it be to have so many clothes you forget which ones you have?!"

"I'd like to forget some of the clothes you have. At what age do you think you'll stop wearing sequins?"

Olivia reached over and mimed a punch at his arm, laughing loudly. Her cackle would have embarrassed Jacob if the room had been fuller. Olivia must have noticed his expression because she mugged a sheepish grin.

"Okay, okay, time to break up the party here," the governor said lightly as he approached the table. "I mean we do have an election to win here."

"Speaking of clothes I'd like to forget, hi, Gov. That was actually Olivia laughing, not a screaming cry for help."

"Very funny, Jacob. Sorry about that." Olivia looked more annoyed than she usually did at his jabs.

He smiled and mouthed, "What?" as the governor sat down.

"Hello there, Marco." Taylor extended his arm to shake the waiter's hand.

"Seriously, Governor." Jacob appraised Taylor's khaki Gap pants and striped shirt paired unsurprisingly with his favorite Great American Vending Machine Company baseball hat, the one he loved to wear because he thought it made him incognito. "I wasn't aware there was a dysfunctional sailors' event tonight. It must have fallen off my calendar."

Olivia's eyes opened wide at Jacob.

"What's wrong with this?" Taylor tugged at his shirt like a young kid. "I got these at J.Crew!" He tried to defend the outfit. "We can't all be fashion mavens like you."

Jacob laughed. Casual clothes were feared among politicians more than election losses. All politicians, male and female, as far as Jacob could tell, were petrified of having to wear anything other than a suit. Wanting to seem real and approachable while not wanting to cross over to anything that could be criticized or would subconsciously turn voters off led all of them to the same ensemble: a shirt, usually polo, tucked into khakis, with an awkward leather belt. He noticed it first about Landon, but as the years went on, he realized it was what they all did, even the women. That and the T-shirts all politicians seemed to wear under their suit shirts seemed like the required fashion faux pas in politics.

"I think it looks nice. Comfortable," Olivia said, eyes widened with every comment to send Jacob a back-off signal.

"Okay, Hallmark. I think you are spending too much time in Iowa."

"Hallmark?" the governor asked.

"Yeah, Olivia's like a greeting card store—she can find something nice to say about anything. If the city was on fire she'd tell you how pretty the red in the flame was."

The governor smacked his hand down on the table with a hearty laugh.

Olivia smiled acceptingly.

"Okay, Wiseass and Hallmark," the governor said, "let's get this show on the road. What have we got?"

Olivia started explaining her lists. "I brought a few," she said, and started telling him about their sources.

"*Institutional Investor* sounds interesting," the governor said, reading over her shoulder. "Let's start there."

Olivia went through the names as if she had written historical biographies on each one. For each one there was a plan of action and a point of contact.

Jacob wrote away on his BlackBerry, answering emails and devising the new scheduling-management program he had been working on for weeks. A system where things were scheduled in a meaningful, logical, and unemotional manner was unheard-of in political campaigns, especially presidential ones, but Jacob was determined to do it. He wasn't sure how exactly he would do it, but he knew with more work, he could get it done. He thought for sure it would be the lasting mark he would leave on campaign life and imagined himself in his corner office years from now hearing from political staffers that he had revolutionized scheduling.

Between emails, and sometimes during them, he would zone back into the conversation. *Whoever said men don't multitask would do well to spend a little time at this table.*

Aside from throwing in a comment or an anecdote here and there, or filling in history with one donor or another, he really didn't need to be in the list conversation. Usually feeling superfluous around the governor left him with an embarrassing dose of insecurity, but with Olivia, it was different. She was his pick, his bet, his *long-shot* bet to be exact, so when she was on her game, Jacob actually felt self-satisfied. He looked up and smiled as she explained how one CEO actually used to date the wife of another CEO, which was the reason they weren't friends, even though everyone else thought it was just because their businesses were competitors.

"How do you know all this?" the governor asked.

"I memorized a book of useless donor facts!" Olivia said brightly.

The governor gaped at the sliders as Marco placed them on the table. "Perfect." He grabbed a small burger, his earlier desire for a steak completely forgotten. "Marco, could I get a beer too? You guys want one?"

"Sure, I'm in." Jacob jumped on board, surprised at how long it had been since he and the governor had sat down for a beer. When Jacob first landed the job, a beer or paper cup full of boxed white zinfandel would have done the trick. "Just something to take the edge off," Taylor routinely used to quip to Jacob with a smile. But soon, it turned into two cups of Chardonnay, then nearly a bottle of pinot grigio. Now standard protocol dictated two bottles of sauvignon blanc per evening. Jacob hadn't really noticed it until now, but things had become more formal. Sharing a beer, like buddies, had become a rare occurrence.

"Olivia?" the governor asked.

"I think . . . ummm . . . I'll just have a coffee, please."

"Super cool, Liv." Jacob shot her two thumbs up.

She shrugged her shoulders and lifted her hands in a self-conscious fashion.

As the governor and Olivia ate and talked, Jacob typed away, almost in awe of the fact that he was getting time to just sit and answer his emails, not to mention do it all with a beer in hand. For the first time since he could remember—*No, the first time ever*—he would be able to meet Sophie without sixty unanswered e-mails lingering over his head. He thought back to the last time he had slept at her house, when he had ducked into the bathroom to catch up on work for two hours while she slept. Tonight, maybe, he'd actually be able to sleep next to her.

He brought his attention back to the governor and Olivia as they laughed through yet another story, and then Jacob stayed involved as the governor ordered up another round of beers.

"Could we get more of the truffle fries too?" Olivia added.

Marco took down the order, shooting Jacob a questioning and slyly concerned look.

Oh shit. Suddenly his well-planned evening was hitting a speed bump. *Olivia's ordering food? We'll be here for hours.* He looked down at his BlackBerry, which was free of unopened messages. Nine fifty-six. He looked around as if he might be able to find a *Mission: Impossible* way out. Sophie's email came as if she were reading his mind.

SophieMoore14@gmail.com: *Five minutes and counting. You close?*

Well, at least she thinks it's nine fifty-five. That's one extra minute. He looked back up to the table almost without a choice. He needed to at least give her a time frame.

He started in slowly. "Hey, just so I can give the briefing guys a timeline of when you need your info for tomorrow, how long do you think this should take? They're happy to use some more time if they have it."

Olivia looked at him, stifling a laugh.

He stared her down. *Lock it up. I know how pathetic that was.* She read the look immediately and turned the laugh into an apologetic shrug.

"Bored already, Jacob?" the governor asked, deadpan.

"Never bored, sir."

The governor flipped through the list. "Are you tired too, Olivia? I could go through some more if you wanted. I think this is helpful, no?"

"It's really helpful."

"I didn't say I was tired!" Jacob interjected emphatically. "I just—"

"Kidding, kidding." The governor threw his hand on Jacob's back. "Seriously, why don't you get out of here? Olivia and I can go through this stuff. It's about time you took a little break. Plus, I think your grandma might stop liking me if I don't get you married off soon. Tell Sophie we say hello."

"Grandma Lee will never stop liking you!" Jacob declared. Part of him wanted to stay, but he knew this hashing of donor history could go on for hours. Plus, this might be a game-changing save for his newly forming relationship with Sophie: to be on time. "If you really don't need me I'm going to take you up on that."

"We always need you," the governor said, less cheesily than that phrase could have sounded. "But if you're gone, we can assign more calls to you."

"Deal!" Jacob jumped up from the table like a high school kid who'd just successfully ditched second period. "Thanks." As he raced out of the room, he doubled back to Marco. "Tab to the room? And thirty percent tip. Don't bring them a bill." He headed out the door as Marco waved him off. "Thank you!"

⸙

Olivia looked over at the television, surprised to find that an hour and a half had gone by since Jacob left. "Wow! It's past eleven thirty!" It was the first time since the finance committee meeting that she and the governor had been alone together. And in a hotel, again. She tried not to think of it. She vowed to focus all her attention on her work.

The governor glanced up from the list he was surveying with a confused and surprised look. "Did a clock just show up somewhere?"

"No." She laughed, realizing she had blurted that out rather bizarrely. "Stephen Colbert is doing his Spor' Repor'."

"The Spor' Repor'! Hot damn. What's better than sports and politics all at once? You want to call it a night?"

"No. I mean, whatever you want. This is great." She needed to get through more lists. And she needed to prove to herself she could be alone with him. Just because her stomach rose and fell with every breath did not mean she could not do this.

"I don't want to keep you working too late."

Olivia laughed. "I'd just go back to the office."

"Seriously?"

"Um, yeah. If I go home before one it's kind of an early night."

"Don't you have friends?"

"Sure, but they've learned."

"Learned?"

"About campaign life. You lose the first layer of them in your first campaign, which actually turns out to be a good thing anyway. The second layer drops out halfway through your third campaign when they realize you are going to cancel on every event. By the fourth, at least for me, what's left is family and really good friends who understand and accept your schedule. Which really is all anyone needs anyway. I think." She stopped, mulling over the matter more than she ever really had. "There's too much to get done in this world for so many friendships."

The governor leaned forward. The honesty didn't seem to trouble him. He brought his hand up to his chin and looked up from under the brim of the baseball hat. She loved when he wore that. Jacob was crazy to make fun of his outfit. He looked so handsome in casual clothes. It showed a side of him that no one got to see. "You guys really do work hard." He stared at her pensively.

"It's so much more than work for all of us." She felt almost helplessly earnest the minute she saw the governor's grin. *Damn it, Olivia. Business.* "Oh, that sounded a lot more cheesy than I meant it. I just mean—"

"No, no." He stopped her before she had to explain. "I know what you mean. And I appreciate it. Actually, I more than appreciate it. It's really one of the vital things that gets me through the day—knowing that we are an army of people fighting for what we believe in."

"You."

"What?" He fixed his gaze on her, seemingly confused by that one word hanging between them.

"It's you we believe in." She couldn't help herself. For two people who never spoke without thinking beforehand, the rare occasion of blunt conversation was immediately recognized and palpable. It left a raw quality in the air. Olivia remembered it from the night of the finance committee meeting. *"I lose myself around you,"* he had said. This is what he meant. At least that's how she saw it. It was that momentary loss of control of your words that could only be comfortably shared with someone who valued restraint just as much.

The governor sat back in his chair. She knew he couldn't be scared, but it was the only thing she could think of to explain the expression in his eyes as he looked away from her. He took a swig of his beer as if an "everyman" gesture that might dissipate the sense that his ego was so inflated he agreed with her. She actually felt a little badly for what she had said. It was a lot to lay on a person. And it was an intimacy she knew she wasn't supposed to foster between them. "I mean . . . I just . . . it's that we all know you can actually change the country and when you think about that, it just doesn't seem like work."

Now he was watching her, letting her babble. He had done this to her on one of the first days they had met. As uncomfortable as it made her, there was something about him when he was like this that she loved. Sure, it carried the awkwardness of walking a tightrope, but it made him seem so in control—like a net that could catch her no matter which way she fell.

"Okay, I'm going to stop now. Come on, we have lists to go over!" She pulled herself up straighter in her chair and tried to take charge of her thoughts, her words.

The governor looked completely pleased with himself. He sat back up as well and grabbed some fries. "Okay, Hallmark."

TEN

Jacob followed the governor into his Miami hotel room. He cringed at the thought of having to hurry him right back out for the dinner Olivia had requested for Alek. It seemed as though they hadn't stopped in days. New York to New Hampshire. New Hampshire to Iowa. Iowa to Miami. Going from New Hampshire weather to the Miami sun in the course of four days should have required a suitcase full of outfit changes. But Jacob had events scheduled so tightly that they barely stepped outside on any of their stops. It was one temperature-controlled venue to the next.

Jacob rubbed his eyes in exhaustion, the effects of the last Red Bull beginning to wear off. *I drink so much I'm probably building up a tolerance to it. I gotta try one of those 5-Hour Energy things.*

"I'm damn near exhausted, Jacob." The governor loosened his tie and threw the jacket he was carrying onto a chair. "Who thought this day was a good idea? You couldn't fit anything else in? Maybe a midnight bike ride?"

Jacob gulped and cracked his neck to the side. He hated it when Taylor chastised him, but it was the worst when he was mad for good reason. Jacob knew the day would be hell and he knew he shouldn't have jammed so much into two days. He tried to think back to his conversation with Olivia. *No. I could've just said no to the Alek dinner.* But before he could come up with the words, Taylor sat down on the couch and glared at him.

"I need you to step it up, man."

The words felt like a pitchfork stabbing Jacob—throat, heart, and stomach all at once. Words seemed so much more piercing coming from Taylor.

"I know, sir." He sat down on the chair next to him, afraid of falling over if he didn't.

The governor went on. "I get it. I know they're pulling at more arms than you have. I know each one of them could manipulate an entire army. Hell, they manipulate me most days. But somebody has got to lead the ship. Someone's got to be able to say no to all of them and it can't be me."

"I know." It was all he could squeeze out. He had let him down.

"It has to be you." Landon gave him a minute to take in his words. "You are the one by my side." He paused again. "You are the one I need to trust."

Jacob looked over at the governor as he continued.

"Listen, Jacob. I know you say you just fell into this when you were waiting for B-school, but you didn't fall into anything. I saw your potential. I saw how good you were. *You* even saw how good you were. You are the only one who can do this job. You're the only one who knows me well enough to know what I need, and you're the only one who can get the rest of them to fall into line. I need someone in my corner, not just making decisions for me, but making the decisions happen for me. Someone has got to decide not to put me on the plane in the lightning storm. You understand."

Jacob began to lift his head. This was one of those serious political lessons that people rarely ever talked about above a whisper. It was the story of candidates dying in plane crashes because someone, or more likely everyone, on a campaign put more weight on the need to get somewhere than on the risk of taking a flight in bad weather. Every campaign was bound to become bigger than the individual candidate, and the candidate's needs were bound to be overrun at some points. But someone had to keep those public needs in check. Long days were fine for staffers who could fall asleep at their desk or flub sentences, but candidates could not be in the public eye for that many hours in a row. Taylor didn't have the luxury of looking or sounding tired. Someone had to stop the candidate from getting on the plane when the wings were icing. Jacob remanded himself: *Someone should have kept him from having two eighteen-hour days. I am that someone.* He had to be in that corner with Landon, for Landon.

"I know I'm asking a ton of you. I get it. I'm asking you to see the big picture and the details all at once, but I know you can do it. You can't let Billy get too traditional and slow and you can't let Olivia bulldoze you with fundraisers. That girl would have me at slumber parties if she could."

Jacob laughed. There was something so heartening about knowing Landon understood the inside aspects of the campaign and the unique personalities of the people on it. Jacob didn't want the governor to dislike any of them, but as terrible as it sounded, even to Jacob's conscience, it was nice to hear other staff members criticized too. Even the slightest put-down of someone else really did make him feel a little better about himself. Moreover, it allied him with the governor as a confidante.

"That would be a whole different kind of fundraising, Gov."

"Yeah. Let's not put any ideas in her head."

"Gov?" Jacob breathed out and took a moment to accept the weight of what was required of him. "You're right. I can do it. I got overwhelmed. I won't let it get to me anymore."

"You know this campaign is only going to get harder."

"Well, then I'll keep getting tougher." Jacob smiled.

Landon smirked, but they both knew this was the truth. It wasn't so much a promise as it was a prediction.

"We're going to do this, Jacob." The governor clapped him on the shoulder. "We're going to do this and it's going to be great."

Jacob had heard that before, but somehow in the hotel room, as he stood with the soon-to-be president of the United States, the promised land sounded more real than ever. It would be he and Landon against the world. Actually, he and Landon *for* the world.

"We are, sir. And it definitely will be great."

"Okay then," Landon said, slapping his knees and standing up, reenergized. "Now get me some freakin' Red Bull."

❦

"Hello, again, Governor." Olivia had barely made it to the restaurant in time to see Alek seated at his favorite corner table. Everything was set just in time for the governor to walk through the door.

"Hello, Olivia," the governor said with a begrudging smile.

Jacob's warning came flashing back to her: *"Alek won't feel very loved if the governor sleeps through dinner."* She looked up at the governor, trying to transfer over some of her energy to him. She scanned her memory for good sports stories, to get him talking, but she hadn't picked up the sports section of a paper or made it home for *SportsCenter* in months. She remembered Jacob once telling her pretty girls put him in a better mood and decided either it wasn't true or she wasn't pretty. *Both possible choices.* She glanced down, knowing she wasn't looking her best. But there had to be something more than that. He thought she was amazing. That couldn't just disappear.

She settled on honesty. "I know this isn't ideal. I promise I'll make it worth it."

"Let's just get it going and keep it moving."

His annoyance felt like an attack. It brought on an onslaught of obsessive thoughts about who else might be annoyed with her and left her wanting to just run and hide, escape from her own body to anywhere. She toyed with the idea of jumping under the nearest table.

I should have listened to Jacob. Jacob's probably angry at me too.

While she walked toward Alek she tried to figure the exact jump she would need to make to slide gracefully and quickly under the tablecloth of the empty table nearby. The governor had stopped to talk to two of the busboys. He was on the side of the room shaking the young men's hands, while the wealthy patrons around tried to conceal their envy of the fact that he was not talking to them instead. A key rule in the world of the social-climbing elite, Olivia had learned, was not to show any traces of interest in anything you might theoretically not be able to have yourself. Of course the efforts never masked their deep desires. They just spoke louder to each other and looked away in a more obvious fashion than if they had been staring right at the governor.

Olivia couldn't help but smile at the woman dripping with diamonds who lost all interest in her table's conversation and even faked a cough in an attempt to catch a furtive glance. It so clearly pained her to see Governor Landon Taylor engrossed in conversation with people other than herself and, worse, people she deemed to be of a lesser station.

It was one of the governor's great qualities: that he could walk straight past even a king's table on his way to talk to the footman. She smiled. The busboys were in their glory, and the governor seemed to have perked up a little. He saw her waiting and caught up.

The governor nodded. "Nice guys," he remarked, loud enough for the lady in diamonds to hear. He put his hand on Olivia's elbow as they reached the table and pulled out her chair before crossing to Alek with a hug and a hello. Alek was sitting in a perfectly tailored, light gray suit with a bright orange Hermès tie and matching pocket square. His cheeks were red, as always, and puffed out like a proud blowfish's.

"So good to see you, man! It has been way too long."

Alek beamed at the attention he had so desperately wanted. He started to talk even before he sat all the way down in his chair. The governor grinned, almost comparably happy to have his attention so desired. He reached over for bread and took a bite. "Sakes alive, this here is some fantastic bread! Olivia, you gotta try this!"

Olivia grinned at the turnaround in his mood. In an instant he had cleared out every negative feeling in the room. *That's what he'll do. He'll make people feel better about themselves.* She tried to make it general, so that it wouldn't seem such a personal feeling. *It's not just me who feels this way. But it's me who gets to sit next to him.*

After the entrées were served, Alek excused himself to the bathroom. The governor slid his hand across the table and touched Olivia's wrist.

"Thank you for making sure this happened. I get so busy sometimes, I forget what is important in life." He continued on. "I know he talks a lot, but Alek, he's a good friend."

"I agree, Governor. Sorry it had to come on such a busy day."

"Ah, they're all busy these days."

She felt settled again in her friendship with him. He patted her wrist, and she longed for each pat to be prolonged for even a second more. His touch was so gentle. She knew it. She knew this was the real Landon Taylor. She knew that his bad mood was caused by the fact that he just was stretched thin to build an enormous, complicated campaign. She didn't need to decode her emotions about him—she loved him. She loved who he was. She knew he couldn't love her back, but that was okay. She got to be this close to him. That would be enough.

ELEVEN

S tephen Bronler had enlisted magazine editrix Eva Bloom to help
with the Martha's Vineyard party. The event—or the "kill," as Addie had come to refer to it after Olivia had burst out one night
into an overtired monologue about how the event would either "kill"
in the slang sense of the word or kill her—had to do six hundred thousand for the campaign to meet their quarterly goal. That thought in and
of itself was enough to send Olivia into a panic mode, and that was before Eva offered to hold the planning meeting at her office. A meeting
at Eva Bloom's office took it to a whole new level. Staffers were never
invited, that she knew of anyway, to the editrix's lair.

To top it off, Aubrey was coming to the meeting. Eva and Aubrey
had become friendly in the last campaign, when the magazine ran a five-
page spread on Aubrey, labeling her "America's Political Beauty Queen."
It was a compilation of photos that were absolutely breathtaking—
mostly Aubrey in couture, and one final one of the whole family walking on the Georgia coast looking like they had been painted into a perfect
beach mural. The campaign had gotten slammed for it, having already
taken heat for being too elitist, but Aubrey loved it and insisted that
Olivia send it to all hosts and prospective donors before they were to
meet Mrs. Taylor.

At first Olivia had ignored the request, thinking it would be seen
as egotistical and totally incongruous with the campaign's focus on the

gap between rich and poor. "She'll never know if I don't send it," Olivia had remarked to Addie.

Sure enough, ten minutes into a meeting with potential campaign donors, Aubrey had started in about her good friend Eva Bloom and was promptly told that none of the six people in the meeting had seen the article, one of whom even unsuccessfully searched his email to find the message that Olivia "thought for sure" she had sent. Olivia apologized profusely afterward and swore it would never happen again, to which Aubrey responded, "I should hope not." And then she added, with folded arms, "You should know I have no bid for incompetence around me."

Olivia now stood in front of the formidable office building, which seemed sleek and elegant even from the outside, waiting for the political queen.

As the black town car pulled up, Olivia peered into the darkened windows to see if she could decipher Aubrey's mood through the glass. Before she could see anything, the door opened and out came Aubrey's purple Christian Louboutin–shoed foot. Aubrey emerged, clad in a purple tweed Chanel suit the exact color of her shoes that hugged tightly around her hips. She was considerably heavier than she had been in her younger days and her plumpness, combined with the wrinkles around her eyes and lips, softened her look. She appeared kind. Olivia chuckled. *Can't judge a book by its cover.*

"Hello, Olivia. Don't you look pretty today." She spoke with a rarely heard sweet tone.

"Hi, Mrs. Taylor." Olivia pulled open the door to the building for her boss's wife; "That is such a beautiful suit." *Translation: I'm sorry I kissed your husband. Please go back to being mean so I don't feel worse about it.*

"Well, isn't that lovely of you. Thank you. Okay then, let's get on with it."

They walked together to the front desk where an elderly man with tiny spectacles sat.

"Oh!" The man behind the visitor's counter jumped up, nearly knocking his glasses off his round face when he recognized Aubrey. "Mrs. Taylor. It's such a pleasure."

"It is *mahhh* pleasure." Aubrey extended her hand to shake his and

Olivia couldn't help but stare at how perfectly manicured her fingers were. Her nails were a perfect shade of pink and just long enough to look classy. Olivia looked down at her own hands, dry and with chipped polish only half-covering her bitten-down nails. She had thought of getting a manicure before the meeting and had even made it to the front of the nail salon when Billy had called with a list of demands, which, as always, he spelled out in the slowest way possible. Knowing her fingers wouldn't be free any time soon, Olivia had turned away from the salon and headed back to the office.

As they stepped into the elevator, surrounded by a handful of gorgeous, leggy thirty-year-olds, Olivia stuffed her hands into her pockets, feeling completely insecure about her go-to Brooks Brothers white button-down, which she had tucked into her black Theory cigarette pants. She had put a gold chain necklace around her waist like a belt, a move that had seemed so fashion-forward in the small, fogged mirror at home but was so obviously pathetic in the clearness of the magazine elevator mirrors. She wondered if she could remove the necklace without anyone noticing.

No such luck. Eva's assistant, Stella, was waiting for Olivia and Aubrey close enough to the elevator when they walked off that Olivia thought the assistant might tumble in. Stella led them to a white conference room, sparsely decorated with a glass tables and chairs. In the middle of the table sat the most beautiful bouquet of white roses Olivia had ever seen.

Other people began to shuffle in: Stephen Bronler's assistant, Lisette, who as always looked like she was taking a meeting at the Cannes film festival, perfectly glamorous and chic, in one of those impossible-to-get Animated Closet dresses Olivia had ogled in a store window and Jimmy, a man too old to be called by a name with a "-y" at the end, but who nonetheless seemed to wear the moniker well. Olivia was never clear on what exactly Jimmy did. It seemed as though he covered everything from marketing to new film development to special events, and since all events that Bronler was involved with were unquestionably special, Jimmy was always in every meeting. Then there were the production people, whom Olivia had worked with once before. They did events like the Super Bowl, and so it seemed a little over-the-top to have them at a planning meeting for an event in Martha's

Vineyard. But they were nice and highly efficient, and Olivia was in no position to turn down help. Each of them greeted Aubrey with reverence, complimenting her suit, her hair, her shoes. Aubrey sat perfectly straight, shoulders back, chin up. *That really does make her look thinner*, Olivia thought. She remembered how her grandma Becky used to always inform her of that fact and she vowed to do it more often herself.

Stephen would be connecting in through a conference call. Olivia watched as Eva's assistant patched it through to the small but perfect-looking silver box in the middle of the table. "It's a Jambox," Stella explained, causing Olivia to hope she wasn't the only one who looked confused enough to warrant the explanation. "It's completely wireless. Eva dislikes wires."

"Very cool! We're barely rid of rotary phones in our offices!" Olivia laughed, only half kidding.

Mrs. Taylor shot daggers at Olivia, who promptly stopped laughing, feeling as if she was a complete embarrassment to the campaign. She shifted the chain "belt" around her skirt and offered herself a small congratulation for understating the problem. *They don't even know the half of it.*

"Hello?" called out a sweet voice from the Jambox.

Lisette answered the voice. "Hi, Ciela. Please have Stephen ready to connect in five minutes."

Olivia looked around, feeling like the nerdy kid in the cafeteria and wondering how Lisette, who wasn't even hosting the meeting, knew in how many minutes the meeting would start but she didn't doubt Lisette did know.

Sure enough, two minutes later, in walked the petite and perfectly put-together editor, Eva Bloom. Her assistant scurried around to her and followed a step behind, introducing the people at the table. Eva said hello to everyone, something Olivia had never imagined in a million years. The Eva Bloom that Olivia envisioned would have ignored everyone and asked Olivia why she deemed it suitable to dress so shabbily in her presence. Olivia had imagined this terrifying meeting so fully, she could almost see Meryl Streep grabbing the necklace-turned-belt from her body, saying, "What, did you bump your little head?!"

She was almost disappointed when she was nicely tapped on her shoulder.

"So wonderful to meet you, thank you for coming," Eva said to Olivia as she moved to Aubrey. The two embraced like sorority sisters. Eva fawned over Aubrey's suit and her last appearance on *The View*. Aubrey thanked her graciously and went on and on about how grateful she was to Eva for cohosting this event.

Eva took her seat next to Aubrey and looked out at the group. "Are we ready?" Her voice was pleasantly quiet.

Lisette piped up. "Ciela, please connect Stephen."

"He's connecting in right now." Two beeps followed and on came Stephen's scruffy voice. Olivia sat impressed and baffled by the efficiency of people outside of campaigns. Never in recent memory could she remember a time when a politician was connected into a meeting or event or anything without massive chaos.

"Hello, hello, everyone. So sorry I'm not there."

"I think we're sorry we're not *there*!" Eva smiled sweetly.

"Next time we hold the meeting in Corfu!" Aubrey added in, and they all laughed.

Olivia had no clue where Corfu even was, but she liked that idea. Especially since apparently these people who were allegedly so feared by all the world were acting so remarkably nice. Being in Corfu with the kind Eva Bloom and the fun Stephen Bronler sounded great.

"So what've we got going on?" Stephen called out.

"Well, I believe we're all set to do the event at my home in the Vineyard. The house is not too large but the property itself is sizeable, and I was thinking we would put a large tent or maybe two out there. I have the most wonderful tent company there. Stella, have you reached out to Caroline and Marielle?"

"I have. They have the date reserved and will have their tents and rental equipment at your disposal."

"Wonderful. Thank you."

What? Eva remembers names? And says thank you! And seems genuine about it. It was almost enough to make Olivia lose focus on what needed to actually be done.

"Great!" Stephen roared. "I've got calls in to Dana Klein. She's fantastic and sings this amazing track in my new movie coming out. I'd love her to sing at the event. A few acoustic numbers. Aubrey, you will love her!" The conversation swirled from entertainment to celebrities to what type of fabric the tent should be made out of, all while Olivia tried to refocus the group on the money being raised and remind them of the expenses, which had to be kept within a tiny budget.

"The tent shouldn't be much." Eva flicked away Olivia's cautions with her hand. "No more than twenty-thousand."

Aubrey was glowing. "I'm sure anything you do will be absolutely perfect! It's so rare for the campaign to have an opportunity to do something so spectacular! Now, don't get me wrong, I do love an Iowa Butter Burger as much as the next girl, but Martha's Vineyard will certainly be a welcome reprieve from the campaign trail!" Aubrey put her hand on Eva's shoulder, something that should have seemed taboo but instead looked warm and loving.

Everyone laughed except for Olivia, who tried to contain her panic. "I'm so sorry," she piped up again, feeling as if she were a constant interruption in their otherwise lovely conversation, "but I can only spend fifteen thousand on this entire event."

"Don't worry, darling," Eva responded with a breezy smile, "I'll cover it."

"No, but you can't." Olivia clarified. "It would be considered a contribution to the campaign and it would be over the limit."

Aubrey looked over at Olivia as if she had just run Eva over with a pickup truck. "I'm sure there's something that can be done, *noooo*?"

Olivia hemmed. "Uh . . ." *Nooooo! It's campaign law! Not to mention, the governor can't be partying under a twenty-thousand-dollar tent while one out of three American families can't put food on their table!*

Aubrey persisted. "Olivia, dear, I'm quite certain something can be done." Then Mrs. Taylor patted Olivia's arm and spoke directly to Eva. "Olivia can make anything work! She's our secret weapon!"

Secret weapon? She likes me? You can't like me. I kissed your husband. Aubrey liking her was not in the playbook. That wasn't how things were supposed to be. Olivia glanced at Aubrey's hand on her arm and then looked up. She felt the weight of every eye in the room on her. And

Aubrey's smile. She repeated Aubrey's phrase to herself. *"Olivia can make anything work." I have to figure this out.* She channeled her inner Tim Gunn. *Make it work.* "Unless"—Olivia started with what she knew should have been more hesitation, if not total pause—"unless you already have the tent up for something else." She hated putting that idea on the table. She knew it was a gray line. *It's totally legal,* she reminded herself. *But it's not right. It's not right, but I need to make this work.*

"I almost always have a tent up! If it's up already it doesn't count?" Eva asked with appropriate confusion at the ridiculous laws of campaign finance.

"That's correct," Olivia answered. "As long as it's definitely for something else."

"Fantastic!" Aubrey lightly clapped her hands, totally pleased. "See, I told you Olivia can do anything!"

Eva smiled. "Aubrey, Stephen, you are officially invited to my tented party on Friday, the twenty-first."

⚬᙭᙭᙭⚬

Olivia was eventually invited to the tented party as well. And on top of that, Eva asked her to be her houseguest. When the editrix first volunteered her guest cottage, Olivia had hesitated, worried that it would be weird or awkward. She much preferred staying at hotels where no one cared or noticed if she worked all night and made a mess of her room. But Addie had gasped and almost smacked her across the face for thinking of refusing the invitation.

"*The* Eva Bloom wants you to stay at her house and you are considering turning that down?!"

Olivia had succumbed to the invitation, more because it saved her the time of finding other options than because she actually wanted to stay there, but as she walked into the two-story colonial, bigger than the one she grew up in, she was glad she had said yes. The term "guest cottage" would only have been fitting if the guest were Queen Elizabeth and "cottage" were another word for "mansion." It was much newer than the main house, which sat right on the water, far enough down the winding road to be completely unseen from the guest quarters. Inside the rooms were painted white from floor to ceiling, but not in the cold, sharp way all-white decor could be. The living room, which opened to a huge kitchen, had two massive white comfy sofas and an enormous, gorgeous mosaic coffee table, which Olivia proudly recognized, having sat through enough of Tim and Ashley's art parties and dinners, as an original Dana Kirkpatrick. Though it seemed to Olivia not to make much sense to use a piece of art as a coffee table, it did make the room look spectacular. *Plus,* Olivia thought to herself with a laugh, *I'm guessing Eva's guests don't eat take-out and French-bread pizzas on their coffee tables every night.*

There was maid service. Croissants and coffee would be waiting for her in the morning and, Eva's assistant explained to Olivia while giving her the tour, "Eva asked me to pull a few things from the office in case you wanted to wear them."

"Wow! That's amazing! Thank you so much."

"No problem."

After the assistant left, Olivia tried on all the dresses, loving each one more than the next and feeling like she had gotten her *Devil Wears Prada* makeover after all. She chose a navy blue, billowy Dior dress that hung down perfectly in that loose way that only really good-quality clothes can do. She went over to the accessories that were also left out for her and slipped a vintage Miriam Haskell necklace around her neck. It lay perfectly against the navy. She heard her sister's voice telling her not to over accessorize, but she couldn't help herself as she pulled a matching Haskell ring onto her middle finger. She had seen both pieces in *Lucky* magazine on the flight to the Vineyard in an article on that great new actress, the one whose name she couldn't remember and whose movie she obviously hadn't seen because the luxury of two unproductive hours was a thing of the past.

Lucky was the one indulgence Olivia still allowed herself, grabbing peeks any time she had a moment to look at something other than lists. She stared at herself in the mirror, thinking she looked better than she could ever remember, minus, of course, the huge bags under her eyes.

Eva and Stephen, whom she was now completely convinced were the most misrepresented people in history, did everything they could to make her feel welcome at the party. This was helpful because Martha's

Vineyard was way out of her league. It was as if Aspen and the Hamptons had gotten together and produced a richer and classier baby. It was
a perfect combination of beach and forest, like a cut of the Berkshires
surrounded by ocean. On top of which, the people had a status all their
own. Olivia figured a big part of that was that you needed a plane to
get there, and the private-plane list was a whole lot different than the
chauffeured-car list.

◌∞◌

Eva's party people, Marielle and Caroline—two beautiful girls in their
early twenties who looked like they should be at a ballet barre—fluttered gracefully around the huge dark-wood tables, making sure each
stem of the cascading white and green flowers was placed perfectly. A
myriad of candles between the flowers lit up the entire tent, which,
Olivia thought proudly, was filled with eighty-two practically perfect
people. There were celebrities ranging from the newest rockstar on the
scene, Leo Davis, to long-known names like Susan Sarandon, every possible power couple—even the Silvermans from Florida made the trip—
and all the New York elite.

When everyone was finally seated at the "kill" event, Olivia moved
to the back of the room looking over the twelve tables. Even though figuring out who should sit where cost her two nights sleep, and it all
changed anyway when Eva announced four hours before the party that
she had six friends staying with her who would, of course, need to be
seated, and definitely not all together, Olivia had to admit the party
looked beautiful. Olivia watched as Aubrey, wearing a gold dress that,
as far as Olivia could tell, was taffeta, sashayed through the crowd
toward her, as if she were still on a pageant stage. Olivia scolded herself
for wanting to make fun of the outfit. *You kissed her husband. You have
no right to say anything.*

"Sweetie," Aubrey said as she arrived next to her. Her pursed lips
pushed her cheekbones up. "You usually do such a good job at seating."

Olivia folded her hands in front of her and smiled politely, proud
of pleasing the unpleasable woman who lately seemed to really like
Olivia. "Oh, thank you."

"And Landon tells me you've been just wonderful."

Landon tells you about me? Olivia felt a rush of nervousness. *What does he tell you? Does he tell you he loses himself around me?* Her eyes fluttered and her thoughts flipped. *Or does he tell you I'm a kid with a crush? Am 'I a joke? Does she know? What do I say to that?* "Thank you"? Yes, "Thank you." "Thank—"

"But this seating," Aubrey said, continuing with a bat of her eyelashes, "is just simply disastrous." She nodded her head, lips still pursed into a half smile. "I mean, you couldn't possibly have thought it was a good idea to sit the Levkoffs next to the Donnellys, could you have?"

I guess I could have since I did. Olivia tried to hide the fact that she was crushed. "Oh, I'm sorry, I—"

"Evvvveryone knows they don't like each other one bit. Jamie Donnelly is frightfully jealous of Jen. But, of course, you know that."

"I'm sorry, I didn't." Olivia looked out at the group of people in front of her, most of whom had already taken their seats. Campaign Lesson #15: No seating dilemma is unfixable. "Would you like me to try to move them?"

"Oh!" Aubrey's hand flew to her chest as if she were Scarlett O'Hara gasping for breath. "Heavens, no! I just wanted to be sure you knew."

"Okay. Thank you. I'll be sure never to sit them together again."

"I'm sure you won't. Thanks, sweetie."

Well, there goes the nice Aubrey. If I were his wife, I would be so much nicer. I'd be a great candidate's wife. Olivia folded her arms, then unfolded them quickly. *Maybe she knows. Maybe she can tell I've kissed him.*

"Wow. This is kinda fabulous." Jacob slid in next to her without her seeing his approach. He leaned back against one of the tent poles.

His words made her flinch a bit, breaking her concentrated gaze from Aubrey. She smiled when she saw it was Jacob.

"A little jumpy, are we?"

"Sorry." She moved back to the wall next to him. "Just a little low on sleep."

"I'd say that's the understatement of the year."

"Yeah, probably true. The other day I tried to count up how many hours I had missed in the past four months, you know, based on that whole 'humans should get eight hours of sleep a night' thing. It's a lot of hours."

"But that's for regular humans. We are definitely not regular humans. Or so I've been told."

"Sophie?" She could sense that the person who had alerted Jacob to his abnormality meant something to him.

Jacob shook his head. "She says I'm in a relationship with Landon Taylor and she feels like the third wheel."

"Ouch."

"I mean, what do I even say to that? We *are* in a relationship with Governor Taylor. Or Taylor 2012. Whatever."

Olivia offered him an empathetic shrug as he went on, pleading his case.

"I never sold her a bill of goods that I was regular. Regular people definitely don't work twenty hours a day. They don't get paid shit and they definitely don't put one crazy guy's needs before their own well-being. She bought the tickets; she knew what she was getting into."

"Yeah." Olivia nodded. Then she thought for a minute. "But the thing is: regular people don't elect presidents."

Jacob smiled. Why that argument, the exact one she had been trying to make for weeks, only made sense to other campaign people was a complete mystery to her. She looked out at the event, thinking about how rare it was to be surrounded by noise and chaos, yet stand in complete silence with someone else the way she could with Jacob. The two of them had become so accustomed to traveling together, passing glances back and forth in the back of cars and planes and giving orders to each other across rooms, it had become like they had an inaudible language all their own. He could tell when she needed a call made, just as well as she could tell when he needed Taylor out of or into a room. They worked together more like teammates on a football field than coworkers.

He furrowed his eyebrows. "So can I run something totally crazy by you?"

"Crazier than 'Do you want a fun job on a campaign'?"

Jacob laughed. "Touché." He motioned to Olivia to follow him to the chairs just outside the tent, where they would be out of earshot. "By the way, we should care more that Leo Davis, James Taylor, and Dana Klein are singing right now, shouldn't we?"

Olivia looked up at the famous musicians joking around onstage and mock-grimaced. She knew it was an exceptionally rare experience and not one she should be ignoring, but every glance at them just reminded her of the logistical nightmare she went through to get them all there. She sat down in the chair next to Jacob as he began to whisper.

"So." He paused cautiously. "How much do you think the voters care about affairs?"

She could hear the words coming out of Jacob's mouth before he said them. She knew that look in his eye. He was about to tell her that the governor was having an affair. *With someone else! That's a stupid thought. There's no affair with you. It's just someone, not someone else. Ugh.* The thought of the words hit her like a steel pipe to the stomach.

"That's a scary question to ask. Do you have something to tell me?"

"Now, I have no real evidence of this. And I haven't told a soul in the world."

Olivia's mouth got dry and she could feel her heart sinking. "Tell me." *Just say it.* Olivia prepped herself, realizing how much she didn't want the governor to be having an affair. And not just because it would be an Achilles' heel to the campaign that was her life.

Jacob took a big breath in, and even though no one was anywhere nearby he whispered, "I think Aubrey's having an affair."

⚬〰〰⚬

Just saying the words aloud, even in a whisper, was a huge load off of Jacob's shoulders. Olivia, in contrast, looked like she had seen a ghost. He immediately tried to calm her.

"I'm really not sure. I mean, it could all be coincidental."

"No, no." She recovered. "I just—I'm surprised, that's all. Why do you think that?"

"Well, it's a couple things." Jacob began to spew his theories. As he did, it all became even more incriminating than it had been in his mind. "The first was that trip to Miami, the one where she simply *haaad* to get away from the kids for a bit."

Olivia laughed at his always perfect impression of Aubrey.

"She was supposed to be meeting friends there, but when I called Shelby, one of the friends she was allegedly 'meeting,' to talk about a local women's event we were doing the week after, Shelby inadvertently made it crystal clear Aubrey had not been in Florida. Definitely. And she had not been with Aubrey. 'Coincidentally,'" he said, with air quotes, "Roger Tiwali—you know the former secretary of state—happened to also be in Miami that weekend. My paranoid self checked. Then there were the handful of times when Roger's assistant mentioned seeing her when she wasn't scheduled to see him. One time I even tried to ask the governor about their meeting, and he didn't even blink. He said they barely knew each other. Also, don't you think it's odd that we'd have the former secretary of state showing up at so many events recently? His endorsement is, according to Aubrey, 'in the bag.'"

Olivia looked more and more amazed as Jacob talked. And she was almost smiling.

"Plus, well . . ." He paused, wondering if he should finish the sentence, but then remembered it was Olivia he was talking to. She was in the foxhole with him. "Gov would kill me if he knew I said anything about this. Actually I don't really even know anything about it. But," he whispered even more quietly than they had been, "Aubrey and the gov, they were kind of rocky for a while there. I don't know the details, but I think he even moved out for a week or something before all the campaigning started."

Olivia looked, understandably, shocked as Jacob continued to seep information. He felt so good telling someone, having someone to share the burden of the secret, the worry and the rationalization. "You are sworn to secrecy on this," he added.

"Obviously. It's kinda funny at this point that we'd have to say that."

"Yeah."

"So, do you think she'd leave him? And during the campaign?"

Jacob looked at Olivia, his relief turning a bit to guilt at saddling her with the upsetting information. "Aubrey? No way. He's the product she's selling in the sale of her life."

"Yeah, I guess." She almost seemed teary.

"You've seen her though enough now. She barely likes the guy."

"Yeah, I guess that's true." Olivia paused and then asked, "Why doesn't she love him?"

"Who knows! She thinks he's lowbrow, not up to par with her. She's constantly telling people he doesn't read books. She comes one step short of calling him an idiot."

"You think he loves her?"

Jacob shook his head. He had asked himself that question so many times, but still, he really wasn't sure of the answer. "I don't know. He definitely needs her constant approval, or wants it. I don't know." He glanced down at his watch. "Shit! I gotta get the speaking program started. I hate this place and its absent coverage. How can I keep track of time without the metronome buzzing of my BlackBerry?"

He sprang up from the chair and headed into the tent.

He called back, "Sorry to drop this on you, Liv. I had to tell someone."

"It's all good," she said, smiling reassuringly. "We irregular people gotta stick together."

⌒◍◍◍◍⌒

As Olivia went to sleep that night she replayed the conversation with Jacob in her head over and over. It had to be true. Jacob knew these things. Plus, there were all those times Aubrey excused herself from events. All those furtive calls she would take. *Poor Landon. That's why he kissed me. He's just lonely. I wonder if he knows. Of course he knows. Who could hide something like that? How could Aubrey not cherish him?*

She tossed and turned, rolling around in the soft Pratesi sheets, wondering what this all meant. She knew she shouldn't follow the thought path to where it was going, but it seemed impossible to avoid. Would they get divorced? Could there be a world where Landon Taylor would be single? She guiltily relished the notion of her dream man becoming a viable option and then quickly batted the thought from her head.

No. She scolded herself. *You like this man. He has kids. A family. He has to be the president. You can't want him to get divorced.*

TWELVE

Conference calls were usually the bane of their existence, but Jacob and Olivia couldn't wait to get on this one early on a Tuesday morning before the filing. The filing was three days away and there was 1.6 million in hand, way more than even the craziest goal they had set. Jacob sat across from Olivia in the conference room as she dialed the call-in number. It was a weekly call, but since the Hamptons and Martha's Vineyard both fell within the last six days, the bottom line—the amount of money the campaign had collected and would report for this quarter—had changed drastically.

"Okay," Billy said in his usual monotone, "everyone on?"

The nine participants—Jacob; Billy; Olivia; the press secretary, Peter; the political director, Ron Mixner; Addie, whom Olivia insisted be included since she had been such a big part of things; and two consultants who had helped on the events called out their names in a totally disorganized fashion. It always reminded Jacob of one of those childhood games where you would try to count to ten without anyone saying the same number at the same time.

Billy found it less amusing and without fail would stop everyone halfway through, saying, "All right, all right, let's just get going." Today was no exception. Jacob smiled, looking across at Olivia and enjoying how excited she was. Her hair had grown long and straggly and fell down over her face, which was visibly drawn and tired, but she remained pretty in spite of it all, and her optimism, though he chided her about it constantly, really had been a welcome addition to their usual campaign tone. He texted Taylor the call-in number one last time, hoping he would join as well. It was a fine line Jacob tried to walk, wanting Taylor to do things he thought would boost morale, but careful not to become a nag. Reminding him of birthdays, weddings, and other such events where a call would make a huge difference to someone had been a big part of Jacob's job, but it had become harder to get the governor to make those calls with each passing day of the campaign. "It's the thought that counts," the governor had started saying with regularity. Jacob hoped it was the pressure of the schedule getting to the governor and not his ego, but on days like this, when he was waiting for Taylor to do something asked of him, he couldn't help but waver in his confidence. Billy broke his chain of thought.

"Since there's only one thing that actually matters now, let's get to it. Olivia?"

Jacob piped up, buying the governor a few extra minutes, asking a quick question about the *Times* story they were waiting on, and hoped no one would call him out for not really needing to know the answer. As Peter answered the *Times* question, the phone beeped in.

"Hi, y'all. Hope I'm not interrupting," the governor said in his booming voice, and Jacob smiled gratefully.

"Hello, Governor. Glad to have you on, sir." Billy spoke with his regular formality.

"Did I miss the numbers?"

"No, sir."

"So let's hear 'em! Did we hit one point three?" Jacob wasn't sure what he appreciated more, the governor's enthusiasm or how thrilled Olivia and Addie seemed that the governor would be on the call for their big news. He couldn't help but congratulate himself for moving a lot of great pieces into a perfect puzzle.

"Olivia?" Billy called on her.

Olivia's voice shook a bit. "Hello, sir. I'm happy to report we haven't just hit one-three, we've surpassed it. It looks like we'll file with one point six."

"Shit!" Peter sounded off first, falling intuitively into the Brook-

lyn nature he had been actively working to sweeten with Southern etiquette, and then quickly retracted the curse. "Sorry, sir. That's awesome,
Olivia!"

"No 'sorry' necessary, Peter," the governor said in his slow, pensive mode. "That is just pheeenomenal, Olivia. And everyone. Team,
this is great, just great. Sakes alive."

Everyone chimed in with their congratulations, and Olivia and
Addie beamed with pride.

"Why don't we do a little party after the event Thursday? We need
to celebrate and thank people."

"Yes, let's do it." Jacob knew it would give him a great reason to
stay a few more days and attempt to make up with Sophie. He had
come to New York for the Hamptons event and worked out the schedule to stay for Sophie's birthday. She wasn't talking to him, but he was
convinced he could save the relationship. *Save the relationship, ha! More
like win her back.* Of course it hadn't gone exactly as planned since he'd
gotten dragged to one of Alek's dinner parties and had showed up,
much to Sophie's dismay, late to her birthday party. He had tried to explain to her what a big deal it was that he was even able to be in New
York for it at all, but like many campaign-related things, it fell on deaf
ears. He would surely be able to fix it now.

"We'll get it set," Olivia said, falling back into her responsible
tone.

Ideal, Jacob thought. *It's all ideal.*

⟡

A who's who of New York socialites showed up to the celebration. People moved around the room excitedly and the air seemed to be filled
with a vociferously festive fervor, despite Olivia's attempts to keep the
party low-key. She had constantly reminded herself, with Jacob's nagging help, that while they wanted to celebrate the filing and thank
donors, they had to be extremely cautious of looking overconfident or
celebratory without cause. Campaign Lesson #13: Celebrations in politics, at least publicly, were to be reserved for elections and nothing else.
There were no balloons, no banners, and definitely, as she could hear
Jacob saying, no sparkles! She glanced at the small cocktail tables, which

were decorated with little white votives that the hotel put out for free and red apples that Olivia had run to the grocery store before the event to buy, in an attempt to decorate as cheaply as possible.

As she scanned her frugally elegant stage decoration, she caught the governor's eye across the room. Alek, in black pants, a black sweater, and a Gucci belt, had him cornered and was barely missing him with the champagne glass that moved with his flapping arms. Alek's short bangs were spread out across the very top of his forehead. She smiled to herself at the sight of the governor looking so sweetly trapped, obviously trying to push Alek toward the end of whatever story he was telling. With one eyebrow raised, Taylor noticed her and silently called for help. Olivia put down her soda and walked swiftly over.

"Hi, Alek."

"Ahhh, se princess!" He flung an arm around her, spilling more of his champagne.

"Such a great night, isn't it?" she said. "And you were such a huge part of it. I keep telling the governor I just followed your lead this quarter!"

Alek beamed at the compliment, which, as all compliments were, amplified when it was said in front of the candidate.

"It's true." The governor followed suit. "I am so lucky to have you as a friend, Alek." He looked at his old buddy with sincerity. "I hope one day I'll have the chance to be half the friend to you!"

Alek almost bowed his head humbly. "Thank you, thank you," he said. "Like you say, it's se thought sat counts, and sat thought counts!" He cackled a bit, drinking more champagne. "Like my mom used to say, 'Ne imey sto rubley, a imey sto druzey.' Don't have a hundred rubles, have a hundred friends."

Olivia enjoyed their preserved friendship but knew she needed to get the governor away for a break.

"I so hate to interrupt you but I need to steal the governor away to take a quick press call."

"Ahhh, of course! Of course, you take him. I just vas telling him we are going to do big event in California." Alek continued on as if she hadn't interrupted.

"That is amazing! Let me get the governor on this call and I'll come back and we'll plan!" Olivia did her utter best to gin up enthusiasm for more work as she gently grabbed the governor's arm and pulled him away.

As they got out of earshot, Olivia's hand dropped off his arm. Taylor caught it and grabbed her by the wrist.

"Nice save." He slid his hand down and squeezed her fingers. "Hold room." He stepped in front of her and let go of her hand. Yanni was walking toward him.

Jacob grabbed her from the other side and slipped a paper into her hand.

"Angel. Calls. Must be made."

"On it, Charlie! But cover for me with Yanni so I can get him out." They worked the room like they were executing a pick and roll. Jacob headed straight for Yanni, and Olivia pulled on the governor's elbow, leading him to the hold room. She looked down at the paper Jacob had handed her. It had about five names and numbers scribbled on it. *Perfect.* She figured she could add three or four of her own calls to the list and have him back out in the party in twenty minutes.

Olivia walked into the hold room, which was actually just another part of the ballroom, sectioned off by a sliding wall they used to divide the huge catering hall when needed. The governor followed behind her. As the door clicked closed, Olivia looked around, surprised at how muffled the noise of the party was from in here. The room was large and empty, save for one table with a phone, four bottles of water, and a bowl of pretzels. *So glad I remembered to set this up ahead of time.*

Olivia headed for the table, but the governor grabbed the back of her waist, spinning her into him like they were doing a tango.

"I—"

"How great is this?" he asked, standing way too close.

Olivia breathed. "It's great, I—" Her mind instantly went to the numbers and the party. She didn't even have time for an ellipse. He pulled her tightly into him. And he kissed her.

His tongue moved hers back and forth. It was softer than she remembered. And it tasted of the pretzels from the ballroom tables, mixed with the spearmint Tic Tacs he was constantly popping. His lips pressed up against her mouth as his hands grabbed her sides. All the exhaustion and excitement came rushing over her. She let go into his arms.

"I—"

"No. Don't say it. Don't say anything." As he spoke she buried her head into his shoulder and breathed in his smell. It was that same scent of the outdoors that she remembered from the hotel in Georgia. "I'm not sorry this time," he was saying into her hair. "This is one of the greatest moments of this campaign and it's you I want to celebrate with. It's you I want to kiss. I see myself differently through your eyes. Everyone picks me apart. But you, you pick me up."

He went back to kissing her and she let him. She wanted to. His kiss was perfect. He was perfect. The party roared outside the door. *The door that doesn't lock! Oh my God. Is it even closed all the way? Holy crap.* She pulled away from him. "We can't do this here."

"Fine, fine," he said in agreement. "But not because we can't do this. We can." He spoke with an authority that thrilled Olivia. For a moment, she stopped arguing the point.

"Come on." She pulled him to the table. "I need you to make a few calls, then I'll let you get right back to that conversation with Alek." She laughed.

"The only conversation I want to finish is the long-overdue one with you," he said. He looked at her longingly and then pushed himself away from her. He sat and grabbed the list from her hand. It was crinkled from the grip of her sweaty palms. He smoothed it out on the table and lifted one eyebrow at her as he began to dial.

Olivia smiled. He made the calls, his feet up on the table, leaning back in a more relaxed fashion than she had ever seen him. She remembered how his shirt lay wrinkled halfway up his back that night in the hotel in Georgia. She sat back in her chair, dazed, watching his eyes watch hers. One after another he made the calls, speaking with a kind of steady energy and focus that gave no hint of the eyebrows he was raising at Olivia. She put her head down, unable to hold his glance without seeming embarrassingly giddy.

Before the last call he put his phone on the table and moved his chair closer to her. He whispered. "I love the way you look at me. I can't wait to kiss you again."

She faced him, staring him square in the eye, suppressing her need to scream out in joy, and said with mock sternness, "Make the call, Governor."

He gave her a peck on the lips. She flinched at the strange familiarity of his kiss. Then he obligingly sat back down and began dialing the number. She listened to him intently but barely heard a word. *I kissed him. He wants to kiss me again.* The words kept replaying in her head so quickly that no other information could go in or out. This time when he was finishing the call, he grabbed her leg just above the knee.

"Let's get this party over with so we can conversate."

She laughed, partly at the word but more so to cover up the rush of feeling that filled her body from his touch. She grabbed up her papers and followed behind him with a skip. *I just skipped. I skipped in front of the governor. What am I, six years old?* As she moved in front of him to open the door he grabbed her shoulder and pulled it back toward him. She could smell his breath on her neck.

"See." He spoke in a jubilant whisper. "You. Later."

⌀⌀⌀

Jacob glanced over Yanni's shoulder as the governor followed Olivia out of the hold room. He couldn't help but grin. The governor looked happy. It had been genius of Jacob to hire Olivia for the campaign. *Genius.* She threw him a thumbs-up, which he knew meant his calls got made. The governor was reaching out to the donors he needed to, endorsements were rolling in, and the fundraising goal that had seemed so outrageous four months ago had been surpassed. Senator Kramer was now their only real challenge and his numbers had been steadily dropping due to his botched appearance on *Meet the Press*. Kramer had made an analogy that did not go over well with the viewers and it had gone viral in minutes. Jacob had even heard from a friend that Kramer would file with only five hundred thousand. It was perfect, and Jacob, though still young, was seasoned enough to feel it.

Campaigns, with all their chaos and ambiguity, were strangely black and white in one way; they either had the magic or they didn't. Like someone in a bad relationship, staffers could convince themselves that it would change, that they could change it, but the truth, Jacob surmised, was that the breaks either went your way, or broke you. It wasn't a luck thing, it was the right candidate surrounded by the right people at the right time. He had been on both types of campaigns.

He thought back to the congressional run he'd worked on years back. No one thought his candidate, a Democrat running in a Republican district with no experience and no name recognition, had a shot in hell. There was a feeling, though, in that campaign office, a feeling of humble invincibility. They couldn't *not* win it. Sure enough, they got every break they could, ending with their opponent getting caught drinking at a college keg party. Other campaigns just didn't have the winning edge, and no matter how much you tried or pretended, you wound up with that looming feeling of impending loss. Jacob stood in the middle of the ballroom feeling almost suspended in time, sure that this was a good-feeling campaign. He inhaled such a breath of self-satisfaction that he reached to email Sophie. Things with her might be good. She had even agreed to come stay with him at the hotel.

Jacob@LTaylor.com: *It's all falling into place.*

He felt more confident writing the words than he was when he thought them. He skimmed through the rest of the twenty-two emails that had come in since he last checked. Sophie wrote right back.

SophieMoore14@gmail.com: *Really? What happened?*

He could almost hear her innocence in the words and felt bad that his reaction to the questions was almost annoyance that he would have to explain himself. He started to type an answer back, trying to put into words the feeling of being in that room and of knowing they would win. *Today we* was all he got out before Alek tugged on his arm.

"Jay-cohbe!" he bellowed.

Jacob felt a pang of guilty relief at the opportunity to procrastinate instead of trying to tell a layperson how important surpassing fundraising goals was. He knew it wasn't fair to not write her back immediately, but he wanted to be able to talk about the filing with someone who just got it, even Alek.

Alek pulled Jacob toward the bar and a beautiful young Russian woman, Marina, who looked entirely out of place. She wore a tight bright blue dress and sipped on a pink drink. Jacob looked at it, hoping Olivia had not ordered an open bar. They talked for ten minutes while

Jacob stood nodding his head in affirmation, pretending to understand what they were saying in their heavy accents. He glanced down periodically as new emails filled his inbox. The unfinished email to Sophie sat in draft mode offscreen. He might have remembered to finish it deep down, but that thought was covered up with the fear of accepting that she didn't understand his life.

"Thesse people," Alek was saying to Marina, "they are my fahmlee."

"You're our family, Alek." He grinned as Alek began telling the story about meeting Stephen Colbert with the governor at a NASCAR race, a story everyone on the campaign knew by heart. Jacob looked to his side and caught sight of Olivia across the room. She was emphatically explaining something to the catering manager of the Sheraton, pointing to one of the bars as if it were on fire. He smirked, watching her start out speaking at a hushed yell and then, as donors passed, instantly transforming her furrowed brows into a perfectly joyous smile.

All campaign staff had been schooled in that loss of natural reaction, forcing responses as they were needed, and he wondered if he looked as stupid from afar when he was doing it. He was in the middle of reminding himself to make fun of her for it when she caught his glance and looked over at him sympathetically, knowing he was about to be stuck, as all people got, with Alek. She winked at Jacob while excusing herself from the catering manager and headed toward the bar.

"Hey, Alek. Hey, Marina." She gave arm squeezes to both of them. "Hey, Jacob. I am so sorry to interrupt." *Brilliant! Not making fun of her for anything now!* Jacob started to move to her, ready to bolt for whatever emergency she "needed" him for.

"But, Alek," she said, "the governor wanted me to introduce Yanni to you. He told Yanni no one joins this campaign without meeting his oldest friend in the game!"

Spectacular. Jacob graciously bid them good-bye, thrilled to be out of the conversation without having to give up his place leaning across the bar. As Olivia pushed Alek away, she turned back to Jacob, who bowed his head and hands in a manner befitting a royal. *Thank you,* he mouthed. She smiled and led them off.

∽⟪⟫∽

As the room started to clear, Olivia shook hands as if she were on her own receiving line. She scanned the thinning crowd with more intent than usual, keeping an eye always on Taylor. In the brief moments she got between conversations she would remember his words. *He loves the way I look at him.* She fidgeted with her white bra strap, wishing she had worn something less plain. Jacob came up behind her while she was saying good-bye to Yanni.

"Alek just agreed to put twenty-five million in my hedge fund. You are officially my golden child." Yanni gave her a huge hug.

Jacob leaned into Olivia as Yanni walked away. "What was that about?"

"Oh, I am so out!" Olivia pursed her lips and nodded with a feigned severity. "Did you know there was a place where you could fundraise and people would stand a chance of getting their money back? And possibly make money? That has to be an easier sell."

Jacob put on his best Godfather voice and said, "But I've always taken care of you, Fredo."

Olivia laughed.

"The good news," he continued, "is not only do we pay you incredibly well, but there are huge perks!" He pulled out a hotel room key.

"You wish!" She laughed out loud.

"*You* wish!" he yelled, and slapped her on the back, laughing and caught off guard at her joke, which he was more prone to have made than she.

"I have a much nicer suite," he said, pulling out his own key and remembering that he'd never finished that email, "which I am hoping I can convince Sophie to join me in. But the hotel comped us two extra suites. I was thinking some of the out-of-towners might need them, but they're all set, so one's yours."

"Wow, that is so much better than making millions raising money for funds." Olivia happily grabbed the key from him. It could not possibly be this easy. This perfect. She hadn't even thought through how she would meet up with the governor, but now it would be easy. *The governor. Landon. That kiss.* This night was getting better by the moment.

"Oh, please. I know you love the opportunity to stock up on hotel soap!"

Olivia hung her head and looked at him with a sarcastic glare. "You don't know me!"

Jacob snickered. "Okay, I'm gonna pull the gov out. You good closing down?"

"Yup, perfect." *Perfect for you to take the governor to his room so I can go meet him there! I'm going to meet the governor. I'm not really.* She went back and forth in her head like she was twisting a Rubik's Cube. Could she really meet him after? It wouldn't be an accident. This time it would be premeditated.

Olivia looked around the room, having lost sight of the governor. She tried to watch Jacob as he walked away, but she was pulled into conversations and good-byes. *Maybe he came to his senses,* she thought, glancing down, hopeful the red blinking light of a new message would spark.

As she pushed out the last two people, young hedge fund brothers who, as always, had consumed too much alcohol, she stared around the empty room. It was quiet but for the clacking of glasses being cleared by the catering staff. *Who picks hotel ballroom carpeting? And why?* Her thoughts were completely useless questions, which she admittedly spent more time thinking about than anyone ever should. Nevertheless, every time she stood in a hotel event space before or after an event her mind was boggled. This one was a dark brown with blue, red, and purple circles.

She went over to a white-clothed corner table the staff had not yet gotten to and pushed the napkins and empty glasses to one side. She plugged in her BlackBerry, which had been beeping with a red low-battery sign for a while now. As she looked down, she realized the signal had switched off because of the battery. As the battery juiced up, the messages started to roll in. Twenty-six new messages. The red messages scrolled in at the top. Six to be exact, the first three with his room number and the last three asking where she was. She couldn't help but smile, flattered. She typed back quickly: **Sorry, battery died while closing down event. Still awake?** She sent it with the bated breath of someone making a lottery pick. A response came in record time.

I'm up. Come here.

Okay, she typed, and hurried toward the door of the ballroom, stopping quickly to thank the catering managers, Ed and Karen.

"You guys are the best!"

"Anytime." Ed shook her hand. "Can we get you a drink or anything?"

"I'm good, thank you." As the words came out of her mouth, she noted how much help a drink would probably be at this exact moment, but she didn't want to take the time.

Outside his door the thought doubled and tripled in her mind. *What am I doing? I'm not really going to do this. I can't. He can't. But then, how can I not? And maybe Jacob was right. Maybe Aubrey is having an affair. So why shouldn't he?* She heard her mother's voice: *"Two wrongs don't make a right."* But *I'm not having an affair. It's just a kiss.* She double-checked his pin message to make sure she had the right room. *What if I knock on the wrong door? What if someone is in there with him? What if Jacob is in there?* She shuffled through her bag to pull out papers just in case she needed an excuse for being at the governor's door at this late hour, while trying to push the thought of Jacob out of her mind.

She stood staring at the brass numbers on the white door and tried, almost physically, not to ask the questions she didn't want to answer. She shifted her bag to one hand and then back to the other. She bit her lip and curled her fingers into a fist. Knocking on this door was a bad move on so many levels. There was definitely a Campaign Lesson here that she was forgetting.

She shook her head a bit, trying to get the thoughts out. It was too much to consider, too much to think about. *I want this,* she told herself in an almost pleading cry from her heart to her head. She gripped the lists and knocked her fist against the door. When it opened, he stood alone in the doorway—head cocked, the corners of his mouth slowly turning up. Her grip on the papers tightened, crinkling them. Bruce Springsteen's "Thunder Road" played quietly in the background.

"Hello, there," he said in the sweetest Southern accent she had heard yet.

Her knees buckled like she had always heard knees could buckle, and all the problems outside the door disappeared in the fog-machine effect of his eyes. *His smile.* He grabbed her hand and pulled her gently inside, closing the door behind her. The room was all windows, and the glow of neon through the dark lit up the room.

"I've wanted to do this for so long." He pulled her close and kissed her. There was more power to his kiss than before. She stood almost stationary, arms hanging awkwardly by her sides, her left hand gripping the lists even tighter.

He must have heard the sound of the pages rustling against her skirt. "Um, was there work you needed to do?" He reached down and took the lists slowly from her.

"No." She laughed at her own gawkiness. "I just—They're nothing." She pulled them back from him and stuffed them in her bag, embarrassed to have even thought through an excuse. *That's the part I thought through here?* she thought, mocking herself, while turning her face back up to kiss him.

Everything about him was right. His white button-down shirt hung out over his suit pants, the bottom of it wrinkled from being tucked in all day. The top three buttons were undone and his white T-shirt underneath showed through. It was big on him but his shoulders pushed out against the top of the shirt. She reached up to them and put her arms around his neck, clasping her hands together behind his head.

He murmured into her ear, "You make me feel so alive." His breath felt warm against her ear. "I haven't felt this way since . . ." His hand came up over her head and stroked her hair. "I haven't felt this way ever."

Me neither, she wanted to scream, but the words seemed stuck in her throat.

She lay her head on his shoulder, trying to collect herself, but as she looked out at the lights piercing the city night, she felt more alive than ever. She could see all the way to the bridge at the southern tip of the city. Her stomach flip-flopped with excitement. *I am in a gorgeous hotel room with the man of my dreams. I have never felt this way either. Never.*

The negative was there; she felt it. But the good was too good to let the questions seep in.

He slipped his arms tightly around her waist.

"How breathtaking is this?" she asked. She reached down to intertwine her hand in his.

"That's a good term for it."

"It doesn't even seem real. It's more like someone dropped a movie set down just for us."

She looked up at him. The blue lights outside seemed to illuminate his face. As they kissed, she closed her eyes tightly, almost in fear that if she opened them, she would wake to find this all a dream. One by one pieces of their clothing came off.

As he lay her down, both of them nearly naked, Olivia's mind almost stopped. Thoughts couldn't even be completed in between his kisses. As he moved on top of her, he stared straight into her eyes. Olivia tried to regain some sense of the world beyond them.

"Wait." She attempted to shift a bit. "We can't."

"Yes, we can."

"No." She laughed at his raised eyebrow. "I mean, we can't be unsafe." It sounded so stupid to her. This was the least safe thing she had ever done.

"Huh?"

"Without protection. We can't . . ."

The governor let out a belly laugh that shook her body. He grabbed on to her.

"Sakes alaaahve," he said, shaking his head back and forth and carrying out the "alive" with a twang.

"What?"

"Sorry, they're not the kind of thing I carry with me," he said more softly.

Olivia laughed, happier than she would let on to know that this wasn't a common occurrence for him.

"Right." She looked past his shoulder, wondering if he was as caught off guard by the mention of a condom as he seemed. He had to be. This kind of thing really was rare for him. She was special. She looked at him, desperate to figure out more about him than the moment could possibly divulge.

"This isn't the kind of thing I do."

"Really?" She stared up into his eyes, looking for a hint of a lie, aware of the troubling fact that she was worried about others when just his wife should have been enough to stop her.

He looked back with an absence of doubt and with an intimate rawness. "Really."

She kissed him and rolled on top of him. She lifted her head up so that her hair hung down around them. She clasped his shoulders and stared at him, with a feeling she could stay right there forever.

She felt strangely relieved. "It's probably a good thing."

"It is definitely not a good thing," he said with a mischievous smile, "but I'll settle for holding you."

She nuzzled her head into his shoulder, relishing the feel of his smooth skin against her cheek, feeling incomprehensibly safe in his arms.

"For now," he added, as they drifted off to sleep together.

THIRTEEN

O livia followed the governor out of the library-like restaurant area of the Brinmore hotel, trying to sneak past Jo and into the elevator bank.

"I have a dayroom," the governor said as he guided her into the elevator and pushed the button for the sixth floor.

Olivia stood almost at attention, nervously stiff against the wood paneling of the elevator. *I wonder if that disgraced governor knew the courtesy was available when he brought that girl to the Days Inn,* she thought. *Of course a reporter caught him there. That's where you go for a seedy affair, right? But the Brinmore? That's for high-powered meetings and big-dollar fundraisers. Ha. Another example of the growing gap between the rich and poor—wealthy politicians can get away with more scandal than underprivileged ones.* She laughed at the ridiculousness of it all.

Feeling sketchy, Olivia followed the governor off the elevator and into his room. "Governor, we can't do this. We can't be here."

"First of all, stop calling me 'Governor,' and second of all, how many times are we going to have this conversation?"

As he spoke, he grabbed her close and began to kiss her neck. She dropped her head back and looked at the ceiling. It was true; the conversation was getting a bit overplayed, even for her. They had been having it every night since the filing party twenty-six days ago. Most of the time it had been on the phone, but this week he had come in on Saturday for the Sunday shows and somehow managed to stay until to-day, Tuesday. Each night began with Olivia saying, "Absolutely not," as emphatically as she could, having spent most of the day thinking of a million reasons she could not be involved with him, and much to her chagrin, each and every conversation would end with her losing the argument. No matter where he started, he always ended up asking her the same things—"Don't you want to be with me?" and "Don't you feel something special here?" As much as she struggled to lie, or just leave his questions unanswered, he always got the "yes" he was looking for.

"I'll tell you what." She put her finger up to his lips to stop him from kissing her. "We can stop having this conversation when you come up with a single logical reason why this is okay."

"I have given you many." He flicked away her finger and kissed her systematically down her neck. As had also become habitual over the last three days, he began to unbutton her top while she argued her points.

"This is so wrong." As the words came out of her mouth, she succumbed to his touch and kissed him on the lips. It was a useless argument really. He could talk her into or out of anything, and it wasn't really fair to blame herself for it. There was statistical data that proved his ability to convince thousands and thousands of people to do things. It was his job. And, of course, there was the key fact that she wanted him too. He was everything she'd ever wanted in someone. He was brilliant, confident, handsome. He spoke with clarity and passion about all the issues she cared about. He took action. He was perfect. Actually, he was so much more than perfect. *And such a good kisser.*

Forty-five minutes later, they were back downstairs for more meetings like it was the most normal thing in the world. *I will say this,* Olivia argued to herself, *the increase in trips to New York is great for fundraising. He is doing twice as many meetings these days.*

She liked her latest attempt at rationalization, or better yet, finding an upside to what she was doing. "What she was doing" was the term she used as she couldn't bring herself to say the word "affair," even to herself. The fortunate thing about keeping something she shouldn't have been doing a secret was that she could use reasoning that wouldn't pass muster even with herself if she had been forced to speak it aloud.

Inner monologues make so much more sense when they are kept to your inner self. Maybe that's what Dad meant by "The heart has reason the mind knows nothing of."

When the governor showed up at her door at ten thirty that night, after a day of important fundraising meetings and escapes upstairs, she again tried to talk herself into doing the right thing, but was overcome with the need to touch him and feel his touch. There was a desperation to be close to him, one she had never experienced before. *It's my heart, totally beyond my control,* she would continue to tell herself for the next month, even though she knew it was a complete lie.

ᏇᎥᎥᎥᎴ

"Liv, I need him back in Georgia!" Jacob roared into the phone. He didn't mean to take his frustration out on Olivia. It was the governor he wanted to scream at, but since it wasn't appropriate to berate the boss, Liv was in the line of fire.

"What do you mean?"

"Apparently we're sending him to do another freakin' Sunday-morning talk show, which is a whole other issue, and now he says you said there was some good event to go to Saturday night. Ahhhhh." He let out a controlled yell that was actually more of a sigh than anything nearing a scream. "There are so many things wrong with this."

Olivia sputtered an excuse on the line, sounding unsure of what he was talking about, which made him even more angry.

"Oh, um, Saturday. I . . . Sorry, Jacob, I just—"

"I can't have you guys all asking him to do things. Of course he wants to go to parties in New York and quench his newfound thirst for million-dollar wines. We all want to do that. But we have a campaign to run. And I am the only one watching out for him."

Jacob heard Olivia trying to cut in but wouldn't let her. He was on a roll and needed to vent. He had spent the entire day, actually what seemed like an entire two weeks, defending schedule changes that he himself didn't even agree with. Three times now the governor had told Jacob they needed more fundraising dates on the calendar. Which was bullshit. Jacob had just figured out the perfect balance of what needed to be scheduled and when. He had dutifully turned things upside down to make the changes the governor wanted and then defended them to the rest of the staff, who had meetings and events canceled for "more money time."

Plus, Aubrey, who seemed to be throwing more tantrums than ever, canceled yet another campaign stop to stay in Atlanta. She had called Jacob at six thirty a.m., twenty minutes before she was supposed to be on a plane, to tell him she had "not been briefed properly for this trip," so she "simply could not go." And coincidentally the former secretary of state was scheduled to be in Atlanta. *Shocker. On top of all the other negatives, getting laid isn't even helping her mood.*

"Peter has him on so many press shows we might as well be paid bookers. We're running for president, not vying for an Emmy!" He continued on for a good four or five minutes, at which point he started to feel worse about his own lack of verbal control than he did about the lack of control he had on the campaign. He took a deep breath. "Sorry."

Olivia, in the calm monotone voice of either a therapist or someone who was paying no attention, broke her uncharacteristic silence. "It's okay."

He repeated his apology, trying to regain some poise. "Sorry. I'm just frustrated."

"I know. Sorry. I shouldn't have said anything to him directly."

"I just need to regain some control," he said, more to himself than to her.

"You haven't lost that."

"Why are you talking so weirdly?"

"I'm not."

Jacob didn't buy it for a second. He looked down at the clock on his computer screen and realized it was twenty past eleven at night and she had been at meetings with the governor all day.

"Shit, Liv, did I wake you up?"

"No! It's only like eleven o'clock. Sorry, I'm just tired today."

"Oh, good. I mean, not good you're tired, good I didn't wake you up." Jacob still wasn't convinced. "Wait! Is someone there with you?!"

"Please, you know the only relationship I'm in is the dysfunctional one I have with this campaign." She said it with a laugh.

"Phew. We'll not have you sleeping around on us."

"Please, I am well aware of the 'no sleeping at all' rule on this campaign."

Jacob laughed. "Yeah, clearly a rule I should break for myself today."

"Jacob, you are doing an amazing job," Olivia said. "Everyone knows how lucky we are to have you at the helm."

"Thanks, Liv. Sorry for my tirade." He really did start to feel better. "Oh, but really, on Saturday, I don't want him going to an event unless you really need him. We can't have him become a New York socialite. Those things don't go over well in places like Iowa."

"No problem at all. I don't really need him there." She paused with a weird laugh.

"Okay, cool. He's got to be in New York for the morning show Sunday, so he gets in Saturday night. I'm going to try to send him as late as possible. If he gets in early enough, maybe you guys could do call time or something? I just don't want him at another party. You know, AHAP—as hidden as possible." Jacob snickered at himself. "Ironic since the trip is for him to do more press!"

"No problem. I can think of something. Sorry again about the party thing. It really was just an idea that spurted out of my mouth. I didn't think through it at all."

"Unfortunately for me, these days your word seems to be golden!"

"Very funny!"

"Actually, Liv, you really are doing a great job. He's listening to you because you're getting things done. You just need to keep in mind that when he starts listening to you on that level you have to be much more careful about what you're saying."

"Okay."

Jacob tried to explain his point further. "I mean, I know it sounds crazy but he takes in so much every day, we just have to filter things before they get to him so we can keep the campaign more focused than any one human could be. The whole needs to be greater than the parts here, even the big part!"

"It doesn't sound crazy at all. Will work on it."

"Thanks, Liv. And thanks for letting me vent."

"No prob, Jacob. Hang in there. Tomorrow will be better."

∽⚭〜

"You don't need me here, huh?" The governor ran his hand down Olivia's stomach as she hung up the phone with Jacob, and she flinched when it tickled.

"Not at all." She turned on her side, facing him, and leaned in to kiss his ear. "It's really more of a want thing."

The governor's arm wrapped around her side and he inched her closer. "So, what was that all about? He complaining?"

Olivia felt protective of Jacob. *Relatively.* She revised her own thoughts since she was lying in a bed with Landon, a move that was far from protective of anyone, most of all Jacob. "That, my friend, was about us almost getting caught! You made me laugh twice."

"Oh please, you laugh all the time."

"Not while you're on the phone! Campaign Lesson number twenty-five: No talking in the background!" She punched him lightly in the shoulder and winced. She hated recognizing that it had become reflexive for her to stop talking every time his phone rang.

"I thought 'No kissing in the background' was twenty-five."

"Very funny. Seriously, we have to be more careful. And you. You have to stop favoring fundraising."

"Is that so?" He started to pull his hand away from her back. She grabbed it back. She loved the feel of his arm around her, his hand grabbing her side.

"Well, at least in such an obvious fashion."

∽⚭〜

While the time Landon put into fundraising was a huge help in reaching her financial goals and she certainly wasn't going to argue about the time they were spending together, the amount of it all was starting to take a toll. She had been in L.A. for three days, and between the time change, work, and late-night calls with Landon, she was just plain tired and thankful to be at the last fundraiser of the trip. As if three straight days of events weren't enough, Aubrey had brought the kids and two nannies out for the trip, which doubled everyone's logistical work and stress.

Olivia was charged with contacting donors to get them special tours at Disneyland, Universal Studios, and anywhere else she could think of. She hated making the calls on so many levels. She didn't have the time for superfluous planning, especially on calls that consisted of her hearing how honored every single person in L.A. would be to be in the presence of Aubrey, Margaret, and Dixon Taylor. *Aubrey, Margaret, and Dixon Taylor.* Saying their names twenty times a day did not go over well with her conscience, which preferred to stay in a state of denial. However, having them scheduled around the city for most of the trip meant Olivia could steer clear of seeing them in person. Until tonight.

The last event of the trip was a fundraiser at the home of Andrew and Liz Herly, championship sailors who had moved to L.A. after their reality TV show became a hit. The house looked like a New England boathouse transported to Beverly Hills. Its high ceilings were vaulted, with exposed wood beams, and most of the walls were covered in navy and white striped wallpaper.

Aubrey and the kids and Landon stood on a makeshift stage in front of a full-wall mural of Liz and Andrew winning the World Cup. Olivia had learned from writing the briefing that the renowned artist Lisa Baglivi had been commissioned to paint it last summer after her solo show at LACMA. As a backdrop to the speaking program, it made the Taylor family look like they were standing in the middle of a beach. As Landon began talking, Olivia's heart sank with the knowledge that she was hurting, possibly ruining, this perfect family.

"Let me tell you"—he looked out at the crowd of about a hundred people—"nothing could make me happier than being here with my beautiful family. Let's have a round of applause for the real beauty and brains of the Taylor operation!" He beamed at his wife and kids, who adoringly looked back at their man, as he went on to recount the tale of their first family trip to California. Olivia had heard the story more than a million times and yet it still sounded like fingernails on a chalkboard. She hated thinking about them as a family at all. *"You can't combine worlds,"* she remembered Jacob telling her. *"Keep them separate or they won't make sense." More like keep them separate or you'll have a nervous breakdown,* she thought. It was so much simpler to see Aubrey as the mean woman who canceled fundraisers hours before they were about

to start. The bitch who looked down on Landon, who didn't appreciate what she had. And Olivia preferred to not see the kids at all. Hearing family stories, no matter how many times Landon told her they
were old news, wracked her with guilt. Olivia walked off to the side of
the living room and headed to the back bar, which had been brought
in and placed in front of a wall of trophies. She needed to literally move
farther away from his words and also was in desperate need of hydra-
tion. *Maybe they have some appetizers left back there,* she thought, knowing full well that she had requested they not serve anything while the
governor was speaking.

She quietly whispered to the bartender, "Sorry to have been bothering you all night, but could I grab a Diet Coke, no ice?"

"No ice?" he asked incredulously, making her even more aware of
the bead of sweat rolling down the back of her neck.

"No ice, please." Like the service of food, ice would make noise, a
totally unacceptable distraction from his speaking.

She grasped the warm soda and fell back into the wall. After two
sips she looked up to the ceiling and questioned the world she had
landed in. She felt barely strong enough to stand up, even with the wall
behind her. As her head tilted downward she noticed the rapt quiet of
the room. The governor's voice was rising,

"Our country used to be about becoming bigger and better. Politicians added amendments to our Constitution to expand rights and in-
clude more people. Now it has become the opposite. Now everyone
spends all their time stopping things—gays can't marry, immigrants
can't immigrate, women can't choose when to start a family. I'm not
arguing the points, though I could. I could go on for hours about how
wrong they are, how racist and closed-minded they are, but then I'd
just be adding time and energy and another voice into a negative corner of the world. It's time to turn the conversation around. It's time to
start talking about—and more importantly working for—good things,
positive things. It's time for innovation. It's time for scientific ad-
vancements. It's time we find sustainable energy sources. It's time we
make our education system one we can be proud of."

Olivia stood as hypnotized by his words as the rest of the room
was. A dropped pin would have been crashingly loud.

"Y'all know where I stand on the issues, and those who don't can look it up on the Internet. I'm not going to spend this campaign talking about what's wrong and how we're going to fight it. I'm going to talk about what's right, what could be, and how we're going to get there. I want a better America and it is not just possible, it is within our reach. Once upon a time in our history, a man stood up and said we could go to the moon, and a nation delivered. Now I'm saying I want to bring us back to earth. Feet firmly on the ground, we will make this country the beacon of light and of advancement that it should be. Together we will reach the greatness we were meant for."

Olivia dropped her drink on the nearest cocktail table. No longer aware of the heat or her exhaustion, she joined in the standing ovation. She looked around at the exhilaration in all the faces. Suddenly the momentous nature of the campaign hit her with a wave of pride. *I better commit this moment to memory,* she thought. *One day people will want to know what it sounded like in person.*

"Wowzers." Mariqua, one of the many rich female donors who swooned every time the governor was around, leaned in close enough for Olivia to get high off her Chanel No. 5 perfume. "That was amaaazing. Ahhbsoluutely amaaazing. I mean, can you stand it? I haaave to talk to him after. I simply muust. Here are more contributions!" She handed Olivia two folded-up checks. "Did you ask him yet if he'll come meet us at Mr. Chow?"

Olivia smiled. "I'm so sorry, Mariqua, he's just not going to be able to go. Aubrey and the kids are heading back to Georgia, and he needs to see them off at the airport." *Like I have told you forty times before,* she thought with new understanding of why Landon always said he was downright frightened by Mariqua.

Actually, Aubrey, with the kids and nannies, would be chauffeured off to their private plane without Landon, but this excuse sounded decidedly better than, "The governor needs to get back to his hotel to cheat on his perfect family with his imperfect fundraiser."

"So sorry," Olivia said, using one of her favorite get-out-of-a-conversation-quick tricks and pointing to Taylor, "I've got to go grab the governor."

"Ahhhh"—Mariqua breathed out embarrassingly loudly—"wouldn't

I love to be the one to *grab* him. Haaaahaaaahaaaahaaa," she cackled absurdly.

Olivia smiled politely and walked away. Even though the indecency of her actions was magnified in this room, she couldn't help the giddy, mesmerized feeling she had. *I do get to grab him, s*he thought indulgently as she glided through the crowd, which didn't seem half as pushy or painful as it did before. She went to the front door to collect more checks as people filed out of the house.

Jacob ran by her. "This was so much easier when we had Secret Service," he whispered as he went outside for the third time to check on the family's cars.

Olivia nodded. She hadn't been around for the last presidential race, when there was security everywhere, so even the one or two guards who accompanied them these days seemed like a lot to her. She wondered how she would be able to be alone with Landon once the Service tracked his every move.

"All set!" Jacob spoke loudly as he reentered the home, motioning to the governor. Landon was thanking the hosts as Aubrey pulled the kids toward the door.

"Good-bye, Olivia." She nodded her approval. "Kids, what do y'all say to Olivia? She arranged the tours for us at Disney and Universal and at the museum."

"Thank you!" The kids spoke over each other. "It was so much fun!"

"It was my pleasure. Glad you enjoyed it. Have a safe trip." Olivia smiled, now positive that she would go straight to hell.

⌒ππα⌒

"Shit." Jacob looked up from his BlackBerry for maybe the third time when they got into the lobby of the West Cove Hotel, a new modern establishment that seemed way too hip for the campaign but was probably the cheapest they could find. There were people everywhere. And worse, paparazzi. He looked past the registration desk to the bar, where people were raucously gathered at the entrance. He turned behind him to see the governor and Olivia following but still at the curb. The crowded bar would not do. Aside from the fact that it was noisy and dimly lit, useless conditions for looking over lists, he would be bothered every five minutes by people trying to get a picture or even a hello. In California, where movie stars were commonplace, other types of celebrities, like politicians, were bizarrely more sought after.

Plus, Jacob thought to himself, the last thing he needed right now was anyone gossiping about Landon Taylor being in a bar with a young girl. *Hmpf,* he thought, laughing to himself, *if any of those idiot gossip columns actually sat with Landon and Olivia during one of their list meetings they'd never write another story about the governor.*

The thought of the grind of the actual work hit Jacob, and he had to hand it to Olivia for remaining so Hallmark upbeat when most of her job was tedium crossed with mind-blowing pressure. *Olivia really is a trouper.*

He thought about her quickly turning to stare out the window stoically when the governor asked if they could go over lists yet again. Jacob knew she appreciated the extra fundraising time, but even she had to be tired of it by now. She must have had a million things she would rather do than be alone with the governor in a hotel hold room, their lists all over the table.

Jacob darted back out to stop Olivia and the governor before they got near the paparazzi. He needed to brief them on the situation. "Major crowd in there and lots of photogs."

"Is there another way in?" the governor asked impatiently.

Olivia took a few steps back, as if Jacob had just told them the reporters had guns rather than cameras.

"Yes. We can go around the rear of the building. If you guys want to head back to the car and drive around, I'll meet you and open the back door. It leads right to the side elevators."

Taylor flexed his jaw in annoyance. "Fine. We should've just gone that way in the first place."

As the governor headed to the car, Jacob turned and hustled back into the hotel to meet them at the back entrance, feeling stung. *Why is he so annoyed with me all the time these days? He didn't even pass off his BlackBerry to me during the fundraisers this week. What the hell did I do?*

Jacob's distress wasn't lessened when the governor slid by the open rear door with a muffled "Thanks," but Jacob chalked the rudeness up to exhaustion. He carefully ushered Taylor and Olivia to the club room he had reserved for working. Billy would disapprove of the added expense, but it was inappropriate for any of them to work in the governor's room, or for him to be in theirs. Jacob thought about the possible consequences of misperceptions in a hotel filled with paparazzi and congratulated himself on avoiding them.

FOURTEEN

The bitter cold somehow made Jacob's dingy New Hampshire motel room seem even worse than it should have, especially after spending the last three days in L.A. Jacob was in room 201 and Taylor in 203, but oddly enough, they were on opposite sides of the floor. That was strange, but not as strange as the waffle maker in the room. Especially given that there was no kitchenette, or even an iron. There was a Bible, and not even in the drawer, as normal hotel etiquette would dictate. It was sitting smack-dab in the middle of the nightstand. *Do you think Jesus loved waffles?* Jacob started to text to Olivia.

He had a habit of texting things to Olivia as if she were standing in the room beside him witnessing the absurdity. Of course, he knew it made no sense out of context, but she always understood. Plus he needed to amuse himself somehow.

The trips seemed to be longer and longer these days, and they moved from state to state so quickly, he barely knew where he was anymore. The campaign was surging—they now led Senator Kramer by at least six points in all the Iowa polls—but Jacob couldn't help but feel more and more defeated personally. The governor had changed. There was no other way to view the problem. He was constantly insisting on being on the Sunday-morning shows. Taylor's charm made it okay and probably even helped with the short-term bump in the poll numbers.

But Jacob saw it eating into his long-term strategy. The path to the White House that he and Billy had so meticulously plotted seemed to have been rerouted by an increasingly reckless Taylor. And then there was Taylor's snobbishness. He had become so close with donors like Yanni and Alek that he was losing perspective.

Unfortunately, Jacob's advice to the governor, particularly when combined with the edge of exhaustion, had not been coming across kindly. Like last week, when Jacob had suggested taking a commercial flight to Iowa. The governor had scoffed at him angrily, "Just call Yanni and get his jet." Taylor had given the order as if instructing Jacob on something as simple as picking up a coffee. "And don't go complaining to Olivia about it either." Their once joke-filled, fun relationship was beginning to show cracks of tension.

Jacob's BlackBerry buzzed. It was the governor. "There's only a bottle of Chardonnay in here, and it's room temp," the governor complained.

Asshole. "Hey, just be glad it's not in a box!" Jacob shot back, unable to control his exasperation.

The governor didn't miss a beat. "That's the difference between you and Eric," he said, comparing Jacob to his lackey and all-around houseboy. Jacob hated that comparison most of all, probably because somewhere inside, Jacob was frightened of becoming like Eric—so far into the Kool-Aid he didn't even realize he was drinking it anymore. "Eric would have already hung up the phone and been halfway to a liquor store by—"

Before the governor could finish his jab, Jacob let himself go too far. "That's only *one* difference between me and Eric. For the record, I don't plan to come over and wipe your ass after you take a shit tonight, either." As the words left his mouth, Jacob threw his head back, wishing he hadn't let them slip. *Jesus! What was I thinking? DANGER, DANGER!* That was the kind of joke he might have made to a guy from college, and even then, it would have meant he hated the guy.

The governor stayed silent on the other end of the line. Jacob immediately backpedaled. "I shouldn't have spoken to you like that. I apologize, Governor. I was just—I don't know how to explain. I was just in an argument with Sophie and I let my emotions carry over." *Lie.* It was true he had endured a fight with Sophie but that was two days ago. His ever-expanding ability to stretch the truth was exactly why she had yelled at him that way. Not calling her back was the other. He grunted as he remembered he had again forgotten to call her.

"Man, you guys are hard on Eric," the governor said, deflecting the apology and, with it, the first insult. "What's that nickname you call him again? Little Prancer or something?"

Jacob exhaled. The governor might not have even paid attention to that last rant, assuming it was all about Eric, or he might just be demonstrating his desire to not confront the reality of their fraying friendship.

"We call him Lieutenant Proctor, sir." Jacob didn't grow up saying "sir"—he was a damn Yankee after all—but maybe the Southern style, he thought, would help mute the annoyance he was feeling. Unfortunately, as it almost always did, his conveyed respect instantly turned to sarcasm. "You know, Lieutenant Proctor from the *Police Academy* movies. The kiss-ass who can't get out of his own way."

"What?" The governor groaned.

"The movie. *Police Academy*. Steve Guttenberg. Bubba Smith. The whole series is classic. Please tell me you've seen them."

"Nope, never seen nor heard of it."

"You mean to tell me you know who won the last three seasons of *American Idol* and who was going to be the next Bachelorette, but you've never seen *any* of the *Police Academy* movies?" It was another example of Jacob's going too far in this strange impulse he felt lately toward familiarity and contempt, but he was too tired to care.

"Put it in my briefing tomorrow, and next time you bring it up, I can pretend to know what you're talking about," the governor said. "But last I checked, I didn't call you to hear about the movies I should watch. You're walking a fine line, Jacob."

"Oh right, the wine. That's what you want. I'll go down to the lobby and see if I can get you a few pieces of ice."

Down in the lobby, Jacob tried to ignore the voice in his head telling him he was becoming more and more like Eric every day. *Running around a dingy motel in . . . where the hell are we anyway? . . . for pieces of ice to cool down the candidate's freakin' wine. What real man drinks white wine anyway?*

"Please, ma'am, I just need a small cup of ice." He pleaded with the woman at the reception desk for the fourth time, unsure of why ice seemed to be such a difficult request in random states. When she finally reappeared with a small plastic cup containing two ice cubes, Jacob looked down and rolled his eyes. He quickly remembered people would see him with the governor tomorrow, and ever-conscious of the campaign's reputation on all fronts, he looked up and thanked her profusely.

He headed to the second floor. As he walked down the long, freezing-cold, and yet incongruously musty hallway, he sighed, troubled by the tone of his last conversation. He felt as though the friendship, the bond, he had with the governor was tearing beyond repair. It was those damn TV shows. They had been arguing about them for weeks. And now, the sarcasm that used to leave the governor in stitches was turning into something only heard as disrespect. Maybe it was Jacob's fault. Maybe he had gotten too close, become too casual. After all, the governor was his boss, not his friend. He knocked on the door and hung his head remorsefully. The door opened slowly.

"Hi, Governor."

"Hey."

"Here's the ice. And, Gov?"

"Hmm?"

"Sorry about before."

"Don't worry. We're all tired."

Jacob looked at the governor's haggard glare. Taylor was disappointed. Jacob realized the cause: the two measly half-melted ice cubes.

"Thanks for the ice."

The door closed swiftly and Jacob walked back down the hall, not quite sure if his discontent was aimed at the governor or at himself.

Among the emails that he had ignored while searching out ice cubes were four from Maggie, the *New York Post* political reporter, the last two of which read *Urgent* but with no other message. Jacob forwarded one of the early ones to the campaign press secretary, asking if he knew anything about it. *Nada,* Peter had pinned back.

I'm sure it's nothing. Maggie's a friend. If it were something truly awful, she would give me a bit of detail. Well, Jacob thought to himself, realizing that he hadn't called her back in quite some time, *she was a friend. Shit. Sophie. Also haven't called her back.* He remembered his last fight with Sophie, when she had yelled at him, "You always choose the campaign before me." A grand gesture was required to soothe that girl, so he called her before Maggie.

"Hello?" The fact that she'd answered with a questioning hello when her caller ID definitely informed her who was calling was a telltale sign she was still mad.

"Hey, Soph."

"Nice of you to call."

"I just left the governor! I called you before I even called the *New York Post* back." The grand gesture had sounded so much more grand in his head.

"Wow. Thanks."

"Sorry." He didn't really have the energy to explain his point, much less argue it. Asking for the slack he needed seemed like a surefire way to start another fight, which he didn't have time for.

"How's New Hampshire?" she asked with somewhat feigned interest.

"Good, good. Polls are looking good. People seem to really be responding to the message." He realized he had reflexively fallen into talking points. These days they seemed to come to him so much more intuitively than normal conversation. "Hey, and I had the most amazing apple cider. One day I'll have to bring you here for it."

"Yeah," she said, unenthused.

"How about you? What's going on there?"

He tried to focus as she started talking, but he couldn't bear just idly listening. He threw her on speakerphone and started replying to emails while attempting to catch the vital parts of Sophie's story about the start of school. As she spoke, he couldn't help but get more nervous about Maggie's messages.

"You falling asleep yet?" Sophie asked.

"No, sorry, Soph. Just tired."

"You should go to sleep."

He didn't tell her there was no chance he was going to sleep any time soon. "I probably should." It wasn't a lie, he assured himself; he was tired as shit. "It's so good to hear your voice though."

"You too." She said it with less enthusiasm than usual, but he didn't really have the time to analyze it. He had to get on the next call. He stopped for a second and then dialed Maggie.

"Hey, Maggie."

"Jacob! I thought you'd never call."

What is with every girl saying passive-aggressive shit like that tonight? He was almost at his apology quota. He had said sorry so many times he felt like Olivia. He begrudgingly apologized. "Sorry, long day in New Hampshire."

"Ohh, good times. You staying warm?"

"You know, it went up to thirty today, but the good news is I'll be back soon so hopefully I can catch some real cold weather."

Maggie chuckled and Jacob smiled, remembering that he loved Maggie's ability to still think all of this was interesting and funny.

"So what's up?"

"I need to run something by you. I didn't mention anything to Peter because it's offhand and I didn't want something turning into a story because of me."

"Okay, I'm braced. Hit me with it. We're off the record, right?"

"Hells to the yeah. Way off on this one. So, they're thinking about running a blind item about a married presidential hopeful sleeping with his fundraiser."

Jacob gasped. "What?! And you think it's my guy?"

"Yeah."

"Oh my God, that's hilarious!" "Hilarious" was the wrong word. "Totally ridiculous. That man is twisted tight around Aubrey's finger. And Olivia. She's not—No way. Believe me, *I* would know if she was."

"Jacob Harriston! Are you telling me the story should be about you, not Governor Taylor?"

Jacob laughed and then decided to purposely not deny it. Let her think he and Olivia were sleeping together. It was a lot better than having any rumors about the governor out there, and he knew Maggie would tell others on the down low if even a question arose.

"Maggie, I'm telling you this is not a story!" He said it in gentle-enough protest to suffice as an admittance.

"Wow, I'm glad to hear this. On many levels. I mean I'm glad you're happy. Are you happy?"

"I'm happy," Jacob said. *I'm not lying,* he told himself yet again.

"Plus, well, the truth is," she said, almost whispering, "I really didn't want to believe he was one of those guys."

"He's not, Maggie. He really is better than that."

"Cool. Thanks for calling back. Sorry to stalk you."

As Jacob hung up the phone, he sat back thinking about the conversation and wondering why he had instinctively steered Maggie into thinking he was sleeping with Olivia. He dismissed it quickly.

Two cups of hotel coffee, a.k.a. sludge, later, Jacob picked up a pin from the press secretary, Peter, asking if everything was okay with the *New York Post.* Jacob flashed back to his conversation with Maggie. All fine, it was nothing, he wrote back with a weird feeling that it wasn't completely true. *Where the hell does this insecurity come from? There couldn't be any truth to the rumor, could there?*

No, there could not. He scolded himself for even the thought. Still, he couldn't help but muse a little. *They do really get along well. And Olivia has been on every trip, even the ones she didn't really need to be on. That's just because she's a control freak. She's a control freak!* He continued to yell back and forth to himself in his head. *She would never let go enough to take a risk like having an affair with anyone, much less the governor. She yelled at me when I wanted to sneak into a second movie on the same ticket that one time. She hates when I cut lines. She doesn't break rules. And Landon. He is one of the good guys.* He tried to reassure himself, with more than a hint of doubt. *Sure, he's changing. How could he not? He's steps away from being president of the United States. It's okay that he likes better wine. Who cares? Really. He is not sleeping with Olivia.*

His head then swerved into a tailspin about letting Maggie think he himself was hooking up with Olivia. What if she put something in the paper about Olivia sleeping with him? That would definitely be the last nail in the nice coffin he was building himself where Sophie was concerned. Fortunately, the campaign's pollster, a known insomniac, called, putting an end to the inner tailspin.

"New poll numbers," Richard yelled through the phone, not bothering to say hello.

Pollsters were a bizarrely unique breed—with few exceptions, brilliant, almost mad scientists. Their lives were spent studying people's hearts and heads. They interrogated people, evaluated them, and formulated strategies to sway them. One would think this obsession with human thought and behavior would give them an above-average ability to read people, maybe even relate to them. But that theory had a huge margin of error.

The Taylor campaign's pollster was an extreme specimen of the breed. He was heavyset, with a comb-over of white hair that was usually plastered with the sweat that rolled down his rounded, bespectacled face. For Jacob, talking to him was a learned skill, as Richard was completely impervious to sarcasm and repeated himself in almost an autistic fashion.

Despite being paid hundreds of thousands of dollars by campaigns worldwide, he dressed like a homeless man, always in a suit that was too big, with his dirty white shirt half-tucked-in, the tail hanging out over his pants. In fact, one time, while Richard was on a corner in New York, waiting for one of his billionaire corporate clients, a family walked by him, stopped, turned around, and gave him a dollar. Richard barely noticed them and took the dollar.

"How we looking?" Jacob inquired.

"We're good, good. It's really looking good."

"Oh, yeah?"

Richard spun into a description of the numbers that only the man from *A Beautiful Mind* could have followed completely. Jacob got the important points. Sixty-two percent of the people thought Landon Taylor would take the country in the right direction. Head-to-head, Taylor beat Senator Kramer by three. Not a lot, but enough. More importantly, in Iowa, his negatives, political shorthand for what percentage of the people had a negative reaction to him, were down to 34 percent. Much lower than they had been months before, when the campaign started running ads.

"The ads are working." Jacob lunged back into his couch and threw his tightened fist up in the air.

"The ads are working!" Richard repeated loudly, sounding somewhat proud.

"Great. Can you come in Monday?" Jacob knew Governor Taylor would want the full report in person, every number, every answer, once he heard of the success.

"Yup, yup. I can. I can. Can do. Will do."

"Okay, great. I'll figure out an opening and let you know. Thanks, Richard."

On the off chance Taylor was sleeping, Jacob pinned him: *Spoke to Richard. Up for a while if you want summary.*

His phone rang almost instantaneously.

"What've we got?"

Like the pollster, Taylor didn't say hello, but unlike Richard's failure at normal niceties, Jacob liked Taylor's lapse. Especially after their exchange earlier. Jacob chalked the nongreeting up to the fact that they had gone back to the conversation they were perennially in the middle of. A five-year conversation that didn't warrant hellos or good-byes, just continued.

"Sixty-three right direction with you and negatives are down to thirty-four."

"Hmm. Okay. That's not so bad." When they went over the polls it was one of the rare times Jacob heard insecurity in the governor's voice, even when the numbers were good.

"That's *great*, Gov. The ads are working."

"Good," Taylor repeated contentedly but with a pondering hesitation. "Let's get Richard down next week for the full run-through."

"I've got him coming in Monday." Jacob loved being a step ahead.

"Great. That will be great." The governor paused. "How you feeling? You good?"

"Me? Yeah, I'm good, Gov." This was the equivalent of an apology from Taylor. Jacob knew and appreciated it.

"You feel good about things?"

"I feel great about them. There's a direct bump from the ads, which means we're going in the right direction. If we can drop the negatives another four or five points, this thing is in the bag."

Taylor sat quietly on the other end. No matter how often he did this, Jacob would never get used to it. *"I'm just thinking,"* Taylor had once explained. For Jacob it was just bizarre, and he often had to make sure the call hadn't dropped completely.

"You still there?" he asked.

"I'm here. It feels good out there too, doesn't it? The energy, it's really moving with us."

"Yeah." Jacob paused himself. The voice he recognized had returned to the other end of the line. The one that belonged to the man he admired. The one that carried with it that thing, that magic that won elections. "We've really got it." The words felt weighty coming out of his mouth. It wasn't just Governor Taylor. It was "them." It was the campaign. It was the sum of the parts coming together perfectly.

"Yup." Landon acquiesced. "The magic."

☙

The clock moved slower than seemed possible. Olivia sat at the table with friends in Hazan's, the hottest new restaurant in New York, trying to seem less distracted than she was, which was difficult, considering how distracted she felt. The governor was due in from New Hampshire at nine, which meant they would meet around nine forty-five. All she wanted to do in the meantime was take a nap, but she hadn't been out with Marcy and Katherine in forever, a fact they had reminded her of with great regularity. She had agreed to meet them and three friends and had begun her overdue apology to them by getting them the reservation. Actually, Alek had gotten the reservation, as he was beloved in every hotspot in town, undoubtedly because he handed out hundred-dollar bills with the same regularity with which most people handed out business cards.

She sat listening to their stories, feeling even more isolated than she had before. Tracy's boyfriend had just proposed to her; Stephanie, who had recently launched her new clothing line, was busy planning Tracy's engagement party, which would be when Olivia's Texas event was held. Another missed event. Katherine had just gotten a new job at a swank book company, Amy was going to open a bakery, and Marcy was getting serious with her new boyfriend, whom Olivia had still not even met.

She was too far behind any of the stories to jump into the discussions, and the whole topic of life-changing events made her desperate to tell her own story. She bit into her lip a bit when Marcy gushed about her new man, wishing she could tell them how Landon's eyes seared into her, how he told her she wasn't like anyone he had ever met. The stories she could tell them swirled in her head and she wished quietly that they could meet him. *They would love him. Well, who wouldn't?* She let herself daydream about his walking in and sitting down. *One day they'll meet,* she told herself wistfully as she glanced down at her BlackBerry.

Need some food and a drink. Where can we go?

Here! She continued on with her fantasy but would never actually consider writing that. Just the fact that he wanted to go out somewhere was a step in the right direction. She loved the excitement of going out with him because being in public together—admittedly while trying everything short of wearing camouflage to remain unnoticed—seemed to give the relationship an ounce of reality, at least in her mind. The logistics, though, were less enjoyable. They needed each time to pick a small place that would be totally empty. A few places by her apartment could work, but it was a Saturday night, so she couldn't be sure any of them wouldn't be filled with unemployed recent college grads or young moms on their night out.

Text me when you're in. I'll look for somewhere empty.

She looked up just in time to catch an annoyed gaze from Marcy.

"Sorry," she mouthed.

"Whatever," Marcy said with a dead-eyed glare.

It wasn't only the guilty feeling that came with her sister's annoyance that disturbed Olivia; it was her own internal struggle. She wanted to be interested in the stories being told. She wanted to care about what shoes she should be wearing, how many carats Tracy's ring was (six, she heard at least four times). She wanted to fit in. But the truth was she didn't. All she really wanted to discuss was whether or not the polling in Iowa was accurate and if Senator Kramer's new ad would have any real effect on the numbers. She looked around the table and wished for one moment when she didn't care about any of that more nerdy stuff.

As Marcy turned her head to order dessert, Olivia looked down again at her BlackBerry.

See you in about an hour.

Olivia couldn't help but smile, knowing in an hour she would be sitting across from someone who wanted to talk about everything she wanted to talk about.

Katherine smiled. "What's so fun on the BlackBerry?"

"Oh." Olivia paused, not used to people catching her inappropriate smiles. She missed only a beat. "Looks like Senator Kramer just went down a few points in Iowa."

"Oh," Katherine said, her enthusiasm diffused.

Unfettered, Olivia continued. "Do you know how many more people vote for *American Idol* than for the president of the United States?"

"Hmmm." The faces around the table looked at her with blank stares, the same ones she had seen all her life.

By the time nine fifteen came around, Olivia was itching to leave. The others planned the next stop, at J. Cooper's, a new bar in the Meatpacking District.

Olivia picked at her dessert. "I'm so sorry, but I have to bail after this. I have so much work to do."

Tracy threw up her arm. "But it's Saturday night!"

Stephanie looked over. "You work for Landon Taylor, right?"

"Yup." Olivia nodded.

"Is he the hot one?" Amy added in.

Olivia bobbed her head again and tried to stifle her ear-to-ear grin.

Tracy leaned in toward Olivia. "So have you, like, met him?"

"I have," she said. She could guess the next question before Stephanie asked it. Olivia had heard it a million times before.

"Is the campaign your real job?"

"It is."

Stephanie continued. "They pay you for it?"

"Not enough for the hours she works!" Marcy chimed in.

"That's definitely true." Olivia acquiesced, wondering why no one ever understood that campaigns had paid staffers. "But it is my job, and there's more of it to do tonight than I could hope to get done. Sorry!"

"So have you met his wife, too?" Tracy looked at Olivia impatiently.

"I have."

"I am obsessed with her. Did you see the pictures of them in *Lucky* magazine this month?"

"Yep." *Yes, I did see the pictures of her looking absolutely gorgeous splashed all over the pages of my favorite magazine this month. And their kids.* Olivia tried to disguise her flinching. Seeing the kids was the worst. She thought back to California and how adoringly Margaret had looked up at her dad, and how Dixon had jumped into his arms on the way out. They were hardly ever on the campaign trail, so Olivia could usually live in complete denial of the innocent victims of her actions. But when they were there, her conscience became a monster inside her head. *They won't be victims.* She tried to quiet the inner admonishing voices. *They'll never know.*

"She is sooooo beautiful. The article said they have dinner once a week at IHOP. Is that true? That is so cute."

"Yes, they do." *Not. They do not.* Olivia grinned at the idea that Peter and the press team could get magazines to print pretty much anything.

Olivia's sister put down her coffee. "I have to say, I was totally wrong. He's not one of the bad guys at all. I just read one of the stories about their relationship. He seems completely devoted to her."

Olivia felt a twinge in her jaw. "Yep." *Except he is one of the bad guys. Well, not bad. He's a good guy. They would understand if they knew Aubrey. He's not like those other guys.*

Marcy beamed.

Olivia couldn't imagine what was making her sister look at her with this level of real affection, even . . . was it pride? Marcy laid her hand on Olivia's shoulder. "Do you guys know Olivia is the youngest finance director of a presidential campaign ever? She's in charge of all the money they raise."

Olivia smiled but her chest ached a little. That's who she was supposed to be. She was supposed to be the youngest top fundraiser in the country. She was supposed to be someone her sister was proud of. She was not supposed to be the candidate's girlfriend. The affair.

Her sister continued on.

Each compliment made Olivia feel worse.

"If he wins, Olivia will totally work in the White House!"

"Really?" Tracy asked. "That would be so cool. I bet his wife will be a total Jackie O. She's so fashionable."

Stephanie jumped in. "Hey, do you think you could get her to wear one of my company's sweaters? My friend James at Bulgari said after she wore one of their watches on *The Colbert Report,* it sold out in two days." She touched the pretty, blue cashmere sweater that hung perfectly on her shoulders. The one that would undoubtedly look fabulous on Aubrey.

"Umm, yeah. I could try. I mean, I don't really know how that works." *Let's see, "Hey, Aubrey, I know I'm sleeping with your husband, but could you do me a favor?"* Olivia squirmed in her chair.

"Thank you so much. That would be totally huge. I'll send you a few Monday." Stephanie beamed.

Thankfully, the conversation came to an end when the restaurant owner, a tall, shaggy-looking guy whom Olivia was sure she had met a few times before, came over and let the group know Alek had taken care of their bill. Olivia was thrilled not to have to spend the seventy-five dollars she probably would have had to shell out and also happy knowing the goodwill would definitely get her out of the rest of the night's plans with much less of a fight.

At the door of the restaurant, which was jammed with people trying to get in, Olivia said her final good-byes. She pulled her BlackBerry out and began walking north toward her apartment. Landon had just arrived at Teterboro and would get dropped off at the Brinmore, where he'd "take a stroll." Jacob, the only person who might question the Saturday-evening walkabout, was eagerly off to Sophie's—to take her up on his third "last chance." The governor could fail to come back to the hotel without anyone's noticing.

Olivia walked around until she found a small bar down the street from her apartment. It was a dive bar, with tables lining the side of the room. In the back was a pool table and a Centipede video game. It was totally empty, probably either because it had just emptied out from the night before or because it hadn't been busy since 1982. Same smell either way. She moved swiftly to a table in the back corner, happy to be unnoticed by the young bartender who was busy yelling in an Irish accent at the soccer game on TV. She took the seat facing out so that the governor could have the seat facing the wall. *AHAP. As hidden as possible. The Campaign Lesson that started out in the twenties but seems to be moving up in importance these days.* She laughed, thinking it was probably a rule of chivalry to let the lady take the seat facing out anyway and decided to let that be the explanation she'd go with in her own head, rather than the one that kept him more inconspicuous.

After surveying the single-page, plastic-covered menu—half of which was taken up by types of beer—Olivia quickly ordered from the young, Irish boy who was at the bar. A tequila for herself, and a sauvignon blanc for him.

"Nope." The waiter spoke rapidly.

"Nope?"

"No sauvignon blanc."

"Oh, okay, what other types of wine do you have?"

"White and red," he said, seeming annoyed she had asked. Between each word he uttered, he looked back at the TV as if the game, which Olivia could see was just starting, was in its final moments.

"White sounds great. Thank you. And we'll have sliders, fries, and a quesadilla. Please." It seemed like a good combination of bar food but Olivia held her expectations low, knowing the downside of finding empty restaurants in New York City was that they were usually empty for a reason.

Olivia hoped the drinks and food would come before the governor arrived, so he wouldn't even have to share a glance with the waiter. It seemed possible, as long as the game lasted at least an hour or two, for them to eat completely unseen.

Twenty minutes later, as Olivia snacked on the fries, which were soggy and as terrible as she had predicted, Landon came in. His Great American Vending Machine Company hat, the one he wore because it made him feel more discreet, was pulled down to below his eyebrows, and his leather jacket hung down just past his waist. She raised her hand a bit. Without another person in the bar, any type of signal was wholly unnecessary, but it was the natural extension of her yearning to reach out to him. He nodded and moved forward with the cool grace she loved. As he sat down, he grabbed her thigh and gave it a squeeze.

"Hey, babe." The corners of his lips went up and she could see just a bit of his teeth. It wasn't like the smile that was always plastered on his face for the press. It was special. Just for her.

She lifted one eyebrow, cautious to keep her reaction tame, even though no one was around to see it.

He looked like a kid when he dug into the slider. "Good place," he said, slyly taking a look around.

"If by 'good' you mean 'empty,' then definitely." She leaned into the table and rested her chin on her intertwined fingers, acutely aware of the difference in feeling from one table—with her sister—to this one, and wondered how she could feel so much more like herself with him than she did with friends or even family. Conversation, as it always seemed, came so simply with him. She loved the way he made talking about serious topics over a drink seem so acceptable.

"I really want you to meet this guy Chad. He's doing incredible work on gay marriage out in California," the governor was saying. "He traveled with us all through New Hampshire today. I was so glad to hear someone stand strong publicly on the issue. It's not good enough to be okay with it, to go halfway. Those guys drive me crazy—'Vote for me because I won't be terrible on the issue.' I'd rather lose an election than elect someone who wavers on their morals. It's ludicrous."

She could do little other than gaze dreamily. He was her favorite textbook come to life, packaged with blue eyes. He wanted her to meet Chad. She knew he would probably never introduce her to him, and if he did, it would be as the girl who worked for him, not the woman he loved, but at the moment, none of that mattered. He wanted her to meet him. And him to meet her.

The smell of the bar and the taste of the food couldn't possibly hamper Olivia's evening. To her this bar became perfect. She remembered the first-date stories her friends had told her that night at dinner. She didn't mind first dates—making small talk was a staple of her job, after all. It was second dates that killed her. On the second, she would have to explain further; they would surely find out that she had only read the first paragraph of the five books she had claimed to have read on their first date and they would undoubtedly not understand anything about polls, filings, or primaries. With Landon, there was no second date, no need to do the whole get-to-know-each-other thing. They had known each other for what seemed like at least a lifetime.

"So, we got back some poll numbers." He picked at a slider.

"Oh, yeah? And?"

"Apparently they're pretty good."

"That the technical wording Richard used?"

He laughed. "Well, I won't know all the numbers until Monday but sixty-three percent think we have the right direction for the country."

"That's amazing!" Olivia spoke with French fries in her mouth. She meant to stop chewing but got excited about the numbers, which were incredibly high for so early. Olivia felt a rush of excitement. She was completely confident they would win, but she loved when outside sources confirmed her admittedly biased feelings.

"Yeah." Landon hung his head like a kid who just got socks for Christmas.

"Are you not happy with that?" She didn't understand why he seemed almost upset.

"No. I am. The other part they told me was my Iowa negatives are down to thirty-four. I'm supposed to be glad about that." His voice wandered off with his eyes.

"Is that a question? Because yes, you are supposed to be glad about that. That's down, what, four from last time?"

"Five."

"Okay, so what's with the melancholy?"

"Look something up for me on your BlackBerry, would you?"

Olivia pushed away her drink and held her device at the ready. She was pleased to be needed but baffled, as always, by his total incompetence around computers and BlackBerrys. It wasn't anything atypical. Politicians were often completely helpless with anything technological. Between being on the road all the time and having staffers who printed out or emailed anything and everything they needed, being able to pull up a website or open a document on a phone was just not a necessary skill. Except of course at eleven thirty p.m.

"Okay, shoot. What do you need?"

"What's the population of Iowa?"

"Seriously?"

"Yeah, and don't tell anyone I asked. It's probably something I should know."

"Wait"—she paused with a mocking tone—"you want me to keep a secret?" She opened her eyes wide.

"Very funny, smart-ass."

"Okay, it's three million seven thousand eight hundred and fifty-six."

"Okay, hold on." He squeezed his eyes closed. "Okay, so thirty-four percent of three million seven thousand eight hundred and fifty-six is around one million."

"Okay," she said, not following.

"That means that a million people, no, over a million people don't like me."

"What?"

"More than a million people don't like me! And that's just in Iowa."

"Landon." She sighed, unsure of what to say. She had never thought about polls from a personal perspective.

"*Hmpf.*" He sat thinking again.

"Landon, if everyone liked you, you would not be standing for anything. You don't want crazy extremists liking you. The only people who are universally liked are people who don't make tough choices, take tough stands."

His voice seemed to lighten a little. "Are you telling me my negatives should be higher?"

"Very funny. I'm serious. Why do you always see the cup as half-empty?"

"Why do you always see it as half-full?"

"Touché."

"Actually I think I see it half-empty because it forces me to look for ways to fill it. A constant need to fix. It's what makes me who I am at my core actually. If you see the world as half-full you have less impetus to fix it." He stopped. "Unless you're you. Then you can apparently see the glass as half-full and still want to fill it."

"Ha! You know, I'd probably pour water in a totally full glass."

"It's one of the best things about you. Speaking of full glasses, another?" He lifted up his empty wineglass.

"I don't know—you've got to be awake for the morning shows. We want them to invite you back." She laughed, as it had become a joke between them that his sacrifice was going on the, as he would put it, "morning trash" just so he could spend Saturday nights with her.

He looked at his watch. "It's only eleven forty-five. I've got plenty of time to sleep."

"Not if I can help it!" She smiled slyly and then put her head down, amazed with herself for even saying that. "Oh, wow, this is bad."

"What is?" he asked, totally amused.

"Do you know how comfortable I must be with you to say something like that out loud?"

"Oh, yeah?"

"Yes," she answered, decidedly more serious than him. "Talking to you . . . it's as natural as talking to myself."

"That's a good thing. It's not supposed to be hard to talk to me."

"No, I know, I just . . ." She struggled to explain her feelings, suddenly ironically aware of her vulnerability. "I just want you to know"—she paused, swallowing down the "I love you" that was pushing out of her lips—"I . . . I feel like I fit in when I'm around you. It's not something I thought I'd ever really feel." She tried to make sense of the words that came out discombobulated, as words often do when they're covering up the truth. "You just, you help me to see my place in the world." She giggled self-consciously, "I think that's a song."

He answered in that unwavering tone that just added to the secure feeling he left her with. "If it is, I want the download."

She welcomed the reprieve from seriousness.

"Okay, I guess I'm just saying you make me really happy."

"Oh, Liv," he said bittersweetly, "you make me happier than I ever thought I could be. I wish things were different."

"You do?"

"Of course. I mean, my situation is what it is, unfortunately, and changing it now . . ." He breathed in. "I would never put you through what that would be."

"Oh," she said. It was nice to hear but it left a pang of sadness for what could never be. She grabbed a few French fries and tried to hide her disappointment.

"Hey, baby." He must have sensed her deflation. "I'm here now."

"Right. I know. Let me get us those drinks." She walked over to the bar and to the waiter/bartender, who hadn't looked up from his game since delivering their food. Olivia stood at the bar for a minute before pressing for his attention and furtively lifted her finger to the corner of her eye, where she could feel tears starting to form. She pressed down, grabbing a tear. *What am I doing?* she asked for what seemed like the millionth time. When the bartender finally turned around, Olivia placed her order. She sniffled and stopped trying to answer her lingering questions. Olivia told the bartender she would be back in a minute and went to the bathroom to regain control.

In the bathroom, which was a more grotesque extension of the bar, Olivia looked in the sticker-clad mirror. She ran cold water on her hands and patted her eyes. She breathed in, careful not to look back at her reflection, sure that if she did, she would begin to really cry. *Not being able to look at yourself in a mirror is definitely not a good sign.* But processing that thought seemed too much to handle. She took her hair out of the ponytail she had tied it in and headed back to the table.

Landon looked up as she sat down. "All okay?"

"That bathroom would need to be painted before they could even condemn it!" she said with a laugh.

When the bill finally came, Landon reached into his pocket and pulled out a small wad of money. He counted out forty-two dollars and put it with the check under a salt shaker. She watched with dismay. Of course he had to pay in cash. She was with someone who couldn't leave a paper trail. The tears she had stopped in the bathroom began to form again. Landon caught the look.

"Liv, you okay?"

"All good," she said, feeling the strain on her jaw as she spoke.

They walked out into the dark night, Olivia staying a few steps away from his side. The weather was getting a bit cooler in New York and the wind blew a plastic bag past them on the Upper East Side street. As they walked around a corner, two blocks from her apartment, he grabbed her hand and she entwined her fingers into his. *Damn, he's good*. She knew he sensed even the momentary drop in her mood.

The public display of affection was risky at a minimum, stupid at best, but as she scanned the street for potential spies, still not wanting to let go of his grip, she realized that no one was looking. That was the thing about New York City: the truth was everyone was so self-conscious about their own situation they didn't have the headspace to notice anyone else's. Maybe that held true all over the world. She kept clasping his hand, relishing the new feeling of his fingers interlaced in hers, until they were inside her apartment.

She locked the door. "Listen," he said, grabbing on to her coat and tugging it, leading her into the bedroom. He took the jacket off and let it drop to the floor. Slowly, he pulled her shirt up and over her arms. "I want you to come to Cartagena with us."

"You're kidding." She began to take his coat from him.

"I'm serious. We're going with the Foreign Policy Committee. Their membership is practically all donors, so I can absolutely justify you going."

"Okay, crazy man," she said. She dismissed him as she unbuttoned his shirt. It was the kind of outrageous thing he might say to make her know he would like her to go, also knowing full well she would shoot down the idea as too reckless.

"Picture this—you and me on a beach in Colombia, away from the press, the world."

"It's a campaign trip! Not a vacation!"

As ridiculous as it was, she couldn't imagine anything better.

"Do you want to go?"

"Landon!"

"Do you want to go?" he repeated with seriousness, grabbing her shoulders.

"Of course I want to go." She held his gaze, knowing that was the wrong answer and wishing the right answers, the ones she knew she *should* give, were easier to come by.

FIFTEEN

When the word "delayed" popped up next to their flight number it seemed to Jacob apropos, if not expected. This was just how things were going.

"I'm just going to grab a coffee. Anyone want anything?" The team—Governor Taylor; Billy; Michael Maddox, who was the head of the Foreign Policy Committee, the group sponsoring the trip; and, of course, Olivia—looked up at him sort of blankly and declined.

Jacob growled to himself as he ruminated on Olivia's presence there. She was the current golden child of the campaign, which shouldn't have bothered him as much as it did, but it had started to drive him insane. He couldn't shake his conversation with Maggie about the rumor. *They're not sleeping together,* he told himself repeatedly in an attempt to force the thought out of his head. *It's just lists,* he reiterated, *just fundraising*. The thoughts grumbled in his head as he rehashed his conversation a week earlier with the governor.

"It's a complete waste of money and the campaign's time to bring Olivia!" Jacob had yelled.

"*My* campaign!" the governor had barked back. "It's *my* campaign time and money. End of story."

Jacob had appealed to Billy, hoping it wasn't the complete end of the debate, but Billy, ever the peacemaker, sided with the governor. Even Billy had changed, it seemed to Jacob. He was always demure, respectful, but he used to be able to tell the governor when he was wrong. Not anymore. The governor had become more brazenly insolent to everyone, even Billy.

Jacob walked past the bookstore and stopped at the display by the door. In between the newest Candace Bushnell and James Patterson books sat stacks of *Toward Tomorrow*, the book by the new senator Henry Morris. Jacob had met Senator Morris in DC a few weeks back. The book was the senator's blueprint for a new way to approach campaigns and government. Jacob had been enthralled by his speech at the Democratic Press Club and the two had wound up talking through a dinner afterward. Jacob felt an instant bond with the guy and saw in him a flicker of the old Landon, the one not skewed by campaigns and by the glamour of fundraising.

Jacob bought a coffee, a bag of sweet potato chips—so he could tell his mom he was eating something healthy—and the book. He headed back to the seats where the team was waiting. Taylor was haranguing Billy to try to get them moved to first class and Billy was nodding with submissiveness. Jacob softly shook his head, unnoticed by the governor, and cracked the book's spine.

⚭

They had only been in Cartagena for forty-eight hours and already Olivia was exhausted. She sat on the patio of the guest quarters of the ambassador's home, staring out at the red sky, and decided the night was not as terrible as she had first thought it would be. She had spent the last few hours thoroughly annoyed that she wasn't included in the dinner at the main house, which was five miles down the stone road, along the beach. The ambassador was a young woman, Maria Teresa. She and her husband, Raj, a well-known American businessman, were famous for throwing the most fabulous dinner parties in all of South America, and tonight's plans sounded like they would be no exception. It was offensive that Jacob had told Olivia it wasn't appropriate for her to attend. She knew he didn't want her on this trip and excluding her from dinner was his chance to slap back after losing the battle over her coming at all. The truth, though, was that she really felt more embarrassed and guilty than she was angry.

It was far from appropriate for her to be along. She knew that. If she were signing the budgets or reporting on the governor, she would have raised the alarm over such a choice. She had decided to fight to come, though, because of her heart. How could she not? Four days in the most romantic place she could imagine, with the man she loved. Logic just seemed to fall down a few notches on the priority ladder.

She loved sitting next to him on the plane, daydreaming about going off with just him. And the moments they caught together—the sides of their legs touching in the backseat of the SUV, walking too close in the streets of the Old City—were better than she could have imagined. But she couldn't help but be swung back into reality every time she caught one of Jacob's knowing looks. He was like the conscience on her shoulder, seemingly more aware than she knew he could possibly be. His stares carried a disappointment that seeped through the air. She knew he had voiced concern with her coming, "concern" being Landon's euphemism for what was probably actually rage. But when Jacob had pulled her aside and told her to stay back tonight, it was the first time he had confronted her directly.

Giving in, she had sulked back at her room and pulled up her emails, deciding she would at least get work done. Emails distracted her from thinking about what she was doing in Cartagena and how it could ruin the campaign, Jacob, Landon. It could ruin everything that meant anything to her.

It wasn't until seven p.m. that a woman came to her room with dinner. She wasn't sure who had ordered it—she had assumed she'd been sent to her room without dinner—but she opened the door and in came the small, stocky woman. She looked around sixty and her hair was tied back in a series of beautiful braids fashioned into a bun and accented with small flowers. Her face had soft curves and wide black eyes that made her appear kind. She pushed a large, old-fashioned silver cart that looked like it came directly from the set of a Humphrey Bogart movie. On it was ceviche served in a thick and wide margarita glass, slivers of avocado covering the pink of the tuna. Two other large plates with silver lids sat next to a basket of bread that could have lasted Olivia for days. There was one large bottle of water and a full pitcher of the delicious sangria-like punch they had been served upon arrival.

It had a stream of coconut rum in it that gave it a perfect tropical twist. The woman took in Olivia's room with a kind of pity, noticing the desk facing the wall, complete with papers, Diet Coke, and Doritos.

"*Afuera?*" she asked, pointing to the door to translate. Without waiting for an answer she moved that way and pushed the cart outside to the patio. The warm breeze blew in, bringing with it a trace of the ocean air. The sky was so red it almost lit up the room. Olivia slowly lowered her head, acknowledging that she had been holding on to her grudge so tightly she'd almost forgot where she was. She followed the woman outside and looked around in amazement.

The woman grinned and spoke in a heavy accent. "From Signora Ambassador."

"*Muchas gracias,*" Olivia said, bowing her head a bit, thankful for the food and even more for the wake-up call.

Olivia sat and sipped the punch, staring happily at the sky, with the realization that it was actually a nice thing to have been left behind. Instead of being at some stuffy dinner where it mattered what fork you used and how straight you sat, she could dine without giving a thought to who she was or how she was acting, something she realized had become a constant in her life.

The loneliness and anger seemed to crash away with the waves that rose up against the rocky beach. She breathed in; pulled her knees up to her chest, pleased to be sitting so improperly and comfortably at a table; and looked out to the east. Her toes pressed down against the cool metal of the chair. The land in front of her wrapped around a bit and she could see the stone walls of the old city. The tops of the buildings were illuminated by what looked like perfect white Christmas lights that connected the bright red of the sky with the gray stone and dark water. As the red turned almost to purple, she opened the silver tray in front of her and found a beautiful lobster, all the meat taken out of the shell and lying atop a corn-and-mango mix. The smell of the butter that was drizzled over it mixed with the warm, fresh air and Olivia breathed in and out, appreciating the silence and feeling a sense of peace. She was in Cartagena, the finance director of a presidential campaign, *the youngest finance director ever.* More importantly, she was in love with a man who loved her.

"A peso for your thoughts?"

She looked up as if she were seeing a mirage. Landon stood at the edge of the patio in his khakis. A crisp white shirt hung down beneath a perfect blue blazer. Two days of sun had added a hint of a tan to his face, making his blue eyes look almost crystal. His hair flopped down as he smiled and the sight sent a tingle down Olivia's body.

"What are you doing here?"

"It's the strangest thing. I got to dinner and just had this aching in my stomach. So naturally I had to excuse myself after cocktails."

"Oh no," Olivia said with fake concern, "not feeling well, huh?" She didn't even care that she couldn't contain her giddiness, which she figured was spread across her face, or that he had run out on a very important dinner.

"Well, see, that's the thing." He approached her chair with deliberate slowness. "I started up to my room and couldn't help but see your light on. And wouldn't you know, at the edge of your patio my ache started to disappear." He moved in toward her and kissed her with a sweet passion that felt as new and sexy as the Colombian air.

"Isn't that remarkable?" She kissed him back. "So I suppose you'll need to eat somewhere?"

"I suppose I'll need to eat here. You up for company?"

Landon sat down and Olivia poured him part of her punch.

"So what was the thought going on in there before I interrupted?" He leaned over and tapped his finger lightly on her head.

"Actually I was just thinking I was happy by myself."

"Ouch." He pulled away from her with fabricated concern.

"No, no," she said to reassure him, "not like that. Obviously I'm much happier with you here."

"Well, that's a relief."

"I just mean I was happy sitting with myself, which I don't think I've ever been before."

"That makes sense," he said. "You've come into your own. Once you get to a point of knowing yourself on a deeper level it's easier to be alone without being lonely."

"Yeah," she agreed, then paused gratefully. "It's amazing how you do that."

"Do what?"

"You add reason to my words. It's why I just say what comes to mind. I don't have to do all the thinking, because you understand before I even explain."

"It helps that your words are always knee-deep in reason."

"No, they are not!"

"Olivia," he said with a serious sincerity, "for as much as you know yourself, and I believe you do, there's so much beauty and intelligence that you miss about yourself."

Olivia was more than flustered; she was a bit in awe. Whatever insecurities she had now melted away in his words. "You know, you actually make me believe that. You make me feel smarter and more beautiful than I have ever felt."

He looked at ease with the thoughts that she viewed as so raw and vulnerable.

"That's what love is, Liv. It's seeing the true beauty of someone and loving them enough to help them see it. That's why real love brings out the best in people. It amplifies the best part of who they are."

There it was. The L-word. He had said it at least three times with such simple honesty.

Olivia put down her glass and stared at him across the table. The sun had gone down and the sky behind him was perfectly dark. The stone wall around the patio now seemed to glow with glistening gold. The breeze blew his hair just a bit but was barely strong enough to move a napkin. She gulped, feeling a dryness in her mouth that seemed to be the result of her breath being taken away.

"I love you, Landon," she said, her voice shaking with vulnerable truth. He looked up at her, almost unaware of the impact of what he had said. Without a word he stood and took her hand.

"Come with me." He led her a few steps off the patio to the rocky beach.

"Where are we going?"

"Just come."

Olivia followed, glad at least not to be stuck in the susceptible silence of the table. As they stepped from the rocks onto a small sand path, Landon started running, grasping her hand tightly. They sprinted out across the sand, Olivia feeling the perfect coolness underfoot and exhilarated at the idea of running with no clue where she was going. He could take her anywhere. Just before they reached the water, they came to a small hut built into one of the rocks. It had two massage tables in the middle and huge vases of orchids lining the inside walls. Olivia recognized them from the tour the ambassador had taken them on the day before. "Our national flower, the orchid *Cattleya trianae*," Maria Teresa had explained. "I was married to Raj among thousands of them."

As Olivia had listened, imagining herself and Landon surrounded by the gorgeous purple of the flower, he had inconspicuously grabbed her hand. Just for a moment. And now, here they were. Together—alone—among the orchids. Just as she had imagined. Landon led her in, still gripping her hand. As they stood almost enclosed in the rocks, the water crashed up against the shore, each wave feeling like it extended into a rush inside her. The smell of the salt water mixed with the lavender of the massage oils ever present in the enclave.

"I love you, Liv. I love you like I've never loved anyone."

When his arms fell down around her, her eyes closed tightly. It was as if the world completely disappeared.

SIXTEEN

Jacob sat at the bar of the Iowa hotel as he watched the hands on the clock tick toward ten p.m. The nondescript bar was empty, save for the three tourist-type women who looked as if they had been invited to an ugly-sweater party. They carefully sipped their cosmos and fawned over the bartender, who was supposed to be getting the drinks that Jacob had ordered. Jacob agonized, feeling like he did the morning he had to take his SATs. *Impending doom,* he thought, knowing that either way this went, it wouldn't be good. He'd thought about confronting the governor and Olivia all the way home from Cartagena and then for the week since, but he had decided for sure to ask the question after he saw Olivia walk out of that elevator bank earlier that morning.

He cursed Maggie for bringing the idea of Landon and Olivia up at all, wishing he could go back to what he now recognized as his oblivion. Maybe if it hadn't been in the back of his head he wouldn't have noticed the voices coming from Olivia's room when they got back from the ambassador's dinner. He wouldn't have caught a glimpse of Landon grabbing Olivia's hand while they walked through that stupid flower museum. He looked over at the elevator banks, remembering Olivia walking out of the wrong one that morning, nearly fifteen hours ago. He shook his head, trying to get the affirming image out, knowing he needed to get the truth. He tried to play out in his head how it would go.

He knew he was supposed to want the answer to be "It is not happening," doesn't read "It is happening" so he could walk away from the campaign out of principle. The truth, though, was that he knew it was happening and he wanted to help. To calm, contain, and control. If the affair and maybe even love were confirmed, Jacob could help them conceal it, and would do a better job than they were doing. *I'm going to help someone have an affair? What kind of person does that? I'm an accomplice.* His mind flashed to Aubrey. He couldn't even imagine what she would do if she found out. *She'd kill him. And me for helping it happen.* Then he rethought it. *It's not like she's not doing the same thing. What if she knows? What if she knows about Taylor and he knows about her? What if they have a deal? Ugh. That's worse.*

He ordered a shot of tequila, needing more time to process the ideas, even in his own head. How could he want to help them? How could he want to cover up lies? *Landon Taylor—one of the good guys. And Olivia. My hire. My friend. All of them have been lying about everything. Fatally. This could kill us all.* He thought about Aubrey's temper again. *Literally.*

He waved to the bartender, who was flirting with the sweater-clad women even more raucously. "One more shot, please." He had downed the first one as soon as he got it.

He's a good politician, Jacob told himself, *and there's too much at stake.* He thought of how much the world had changed for the worse under the current leadership and how Jacob's decisions, his actions, could keep that administration in power. Even though it seemed morally incongruous, he wasn't ready to risk that. This wasn't just his job. This was his country. Resolute in that, he took a swig of his tequila, grabbed the two glasses of wine, and headed upstairs.

He stood at the door, drinks in hand, and looked at the number. This was it. The moment he would accuse his boss, his hero, of cheating with one of his best friends. And putting the fate of the country in the balance. He hesitated. He closed his eyes.

The door opened the second Jacob knocked. The governor stood without his shoes on, seeming shorter. His hair hung a little over his eyes. *We need to schedule a haircut,* Jacob thought, and then scolded himself for contemplating a detail like that at a time like this.

"What's this you need to talk about?" the governor asked.

"Could I come in?"

"Of course. Wow. Sounds serious."

The governor pulled the door open and walked to a chair by the window, the one that made his room a suite. Jacob followed, wishing he had brought the bottle of tequila with him. Jacob put the wine-glasses on the table and sat down on the bed. "I don't know how to say this," he said.

"Spit it out. When have you ever had a problem saying anything?"

Jacob looked at the governor. What did he hope to see? *Does the governor look nervous? Like something is weighing on his mind? Does he need my help?* "Governor, are you having an affair with Olivia?"

The governor looked at him angrily. "What?!"

This was not the reaction Jacob had practiced for. *Why didn't I think he might be angry?* He had prepared for laughter if it wasn't true, sadness if it was, maybe even anxiety.

Instead, the governor lunged forward in his chair.

I'm right to be bringing this up, Jacob reminded himself. *He needs my help. I'm the one to tell him not to get on that flight.*

"Gov." Jacob searched for a shred of their old friendship some-where in Taylor's eyes. "It's okay. I know you are. I want—"

"Jacob." The governor sat back more slowly and in a calmer fash-ion, but he was looking away. "That's ridiculous."

"I—"

"Please. We've had long days. You're tired. You don't know what you're talking about."

"Gov, I saw her coming out of the elevator bank this morning. And the *Post* had a rumor of it that I shot down."

The governor crossed his legs and his arms. "Since when do you base your knowledge on *Post* rumors? Whose team are you on?"

"Gov," he pleaded, knowing he shouldn't have mentioned the *Post*. He tried to catch the governor's eyes. *He can't look me in the eye. Damn it. He's lying.*

"Jacob, this is stupid. Olivia dropped off a copy of the budget this morning. I'm sure that is when you saw her."

This was not the answer Jacob wanted on so many levels. It was spin. *Landon's spin.*

He stood up. "Okay, boss." He wanted to be careful not to apologize or agree. *If I have to be on the outside at least he's going to know I know.* "You asked me to step up once. You said you needed me to be in control. I was just trying to do that."

"I said step up, not step out." The governor stood too, still avoiding eye contact. "Just try to do your job, Jacob." He tried to take the edge off in a way that had the opposite effect. Scratching the back of his head, he walked to the door and opened it. "You're doing great. Just keep your eye on the ball. I still need you."

"Right." Jacob looked at him squarely in the eye. He was infuriated. And crushed. "It's a good thing, you know, because you and Mrs. Taylor have such a *special* relationship. I mean, I was worried about her and Secretary Tiwali, but I was probably just as wrong in that case. Eye on the ball from now on."

"Okay." The Governor looked as pale and worried as Jacob had wanted him to be at the beginning of the conversation. Jacob hadn't wanted to resort to something so passive-aggressive but it just came out. *That was more aggressive than passive anyway,* he thought.

"Step it up," Jacob mumbled to himself as the door closed behind him.

⌥⌥⌥

Waking up had rarely been so excruciating. Olivia tried to reach for her BlackBerry to silence the annoying alarm that was trying to alert her to the fact that it was ten after six, but her arms felt as if they had been weighed down with dumbbells. *Mono of the arms.* She turned over, flapping her right wrist down off the side of the bed, attempting to talk her muscles into moving. The knowledge that there was no time in the foreseeable future to catch up on the missing hours of sleep made it even harder to succumb to the day's start. She remembered her brother telling her she lived every day like it was Wednesday, equally far from and to the weekend. He couldn't have been more right.

She pushed on the remote and the familiar voices of CNN started to register as she slowly forced her obstinate eyes to open. *Six eighteen. Okay, I'll just sleep until six twenty-five. Who am I kidding? I won't wake back up in . . . How many minutes is that? Oh God, I can't do simple math anymore. Seven minutes. What difference is seven minutes going to make?*

She looked begrudgingly at the clock. *Six minutes.* The figures on TV started to come into focus. Aubrey and Landon. The reporter pointed to the IHOP where the "perfect power couple" was having breakfast. *Good morning to me.*

She rolled off to the side, feeling as if she were leaving her long-distance lover, and took her BlackBerry into her hand, aware that even it seemed heavy this morning.

She scrolled down through the twelve new messages, angry at the fact that there could be twelve new messages between the hours of two and six, and even angrier that none of them were red messages from Landon. It had been three weeks since Cartagena, also known, to no one but her, as the Best Four Days of Her Life. Life since then had changed drastically.

She hated to admit it, but the amount of work she had missed while away, as Jacob predicted, had taken an intense toll on the fundraising efforts. Two events had been dropped completely because the hosts had not heard from her, and the host committee for their New York gala event hadn't come together as it should have. This would undoubtedly leave an irreparable budget hole.

Getting into the shower, she felt her head spin. With every drop of water she seemed to remember a new thing to do. Fearing her memory would fail her, she leaned out, wiped off her hand, and typed notes into her BlackBerry. She tried to focus on the notes and the growing fundraising hole, but undermining everything was the wrenching feeling that her relationship with the love of her life, the one that had seemed to hit a peak of perfection just twenty-two days ago, was disappearing before her eyes.

She hadn't heard from Landon in three days. She thought nothing of it when she didn't hear from him the first twenty-five hours after they returned, but then his pins started to come in more sporadically. He had taken her on the trip to Iowa, but since then it had been nothing but bad news. No I-love-yous. Barely even a "sweet dreams." Back and forth in her mind she swerved, trying to play it cool, then wondering if everything was okay, and on and on. Last weekend he'd canceled his trip to New York with a **Sorry, Jacob says too many morning shows** pin. When she replied with a **Disappointed**, he sent: **Thinking about you, and you know what they say, it's the thought that counts.** She tried, as she had been doing since they returned, to figure out what had gone wrong.

Every time she spoke to her sister she longed to seek her advice. Surely someone would know what to do. But the secrets she had kept for months had walled her in isolation. The real shift, she decided as she entered her office, came when Aubrey decided to travel with him. She was everywhere, at the speeches, the dinners. And worse, when the Taylors were on the road and Olivia was back home, Olivia could count on each newspaper and TV channel to bring her a live feed of Aubrey and Landon's every move. Olivia knew Landon had to have been part of the decision to have Aubrey travel more. It felt like a dagger to the heart. And that made Olivia feel even guiltier. She reminded herself painfully that she was the dagger, not Aubrey. It was Aubrey's relationship she was ruining, not the other way around.

What am I doing? He should *be with her, not me.* These thoughts were repeatedly interspersed with the chiding ones that screamed at her for her overdramatization. *So he's not writing you every minute or calling? He's running for president. He has a few other things on his mind.*

Neither of these theories, nor the hundreds of other guilt-ridden, self-deprecating ones, did anything to alleviate the fact that she felt as if a jackhammer were going off in the middle of her chest. She tried to focus on the job ahead. With six weeks to go, she still needed to bring in seven hundred and fifty thousand dollars.

When she saw his number flashing on her BlackBerry that evening, she answered with irritation. "Hey, stranger," she said.

"Hey, babe." The sound of exasperation in his voice made her regret the way she had answered.

"You okay?"

"I gotta tell you, babe, I am tired. And I got this cold."

He sounded hoarse. *Of course he hasn't called, he's sick!*

"A cold? That sucks. You sound terrible. Sorry." It was so annoyingly hard to stay angry with him.

As he spoke about Iowa, Georgia, and New Hampshire, she couldn't help but feel glad to be included, to feel like she still had a piece of him.

"Landon," she said somewhat weakly as they neared the end of the conversation, "I miss you."

"Oh, baby," he replied. It sounded like reciprocal longing. "You don't know how much I miss you. I cannot wait to be back in that bed of yours. I'm coming in for the shows on Sunday."

"Can you come Saturday night?" She hated sounding needy but she wanted him there.

"I can't, baby. I have this thing." Olivia hated the sound of the excuse, not only because he wasn't making the same effort he used to make to be by her side, but also because he was being vague about the reason, and the only other times she remembered vagueness escaping his lips was when he was talking to someone else about time he was spending with her. She hated knowing how easy it was for him to lie.

"Okay," she said, conceding, "see you Sunday then?"

"Yes, ma'am." He added in a "Love you, babe" quickly. She hung up the phone, only minimally aware of how far out on a lonely limb she was hanging. She held her pillow close to her chest, fragile enough to feel comforted that the person she shared her secret with at least remembered there was a secret to share.

༄

By the time Sunday came, Olivia was on her last nerve and his pin worked it further.

I'm just wrapping up, will be there in 20/25.

Olivia sat down on the couch. *Twenty, twenty-five minutes?* She had been watching the show. His segment had ended at least ten minutes ago. *It's a whole process,* she reminded herself. *He takes forever to get anywhere.* As much as she tried to reassure herself, she couldn't shake the feeling that he was lying. Maybe it had been pretaped. It had to be on a little bit of a delay, right? Which would leave him more than forty minutes. Her mind raced to theories of where he could be. *Maybe there's someone else. That clothing designer, Edie, was on the show too. She's so pretty. Maybe he's sleeping with her.* She seemed to remember Page Six saying that before she had even met him. Maybe he did this all the time. Maybe she was one of many.

Oh, Olivia, what are you doing? She changed her shirt for the fourth time. She stood at her closet, hating the small, cluttered space. Clothes hung half on hangers, others fell down over the mess of shoes at the bottom so you could hardly see anything.

"Argh." She threw a hanger down in disgust. "Why is it such a mess? Why can't I see anything?"

As she bent to pick up a few shirts, she thought through the absurdity of wanting exclusivity with a married man. *That would be classic. Hey, married man, do you want to be exclusive with me? I mean aside from your wife?*

She shook her head. Everything had turned terrible. Even if Landon wasn't seeing someone else, the simple fact that she was questioning whether or not he was pointed to a problem. The fact that her mind instantly went to how many lies he could tell when she heard the phrase "be there in twenty minutes" was a problem. That wasn't the person she wanted to be and those weren't the thoughts she wanted to have. Unfortunately, it was consuming her mind. She was around so many secrets, keeping so many secrets, she couldn't fathom everyone not having as many. Twenty minutes later, expecting him to walk in, she heard the buzzing of a pin instead of a door buzzer.

Babe, got caught up here. Can we meet at Brinmore instead?

"Ugh!" she yelled again, to no one.

⌒ᴍᴍᴖ

Another twenty minutes later she sat in the Brinmore restaurant waiting, feeling tired and annoyed that he wasn't already in the seat across from her, reassuring her that everything would be okay.

"Hey, Marco. Sorry." She felt like a burden for tying up a table for so long without ordering anything. Even Jo's empathetic smile seemed to be waning.

"No problem. Can I get you something while you wait?"

"Sure. Ummm . . . a coffee would be great." She stammered, "And . . . umm . . . the boss should be here any minute, so one for him would be great too."

"Big-time!" Marco said happily, and disappeared.

She looked down at her BlackBerry, considering writing Landon a pin, and then heard his voice. She smiled at the familiar tone but looked up to see him walking in with another couple.

"Olivia!" He walked toward the table with the people, who were dressed as if they had just come from Sunday Mass. "These are my good friends Nora and Alex from Atlanta! We haven't seen each other in years and we bumped into each other right in the lobby. Is that a small world or what?"

"The smallest!" Olivia said, trying to sound enthusiastic and standing to shake their hands. She wished she had worn something more businesslike than her gray V-neck T-shirt.

"Nora, Alex, this is Olivia Greenley, my finance director. She works for me. She's one of the best fundraisers in the business."

Olivia smiled, then looked down at her bag, wishing it, like her shirt, would have given even the slightest appearance of having business use. She kicked it slyly under her seat and tried to chime in gleefully as Landon explained the great trajectory of the campaign.

While he talked, she looked at Landon, wistfully remembering when they first met. She had been so proud to be in public with him then. She had been thrilled to be seen as his confidante in front of other people. She distinctly remembered seeing people staring, clamoring to get a moment with him and the total elation she felt at being the person by his side. So much of his persona that she loved had slipped away. Now she longed to be alone with him, to be sitting here or in her apartment, or anyplace where they could have that intimacy they used to have. *The one he got lost in.*

"Oh, Olivia, you had to have seen their faces!" The governor slapped his knee loudly, bringing her back to the conversation. She wondered if he knew she was completely zoned out.

"I can just imagine!" she said without hesitation and without a clue of what they were talking about. "I can just imagine" was one of those great phrases that covered you no matter what the story was.

"I mean Aubrey and I . . . anyone who knows my wife . . . well, you know Aubrey." The words in between "my wife" and "Aubrey" seemed fewer than those between "Olivia" and "works for me."

Then it got worse. Landon started pulling out pictures of his kids from his wallet. Her stomach churned. *It's literally making me sick. Not it. Him. Me. This situation. I can't believe I'm doing this to kids.*

When the four of them got up to leave forty minutes later, Olivia's cheeks hurt from her forced smile. She wished she had just stayed in the office to work. The minute the governor's friends walked around the corner and out the front door of the hotel, Landon leaned in toward her. "Sakes alive, baby, you look gorgeous." He looked her up and down. "I thought they'd never leave us alone."

Olivia thought he must have been at an alternate table or in an alternate universe. "Seriously?"

"What, baby?" he whispered, looking around. She knew he was checking to be sure no one caught her inappropriate, annoyed look. That infuriated her even more.

"Please stop calling me 'baby'."

He leaned toward her and slipped his arm around her shoulder. "Feisty this morning, huh?" His words fell with an annoyingly teasing tone.

"I waited an hour and a half for you between home and here. And then I listened to you spend an hour clarifying the fact that Aubrey's your wife and I work for you. I think 'pissed' is a better word."

"Babe—" He caught himself midword. "Liv, what could I do? They took forever getting me off the set, and then Nora and Alex were right outside the hotel! I couldn't just ignore them."

"It really took you an hour to get out of there?"

"Scout's honor. Where else would I go?"

"Who knows where you would go." She said the words bluntly, with a sharp edge.

He looked at her seriously. "Liv, you know you're the only person I ever want to go see. You know me, baby."

"Yeah." She couldn't help but let her annoyance simmer over. "Unfortunately, I know how well you lie."

The governor sat back in his chair, looking surprised at her boldness. She felt a pang of guilt at being mean. Who was she to talk any-way? She was lying just as much as he was.

"Let's not do this here." He waved over to Marco for a check. "Come on, I have a dayroom."

She bit her tongue, hating the idea of the "dayroom" more than ever.

Marco came over. "You're all set, boss. No check."

"Thanks, Marco." The governor pulled a twenty from his wallet and left it on the table.

"Always my pleasure, boss." As Olivia started to get up, Marco turned to her and asked, "All okay, girly?"

She immediately plastered on a grin and picked up her tone. "Oh yeah, totally. All is good, Marco. Thanks. I'm just tired today!"

Marco smiled right back. "Good, good. Sleep after the election, right?"

"You got it!"

She and Landon walked out of the lounge to the lobby and Olivia turned to the governor, her smile still glued to her face. "I'm going to just go home. Clearly I'm not myself today."

He furrowed his brow. "Olivia." He sounded like a mad parent scolding a kid. "Let's not make more of a scene. Just come up and we can talk about it."

"Fine." She followed him into the elevator, knowing she shouldn't go, but she needed more of the conversation.

As they stepped into the room, he closed the door behind her. Olivia shook her head, not knowing which argument to go with first. "I just—"

He cut her off with a hug. "Baby, I'm so sorry."

There were a million things she wanted to say but at first all she could do was bite her lip to prevent herself from crying. "It just sucks. You know, I mean, this is wrong. And I deserve more," she said.

"I know you do. God." He didn't let her go. "You deserve so much more."

"We all do. You do. Aubrey does. *Your kids do.*"

Landon closed his eyes and shook his head but would not release his hold on her.

She hit her head into his chest. "When did I become this? When did I become the other woman?" She didn't want to be saying this to him but she had no one else to say it to.

"You're not the other woman."

"Yes, I am."

"You have my heart."

Tears started to stream down her face. She wanted his heart. She wanted to stay in his embrace forever. She wanted the rest of the world, with all its complications, to just go away. "It's not enough."

He held her tighter. "I know."

಄ಮಾ

She walked down the subway steps, recognizing it was probably not the safest idea to be taking the subway home from work at quarter to one in the morning. *Who cares,* she thought, figuring she had enough pent-up anger to fight off anyone trying to attack her anyway. *And I'm going from midtown to the Upper East Side,* she reminded herself. *It's not exactly the most dangerous route in the world.*

When she got to the platform, she simmered in annoyance. The governor had left earlier in the day for his all-American holiday vacation to the Grand Canyon with the family. She knew she had no right to be irritated, but the jealousy brewed anyway. On top of that, they were in real trouble for the filing.

As she waited for the train, she paced, going over names of potential saviors in her head. They were $180,000 away from their goal—$180,000 that had already been spent. On staff in Iowa, on media, on things that couldn't be returned. She had insisted to everyone all day that the last dollars were a cinch, and with every affirmation, she felt as though she were digging one more level down in the ditch she was making. *Someone has to come through. They have to.*

When the train finally arrived, she took a seat, thinking of the first conversation she had with Landon. *"I need you to tell me if we're going to miss our numbers,"* he had said. Maybe she should have said something back then but she hadn't. *Screw him.* He had totally abandoned her. On the other hand, this was her job. Not reaching the numbers was not an option.

She pulled out a list from her bag and started writing names of other people she could call. *I'll do this,* she told herself.

As she walked out of the subway, her BlackBerry started buzzing with loads of messages: Phil Sofia couldn't get his check in by the thirty-first; Dave and Lauren had left for Paris already; out-of-office reply from the Comanduccis; Morris Gregerson wouldn't be a host for the event; Aiden, Hailey, Riley, and Amy were all unavailable to talk today; Simon and Jonah were in London for the holiday, so they wouldn't get their contributions in before the New Year.

Olivia pressed her teeth together as hard as she could. Then the red message came through.

Hello there.

"You have to be kidding me," she said aloud.

Another one came in a minute later.

How you doing?

How am I doing? she thought. *I'm terrible! Thanks for checking in on the life you ruined.* She knew he'd never stop; he could be as stubborn as Ferris Bueller calling Cameron if she didn't respond. Like clockwork, her BlackBerry buzzed with a private number calling. She hit IGNORE as fast as she could, so maybe he would think she was sleeping. She definitely was in no mood to talk. Again he called. She wondered what it would take to report him as a stalker.

Sorry I missed you. Just got out of subway. She sent it hoping a response would put a stop to his efforts, but it didn't.

The BlackBerry buzzed again. She looked down, refusing to pick up the call, knowing it would be impossible not to fall apart in either anger or sadness and knowing she would regret it in the morning.

Baby, pick up.

I'm really tired. Talk tomorrow?

Okay. Don't go on the subway by yourself so late. Thinking of you. Miss you.

Okay? she thought. *Everything is definitely not okay.*

It took everything in her not to throw the BlackBerry on the pavement. *I wouldn't have had to take the subway if I wasn't working twenty-four/seven on your campaign or if you hadn't held my last two paychecks. And don't call me baby!* She fantasized about writing that and so much more but would not consider letting her emotions overrun her logic. Plus he was her boss. That was really the bottom line. That was why she had to end the relationship for good this time. She grabbed her mail from her tiny metal mailbox and threw it into her bag, walking up the stairs with so little energy that she had to take a breath between each step. When she got in, she dropped her bag and stared into the emptiness of her refrigerator. She knew she should have stopped downstairs for food, but the idea of walking the stairs one more time was too much to take, and her hunger wasn't enough to warrant the trip.

She splashed water on her face and swished mouthwash around in her mouth. *Good job, Olivia, not only will you be out of a job in no time, but you'll have no teeth and adult acne.*

She straightened up in the mirror and got out her face wash determined to put a stop to the little pity party she was throwing herself. She would take care of herself. She washed her face thoroughly, brushed her teeth, and put on her favorite comfy blue flannel pajamas.

It will be okay, she told herself. *You can do this.*

She grabbed the mail and flopped onto her bed. Junk mail covered up a *Newsweek* magazine and the minute she saw it she wished she hadn't looked. There on the cover were Landon and Aubrey looking perfectly gorgeous together. The top read AMERICA'S NEW PERFECT PAIR, and the bottom had a line about their perfect family vacation.

I will not break, Olivia told herself as she pushed the magazine onto her night table. She started opening the rest of the mail. An envelope full of coupons kept her attention for a minute as she looked through the things she would definitely do as soon as the campaign was over, as soon as she had some money. Then two notes from her grandma and her aunt, thanking her for the Christmas presents, sorry she missed so much of Christmas, and telling her how worried they were about her, how pale and tired she looked. She felt another dose of tension creep into her aching neck. The last piece of mail was an envelope from her old car insurance company. She hadn't owned a car for as long as she lived in the city. *Oh, please don't let it be another bill,* she thought.

Just a piece of paper, she realized with a sigh of relief. Then she read down.

Dear Ms. Greenley,

We regret to inform you of the death of your insurance agent, Eugene
Tesserman. Eugene will be missed and our thoughts are with his family.

We assure you service will be uninterrupted and a new agent will
be in touch shortly. Should you have any questions or concerns in the
meantime please don't hesitate to reach us at 212-555-1818.

Sincerely,
Dominick Satorelli

Olivia looked down at the words and a tear quickly turned into
sobs. She looked over, in between sobbing breaths, to see Jacob's number buzzing on her BlackBerry. She reflexively picked up the phone.

"Yes?" She tried to sniffle in her sobs.

"Liv? You okay?"

"Yes, I'm fine." She tried to get her voice to sound less shaky and
wished her jaw would loosen a little.

"Are you crying?"

"Yes. I am. Okay. I'm crying." She couldn't help it; the tears were
flowing faster than she could catch them.

"What happened? What's wrong?"

All of a sudden she let loose a sob from her gut. "My insurance
agent died," she said through the gasps of breath.

"Oh my God. Liv, I'm so sorry. What happened?"

"I don't know."

"So it was a surprise?"

"Yes."

"I'm so sorry. Were you very close?"

She sniffled, more upset that she had lost control. "No, I didn't
know him at all." Saying the words out loud, combined with Jacob's silence, turned Olivia's sobs into hysterical laughter. "I never even knew
his name!"

"Holy shit, Liv, you've finally totally lost it."

"Seriously, Jacob, I think I may have." She couldn't stop laughing.
"Sorry . . . I just . . ."

"It's fine. I totally get it."

Even though she knew he didn't *totally* get it, she appreciated knowing he came close to understanding. And even more, she appreciated not having to explain herself.

She breathed in and wiped her cheeks. "So what's up?"

"Gov wants to do a call tomorrow morning to go through the numbers."

She laughed to herself, thinking how predictable Landon was. She wouldn't talk to him personally so he would force her to talk to him professionally.

"Did he just call you and ask for that?"

"Yeah," Jacob said knowingly.

"That's fine. My whole day is calling and collecting so I can do any time."

"Okay. Thanks." He paused, sounding like he wanted to say something. Then he said, simply, "Sorry, Liv."

She didn't want him to worry about her weariness. "It's not your fault. He can just be such an ass sometimes."

"I'm thinking more than sometimes these days."

Olivia was a little shocked that he was expressing this, even though they both knew it. "Yeah, I'm sorry too. I know it hasn't been so great for you lately."

"Liv?"

"Yeah?"

"I'm thinking of leaving."

The mail fell to the floor as Olivia sat up abruptly. "What?"

"Yeah. That senator I told you about, Morris, offered me a job."

"You're not seriously considering it, are you?" Olivia knew the situation between Jacob and the governor had gotten bad, but the thought hadn't even crossed her mind that Jacob would quit. That was the thing in campaigns, the thing she thought she and Jacob shared completely, loyalty. Once you were part of a team you didn't drop your candidate even if he or she were going down in flames. Loyalty was Campaign Lesson #1.

"Yeah, I guess not," he said with less-than-convincing sincerity.

"I can't be here without you, Jacob. I mean, screw *me*, no one can be here without you. You *are* this campaign."

Jacob was quiet, a rare occurrence.

"You pulling a Landon on me?" she asked. "All quiet over there?"

"I'm just not sure this campaign is who I want to be anymore."

Holy shit. I did this. I've crushed Jacob. The campaign. Me. I should have never let the governor kiss me. I should never have kissed him. "Jacob, I'm so sorry."

"Liv, it's not your fault."

"Some of it is." She couldn't bring herself to say the words even though she was dying to get them out.

"It's not."

He knows. He knows it's me. I'm going to fix this. "Okay. Jacob, tomorrow will be better. I'll get the money in, we'll get through this filing, and it will be okay."

"And then what?"

"Then we go to the White House!" She tried to muster excitement, but even the thought of the presidency seemed less thrilling. She was too disappointed in Landon. And in herself.

"Yeah." He shared her attempt to make an effort. "Okay, we should definitely get some sleep."

"You think?" She laughed. "Sorry about my breakdown."

"Please. Like you always say, tomorrow will be better."

"Good night, J."

"Good night, O."

SEVENTEEN

The tears welled up in Olivia's eyes as she read the email from the governor: *How could we be 30k down? Olivia, you have to find this money by tonight. We've bought the media. It's unacceptable.* She scrolled up and saw the cc's. Jacob, Peter, even Addie, and on and on. People she worked with, she worked for, she was friends with. Her head fell down to the desk.

Find this money? Jerk. Where would I be finding him money? She screamed into her arm, but the truth was she wasn't mad. She was sad. She had let everyone down. Even him.

She stared at the money-out spreadsheet in front of her, the names stacked on top of each other with the promises these people had made and never kept: 5K, 10K, 2,500. *They told me they'd have the money in. They lied.* But as she berated the donors, the tears came streaming. How did this become her responsibility? How did the fault fall solely on her shoulders?

She stared at the draft filing on her desk. The day of the filing they always printed it out to look over and catch any errors. She had distributed hard copies to four people, the only four trusted to be a last vet. $1,968,056 for this quarter. She pushed the hair out of her face and started typing.

"We're almost there," she wrote with the "To:" box filled with donor emails. "We need your help."

She could have written this plea in her sleep.

"If all of you could give one more time, we would be there."

Billy called to "touch base," which she knew was Billy's way of making sure she was okay. She kept up the façade while talking to him. "I'll get there, Billy," she promised.

When she hung up, she looked through the names one more time and felt the tears coming back. *Stop it,* she told herself. *There's a little dignity left. Hold tight.* That thought just made her cry more. She stared at the wall.

∽∿∾

Jacob stared at his computer and then at the wall. As glad as he was to not be the one getting hit on that email, it was almost as awkward for it to be Olivia. It was like when his wrestling coach used to berate his good friend for running too slow. He looked back at his computer. Six new pins from Landon. When he got in this mode, it was like gun spray. One by one Jacob answered them.

Yes, the meeting with Mayor DePasto is set. His crazy daughter will not be with him.

Yes, I made sure Amanda, Dylan, and Ryan were invited.

No, Samantha and Julia can't make tomorrow's event, and yes, I made sure they knew you wanted them there—they're out of town.

Yes, I called Luke from the *Merrick Times* back. He's running the story.

Playing phone tag with Rachel and Mike.

Barbara and Bruce will be at your speech. Their daughter, Dev, wants you at the fundraiser for her organization, Lil Ruggers. I sent it to scheduling.

Yes, the policy piece was edited. Madrick was consulted.

Yes, Scott and Jack have been called. Chase and Jordyn, Chris, Hanna, and Jared as well.

He glanced at the sent messages, wondering if his quick responses would be understood or somehow be seen as wiseass. The other issue with this mode was that you were perennially in a lose-lose situation. If you didn't respond immediately, you weren't on your game and ran the risk of getting screamed at or, worse, replaced. *Although, that might not be so bad right now.* If you did write back as quickly as you received them, you'd be tagged as answering without thinking.

Don't placate me with yeses. This isn't a damn dog-catcher race.

Jacob looked at the wall again, feeling responsible for getting Olivia into this campaign. *Maybe I should've warned her more before she took the job. Maybe I shouldn't have had her take the job at all.*

☾₥₥☽

Olivia kept typing. "We're inches away from our goal." Never list how much you need, never write your goal in an email. Those were sure-fire things to end up on a blog, even if you sent them to yourself. "I know you've already done so much." Make sure they're thanked before you ask. She scrolled through the rules Gabrielle had implanted in her mind, but didn't stop the tears. She sent it to fifty-two people and then started to compile the next list while waiting for replies with bated breath. She needed fifteen people or eight couples. *Or one really big miracle.* She reached for the phone and dialed the only person she could think of.

"Hey, Yanni."

"Hey, girly. What's going on?"

"You have a few minutes?"

"Sure." She could hear him covering the phone and yelling numbers out at an employee. Then he came back to her. That gave Olivia more time to compose her thoughts.

"Okay, so the filing is tonight."

"I know this from your spam-like daily emails."

"Ha. Sorry about that. Here's the thing though. My last one about being really close to the goal?"

"Yep," he said, distracted.

"It was really true; we're thirty thousand away from hitting two million."

"Thirty thousand? Shit." He was suddenly at full attention. "Do you have it?"

"Well, yeah, I have sixty pledged but they're not coming in. I'm worried I'm not going to get there."

"Okay, come to my office. Bring the list of who's left."

He hung up the phone before Olivia had a chance to ask for an explanation.

As she gathered her stuff, she questioned the use of her time but then realized it was three p.m. already and anything would be better than waiting in her office. He wasn't the finance chair, but she knew him better than Henley. He would help. He always came through. She glanced down at her hand, which trembled as it picked up her laptop. *Didn't eat breakfast,* she rationalized, knowing that the stress was much more impactful than the lack of food. She bundled up in her big puffy jacket and a scarf that she felt like wrapping around her entire face.

Her hands didn't stop trembling even at Yanni's, and as she walked past the rows of young men yelling toward Bloomberg Television, she felt her knees go weak. Her teeth hurt but she couldn't get her jaw to loosen. *Nervous breakdown. That must be what this is.* It wasn't a helpful diagnosis as it just seemed to worry her more, but it was the only thought she could hold on to. She knew there were tears welling up in her eyes but she couldn't even deal with them. She kept walking, one foot after another. *Get it together,* she thought, berating herself, as she walked into Yanni's office. *This is your mess and you will fix it.*

"Ugh." Yanni looked up from his screen and immediately his face went to pitiful. "You look more pale than normal."

"Ah. I knew coming in here would make me feel better." She flopped down on the brown leather sofa, relieved not to have already fallen down.

"I spoke to Landon. Apparently we really do need this money," Yanni said.

Thoughts rushed back through her head. *He couldn't call me but he called Yanni. Great. Nice love of my life. Swell. Super freakin' swell.*

"Hey. Liv. You there?"

"Yes. Sorry. Okay, yeah, so we are thirty K down. I have ten but I really don't know where the other twenty is coming from."

"Okay, let me see your list."

Olivia pulled out the spreadsheet. She knew the money on it wasn't coming in. It was bullshit. People who always promised and didn't come through were on there. People she had been chasing for weeks. Still, when Yanni took the sheet and started crossing off names, labeling each one bullshit, it hit Olivia like a bat to the stomach. As much as she felt like doing the same thing, having Yanni do it seemed like a teacher failing her on exam after exam after exam.

"You thought Vince was actually going to come through with five thousand?"

No. He's an asshole and I never thought I'd really get it. "He promised me," she said weakly. "He came through last time and Senator Farkas's people said he's been writing checks lately." Campaign Lesson #27: When looking for fundraising validation, always refer to Senator Farkas. Olivia found herself in a run of defenses that wouldn't end. She had to have had reasons for keeping these people on the list; otherwise she would be thirty short. "I'm sorry." Now she could feel the tears.

Yanni looked up and shot his head right back down, like all hedge fund managers would do. Shouting he could take, but tears were not in his game book. "Kiddo," he said, "don't worry. We'll do this."

Embarrassingly, the crying began in earnest. "Sorry." She wiped the tears more quickly than they fell. "I just—thank you."

For the first time in days she didn't feel completely alone.

"Listen, you go to Vince's office. Just tell him you're there for the check and don't leave till you get it and then come right back here."

"Okay." She pulled together her stuff, not even thinking about what he had just said. There wasn't a thought left in her brain, so being told what to do was a relief.

She walked out, head down so no one would see the red in her eyes, glad that she never put on makeup so at least there was no chance that black mascara would be running down her face. The cold air woke her up a bit, but it wasn't until she saw Vince's assistant Amy's horrified look that she realized how totally inappropriate it was that she had just shown up at their office to collect a check.

"It's filing day," she said, knowing full well that the term meant nothing at all to anyone who didn't have a candidate breathing down her neck. The assistant disappeared for fifteen minutes while Olivia fired off emails asking other people to help. Begging them actually. In the middle she emailed her old boss, Gabrielle, for reassurance.

LivGreenley@gmail.com: *How crazy is it that I just showed up at Vince Tilewitz's office to collect his check for the filing?*

Even though she knew what Gabrielle's response would be, some small part of her hoped she would respond with reassurance, but instead she got the expected dose of reality.

Gabrielle@aol.com: *What? Why???*

LivGreenley@gmail.com: *Yanni told me to.*

She wrote knowing exactly how stupid it sounded and laughing to herself at the ridiculousness of it all. Then she stopped and wrote the words that it pained her to type.

LivGreenley@gmail.com: *I'm 30K down.*

Her jaw started to hurt again. Twenty-two minutes had passed. She wondered how many minutes she should let pass before leaving. Then she thought of getting back to Yanni's without a check. *How did I become such a failure? Maybe I could be like Nora in* A Doll's House. *Just disappear. Leave. Where did Nora go? I could go to Massachusetts. How would I even get there? Where would I live? It would be a great Kate Hudson movie. Live in my car, find a job in a restaurant, meet the local ski instructor, and live happily ever after. Hmmm.* She didn't even have enough money in her bank account to rent a car, much less buy one.

Her bank account. She thought about the twenty-six dollars in her savings account and the thirteen in her checking account. She had never been good with her own money, but this was a low point. Her next paycheck wasn't for two weeks. How could she live on thirty-nine dollars for two weeks? She desperately didn't want to ask her parents. Just then, Vince's assistant came out like a much-needed end-of-day school bell, stopping the downward spiral of thoughts. Olivia glanced up at the envelope in the assistant's hands with a spark of hope.

"Here you go," the woman said with a touch of kindness.

"Oh, thank you, thank you so much."

"He's sorry he was late with it."

Olivia tripped over the assistant's words. "No, no, I'm sorry. I'm so sorry to just show up like this. It's just that we're so close to our goal. And it means so much. Thank you."

"That's okay," she said, "I understand."

"I hope for your sake you don't," Olivia said with a smile. "Thank you again."

She looked down at the envelope. Both twenty-five-hundred-dollar checks. One-sixth of what she needed, and yet it wasn't lost on her that this amount of money could cover all of her personal expenses for a good, long while.

She trudged the eight blocks through the remnants of the snow back to Yanni's office, making calls so continuously that she barely had time to even consider trying to hail a cab. Inside the lobby she stopped at the newsstand and picked up a bag of Doritos. She fished through her bag for change to see if she could add in a soda. *One dollar and thirteen cents.*

"Just the Doritos, please. Thank you."

Yanni's office seemed the same as when she'd walked out of it that afternoon. It hadn't emptied even a little, like most of the offices in Manhattan would at this hour. Actually, she realized, Yanni's money management firm always looked the same. Always the same amount of busy buzz. The stark white walls reflected the same amount of light whether morning, noon, or night, and the brightness of the neon paintings, the best and newest in modern art, of course, kept it always looking like a sharp day. It was much louder than the offices she worked in. A long row of young guys and a few girls sat in clear glass cubicles utterly focused on their changing computer screens. They seemed like Goldman kids in training to her, with their knees bouncing against the bottoms of their desks and their loosened ties, even at the start of the day. She wondered if some of them actually put them on already loosened.

As she walked back to Yanni's office she noticed two men yelling back and forth to each other while also on their Bluetooths. *What's the plural of "Bluetooth"? "Blueteeth"?* Just walking through gave her a little boost of energy and she thought, as she often did, it would have been much more fun to work in these offices. *Maybe Yanni will give me a job since I'll clearly lose mine tomorrow. I will lose my job on New Year's Eve.*

"Hey, Yanni." She flopped down on his couch as if she had just returned home. "Got 'em."

Yanni looked up, putting his hand over the microphone part of his headset. "You look like shit."

"Thank you," she mouthed back. Usually this would have made her feel worse, but she couldn't have cared less at this point. She opened her bag of Doritos and threw her head back while Yanni screamed numbers over the phone. His knee against the desk was almost like a metronome too. She tried to breathe along with it. Finally Yanni pulled off his headset and stood up.

"Are you okay?" He looked as if he really wanted an answer.

"Hell no!" she said uncharacteristically. "I've got this, plus the five hundred and eight dollars that came in the mail today. No one has responded to my begging emails, my boss is about to kill me, and the campaign hasn't paid me in four weeks, which means this bag of Doritos needs to last me until I get my impending severance pay." *Oh, and,* she added in her own train of thought, *the boss who is killing me is also the love of my life.*

"What do you mean the campaign hasn't paid you in four weeks?"

Olivia looked up at him, knowing she should not have just spilled her guts like that.

"Oh, it's nothing. Sorry, I'm just being a drama queen." She sat up and bit into a Dorito. "It will all be fine. Provided you have a plan!" She laughed, trying to turn the conversation from where she had brought it.

"I do have a plan," he said calmly, not laughing and uncharacteristically focused, "but I want to hear about this. Have they really not paid you?"

"Yeah," she admitted, but then tried to cover up what she knew was a totally skewed but completely normal practice of all campaigns. "But it's totally fine. All campaigns do it. They want to show lower expenses for the quarter, especially when we're so close on our numbers, so they hold off on staff pay for the last few weeks and then pay them out after. It's not a big deal. We volunteer to do it. And," she said in a self-deprecating fashion, "if I didn't have us so close to the numbers, it wouldn't be necessary."

"Bullshit!" Yanni hit his hand on the table incredulously. "How much do you make a month?"

Olivia thought about not telling him. It wasn't such a small salary, but for living in New York City it was minute. With her $2,000 rent and the taxes she owed from last year, it was just barely keeping her out of debt. She hated the idea of anyone knowing the financial strain her life was constantly in, but she was already in too far.

"I get paid five thousand a month," she said sheepishly. "Plus I get a win bonus."

"A win bonus?"

"Yeah, if we win I get an extra ten thousand."

Yanni looked at her as if for the first time he was trying to figure out who she was.

"Let me get this straight: they are skimping on five thousand dollars? That's absurd."

"Well, it comes to more. I mean, there are a few of us who are doing it." She lied, knowing full well only she and Jacob had agreed to do it. "It's okay, Yanni, really. I'll be totally fine."

"Of course you will." He got up and went to his desk, shaking his head. "Okay, let me make two more calls to finish my master plan." He moved his hand like Vanna White over his desk, which was covered in neon green Post-it notes.

"What is all that?" She felt relieved just by his calm.

"I call it the Post-it Plan, but you can call it the Yanni Is a Genius Plan." He laughed out loud. "I'm starved. You want dinner?" Without waiting for an answer he screamed for his assistant. "Robin!"

The petite blonde woman who seemed to be on constant call to his screams showed up instantly in the doorway.

"Let's order dinner! How about Philippe? That work for you, O? Will you grab us a menu?"

These were the times when Olivia loved people who didn't wait for an answer. Philippe was one of the best restaurants in the city. She had gone once for an event and had never forgotten the taste of the crunchy seaweed salad and the velvet chicken, which literally tasted like velvet in food form. Delicious food form.

"That sounds amazing. Thank you. I'm just going to run to the bathroom."

Breathing steadily for the first time all day, she knew she needed to compose herself, a good thing since her hair was just as messy as she had imagined. She splashed water on her eyes, which drooped from the lack of sleep and the wealth of tears. Robin stopped her on her way back to Yanni's with a printed-out Philippe menu. There were circles and checks around nearly every dish.

"I brought it around to everyone, so we've got almost all of them," she said, confirming the thought, "but make sure we have what you want."

Olivia smiled, even more grateful that she didn't have to make a decision. "I'm good with all of this."

"Great, I'm ordering a few extras of the velvet chicken and stuff, so there will be plenty. We have drinks in the kitchen."

"You are my hero right now."

"Hey, do you want a coffee or anything? We just got this amazing Italian version of a Keurig. It makes sick mochas."

"Um, yes! Seriously heroic. Do you want me to make it?"

"No! I love doing it! Plus"—she lowered her voice a little and leaned in—"you're the only one around here who has said thank you to me all day." She smiled, but Olivia could see the disappointment in her face, especially as the clock ticked to six p.m. on the day before New Year's Eve.

Olivia walked back into Yanni's office and sat down, watching him pace, back on the phone.

"I just need the number." He spoke quickly, with an agitated tone. Then he listened, scribbling down on one more of the green Post-its that were covering his desk.

The mocha, delivered to Olivia within minutes, was as good as Robyn promised. As Olivia sipped the chocolate coffee, she hoped for a moment that Yanni would never get off the phone and she could sit there, melted into the couch, forever. When he hung up, he sat down with a self-satisfied grin.

"You look better."

"Your office is better than a day spa."

Yanni smiled, again pleased with himself.

"Okay, okay, so what's your plan?" she asked. With all the comfort she had almost forgotten the disastrous situation she was in.

"Check out the Post-its."

Olivia got up and walked over to his desk, scanning his chicken-scratch scribble. There were at least eighteen Post-its, each of them with tons of numbers and a few initials.

"Ummm, are you going to turn all Rain Man on me and win us the lottery?"

"So much better than that. Each of these Post-its is someone's credit card and the amount we can charge up to on it."

Olivia's eyes shot open in disbelief. "What?! Seriously?"

"Seriously." Yanni was overflowing with pride. "It's no big deal."

"Yanni. This is such. A. Big. Deal. This is a huge deal. This is . . . I mean . . . you did it." She was almost overwhelmed with relief.

"Okay, don't start that crying thing again."

Olivia laughed. "I promise. No more crying."

"Good. Then take this too." He handed her an envelope.

"What is it?"

"Just take it."

Olivia took the envelope and looked in. It was a check for five thousand dollars. Then she looked closer. It was a check for five thousand dollars written out to her.

"Ohmygod. Yanni, what is this?"

"It's a bonus."

"Yanni, you can't pay me!"

"Fine, it's a gift."

"Yanni, I can't take this."

"You can too and you will. It's offensive what they pay you and it's unbearable that they're holding out payment on you. I'm going to talk to Landon about that."

"No, no, Yanni, please don't. He'd kill me if he knew I told you. Actually there will be a line to kill me if anyone finds out. I so should not have said that aloud. And this is way too much. It's so kind of you but really, I can't take it." She held out the envelope across his desk.

"Fine, I won't tell a soul. It'll stay between us, but it's a gift. It's rude to give it back."

Olivia hesitated, thinking about her thirty-nine-dollar account balance.

"Plus your introductions have brought more money into this firm than most of my employees, and they get paid much more than you. Actually, if I knew you were this cheap, I would have tried to hire you away months ago."

Olivia started to protest.

"Liv. I'm not talking about this anymore. I spent more than that on dinner last night."

Olivia looked down at the envelope, knowing that was true. Knowing that this check that could pay her bills for two months would not even be a blip on his screen. Literally.

"Wouldn't you do the same for me if the roles were reversed?"

"I . . . Yes."

"So stop being a little bitch and take the money. Consider it me taking you out to dinner."

Robyn popped into the doorway. "Philippe is here!"

Yanni laughed. "Okay, consider it me taking you to dinner twice."

"Thank you, Yanni." Olivia went over to give him a hug.

"Sure thing, kid. Come on, let's get some food and pick out who's gonna pay what."

EIGHTEEN

When Olivia had told a donor, Jason Sackton, she worked twenty-four/seven, she was exaggerating. And when Jason said he would "max out," give the maximum amount allowable—twenty-five hundred dollars—if she was at her job at midnight on New Year's Eve, he was joking. But it was a joke they had taken farther than it should have ever gone. At 11:59 on December 31, as promised, Jason Sackton called the office, and as promised, Olivia sat waiting for the call. She didn't need the twenty-five hundred dollars and she didn't have, as she had told her friends and family, piles of work to climb out from under. The truth was she just wanted to be alone. She was never one for New Year's celebrations but this year it seemed simply intolerable. She was exhausted, sick of people in general, and with her secret relationship in shambles, she had a broken heart that she couldn't share with anyone. She talked with Jason as he gave her his credit card information in bewildered amusement at her insistence on staying in the office.

"You should come down here to St. Barths! Everyone's here. You could stay on our boat—we have three extra rooms. I saw Addie on the beach today. You wouldn't have to pay for a thing. We're going from here to Ibiza, but I'm sure you could bum a ride home on someone's private plane."

"Bum" and "private plane" just don't seem like they belong in the same sentence, Olivia thought. She laughed as he went on, describing the

beaches, restaurants, and of course, shopping, thinking that fabulously posh place was her worst nightmare. Just the thought of having to be around all those people made her grateful that she had been able to convince everyone that the office was where she wanted to be. She pulled the hood of her sweatshirt over her head and sat back in the silence. She looked down at her BlackBerry.

Marcygreenley@gmail.com: *Happy New Year! Miss you!*

She wrote back, thinking of what Marcy would say if she knew Olivia had scoffed at a paid trip to St. Barths. *It was stupid. I mean, who wouldn't want to go to St. Barths? Me.* She looked at the clock and then down at her BlackBerry, wondering if he would text her. As the clock turned to 12:06 she swallowed her pride and pinned him.

Happy New Year, Landon.

The response pin came back quickly and was painfully innocuous.

You too, babe.

"Uch. Ew." She was so irritated, she said it aloud to really get the effect, unsure of whether she was annoyed at the response or the fact that she knew that would be the response, the whole response, and had sent the pin anyway. It felt like she had just given him the upper hand in the emotional chess game she had worked up in her head. She felt totally helpless and did the only thing that made her feel better. She leaned forward to reach her iTunes and found Eminem's "Not Afraid." Turning the volume higher, she sat back deeper in her chair and tugged at her sweatshirt hood, trying to pull it farther down her forehead.

There was something about knowing all the words and being able to say them in time with him, barely breaking for breaths, that always turned her bitterness into some kind of empowered anger. Two minutes in, she was so lost in getting the words right and wondering who she was competing against, she didn't even hear her door move from a bit open to completely open. The knock startled her into a scream.

"Whoa, Eminem. Didn't mean to scare you."

"Holy crap, Jacob!" In the seconds it took for her heartbeat to get back on track, she held her throat and looked at him. His floppy brown hair, longer than ever, hung over his eyes. Dressed in dark jeans, a vintage-looking T-shirt, and a heavy blazer, he looked almost adorable. He took some steps in and placed an open bottle of tequila on her desk.

She smiled. "What are you doing? Why are you here? You scared the living daylights out of me."

"Sorry 'bout that. I was at a party having stupid conversations with stupid people. And then I went to get a drink and this bottle of Patrón was just sitting there, so I took it and left."

Olivia laughed. "Why did you come up here? It's New Year's!"

"It's so stupid . . ."

"Ummm, you did just walk in on me singing Eminem in a hooded sweatshirt at my desk on New Year's. The bar for stupid is pretty low at the moment."

"Seriously, you are gangster."

"Okay, so lay it on me. What did you do?" She grabbed two mugs, looking into them to make sure they were clean—*well, clean enough*—and started pouring the tequila.

"Sophie and I had planned to go to this party for ages. I laid out the two hundred dollars in September or something and, yes, I am acutely aware of the fact that we broke up, but I don't know, I just thought . . ."

"That's not stupid, Jacob."

"Liv, it's moronic. Despite the teachings of *The Secret*, you can't just visualize something and make it happen. Real life requires effort."

"So she wasn't there?"

"Worse! She was there with the new guy she's dating. Josh. Ech. He works in the state treasurer's office. They've been dating for a month! I hadn't even realized it had been that long. I swear it's like we're in a time warp."

"Oh, I am so sorry. That sucks. Cop a squat. I'll start pouring."

Jacob sat and threw his feet on the desk. "My goal was actually to drag you out to a bar. What the hell are you doing here anyway?"

"Well, Jason said he would max out if I was actually here at eleven fifty-nine . . ." She started in on the excuses like a broken record but stopped, knowing Jacob knew too much to believe any of it. "Okay, I couldn't deal with people. That is the sad, sorry story. I just didn't want to be around anyone. I should probably buy a few cats and call it a day."

"Here's to campaign life." Jacob lifted the glass of tequila and swallowed it down in two gulps. "So did Jason even call?"

"Yup. Told me I should fly down to St. Barths immediately."

"Gross."

"Ha!" Olivia laughed out loud. "You think we are the only two people in the world who think an all-expenses-paid trip to St. Barths sounds terrible?"

Jacob laughed with her. "It's pretty ridiculous. I've never been, but it sounds like the Hamptons on crack."

"Totally."

"So how are we looking for the filing?"

"Great. Over two, so we're just super great." She said it with the annoyed sarcasm she felt.

"That's amazing, Liv. Really. It's awesome."

"Thanks. I know it's good." She then downgraded the compliment, as she had been doing all her life. "It feels shitty though."

"I know."

There wasn't anything else to say, and Olivia appreciated that Jacob didn't try to add to it, explain it, or defend it. It was what it was.

"I guess it just is what it is," he said.

They smiled in joint recognition.

"Let's get out of here." Jacob stood up and smacked her desk. "Call this year over."

"That," Olivia said, shutting down her computer, "is a great idea."

As they stepped out into the street, Olivia felt like she was walking out of a dark movie theater, her eyes taking time to adjust. The lit-up sidewalks bustled like Christmas on Fifth Avenue, people walking in every direction, dressed in every which way, all of them with an intense (often drunkenly intense) mission. Get to the next party, find the next bar, find a cab. All of it seemed to be going on in a world Olivia wasn't part of. It made her feel like she was walking in a hall of mirrors, where everyone around was a version of herself, a version she may have been once or might be next year but definitely wasn't at that moment. She looked at the gaggle of girls on the corner dressed as if they were auditioning for *Sex and the City*. Tiptoeing to try to prevent their super-high heels from touching the snow, they flailed into the middle of the street, arms raised in an attempt to hail a cab.

"This is like soooo annoying," one of them whined. "Why are there, like, no cabs?"

"Um, heh-lowww, because it's New Year's Eve!"

Then they all squealed together, "New Year's Eve!"

Olivia couldn't help but comment. "Uch. Why are people so annoying?"

Jacob laughed in agreement. "Want to walk a little? I'm staying at the Brinmore, obviously."

"Yeah, that would be nice. I could go for some fresh air. Plus if I get home too early there's a chance someone will try to convince me to go out. Hmm." She smiled with self-degrading mockery. "It really is a mystery why I'm single!"

They started to walk up Park Avenue in a silence that seemed to please them both. People flanked them in festive clothes and hats, blowing noisemakers and having idiotic conversations, all of which reinforced for Olivia her choice of a quiet New Year's. She looked up at Jacob, who seemed just as dazed as she felt.

"Hey, thank you for the tequila tonight. I'm sorry it came at the cost of a bad New Year's."

"Want the truth?"

"Rarely. But sure."

"I think I probably came more for me than for you. I just needed to be around someone who didn't need an explanation."

"Yeah, I get that."

"Why are you the only one who does?"

"I'm not. We just don't get out much."

Jacob laughed, tripping a little bit over his own feet.

"You okay there?" Olivia grabbed at his arm and he spun around into her. Their faces were together in that awkward place that left them too close to talk.

"Liv." Jacob looked down at her, his eyes more puppy-dog than she had ever seen them. His hand reached down to hers.

Oh no, no, no. She shook her head and took a step back. "Jacob, I can't."

"Why?"

"Because."

"Say it, Liv."

"Say what?"

Jacob held his stare, scrutinizing her face, which was still way too close to his. "It's him. Isn't it? It's true."

"Yes." The word fell out of her mouth. Guilt and relief.

"Liv. You can't." His response was more serious than she expected and reeked of desperation, as though hearing her say the words finally slammed the door on the excuses he had been trying to make for the governor. "Don't do this, Olivia. Don't do it to me. To him. To you! How do you think this is going to end?"

"I don't know. I think it might have ended already."

"Well, I do know how it will end, so let me fill you in. It's going to end one of two ways: the first is you will be caught and this whole campaign plus both of your lives plus mine plus a million more will go up in a huge fiery blaze that *you* started."

"It's not going to." She pushed out the words more to stop him than to actually say anything she thought had a bit of truth in it.

He continued with no regard for her protest. "The second way is he will be president and Aubrey will be first lady and you will not. You will be left in the dust of a campaign."

He meant it as the lesser of the two evils, but the latter choice filled Olivia with a fearful sadness. She had been saying it to herself but she didn't believe it.

"It's not like that. You don't understand."

"Yes, Liv. I do. They made a deal. She gives up Tiwali and he gives up you. That's why she's been on the road with us. That's why he hasn't been to New York. They don't care about people. It's all about the campaign."

Olivia looked at him in silence, the words hitting her like a sledge-hammer, as he continued.

"Liv, he'll never be able to give you what you deserve. And you deserve so much. You are not the other woman. You should be *the* woman. You deserve someone who will shout your name from the rooftops. You deserve to be with someone who doesn't have to go silent every time he picks up his phone. Someone who will be there for you. All the time. You deserve the moon and the stars and then some. He'll never give that to you, Liv."

She knew he was right but wouldn't let herself admit it.

"What am I doing?" he said, more to himself, filling in her dazed silence. "Liv, I'm not going to stick around for this. That senator I told you about. The one who offered me a job. I'm meeting with him next week."

"What?! What is that, a threat?" It was too ridiculous to be true.

"No, it's not a threat."

"Okay, you're going to leave a presidential campaign to go work for a senator? Give me a break, Jacob."

"No. I'm going to leave a man who doesn't have a tenth of the morals he had when I signed on, for a man who has double what Taylor may have ever had."

"He has morals, Jacob." Olivia went on the defensive with whatever conviction she had left to conjure up.

"No, Liv. He had morals. Trust me, I believed in him more than anyone. But somewhere in between Georgia and here he lost his way. I'm not going to keep following the guide when I know he's lost just because he's the guide. I'm finding a new way and I want you to come with me."

"I can't just leave, Jacob."

"Yes, you can."

"You don't know him like I do." The minute she said it, she wished she could take it back. It was like she saw the words coming out of her mouth and she raised her arms to reach for them. "I don't mean that. I just mean it's not the same."

"Yeah. You know what, Olivia, that's the first thing you've been right about in this conversation."

"Jacob, I didn't mean—"

"No. I'm not offended. I don't know him at all anymore. And I don't want to."

He looked so resolute, it hurt her heart. Olivia was almost glad that they had arrived at the doors of the Brinmore.

"I'm so sorry, Jacob." She had just let down the last person in her corner.

"This, Olivia, is not something to be sorry about. It's something to get out of. You're a kid, and he's taking advantage of you. He's taking advantage of us. We deserve better. And," he added in, "the world deserves better."

Olivia walked the next twenty-five blocks home by herself with an unbroken stream of silent tears. They weren't the hard kind of tears that fall in anger, and they weren't the sobs that stop your breath; they were just plain human sadness.

NINETEEN

Olivia stared down at her vibrating phone as Alek's number flashed in front of her. She looked at the clock, wishing he wasn't calling at 11:54 p.m. For three days now she had served as friend, adviser, and therapist, and she wasn't sure she had another pep talk in her. Plus, it was late. She was tired. *Exhausted.* It was only a week after New Year's, and Olivia's life had gone decisively downhill. The governor was trying to make up for his pre-filing behavior, but instead of making anything better, it had left her on an emotional roller coaster and the only person who understood any of her life, Jacob, was as far away and distant as all her other friends.

To top things off, three days ago the press had accused Alek of being the head of a Ponzi scheme. The accusations, all of which Alek vehemently denied, turned into an indictment. The campaign was in a flurry over it. Alek had called Olivia, originally trying to get a hold of the governor, but, as usual, Landon wasn't calling him back, and Olivia was the stand-in.

She closed her eyes, shook her head, and begrudgingly picked up the phone.

"Hi, Alek." She had the deflated tone of someone who knows they're about to have a trying conversation.

"Oh, Ohhhlivia. Se princess." His voice shook with worry.

"How are you holding up, Alek?" She knew the answer. She also couldn't stop thinking about whether or not her every word was being monitored. There certainly had to be a Campaign Lesson about not talking when the FBI was likely to be listening.

"I can't believe they are doing this to me." He spoke with desperation. "They're ruining everything. They just want to destroy me."

"Who do you think is behind it?" Olivia asked the question less for the answer than to just have something to say.

"It's se media. They just want to hurt me." His voice started to crack. "After all I have done for this country. I have built schools. Everysing you have asked me I have done. Nó? And now sey want to juss take me down." His accent became thicker as he became more upset.

Olivia rubbed her forehead, wondering how she was the one left talking one of Landon's oldest friends off the ledge.

"Listen, Alek," she said in the most calming voice she could muster, "the truth wins out in the end. Reporters can certainly make a mess but they can't infiltrate the justice system." She remained conscious of her word choice. "It's late. Get some sleep. You'll go tomorrow and you'll prove to them you're not guilty." She knew there was a lack of confidence behind her words and hoped he didn't detect it. She wanted to believe him. She couldn't imagine how anything they were saying could really be true. This was Alek. Landon's friend. Her friend. He couldn't be a scam artist. It couldn't be a Ponzi scheme. Still, the lingering doubt hung in the back of her mind.

"No. They ahave ruin everysing." He spoke bluntly enough that it scared Olivia.

"Alek, you know what they say—the best way out is always through."

"Yes." He said this more as a sigh than a word.

"You just have to hang in there. One foot in front of the other and pretty soon we'll be back at Hazan's!" She tried to lift her voice into a pep-talk tone.

"You har very good friend. I want to sank you. You've been so very good to me."

"You've been a good friend to me, Alek." It was true, she thought with a pang of guilt for feeling so reluctant to talk to him when he was so desperate. He had been a very good friend. He had been there every time she called desperate for donations. He had gotten the campaign whatever they needed, from plane rides to restaurant reservations. Whenever they needed it.

"What's your address? I have to send you a sank-you. Oh, never mind. Sere is no pen. You tex me your address, yay?"

"Yay." She reflexively answered with his mispronounced version of "yes." "Yes," she said, correcting herself, "yes, I'll do that right when we hang up."

"Oh, se princess. You take care of everything."

"Just try to get some sleep, Alek. Things always look better in the morning." Olivia hung up the phone, hoping her adage had even a shred of truth to it. She sat in the silence of her apartment, holding on to her BlackBerry, desperately needing to reach out to someone. She started an email to Jacob, first with humor, then with seriousness, but no words seemed appropriate. Then she moved to Landon's name.

Hey, she typed in red.

No, you cannot do this, she thought. *You have to cut the cord.* She erased the word. How had it become so hard to reach out to anyone?

She sat there for a few more minutes, thinking about Alek and the campaign, then pushed herself up off the chair and propelled herself into the bathroom. *Sleep is the only appropriate way to go. It'll be better in the morning.*

As the shower water fell down on her head she thought through the worst-case scenario. If Alek were guilty of what they said, the campaign would take a huge hit. If she had stayed out of the fraying of the governor's friendship with Alek, the governor would have never called Alek back, never seen him for dinner. Alek would have been a distant friend of the campaign, not a key player. Why couldn't she have just stayed out of it?

She climbed into bed and tried to get comfortable, but nothing worked. She ended up on her side, staring down at the BlackBerry that lay on her pillow. She picked it up and started to write, wracked with a feeling that she could not just write for the sake of writing, as she would have two months ago. She scrolled to her saved messages and looked at the one from Landon with all X's and O's. It felt like a distant time and another person, but she longed for a connection to something about it, anything.

Hey. Spoke to A. He swears he's not guilty. I'm so sorry for the mess.

As she wrote the last line she gulped to catch her breath and not start crying again. SEND. She lay staring at the ceiling for a minute, her heavy gaze broken by the vibration of a private number calling her phone. As much as she wanted to talk to him, she didn't. She knew he would be logical and that she would have to be linear about it. All she actually wanted to do was melt into a thousand pieces in his arms. She hated both to need something from him and knew that he wouldn't give it to her.

"Hello."

"Hey." He was talking in a hushed voice, which meant he was somewhere in the house and not somewhere safe for him to be calling her. "You okay?"

"Yep." She said it quickly enough to cover up the lie, sad to be closed up to the one person she thought she could say anything to. His hushed voice and question were sure signs he wasn't looking for any other answer than that.

"Okay," he said, as if he had just checked off a box on his to-do list.

Olivia straightened up in bed, feeling almost offended by the call she'd wanted so badly. "I just—I'm really sorry for the mess. Alek says he's not guilty. He says it's all a big miscommunication."

"I'll say."

"And the thing is," Olivia said, feeling like she needed to be on the offensive and knowing the governor would appreciate the unemotional thought, "if it turns out he is guilty, every campaign across the board has taken money from him, along with most of the major nonprofits. Plus we have only taken twenty-four hundred dollars directly from him, which we could obviously easily give back."

"You think he's guilty?"

"God, I hope not."

"Yeah." The governor sounded less convinced or even hopeful.

"Have you talked to him at all?" she asked rhetorically, knowing full well the answer was no.

"No."

She bit her lip, not wanting to give up the control she was holding on to by a thread, and let him sit in her uncharacteristic silence.

"We're supposed to be in town tomorrow."

"I know." Olivia pinched her hand to keep herself from getting as emotional as she wanted. She hated him for everything that was going on and at the same time inexplicably almost ached for him to just hold her.

"Jacob thinks maybe I should steer clear, just until this blows over."

"He's probably right." Even if she had wanted to, she didn't have the energy to argue the point.

"You sure you're okay?"

She listened to the phone, to his whisper, trying to grasp even a nanosecond of sincerity in the question. It was like he was pushing himself to ask her a second time to make himself feel better. He knew her well enough to know the answer, which made the asking even worse.

"I'm fine." She pounded it out resolutely. She wasn't fine, but she would be. Alek would go through the paperwork and it would all be okay in a week. "It'll all be better in the morning," she said once again.

"Get some sleep, baby."

"Good night, Landon." She said the words succinctly, hanging up before he had a chance to finish his "good night." It was passive-aggressive to say it like that with his name, and she knew it, but she didn't care. She was alone and wasn't getting the hug she so desperately needed today or tomorrow. Tired and annoyed, she resolved to be independent. She thought of Alek and remembered that he had asked for her address, so she typed it out to him. *When you get to the end of your rope, tie a knot and hold on,* she added at the end, taking comfort in giving the advice she could use herself. Her BlackBerry buzzed and a red message popped up,

You didn't sound okay.

Duh. "I'm not okay!" she screamed to the wall. Then she picked up her BlackBerry and typed the only thing she wanted to share with him.

All good.

The next morning came quicker than Olivia would have hoped. Her nightmare of trying to get Alek seated next to Landon at an event was too obvious to spend even a minute trying to process. Nights when she dreamed like that, and they were many, were worse than not sleeping at all, since it felt like she had just gotten off work, not woken up.

She picked up her BlackBerry and saw the flood of emails. Annoyingly disappointed not to see one from Landon, she once again cursed the idea of being disappointed. She answered the emails that needed responses and walked past the outfit she had laid out the day before, when she thought she would be seeing Landon. She threw on jeans and a baggy, comfortable sweater. *Jerk,* she thought to herself, reminded of how insincerely he had asked about her in that late-night whispered call.

Her coffee didn't have enough sugar, and the subway, of course, took forever to come, so by the time she got to the office, she was antsy with agitation and in no mood to explain to Addie why she hadn't put on any makeup, all of which Addie clearly recognized.

"Um, hey, are you okay?"

"Hey, Addie. Just didn't get much sleep." Olivia took a sip of her coffee. "And my coffee's shit." She said it with an accepting smile, sorry to be starting off Addie's day with misery.

"I'll make a Starbucks run!" Addie chimed in cheerfully, probably more to get out of Olivia's way than anything.

"That actually would be great, Addie, thanks so much."

"No problemo! Skim mocha with whip?"

Olivia appreciated the care and waved Addie away with a twenty, cognizant for the millionth time of the profound effect Yanni's extra five thousand dollars had had on her life.

The crazed monotony of the day started in as always, and it was already ten thirty when Olivia realized she hadn't heard anything from Alek or anyone connected to the case. She did a quick Google search that had only yesterday's news. She crunched her neck, feeling the crick in it harden. Just then her phone rang and Theresa, the fundraiser she worked with in Miami and Pennsylvania, the one who was also close with Alek, spoke quickly on the other line.

"Hey, Liv."

"Hey, Theresa."

"Question for you—when was the last time you spoke to Alek?" She asked calmly but there was an edge to her voice that made Olivia worry.

"Um, last night, why? What's up?"

"Well . . ." She breathed in. "He's missing. He didn't show up for his arraignment."

"Ohmygod." Olivia's heart hit the floor. That was worse than the worst-case scenario. "Where have they looked? Has anyone heard anything? Ohmygod."

"Yeah, I know." Theresa stayed calm and continued. "They searched his apartment and there was nothing there at all."

"Empty?!"

Addie came to the door with a frightened look on her face, waving Olivia off the phone.

"Hold on a second, Theresa." Olivia attempted to reclaim her composure.

Addie started in with rapid agitation. "Alek's lawyers are on the phone. There are two of them. They said it's really urgent. They sound scary."

"Okay. It's okay, Addie." She clicked back to her call. "Theresa, let me call you right back, okay?" The need to calm Addie superseded her own worry.

"What's going on?" Addie asked.

Olivia needed to be calm so that those around her would stay calm. "I don't know exactly. Transfer the call and don't talk to anyone until I'm off, okay?"

What would Jacob do? *Calm, contain, control,* she reminded herself, missing her friendship with him more than ever. He had barely spoken to her since New Year's.

"Hello?"

"Ms. Greenley?"

"Yes?"

"This is Yael Utt. I'm Alek's lawyer. I need to know if you have any idea where he is." The lawyer said it sternly, and even worse, as any campaigner feared the most, like she was saying it for a taped recording.

"I just heard he didn't show up today. I have no clue. Has he not contacted anyone?"

"Indeed he's missing," Yael said like a strict principal. "When is the last contact you had with him?"

"Last night." Her panic grew as her mind wandered to her conversation with him. "He was very upset. Oh, no."

The lawyer didn't leave any hesitation for emotion. "I'm going to give you all our numbers here. If you hear from him we need to know immediately."

"Okay. Of course. Of course." Olivia wrote down three different numbers, as well as the lawyer's assistant's name and cell phone.

"Thank you." The phone clicked off. *Crap.* Without logic, she tried Alek's cell, which went straight to voice–mail. She banged her head down on the desk. *How is this happening? Where is he?* She tried to keep her mind from going to the dark place it was now heading toward. She opened up her email and then closed it. Instead, she picked up the phone.

"Jacob?"

"Hey, Liv, what's up? I'm about to get on a plane to New York." She wished more than anything that the edge to his words that had developed since New Year's was gone, but he was as crisp as could be.

"Governor's not with you, is he?" She asked the question despite its irrelevance and despite already knowing the answer.

"No. Billy and I decided it was better for him to lie low today. He's going to do some community events."

"Good." Olivia was actually thankful that everyone was more logical than she. Keeping him in Georgia was a good idea, especially since this was going to be even more of a mess. "So . . ." The words seemed hard to say. "Alek's lawyer just called me."

"Oh, yeah? What'd he say? What's going on?"

Olivia could tell Jacob was only half listening.

"Jacob. Alek is missing. He didn't show up to the arraignment, and no one knows where he is."

"Shit!" Jacob yelled into the phone. "Are you kidding me?"

"No. I'm—"

Addie ran into the office looking like she was on fire.

"Olivia! Someone from the Pennsylvania attorney general's office is on the phone."

"I gotta get this, Jacob. I'll call you right back."

"I have to board. If I'm in the air, call Billy and Peter. Make sure they know the details before anything leaks to the press."

"Okay."

She switched lines without taking a breath. "Hello?"

"Is this Miss Olivia Greenley?" She was beginning to hate that question.

"It is."

The man on the line introduced himself as Bryan Caplin and described quickly his titles at the attorney general's office, all of which slid past Olivia's hearing.

"I assume you have heard that Aleksander Yerkhov failed to appear at his arraignment this morning?"

"I was just informed of this by his lawyer." Olivia tried to talk in legalese, which to her just meant more direct words and in actuality probably just resulted in her pronouncing syllables more emphatically.

"Miss Greenley, do you know where Alek is?"

"I do not." Suddenly she was aware that her legalese was sounding more robotic than legal. "I have no clue," she added in. "I'm really worried." *Too far?* It was true though, and blurting it out was like exhaling.

Mr. Caplin's voice didn't waver. "Miss Greenley, we had a wiretap on Mr. Yerkhov's phones. You are the last known person he contacted, and we know he asked for your address."

"Yes. He did." She felt like she was in the midst of a bad cop show. "He wanted to send me a thank-you for being his friend." It sounded so stupid out of context.

"Miss Greenley . . ."

Olivia wished everyone would stop calling her that.

"I am not your lawyer but I need to advise you, as of ten o'clock this morning, Alek Yerkhov became a federal fugitive. If you are hiding him or helping him get away, you are aiding and abetting a federal fugitive, which is a federal crime."

"Ohmygod!" Her mind was good at thinking about possible outcomes, but this one came totally out of the blue. "No! I'm not! I mean, definitely not. I have a one-bedroom walkup. I wouldn't even have anywhere to put him!" The outlandishness of that explanation didn't even faze Olivia. It was true. A fugitive. Her, hiding a fugitive? It was so surreal.

"Okay, Miss Greenley." The stagnant-toned man continued, seeming to believe her. "If you do hear from him or have any information regarding the case, please contact me at once."

"I will. Of course. Yes." Olivia hung up, shaken to the bone. She dialed Jacob immediately, but it went straight to voicemail. She tried Billy next, who listened intently and brought Peter in on the call for the press part.

"Press hasn't caught word of any of this yet, to my knowledge," Peter said, trying to reassure them.

Olivia hadn't ever heard Billy so silent. As she hung up the phone she had the crushing feeling that she, the young, inexperienced New Yorker, was bringing scandal and evil down on this nice, down-south campaign. She went to her door to close it and stood with her back against it, as if she could keep the world out by pushing hard enough.

⁕

Jacob landed in New York to the worst kinds of emails—a barrage from Olivia, Billy, Peter, each one containing the simple phrase "call me." They might seem to be the best type of email to get, having no long message and requiring no response. But to Jacob, "call me" meant it was something bad enough, urgent enough, that it couldn't be put in an email or even a pin. He walked through the airport, head down, thinking about how thankful he was that he had been able to convince the governor to stay in Georgia. It wasn't great that he was missing the Service Employees International Union meeting, as they were one of their biggest and most important union supporters. Okay, it was terrible that he was missing the meeting, but now, with Alek on the run, the last place the governor needed to be was in New York, where the press would be all over the story. *And the other last place I need him to be is at Olivia's.* The thought of the press finding Alek contacting Olivia was bad enough, but to tie in the governor with Olivia would be the beginning of the end. A federal fugitive and an affair. How the hell did he wind up in this mess? How did his perfect campaign wind up in such ruins?

Fuck it. He couldn't hold in his cynicism. *Maybe I want the whole campaign to be taken down.*

The montage in his mind of Landon as his political hero was long gone. Now all he could see, despite trying to block it out, were the lies. He had made a deal with himself, something he had found himself doing more and more of late. If Taylor insisted on going to New York, Jacob would quit. It would be the proverbial straw that broke the camel's back.

As had been happening though, the few times Jacob thought he would draw a line in the sand, Taylor had made the right choice. A growing part of Jacob wished Taylor would do something that would force Jacob to leave. Maybe Alek would be the final break.

Scrolling through his emails, Jacob felt an overwhelming sense of exhaustion. He got in a cab and leaned his head against the window. Even his mantra of *Calm, contain, control* seemed futile. On a campaign, when the dream was gone, the work became simply unbearable. And now he would have a federal fugitive to deal with. There would be lawsuits and drama. Just as he was pulling up to the Sheraton, home to all political events, his BlackBerry buzzed with Billy's number.

"Hey, Harriston."

"Hey, Billy. Any fallout from Alek yet?"

"Uh, no." Billy sounded weirdly uninterested in the situation. "Y'all spoken to the governor this mornin'?"

Jacob had to think for a minute as the days seemed to run into each other more often than not. "We texted early, like six a.m. Why? What's up?"

"Just haven't heard a peep from him and I spoke to Aubrey, who told me they had a fight and also that we wouldn't be getting Secretary Tiwali's endorsement, though I haven't the foggiest idea what one has to do with the other."

Jacob bent his head forward, wondering how Billy could still be so in the dark. And now Jacob himself was lying to this lovely man. He had joined the circle of liars. "Ugh, Billy, I'm sorry. I'm sure he's just getting some air and she . . . well . . . ."

Billy sounded more jadedly accepting than Jacob had ever heard him. "Yeah. You're probably right." He paused, then regained his comforting fatherly tone. "You okay up there? You need anything?"

He lied again. "No. All good, Billy. Thanks."

෨෨෨

Olivia stared at the email open on her computer for a good ten minutes. The routine continuation of the day did nothing to take her out of the dreamy haze that filled the air around her. After explaining the situation calmly to Addie, Olivia had gone into linear mode.

They had two events the week after Iowa, one in New York and one in DC, both planned to play on the impending Iowa win. Addie needed to call through the RSVP lists, and Olivia needed to hammer the hosts to come through with their commitments. None of it did what Olivia really intended it to do, which was to distract her from the situation with Alek. And her isolation from the governor. She got up to get coffee, but as she walked through the hallways, the world seemed even more hazy. She could hear phones going off and people talking in the background, but the sounds were so she felt she would surely pass out. *That would be a solution,* she thought, laughing to herself.

She got her coffee and scrolled through her BlackBerry. "GLT" came up in red. She stopped and closed her eyes before reading it. *Please don't let this be bad.* She hadn't heard from him all day.

Hey, baby. Where are you?

She didn't know whether to scream or cry. What world exactly was he living in?

It's 5:30. Shockingly I'm in the office. She couldn't help the sarcasm. A response came immediately.

Go home.

Huh?

Leave the office and go home, there's something there for you.

What is it? Not in the mood.

Olivia, go home. He sent this text twice and then added in that it was an order. She finally gave in.

OK. She rolled her eyes, imagining throwing the bouquet of flowers he sent into the East River. The thought of getting out of the office, which felt today like a cage, was good even if it was for fifteen minutes. She walked to Addie's office.

"Addie, I'm calling this a day."

Addie looked at her with a sorrowful helplessness. "I'm really sorry."

"No, please. You've been a huge help. I just think we should cut our losses on this one. Go to dinner with your boyfriend or something fun. No work the last half of this day."

There was too much to be done to be leaving at five thirty p.m., but Olivia was at her breaking point. She'd go home, see whatever stupid thing Landon had delivered, and then come back to work. She relished the idea of coming back and having the office to herself. Addie was smart enough after six months of campaign life to leave immediately when given the option and not risk a mind change or, worse, a phone call that would cancel the decision. Olivia, on the other hand, had no alternative to taking her time; her body was moving in slow motion. She dragged herself out of the building and jumped in a cab. *Stupid Olivia, you probably won't have a job in one month. Now is not the time to take a cab.*

At her building, she stopped at the Italian restaurant downstairs.

"Hey, Gianni. Did something come for me?"

"No, no, *cara. Non ancora.* Not yet."

"Okay, thanks, Gianni." *There's not even flowers,* she complained to herself. She started to walk into the building, but a familiar voice stopped her.

"Hey, baby."

Olivia's whole body felt as though it was crumbling inside.

"Landon." He stood behind her, two plastic grocery bags in hand, wearing jeans, a sweater, and his Great American Vending Machine Company baseball hat pulled far down, almost over his eyes.

"Let us in so I can give you that hug you need."

He didn't give me up. This is what they mean when they say people melt, she thought as she felt her insides dissolve.

She opened the door and pushed into the lobby, where he dropped the bags and bear-hugged her. She bit into her bottom lip and grabbed on to him with whatever strength she could muster.

"What are you doing here? I thought . . . Jacob said . . ."

"Coincidentally Henley was on his way to New York, so I asked him to stop in Atlanta and let me stow away." He grinned.

"But they canceled your stop in New York. Does anyone know you're here?"

"Henley, and now you. Come on." He led her up the stairs. "It took you so long to get here, the Chinese food might be cold."

"Well, if I knew this was the delivery, I might have moved a little quicker."

"What were you expecting?"

"I have no idea. Flowers?"

"Didn't have a chance to get those."

"This is *soooo* much better."

As they got inside, Landon turned her back to the door and kissed her. It was one of those long kisses that consumed her. She pulled herself away, almost afraid of losing herself completely. She was mad at him, so mad at him, but she loved him. She knew she shouldn't. It wasn't right, but it was everything.

"I'm so sorry."

"Baby, this is not your fault."

"It is. I made you stay friends with him. I forced him on the campaign. I should have seen this coming."

"It's not your job to vet them. I've known the man for years. No one could have seen this coming. Come on. Let's have some food."

Olivia smiled, so glad to have someone there with her. *Not someone; Landon.* The anger slipped away, replaced by the primal need for this person who needed no explanation of what was at stake, who knew Alek, who knew her. She cleared off the mess on her coffee table and started to spread out the meal. As always, it was exactly what she would have ordered, a million different things that didn't make sense together at all.

"The thing is," she called to him as he pulled out the vodka he had left in her freezer, "I know I should be mad and afraid, but really I'm so worried about him."

"Of course you are. I am too, baby."

"How do you do that? How do you always make my crazy okay?"

"'Cause I like your crazy. Alek has been a good friend. And he's not guilty as far as we know." He poured out two vodkas as he talked. She looked at him longingly until he kissed her and grabbed her around her waist, pulling her down to the couch. She leaned her head on his shoulder. "Come on." He patted her on the knee. "Let's dig into this food. I'm starved."

She sat back with a plate of chicken and broccoli and pulled her feet up under her. As he leaned forward to get his own plate of dumplings, she reached out to touch his back. It was almost a subconscious move to prove to herself that he was real. He turned his head and grinned at her.

"Hey, baby," he said with a comforting tone, as if he knew exactly what she needed.

"Hey." She smiled, caught. Then she paused and looked at him. "Hey, Landon, thank you."

He put his plate down and ran his hand through the top of her hair. "I love you. It's going to be okay."

And with that she almost believed it would be.

⌒⌒⌒

Forty-five minutes into an episode of *White Collar*, the buzzer at her door rang. Landon shot up, jarred by it as much as she was. She walked over to the intercom, head rushing with what she would do if it was Alek. Or Jacob. She closed her eyes and pressed the button.

"Yes?"

"*Ciao, bella.*"

"Oh, hey, Gianni." The relief swept through her body.

"That delivery you were asking about, the UPS? Ronnie just came with it. Eets here."

"Okay, thanks, Gianni, be right down for it." She turned to Landon. "I bet it's Jonah and Simon's contributions. They said they would send it here instead of the office."

She bounced down the steps and entered the restaurant. It hummed with a vivacious dinner crowd. Olivia looked around, happy that people were out and about. The world was going on and she got to go back upstairs and be with the man she loved. Gianni handed her the UPS envelope, and her eyes traveled to the sender: Alek Yerkhov. She tried to say thank you without letting her horror show as she turned around and left the restaurant. On the walk up the stairs she warily pulled the paper tab from one side to the other. Landon stood up as she walked in, clearly moved by the whiteness of her face.

"What is it?"

"Something from Alek." He moved in to her as she pulled at the letter. Her eyes scanned down the sentences, processing them in a manically quick way.

"To whom it concerns . . . Can't go on . . . made mistakes . . . so sorry." Then the last line, "I don't want a funeral. I just want Olivia Greenley to handle my remains."

Olivia moved reflexively to the couch and fell back. The letter slipped down to the tips of her fingers and onto the ground as tears began to fall. Landon stayed standing, immobile.

"It's a suicide letter. He's going to kill himself." She spoke quietly, unsure of the gray emotion that was swirling around her body. "I . . ." She looked up at Landon, hoping he was falling onto the couch with her so she could bury her face in him. Instead he was slipping his arms briskly through the sleeves of his jacket and stepping into his shoes.

He looked at her, shaking his head. "This isn't good. You've got to call the campaign lawyer. Yes," he said, confirming his own thought, "call Ethanson."

Olivia looked up at him in shock. The haze that had filtered around her now seemed to condense into quicksand.

"You what? I what?" The words barely came out of her mouth.

Landon didn't stop. "Call the lawyer right away. I can't be here." He had rare panic in his voice as he opened the door and walked out.

Olivia looked down at the note on the floor, up at the closed door, and back down again, feeling a total inability to comprehend the pieces of the last ten minutes.

"But he's your friend! Your friend is going to die!" she pointlessly yelled at the door.

Pull yourself together, she told herself, her hands visibly shaking. *He's right. Call the lawyer.* She picked up her phone, looking for Jackie Ethanson's number, and began to scroll down the list of contacts. She stopped at Jacob's name, remembering he was in New York, and dialed.

"J?"

"Liv? You okay?"

"No."

"Another insurance agent die?"

She let out a breath and tried to compose herself. "Alek sent me a suicide note."

There was a heavy silence on the other end of the line. "Shit."

"Yeah." She felt the gravity of the moment, that all kinds of new horrors would be born from this, that her life had changed forever.

"Where are you?"

"At my apartment."

"Okay, I'm across town. Don't do anything. I'll be right over."

"Thank you." The words fell from her mouth, accompanied by the last drip of composure she had left. She dropped the BlackBerry on the couch and grabbed a pillow.

When Jacob buzzed in, she tried to wipe her eyes, but seeing him at the door caused her to lose it again. He moved in toward her and gave her the hug she had so desperately wanted from Landon. She grabbed on to his shoulders and squeezed him as tightly as she could. Tears streamed down her cheeks, falling onto his jacket.

"I'm sorry," she whimpered, finally releasing her grip on his shoulders. "I'm getting tears on your suit." She wiped at his shoulder and then at her eyes. "I'm so sorry, Jacob."

"It's okay, Liv." He hugged her back. "Where is it?"

"Here." She handed him the letter. "I'm supposed to call the lawyer. Landon said to call Ethanson."

Jacob stopped, looking around the room at the two plates of half-eaten Chinese food, and then his eyes darted to the side of the couch. "Landon?"

Olivia watched him look at the floor at the Great American Vending Machine Company. She looked up in admission, too scared and sad and angry to make a quick excuse.

"Landon was here?"

Olivia looked at him again. "I'm sorry."

"Where did he go?"

"I don't know." She shook her head. "He saw the letter and took off."

"You got a suicide letter from *his* friend and he walked out?" Jacob's fury started to build visibly.

Olivia tried to calm him down even though that was the exact question she had been repeating in her mind since he walked out. "I understand. I mean, he can't be here. He shouldn't have been here in the first place. He had to leave."

Jacob looked at her, believing the words even less than she did.

"Damn it, Olivia. Stop making excuses for him. I know he used to be a good guy. No one knows that like me. But he is not a good guy anymore. Liv. He should have stayed. Or he shouldn't have come at all. He should be the one getting this note. He should not be the one to leave."

She stared blankly back, knowing it was true. Jacob spun into work mode, calling Jackie to handle the legal and Peter to handle the press. The next hour raced by so quickly and ferociously that Olivia barely moved. She went through the motions without taking in anything, saying only what Jacob and Jackie and Peter told her to say. A friend was about to die. Or maybe he was already dead. He was guilty of everything she had hoped he wasn't. And as much as she tried to focus on that and as much as she knew that was what was important, she couldn't help but recognize the parallel message it carried for her relationship. Landon was guilty of everything she'd hoped he wasn't too.

TWENTY

Jacob marshaled the last dose of calm he could muster as he walked out of Olivia's apartment at seven thirty in the evening. "Get some sleep." He hugged her again. "It will be better tomorrow."

The minute he stepped onto the sidewalk, free from the worry of upsetting her, his fury simmered over into a loud grunt. He walked vigorously, composing the speech he would scream at the governor when he saw him. He found himself muttering loudly like a crazy person as he headed down the street.

"Liar." He almost twitched.

As he said the words, his BlackBerry started buzzing. "Crap." He looked at the phone, not wanting to answer Billy's call. He had been so busy practicing his rage-filled speech he hadn't decided how he actually wanted to handle the situation. The phone buzzed again.

"Hey, Billy."

"You still with Olivia?"

"Just left."

"Good, good." Billy spoke slowly. "I got good news and bad news."

Jacob wasn't really in the mood for either.

"Okay, give it to me."

"The good news is we found the gov."

"I take it that's the bad news too?" Jacob asked, knowing the answer but now confused at how this would unfold.

"It is." Billy's Southern accent seemed so much more prominent when he was stressed. "Governor decided to get on a plane to New York. He's just landed."

Liar, Jacob screamed internally. "Really?" he asked, trying to stay composed.

"Indeed. Apparently he decided the SEIU conference shouldn't be missed, so he caught a flight and will be there for the dinner. He said to let you know you should meet him there."

"Ha." Jacob let out a sarcastic laugh.

"I know," Billy said like the teacher trying to calm the kids on the playground. Billy knew Landon and Jacob had been fighting, but as far as Jacob could tell, he didn't know anything of the bigger issues. "I know it's not ideal. We're almost through this patch."

Jacob wasn't about to be the one to spell it out. He had dealt with enough today. "It's not a patch, Billy."

"Jacob," Billy said with almost stern stillness, "you go meet him at that dinner and for tonight, just do your job. I promise tomorrow we'll get to the bottom of this and get it fixed."

Jacob wanted to fight, wanted to scream through the phone and quit right then and there, but he had a pang of sympathy for Billy. It wasn't Billy's fault and he had been through enough to last him the year.

"I know, Billy." He thought to himself that this would be the last conversation before it all changed. "You know I have the highest respect for you, Billy."

Billy seemed to understand that these were words of resignation, in all senses of that term. But he didn't try to justify the importance of the race or tell him how lucky they were to work for the governor. Billy might not have known the details, but he knew the governor had changed. Drastically and irreversibly. All Billy said was, "Okay."

⌘

"Look who decided to show up!" The governor moved jovially toward Jacob in the crowded hotel ballroom and elbowed him a little in a friendly jab.

"Actually, sir, it's your showing up we're all surprised by," Jacob said. He grinned, showing full teeth to emphasize his mockingly polite sarcasm.

"Yes, well," the governor replied with a smile, his agitation only visible to Jacob. "It is my campaign, my schedule. Listen." He pulled Jacob in close to him, away from the group of large men that stood behind him, debating the new minimum wage bill. For a minute Jacob thought he might come clean, might say something, anything, that would make this better. "I want to be out of here in thirty minutes tops."

Jacob started to respond with a diplomatic but totally insincere, "Of course, sir," but Ralph, one of the union leaders, walked over to say hello.

"We are just absolutely thrilled that you could make it today," Ralph said. He looked a lot like a much older, balding Chris Matthews. He shook the governor's hand in an almost frantic manner.

"I am so happy to be here. SEIU has always been one of my top allies and I'm hopeful we'll be able to strengthen that relationship."

Jacob took a step back.

The governor continued his expressions of support and seemed to get faker with every word. "I'm just sorry I can't stay for the whole dinner." He looked at Jacob like he had done so many times before, expecting the all-but-reflexive answer of *Yes, we need to get to something else,* but Jacob saw his first opening.

"Actually, Governor"—he smiled broadly as he gently grabbed Taylor's arm and squeezed—"you don't have to be anywhere after this. I just double-checked and we're all good to stay for dinner."

The governor smiled back through gritted teeth. "You sure about that?"

"Super sure. Checked with both Olivia and Peter."

The governor didn't flinch. Eyes straight ahead, he looked at the heavyset union man in front of him and smiled. "Looks like I am all set to stay."

Unaware that anything was amiss, the union guy grabbed Jacob's hand. "Great, great. We have a seat for you too, Harriston. Great."

As the governor and Jacob followed the man to their table, Taylor leaned in to Jacob with fury. Under his breath, he said, "What the hell are you thinking?"

The governor's face turned a shade redder, but before Jacob had the chance to respond, another union leader pulled him away. The dinner was so packed that for the next two hours not a word passed between Jacob and the governor.

Jacob knew it was childish, but he couldn't help indulging. He said audibly, "We're all good on time," and "Nowhere to go after," enough times that the labor union kept the governor for three hours, longer than he would have ever stayed.

When they finally left, they walked in a heavy silence until they turned the second street corner away from anyone who might know who they were. The governor grabbed Jacob's arm and spun him around. "What the fuck do you think you're doing?"

"What am I doing?" Jacob asked with irreverence. "I'm quitting! That's what I'm doing."

"You can't quit." Taylor's voice rose with anger.

"Yes, I can." Jacob looked at him resolutely. "You're a liar and a cheat."

"You don't know what you're talking about."

"Yes I do. You know what's funny?" Jacob paused and almost smiled. "I thought I'd quit because you were with her, but it turns out I'm quitting because you left her."

"Oh, that's ridiculous."

"I gave you everything I had. I gave you my life."

"You work for me!" Landon screamed, losing control.

Jacob composed himself. He said a monotone, "Not anymore. I quit."

"You think you're going to leave this campaign? Ruin it? You think you're going to ruin me?" He pushed his hand into Jacob's chest. Then he stepped back and ran his hands down the sides of his suit jacket. "You won't touch me, Jacob. I'm going to the White House and you will not get in my way. You want out? You got it. Have your shit cleaned out tomorrow."

Taylor shot him a look of complete hatred and turned on his heel to walk through the now quiet street. He waited for a minute at the DON'T WALK sign and then stormed across the intersection, vigorously pumping his arms.

I was supposed to storm away. For minutes Jacob couldn't move, paralyzed by fear of what had just happened and the actual consequences that would soon be upon him. And then by immense sadness. Who was that person? That man he knew so well, the guy who had been like an older brother, who joked, who inspired, who knew his family, whose family knew him—that guy was gone. This guy was unrecognizable. Five years of Jacob's life and all the plans he'd had for the next six had disappeared with the silhouette of Landon fading down the dark side street. Jacob stood in the coldness of the January night. His hands trembled with a mix of sadness, anger, and also, relief.

TWENTY-ONE

Please come to Iowa. I need you.
    It was the twenty-second pin Olivia had gotten in two days. She sat on her couch, where it seemed she had been sprawled since Jacob left. That wasn't actually true. She had gotten up for Alek's funeral, where she sat alone in the church with a group of people. Smaller than the number who had called themselves his friends before everything had shattered. Jacob of course, had shown up and slid in next to her. They barely spoke, knowing there was too much to say. Jacob had signed on to a new campaign already and was staying in New York for a few weeks to regroup before he started.

"I haven't forgotten how many drinks I owe you," she had said, "and the number should probably be tripled after last week."

He smiled, seeming calmer than she had seen him in so long, and she envied that calm. "I'm at Quality Meats almost every night these days. You would be surprised how much tequila helps with recuperation."

"Sure," Olivia had said.

She knew she should be regrouping and figuring out how she was actually going to deal with the fallen pieces of her life. But as she sat on her couch, she knew she wasn't ready yet. Billy had insisted she take a few days off. Landon, on the other hand, had come just short of stalking her. His apologies, his regrets, his love notes all came over pins, whose red lettering that once thrilled her now seemed the modern version of a scarlet letter on her BlackBerry. This morning he had started in with the pins about meeting him in Iowa. Though most of Olivia was thinking about throwing her BlackBerry out the window and hoping Tara from Page Six would walk by and find it, there was a small, admittedly dysfunctional part of her that wanted to go. She reprimanded her heart for being so stubborn and immune to logic but knew that it was also just a side effect of her exhaustion and sadness. At one fifty in the afternoon her buzzer rang.

"Hello?" she called into the monitor, wondering who it might be.

"Hey, Olivia," said a familiar sweet voice, "I'm so sorry to bother you but it's Robin."

"Robin?" Olivia wondered if it was really Yanni's assistant at her door.

"Yeah, it's me."

"Umm, okay, come on up." She buzzed Robin in, completely confused as to the cause of the visit. She scanned the mess that there was no time to disguise. Her *Lucky* magazines, scattered around dirty clothes, were outnumbered only by Chinese take-out cartons. She opened the door, embarrassed.

"Hey, Robin. I'm a total mess and my apartment is worse."

"Oh, please, don't worry at all. I'm sorry to intrude. I wouldn't be here if Yanni didn't insist. I tried to advise against it."

"He's tough like that," Olivia said with a smile, remembering walking into Vince Tilewitz's office, mortified to be there for the check Yanni demanded she get. "Anyway, I'm sorry for the mess, but please come in. What's up?"

"Well . . ." Robin threw a Barney's bag on the coffee table. "I was instructed to get you clothes for Iowa and, well"—she stammered a little over the words—"invite you to go to Iowa with Yanni. He's leaving from Teterboro in two hours. Just going till tomorrow. He said Landon wants you and him there."

Olivia stood dumbfounded.

Robin filled her silence. "I heard about that guy, Alek. I'm so sorry. I'm guessing you don't want to go anywhere, but Yanni and the governor actually sounded really nice about it. I know Yanni's just Yanni, but it's pretty amazing—I mean, Landon Taylor is about to be president and he just wants you guys there."

Olivia smiled at Robin's naïveté and at the pure ridiculousness of it all.

"Yeah," she said, only to make Robin feel less uncomfortable.

Robin pointed to the bag. "I got lots of stuff at Barney's. I only had about fifteen minutes so I hope it's okay. It was actually really fun." She smiled. "I figured jeans, sweaters, and I didn't know your size exactly so I guessed. The receipt is in there so you can exchange anything or I can go back for you."

"I'm sure whatever you picked is great. But this is completely unnecessary. You should take them back, Robin."

"No way! Yanni would kill me. Besides, it's great stuff! He lets me take the Barney's card for my birthday every year. I love that place. Anyway, he's sending his driver to pick you up in an hour."

Olivia was so caught off guard and dazed she didn't know what to say, and somehow "Okay" came out.

After Robin left, she looked through the bag of clothes. She pulled out an eighty-four-dollar plain long-sleeved shirt and put it on. It was the softest thing she had ever worn. She thought about calling Yanni, arguing the point, and then she rethought it. *I'll just go. It'll be closure.* Although she secretly hoped Landon would say something, anything, to change the ending.

She showered and put the shirt back on, pairing it with her favorite jeans, and then pulled out of the bag a thick, maroon cashmere cardigan that fell perfectly to the top of her thighs. It was the exact one she had coveted in this month's *Lucky. What the hell? Yanni will never take the stuff back anyway.* She wrapped it around herself and stuck her hands in the deep pockets, feeling warmer and cozier than she thought possible. She looked down at the other bags and figured she should leave them as is, quite sure she would be without a job and income next week. It was part of the reason she had been quick to take Billy's advice not to make decisions. She knew she couldn't stay, but aside from everything else, the simple fact was, she was living paycheck to paycheck, and the thought of losing her next one was too much to handle at that moment. She brushed her hair, put makeup on, and obligingly got into Yanni's chauffeured car at three thirty in the afternoon.

When they got to Iowa Olivia was glad she had come. Regardless of the circumstances, the cold, crisp Iowa air was a good break from the stuffiness of her apartment. Olivia opened her window and leaned out a little as they drove to Marshalltown for the get-out-the-vote event, grateful that Yanni had been on his cell phone nonstop. When they arrived, Yanni went straight in for the governor.

Olivia saw Peter, the press secretary, standing in the corner with a blond woman she didn't recognize. She pointed over at him. "I'm just going to say hi to our press guy," Olivia said, buying herself some time. She still wasn't sure what she was doing there or even how she felt about Landon. She walked to the side of the room and found Peter huddled over his BlackBerry.

"Got any good stories?" she said, coming up behind him.

"Hey!" he called out, clearly surprised to see her there, and gave her a big hug. "What are you doing here?"

"Yanni wanted to go out on the road and insisted I come."

Peter excused himself from his conversation and walked Olivia toward the chairs on the side of the room. "It's so good to see you. Hey, I'm sorry we couldn't all go to the funeral."

"No, don't worry. I totally understand." Olivia played it off, when in truth she didn't understand. Friendship was friendship, and the governor owed Alek so much, at least enough to honor the man's life, even if he had made mistakes. Game face on, she said believably, "It was totally fine. Glad it's over."

"Yeah." He paused and looked over at the governor, who was stuck in a photo line. "We are losing it without Jacob on the road. Have you spoken to him?"

"A little. He's starting that new campaign in a few weeks."

"Oh, yeah, right. Man, that's crazy. I still haven't even heard what happened with him."

"Yeah, I don't know. Hey," she said, attempting to change the subject, "who's the blonde? Your new campaign hookup?"

Peter shook his head. "I wish. That's Brianna. She's some Web blogger or something, who, I guess, is going to start traveling with us."

"Really?"

"Yep. I'm totally against it. She seems crazy to me, but the gov thinks it's a good idea. And without Jacob here there's no one to say no. You know how that goes."

Olivia nodded in agreement. "Yeah, I do."

Peter's eyes followed the governor as he neared the exit. "Okay, well I gotta go grab the governor. We're going to do drinks in the bar tonight—Ottingly and the other county volunteers will be there. Come join us!"

"Will try," Olivia said, knowing full well she wouldn't.

Yanni came back to her, tapping her arm. "Come on, we're jumping in with them. We'll go get dinner."

Olivia followed politely to the parking lot, feeling every nerve in her body as the governor came into sight. They walked to the two SUVs where Taylor was convening with Peter, the blond woman, and four or five other staff members. Yanni pushed through to the governor, who looked up at them.

"Liv," Taylor said apprehensively as he reached to give her a hug. "I'm so glad you came."

Her body stiffened. His touch felt oddly foreign to her and, more significantly, so fake.

"Yeah," she replied quietly.

He instantly moved to avoid the awkwardness. He was so unaccustomed to anything but adulation.

"Let's go get some dinner. We can go right to the hotel."

They all jumped in the SUV, and thankfully, Yanni talked the governor's ear off for the entire ride and the subsequent dinner. As soon as it seemed acceptable, Olivia said her gracious thank-yous and excused herself, claiming tiredness, to her room. She sat down on the bed, looking at the door and wondering if she would ever feel comfortable in her own skin again. She had sat down crying against the same heavy, beige hotel door a floor below three months earlier. She had wondered how she had gotten to that state of sorrow then, never imagining that circumstances could have gotten worse. She closed her eyes, knowing she wanted this to be the last time she cried behind a hotel door.

When the knock came, she picked herself up off the bed and wiped the tracks of tears that had since subsided. She opened the door.

The governor stood there, his overcoat on, an expression of sincerity on his face, but she had seen him pull out that expression at any number of town hall meetings, on any number of talk shows.

"Liv," he said pleadingly, "I'm so glad you came." He moved in to hug her but she shifted away.

"I don't know why I did come here."

"You do too. I love you."

She looked at him, wondering for the first time if she ever really did love him, or if she had just loved what he represented, what he pretended to believe.

"Here," he said, and he handed her a bag. "I'm so sorry. I promise I'll make it up to you. This is just the start."

She looked down at the Saks bag, which held a shoe box, wondering what on earth he might have gotten her. Without saying a word she opened the box. It was a Jimmy Choo box. She slowly took off the cover and revealed a pair of the most beautiful shoes she had ever seen. They were covered in tiny pieces of what looked like diamond chips.

"Glass," he said as she quietly stared at them. "They're the closest I could find to glass slippers." A tear started to roll down Olivia's cheek as he continued talking. "I swear, baby, I'm going to treat you like a princess for as long as you'll let me."

Olivia didn't look up at him. "Alek called me the princess," she said sadly, remembering his smile and accent.

"I'm sorry, Liv."

She gazed into the governor's eyes, which now seemed less than perfect, and tried to hand him back the bag with the shoes.

"The fairy tale, Landon, was never about the shoes. The fairy tale was the prince. The fairy tale was a love that fit, not a shoe."

"Liv, it's the thought—"

She cut him off, suddenly furious at the phrase she had heard him say so many times before. Her anger and hurt spilled out as rage. "Don't say it! 'It's the thought that counts.' That phrase. You know how many times I've heard you say that?"

"Olivia, why are you getting so mad?" He started to speak in that slow, condescending tone he used when he was trying to calm down one of his children.

"It's not the thought that counts, Landon. Whoever made that up was totally full of shit. It's what you do that counts. It's where you show up. It's when you don't. That man was a great friend to you. You didn't even go to his funeral. Who gives a shit if you were thinking about him? You weren't there."

"Olivia, you are making a much bigger deal of this than it is. Lower your voice."

"No, Landon. No. This is a much bigger deal than you're making it. He was your friend. And I was . . . God, I don't know what the hell I was. But you left me. You left me with that suicide note. You left me at that funeral. You left me to cry alone." She knew this wasn't the argument she meant to be making, but the words just kept coming out.

"You know I couldn't go to that funeral."

"Oh, it is so not about that!"

"You are being crazy, Liv."

"I know. Actually no, I'm not being crazy, I am being completely insane! I am here still talking to you and that, Landon, is insane. It doesn't matter what you think you could do or couldn't do, the bottom line is you didn't show up for Alek, you didn't show up for me, and you never will."

"I—"

"Don't argue with me. Don't explain it away. I know better than anyone how you can spin lies. I don't want to hear any of it. Damn it." She stomped her foot. "I'm too good for this. I deserve so much better." She heard Jacob's voice in her head and repeated his words more for her than for him. "I deserve someone who shouts my name from the rooftops, someone who makes me feel good about myself." She stopped and collected her spinning thoughts and took a breath in and out. "I fell in love with you, Landon Taylor, but mostly I just fell. And it is way past time for me to pick myself up."

"Baby—"

The minute the word came out of his mouth the anger in her dissipated into incredulousness. "'Baby'? That's what you say?" She shook her head and pushed the shoes into his hands, and she pushed him out the door. She shut the door and made sure the bolt locked. Then she leaned against it and slid down to sit on the ground. But this time she wasn't crying.

⌒⊶∽⌒

Olivia gazed out the cab window as she approached the New York City skyline from Teterboro. When the taxi got to her corner, she got out of the car and looked up at her apartment, flashing back to Landon walking in, Landon walking out, and then to Jacob. She stood in the street thinking about him and then simultaneously raised her hand for a new cab.

"Quality Meats, please."

She walked into the bar, grateful for the familiarity, and felt her stomach drop in that good type of way at the sight of Jacob's back at the bar. He was in a blue T-shirt and dark jeans and his long legs hung down off the bar stool, touching the ground. His head turned from the television down to his papers on the bar. CNN was covering Landon's speech, and the Iowa room the governor was in seemed almost fake, or at the least worlds away. She stopped for a minute, smiling, proud of herself for the first time in what seemed like months.

She breathed in and walked toward Jacob without a second thought and with a poignant absence of insecurity.

When she pulled back the bar stool next to him, he looked up, his shock lasting just a moment, and then promptly his expression turned into one of happiness.

Leaning over the bar, she called to the bartender, "Dave, I owe this guy a tequila."

"Dave, this girl owes me a bunch of tequilas." He turned toward her and pulled in the bar stool behind her so she could sit as Dave passed over their drinks.

"What are you doing here?"

She smiled, knowing he didn't actually need an explanation. "You were right."

He had a shit-eating grin. "I know. But about which part?"

"About it all. Campaign Lesson number one was always loyalty," she said. "Just took me a little longer to figure out who I was supposed to be loyal to."

"So you're done? Out?"

"Done."

"You know," he said, looking up at the governor on TV, "we could take this guy down."

Olivia smiled. "We could. We really could."

The two sat for a moment in that thought and relished the notion.

"But he doesn't need us for that," she said. "He's at the bottom; the world may not see it now, but they will. His true colors will show. They always do, eventually."

"Yeah, I know," Jacob said. "Let's just hope they do before he becomes the leader of the free world."

"Well, if it gets too close, we'll reconsider!" She laughed.

"Agreed."

She looked down at the papers in front of Jacob, campaign information for that senator he had been talking about.

"That the new gig?"

"Yup." He laid his hands reverently on the papers like a religious zealot would his Bible. "I think this one could be the real deal."

She looked at Jacob. She realized how much she'd missed the glow that was animating his eyes. "You think they have room for an out-of-work fundraiser?"

He slid the papers toward her and she caught the edges, taking a sip of her drink before reading. Putting her tequila down, she picked up the first page. She scanned it and looked to Jacob, who had moved close enough so she could see him out of the corner of her eye, watching her.

She caught his glance, and they shared an easy, comfortable smile. "Hope and change, huh? I think I could use some of that."

ACKNOWLEDGMENTS

This whole process started with my friend and colleague, Josh Brumberger. His stories, ideas, words, and, most important, his friendship were integral to the book. It also couldn't have been done without his amazing support team—Jill, Clay, Bruce, Barbara, Dev, and Cassius Brumberger.

Thanks to Harvey Weinstein, whose genius I am always in awe of and whose kindness and support I am always grateful for. Biz Mitchell, my incredibly talented and brilliant editor, made my words into a real story. Judy Hottensen liked the idea from the start; her friendship and guidance have been invaluable.

Thanks to the team at Weinstein Books, especially the powerful publishing duo of Amanda Murray and Georgina Levitt. Ryan Fisher-Harbage, my agent and friend, believed I could do this even before I did and taught me how to turn an idea into a book.

I'm grateful for the team at Perseus, especially David Steinberger and John Radziewicz, who went above and beyond the call of duty with his editing and publishing support.

Thanks to Sandi Mendelson and David Kass, who I know will give a great voice to this story.

I have a huge family, all of whom have supported me in ways too numerous to count throughout my life and especially in this endeavor: my parents, of course, to whom this book is dedicated, have been there for me every step of the way; Grandma and Grandpa Hanley, my resident king and queen; my brother, David, who always stands by me; Lauren, and Ciela; my sister Jen; Brett, Amanda, Dylan, and Ryan; my sister Wendy; Jason, Samantha, and Julia. I thank Melissa, Brian, and Luke; Danielle, Bill, Scott, and Jack; Lisa, Jim, Hanna, and Chris, Kathleen, Jim, Rachel and Mike and Aaron and Angela; Gerry, Donna, Caroline, and Marielle; Aunt Sue; Marci, Jon, Hanna, and Jared; Ina, Andrew, Jordyn, and Chase; Kathleen and the Jones and Burris families. And Marcy, who is kinder and much more patient than any character in any book. From naming the Brinmore to giving me endless support, she has been more than I could wish for as family and more than I could ask for as a friend.

My friends have not only been there for me during the writing of this book, but also throughout the many campaigns that inspired it and so much else in my life—Dana Kirkpatrick, Dana Klein, Chad Griffin, Raj and Maria Teresa Kumar; Liz, Andy, Mira, and Peter Herlihy; Bryan and Yael Caplin; Mike Maddox, Greg Morrison, Mike Taylor, Dennis Cheng, Amy Hayes, Dara Freed, Deirdre Frawley, and Dani Super. Marina Giyasov and her dad, William, added the perfect accent to the story. An extra-special thank-you to the friends who, on top of all that, read and critiqued my book, some of whom even redlined it—Katherine Riley, Gabrielle Fialkoff, Ashley Cotton, Jackie Mishler, Justin Cooper, and Peter Ragone. The Hazans—Al, Lisette and, also Dave—who taught me that too good to be true can be true.

I have been lucky enough to have a council of wise people always around to offer support, advice and endless generosity: Michael Del-Giudice, Brian Snyder, Andrew Farkas, John and Donna Marino, Dan Hedaya, Blair and Cheryl Effron, and Jeff Madrick. It's led by Orin Kramer, my patron-godfather—it is because of him that I was able to follow my dreams, and I am eternally grateful.

I'd also like to thank the two English teachers who instilled in me a love of writing—Eliot Eigen and Margaret Stetz.

I may not have painted a great picture of politicians in this book, but in the nonfiction world I have been, and continue to be, inspired by people who have changed the world. Fortunately for me, a few of them have also changed my world. They are the people who truly see a better horizon, and I am grateful to have worked for and with them: Secretary of State Hillary Clinton; Governor Andrew Cuomo; Governor Mario Cuomo and First Lady Matilda Cuomo; Terry McAuliffe; New York City public advocate Bill de Blasio; Kerry Kennedy; and New York State attorney general Eric Schneiderman.

Thank you to the many great friends I have met on campaigns who inspired me with stories and anecdotes.

Finally, there are some special people who, I think, would have really liked this book had they still been with us. They inspire me always and I am grateful for that—Grandma Lee, Uncle Steve, Ryan, and Professor Joseph Lepgold.